IT'S A WORLD OF C… EXPLODING OVER T… AND CH… IS OUT T…

ARCHIE OGLE: For forty … corruption. Now he's hiding … Malta—waiting for Charlie Dance to save his … bling turf. . . .

SADLER: He's scheming to turn a money-laundering operation into an international financial empire—by stealing from the Mob. But Charlie Dance has come to shut him down. . . .

WALLY HAROLD: He's a hardcase hood with a case of the doubts. His job is to keep Dance out of his brother Connie's way—but a beautiful South African blonde makes him think about staying alive. . . .

NAOMI: Tall, beautiful, and rich, she has her own business interests to look after. But when she falls for Wally, a Mafia footsoldier, she plunges into the heart of Mob warfare. . . .

LEMMON: He's a career cop looking for the loot from a million-dollar train heist. All trails lead to Charlie Dance—and to corruption in the highest echelons of the force. . . .

MARGOT: She's Sadler's wife and prisoner. Suddenly her world is filled with strong and brutal men—and she has the key to what they want. . . .

THEY HAD ALL MADE A DEAL WITH THE DEVIL. NOW THEY WOULD DANCE WITH DEATH!

Books by Tom Barling

Dance With Death
Dance With the Devil

Available from POCKET BOOKS

DANCE WITH THE DEVIL

TOM BARLING

POCKET BOOKS

New York London Toronto Sydney Tokyo

Originally published in Great Britain by Transworld Publishers Ltd., 1986

Another *Original* publication of POCKET BOOKS

POCKET BOOKS, a division of Simon & Schuster Inc
1230 Avenue of the Americas, New York, N.Y. 10020

ISBN: 0-671-64574-9

First Pocket Books printing June 1988

10 9 8 7 6 5 4 3 2 1

Printed in the U.S.A.

PROLOGUE

Spring 1963

AT AGE 73, ARCHIE OGLE HAS BEEN THE UNDISPUTED OVERLORD of the London underworld for thirty years, and he is grooming Charlie Dance to take over his Mayfair casinos and the West End territory when he retires to Malta with his wife Queenie. His recently stated ambition to control the new international drug market in partnership with the Tonna brothers from Toronto and the Chinese Triads from Hong Kong worries Charlie Dance, but his loyalty to Archie outweighs his deep concern.

On a site visit to the new building complex Archie is raising to replace the slums of his birth, he is buried beneath the rubble of a bulldozed building, and Charlie is injured pulling him out. Interviewed by Detective Inspector Lemmon and Detective Sergeant "Prophet" Quill at the hospital where his broken arm is set and Archie undergoes emergency surgery, Charlie is told that the demolition contractors work no Sunday shifts. The "accident" is no accident, but the work of an unknown assassin.

Taking to the streets, Charlie finds himself in a dark new

world where the old loyalties have been swept away. Archie Ogle is finished in the eyes of the coming men who want his power for themselves.

Tommy and Jesse Troy from Bethnal Green have smarted from Archie's heavy hand in the past and want his Mayfair casinos. Connie and Wally Harold from Camberwell, south of the Thames, are tired of being bottled up and have designs on the West End. The gangs of North and West London remain neutral, but a shadowy City financier, Malcolm Sadler, courts both the Troys and the Harolds in his bid to take control of all Archie's holdings. If Sadler is successful, and the two gangs come at him in tandem, Charlie knows Archie is finished, his own days numbered. Archie's near fatal "accident" prompts the Tonnas to cancel their trip to London, leaving Charlie with a bare handful of loyal friends as allies. While visiting Archie at his country convalescent home, Charlie and Queenie are shot at, only narrowly escaping the volley of high-powered bullets.

Ingrid Dakin, Charlie's current girlfriend, is a croupier at the Philadelphia House in Mayfair. She recognizes the father who abandoned her as a child in the company of Dirk Jorgesson, a South African who has lost heavily at the gaming tables. Ingrid's father, Vic Dakin, is a confidence trickster who specializes in founding phony banking houses and fraudulent credit companies. Having massively defrauded three major airlines, and bankrupted as many Milanese stocking factories, Dakin has been in hiding on the Continent under assumed names. On the run from the Troys, the Harolds, and the Fraud Squad, Dakin has returned to London out of sheer desperation. He hopes his daughter Ingrid will talk Charlie Dance into financing a grandiose mining scheme in the undeveloped tribal territories of Namaqualand.

Before Dakin can approach Charlie directly, he is picked up by the Troys, who intend to kill him for trying to sell them phony Old Masters in Italy three years before. Convincing them of the riches to be made from the mining venture saves his life, and with Limehouse Lou to guard him, Dakin is hidden in Camden Town while the Troys check his story out.

Connie Harold also gets wind of Dakin's return, and sends his brother Wally to bring Dakin back to Camberwell to face retribution for creaming too much profit from the Milanese micromesh stocking swindle. Wally Harold overwhelms Limehouse Lou, and is bringing Dakin out to his car when Charlie and Ingrid arrive. Charlie puts Wally into the hospital with a blow of his plastered forearm, and spirits Dakin away to pump him about Jorgesson and his mining concessions. Confronting Jorgesson with his markers for £50,000, Charlie forces him to sign his holdings over in lieu of payment and offers Dakin, Jorgesson, and the contracts to Connie Harold for that exact sum, despite Archie's fury over the matter.

Connie Harold agrees to meet Charlie Dance at his Windmill Street office with the cash, meaning to take what he wants at the point of a gun. But informed by an anonymous source that there are illegal drugs on the premises, Quill's squad raids the place, foils Connie's holdup, and enables Charlie to get the £50,000 away through a back window.

Back in Camberwell, Connie Harold tortures Dakin with electrodes, and lays plans to exploit the South African mining project with his new partner, Dirk Jorgesson. Raising the capital needed diverts his attention from the West End, just as Charlie had hoped. Connie employs Sad Sidney Salt, a professional arsonist, to burn two empty warehouses. A fraudulent insurance claim for £250,000 as compensation for the nonexistent goods will finance the first year of operations, and he is deaf to his brother Wally's objections to the whole mad scheme. Wally leaves, and sets up a one-armed bandit circuit with his friend Pimlico Johnny Parsons, despite the fact that Pimlico is backed by Charlie Dance.

Ousted from the Troy firm for losing Dakin to "persons unknown," Limehouse Lou gets drunk enough to seek the Troys out and demand reinstatement, and is caught in a fire-bomb attack on their Mile End pub, the Martyred Thomas. Hospitalized, Limehouse is visited regularly by Helen, Tommy Troy's young wife. Their attraction for each other grows into something deeper, but they know they can have no future together without leaving London and the Troys far behind. To get the money needed, Limehouse agrees to help Sad Sidney Salt burn the Harolds' warehouses.

Convinced that Charlie Dance and the Ogle firm are too weak to have mounted the attack on the Martyred Thomas, the Troys lay the blame squarely at Connie Harold's door. In fact, Charlie employed the Irish free lance Dublin Gerry to fire-bomb the pub for him, and has destroyed any chance of a Troy-Harold alliance, earning himself some much-needed breathing space. Also, with the help of Kensington Kate, a gay club owner, he has introduced a spy into the Troy fortress.

Suspicious of her daughter-in-law's long absences, Ida Troy sets Gay Gordon to watch her, and discovers Helen is seeing Limehouse Lou. Incensed, Tommy beats Helen so badly, she suicides at the very moment Limehouse and Salt burn the first Harold warehouse.

Convinced that Dakin is of no further use to him, Connie Harold sends Vic to the Mitre Street warehouse on the pretext of needing him to prepare some urgent money transfers. Almost overcome by fumes, Dakin makes his break down the fire escape just as Limehouse Lou fires a rocket into the basement. Bowled over but unhurt by the massive blast, Dakin makes for London Airport with enough bank drafts to bankrupt the Harold firm. Sad Sidney Salt is killed in the explosion. Knocked unconscious, Limehouse is taken to Doc Rudge's in Spitalfields by a CID man in the pay of Charlie Dance. Overhearing Rudge and Dance talk, Limehouse learns of Helen's suicide and plans his own revenge on the Troys.

Still searching for the assassin who put Archie into the hospital, Charlie goes to Brighton to see Kosher Kramer, a onetime rival of Archie's. The meeting is friendly on the surface, but Charlie and his two minders are attacked on the train journey home by a mixed gang of Troy and Kramer free lancers. Charlie fights his way to the guard's van, where he has a superior force in hiding. The defeated gang is taken off the train and transported back to London in a refrigerated lorry, and, stripped naked, are kept overnight in a coldstore in Smithfield Market.

Alerting Lemmon and Quill anonymously by telephone, Charlie has them witness him shooting out the windows of the Troy fortress, and subsequently discover the naked men in the refrigerated lorry parked outside. Still in mourning, Tommy Troy can do little but call Chief Inspector Arthur Ax, who reminds Lemmon he has no authority on his patch, and sends him and his squad away under threat of disciplinary action.

For some time, Charlie Dance has been hearing rumors of a planned mail train robbery, and needs to make certain none of the money involved gets into the hands of his enemies, who could use it to buy him trouble. Bonar Tree and Ollie Oliphant, two of the men involved in the proposed robbery, make a deal with Charlie; they will take the money out of the country if he keeps the Troys off their backs. The robbery is successful, and greedy for a lion's share in the massive two million–pound haul, the Troys begin tracking down the men involved. Charlie Dance keeps his word to Tree and Oliphant, and protects the train robbers who come to him.

Meanwhile, D.I. Lemmon is brought in on the investigation of the mail train robbery by his old school friend Bunny Halliday, who orders him to put his squad at the disposal of Detective Chief Superintendent Cotton of the Flying Squad. Convinced that Charlie Dance is somehow involved, Lemmon puts his men to work. They find the farm where the gang hid after the robbery, and it is rich with forensic evidence because Sad Sidney Salt died before he could burn it to the ground. Sergeant Quill keeps some of the evidence with the hope that he can plant it on Charlie Dance, and the squad begins tracking down the gang members who have not left the country.

Pimlico Johnny Parsons had been a driver on the robbery, and although he had destroyed any evidence linking him to the farmhouse, he knows all the other gang members are in extreme jeopardy. When Smiler Tree is arrested, and Popeye Greenland and his sister Elsie are brutally tortured by the Troys into revealing the whereabouts of his share of the haul, Pimlico mistakenly believes Charlie Dance has betrayed them for his own ends. He cannot confide his suspicions in Wally Harold, who has joined his brother in South Africa, and Pimlico's wife Dotty is suffering some kind of mental trauma, and cannot be approached on the subject.

What Pimlico doesn't know is that two blacks he had served time with in Durham Prison were released, and had kidnapped Dotty to force him to give up his share of the train robbery money. Charlie had taken Pimlico's place, and after luring the two men to a remote part of Essex where he said the money was buried, killed both men and brought Dotty home physically unscathed.

Only when Brixton Billy, one of the train robbers, tells Pimlico the truth of the matter does Pimlico wonder how he can make amends to Charlie Dance for his unwarranted accusations.

D.I. Lemmon and D.C. Bulstrode arrest Brixton Billy at Dover, but are ordered to hand their prisoner over to D.C.S. Cotton. Their success has made them enemies in high places, and they are off the case. Others will take the credit for the arrest and conviction of the men involved in what is described as "the crime of the century."

Queenie has taken Archie to recuperate in Malta, leaving Charlie Dance to cope as best he can. Oblivious to the shaky state of his tottering empire, Archie's only thought is to legally adopt Charlie as his son. Only Charlie seems aware of the unresolved problems, and with the summer gone, and winter coming on, he stands alone. . . .

BOOK I

CHAPTER 1

WALLY HAROLD USED THE SHOWER AS A BLUDGEON TO BRING him awake.

The embassy party came back with the streaming water as the woman on the bed ordered breakfast in Afrikaans and asked "Walter" how he liked his eggs. Wally knew he had boxed her compass handsomely on the spinning bed, but her nameless face was lost in the mad kaleidoscope of the last month. He toweled feeling into his legs and brought focus to the whirl of ministers and dignitaries Connie and Jorgesson had rubbed shoulders with the previous evening. The prime minister of South Africa had been there, and champagne had flowed like lemonade for the two hundred guests.

Wally ignored the woman's sleepy "Good morning, Walter" and padded out onto the hotel balcony.

The sun was already hot, and white puffballs of cloud beat gentle fists against the blue vastness above Johannesburg. The air was dry and clear, and traffic purled in orderly rows fourteen floors below.

Wally forced himself through fifty press-ups.

The sun beat on his freckled back as he pumped blood to

his muscles and sense to his head. Then he showered again and lit a first cigarette. Connie was right about the terrific climate, but entertaining these plonk-swilling Dutchmen was costing the Harold firm a financial arm and leg. Even Kelly had cabled her concern in snappy language, and Wally had to admit that even though she wasn't his favorite person she was in Connie's corner when it mattered. Definitely.

Kelly was not only keeping the scrap, demolition, and finance firms afloat without help from Connie, Harry, or Sailor, she was also mothering Connie's kids in Denmark Hill, and doing a better job than daft Pauline ever had.

Not that Connie could see that; he was too blinded by the high life and the trips up-country, where he'd actually picked diamonds up off the ground. Connie was all talk about this company and that company, talking internationally as if he was straight and had a million in cash tucked down each sock.

Wally blew moody streams of smoke.

Connie had also gone soft in the head over Jorgesson's wife. He'd bought the happy couple a house and loaded it with antiques as if pound notes were gum wrappers. Alicia Jorgesson just fluttered her lashes and had Connie reaching for money he didn't have just to see her smile. One look would tell Kelly what was happening.

Wally flicked his spent cigarette over the balcony and watched it sail into invisibility.

Knew he was doing no good being in South Africa.

He could see Connie had no way of controlling the people he was dealing with. Ministers and justices who owned the police could spit Connie out with their morning mouthwash. And Wally knew the South African police used nutcrackers on a man's family jewels when they went for a confession. Just for openers.

Wally lay on the hot terrazzo and bucked through fifty slow sit-ups to tighten his stomach.

Everything was too big. Too foreign.

Jorgesson had talked Connie into flying an English geologist out to assess the Mkuse site, and now there was serious talk of bridging a river and building a bloody airfield. And there were Harry and Sailor, dripping shooters and bandoliers like regular Buffalo Bills, rounding up Kaffirs to dig exploratory trenches for perlite and clear the bush to start the airfield. And the only laugh for Wally had been teaching the Zulu workers to sing "All Coppers are Bastards" as they worked in sweating black rows.

Wally refused to grunt as he strove toward fifty.

Fighting the hangover.

Driving himself to sobriety.

And of all the companies in the world only one could supply a machine to expand this perlite stuff into usable commercial form. Just one company, and it just happened to be Hungarian. A communist company the South Africans wouldn't touch with a dozen ten-foot poles. Wally knew Charlie Dance had been smart to hand Jorgesson over without a murmur.

The woman watched Wally exercise.

Her hair was long and sun-bleached, and her body was lush and toned by swimming. The crests of her full breasts were untanned, and the appendix scar on her taut belly lost itself in the fine down of her pubis. Only the slight gauntness of her neck showed she was close to forty. Cleansed of make-up, her eyes were light amber with understated white lashes.

"You keep yourself in good shape, Walter. I admire that. Too many men grow fat with their wealth."

Still wondering what her name was, Wally flopped on a lounger, lit a second Stuyvesant, and figured something had happened inside Connie's head when their old mother had died. Connie had bottled up his feelings when brother Danny drowned in the Thames. Hadn't even broken stride when the old man had popped his clogs. But he'd sat with the old mother all through the night until she'd gone, and hadn't let the priest anywhere near her until it was all over. Connie laid her out alone and gave Wally a right royal beating when Wally caught his big brother weeping.

The woman put on a toweling robe to let the breakfast trolley into the suite, and wheeled it to the bed, nibbling toast.

"Have you ever been with a Kaffir woman, Walter?"
"Have I bloody what?"
"Had a black—"
"No! Nor Hindus nor Eskimos, neither. Two of your embassy faces pumped me about that last night. Wouldn't believe we wasn't throwing black bimbos to the ground every five minutes just because it ain't against the law back home. There may well be some who like making coffee-colored kids, but not this kiddy, and nobody else who's true-blue white neither."

Wally shook his head. What was he doing around these people? People who Connie thought enough of not to drop his aitches like a Christian cockney anymore? The woman said something in a half-amused way that she wasn't really smiling about.

"What's that?"

"Naomi. My name is Naomi. I thought you'd forgotten. You really are rather a brute, aren't you?"

"Naomi. Right."

"And *you* are a complete rotter."

"Well, that's as may be. But you wouldn't be here if you wasn't partial to a bit of rough trade, would you? Or are you minding me for the syndicate? Seeing I don't steal the silver or goose your Kaffirs?"

"Rather than goose me? A gentleman wouldn't even *think* that."

"You see any gentlemen, Naomi?"

"Only a boy in a man's body. You'll burn if you stay out there. So many muscles and such tender skin. Have you forgotten you're to take me to a luncheon party?"

"Get one of your svelte gents to take you and come back after dark."

Wally left the balcony to burn his mouth on freshly brewed coffee.

Naomi sat on the bed to decapitate a boiled egg.

"Conrad flew to Durban this morning and left you as my escort. Being boorish with me won't bring your memory back. Or cure your hangover." Naomi's tongue found the smear of yolk on her upper lip. "I'm no cheap pick-up. And

I'm not trying to trap you into any act of indiscretion either."

"Who said you was?"

"You. Last night. At great length. And again just now. Are you usually so paranoiac? Or is that a goody you save up just for me?"

Wally grinned at the composed woman.

"Drink and the devil, lady."

"Naomi."

"Naomi. Keep me off the sauce and I'm a darling."

"You'll need to be. We're going to the De Wits' with Clive Spring and the Jorgessons."

"Dirk? I can't stand that face. Nor his bit of a wife."

"Nor can I much. She's my daughter. He's my son-in-law." Naomi wagged her spoon. "And no remarks. Alicia was seventeen when she married."

"No cracks. But she could have done better."

"She likes money as much as I do. But I was less blind. I was spring married to winter. Now I'm widowed and pleased with my lot. I can afford to be diverted by young men like you, and I have no thoughts of remarrying. Honest lust with partners of my choice will do until I feel the need for a companion to accompany me into extreme old age. Until then . . ." Naomi tossed her head.

Wally scratched a pectoral.

"I've never had a woman come straight out with it before. Maybe you're all right after all. Yeah, could be."

"I'll take that as a compliment. Money breeds directness in certain circles. You have much to learn about society, Walter."

"And you'll learn me, right?"

"The word is *teach*. And 'possibly' is the answer to that question. *If* you're sweet to me in or out of company." Naomi lay back to show a lot of tanned thigh. "And you could start now."

Wally lay on the bed and leaned on an elbow.

"Lesson for lesson, lady."

"I'm bargaining with a shopkeeper." Naomi sighed.

"Tell me about this De Wit character?"

"Colonel De Wit? He's a sort of policeman. Just accept that you and your brother need him if you want to keep your mineral rights and drilling concessions."

"Another copper after a payoff. There's one around every corner, even here in sunny South Africa."

"If you mean he's dishonest, you're very wrong. That notion is meaningless here. Take my word for it, and take care you never say anything of the kind to his face."

Wally scratched his cleft chin.

"You looked . . . scared, really scared, when you said that."

Naomi rolled Wally on his back and straddled him. Her face hovered above his, and her breasts were as warm as muffins against his chest.

"And rightly so. Keep your right and white mores to the fore in that man's company if you wish to prosper on your brother's behalf. He can destroy you both with a single telephone call. Now, ask me nothing more. Please?"

"Yes, ma'am."

Wally thought Naomi shivered with more than rising need. She buried her face in the pillow and covered her fear with a show of levity. "Shut up and consume me with fire."

"Don't take the piss, love. I'm only one man. And I ain't got my Boy Scout kindling-sticks with me."

"Second best again, huh?"

"Maybe *you* should try a Kaffir."

Naomi's back ridged under the toweling.

"Don't talk like that."

"We're all the same in the dark, right?"

Naomi's nails bit into Wally's shoulders.

"Some more than others, brute."

"Easy with the spurs, lady. Soft skin, remember?"

"Only in parts, Walter. Only in parts . . ."

The house was white stucco with a portico of slender wooden columns, a roof of red Spanish tile, and tall shuttered windows. The manicured lawn sloped to embrace a pool of jade water scintillant with dancing stars of light. Jacaranda, yucca, and palms bowered between ancient quiver trees, casting shade over the marbled terrace where the luncheon party gathered among loungers and sunshades. The blooms of the flowering shrubs were raw flames of pigment, too harsh for eyes accustomed to the mellow autumnal shades of London parks and the dismal prospects south of the Thames.

Wally sat on a recumbent concrete lion with a beer he didn't want, seeing why Jorgesson's commissions and expenses grew higher with every demand as he strove to keep up with Johannesburg society. The guests smelled of money, and their self-confessed God-given right to minority rule made them walk high, wide, and handsome without the natural grace of the real nobility back home.

To Wally they all seemed to wear uniforms under their clothes.

Their arrogance isolated him, caused him to miss British beer and drizzle, red buses with steamy windows, saveloys and meat pies at a coffee stall, and the grind of barrows on cobbles.

"You aren't swimming."

Naomi dripped over Wally's shoes.

"With scratches up my back and a lovebite the size of a hubcap on my shoulder?"

Wally poured beer into the flowerbed to see it darken the red earth.

"But you have spoken to De Wit?"

"I've listened to De Wit. More like 'Twenty Questions' down at the copshop than talking."

Wally watched De Wit, a man with a farmer's face and a soldier's bearing, ordering drinks from a Bantu houseboy.

"He quite likes you, I think."

Naomi dried herself with a fluffy towel. Made Wally want her again as her breasts moved with her arms, heavy inside the scrap of a bikini, the fine grain of her skin the gold of sandstone.

"He called you a rough diamond."

"I'll bet he did."

De Wit handed Malcolm Sadler a tall Pimms. The Englishman was heavier than Jorgesson and shorter than his host. His Mayfair accent and sober suit set him apart from the Afrikaaners as surely as Wally's dark mood excluded him.

Wally figured Sadler for a smiler you could strike matches on for a century without getting a spark. He was all the things Vic Dakin had pretended to be. But Vic was dead and Malcolm Sadler was very much alive, and was no friend of Connie's or Wally's. Wally could see that plainer than Naomi's big breasts, but Connie was blind to it, like so many other great truths.

"Sorry?" Wally had missed Naomi's last remark.

"He's my daughter Alicia's godparent. He thinks the world of her."

"Who, Sadler?"

"Colonel De Wit."

"That why he puts up with Dirk?"

Jorgesson showed off on a low diving platform. His small and dark elfin wife ignored his clowning with her hand over De Wit's, their heads together like conspirators.

"He likes her all right."

Wally took a passing Manhattan for something to hold. He was the only smoker there and was shy of lighting up.

"Winter and spring again, Naomi?"

Naomi's face was sun-dried bone.

"If you swallowed your spit, you'd poison yourself."

"Would I? What about Alicia and your precious colonel? Cuckolding Dirk without undoing a single button. Doing it with their eyes."

The light seemed to burn the flesh from Naomi's skull. She turned away with an abrupt strangled noise.

"I only guessed, lady. You've made it obvious. And don't let the servants see you cry. I hear they love to gossip."

"You foul-minded, unprincipled . . ."

"Maybe. But that don't change what's happening."

Wally swallowed, and the alcohol hit hard. His constitution no longer bounced.

"You just had to use my own words against me, didn't you?"

"I didn't give your daughter appetites like her mother's. Like you, she's going for power first, and down the road'll buy herself a toy-boy to play with on the beach. You're all hungry for something, you, De Wit, and Sadler. And, God help him, my brother, Con. You all play the end against the middle and want the biggest slice of the pie for yourselves. And, apart from all of you screwing each other for sex or money, the biggest prize right now is my brother's tail, right?"

"Why are you here if you think that?"

"Ain't that a question and a half? What *am* I doing here, apart from not a lot? Nothing is all. You wanna leave with me, like now?"

"I've had more than enough of your diseased mind for company, thank you."

"Your choice, lady."

Wally watered the flowers with the Manhattan and set the glass between the lion's paws.

"Tell Connie, not Conrad, I said my goodbyes like a proper chap."

"Tell him yourself."

"Okay."

Jorgesson had flopped into the pool and was a silver ghost in the glittering water. Clive Spring had joined Alicia and De Wit, and they quoted poetry at each other with practised ease. Spring's Welsh accent reminded Wally of Dylan Thomas's radio voice. Too well oiled to be authentic. Sadler said something clever enough to make the company laugh and Jorgesson spurted water into the air, his hair wet straw against the jade tiles. Their laughter wound down when Wally's shadow cut between them.

"Gotta go. Something came up. Business."

Wally and De Wit cracked knuckles in a hard handshake.

"You'll come to dinner when your brother returns from Cape Town."

"Sure, except Con's in Durban."

"And it's business before pleasure. He's very single-minded."

Sadler waved a long drink in a plump hand.

"I can vouch for that. A lurcher after hare."

Spring found that funny until Wally looked at him. Then he found the foliage in his drink fascinating.

Wally was close to dropping Spring in the pool a limb at a time. There was a slyness about the man that angered Wally. The way he sniggered and took photographs when his subjects weren't looking. As if he possessed them along with their images.

Wally stared at Spring and said: "Hares are only fast rabbits. Thanks again, Mr. De Wit."

"My pleasure."

De Wit didn't react to Wally's dropping his military title. His was just another face in the sunlight and could have been seeing far vistas or dark cells. There was nobody home behind the hooded eyes. Alicia had the same look when she watched her mother come up to take Wally's arm.

"Actually it's me, darlings. I have this frightful head, and Walter has offered to drive me home. I'll call you later, Alicia. Tomorrow."

There were the usual goodbyes, and Naomi threw her car keys at Wally in the carport, slapped the roof of her white gullwing Mercedes, and snapped, "I suppose you can drive one of these?"

"If the rubber bands ain't perished."

"I thought for one dreadful moment you were going to hit . . ."

"So did Spring."

Wally drove between confident estates and small exclusive houses in the weatherless weather. Found his way out onto a highway where knots of black children offered fruit and small birds for sale. He turned off into scrub land and let the motor idle above a deep kloof tangled by nondescript thorn. The air conditioner hummed and the car ticked in the blanket of heat.

Wally lit a cigarette.

"What's De Wit's angle with Connie?"

"What could it be?"

"I'm asking you, lady."

"Nothing other than the desire to see your mining venture succeed. This is still a pioneering country. We all admire self-made men."

"That's as phony as your headache, Naomi."

"And as phony as you threatening Clive Spring. And as silly as your not calling De Wit 'Colonel.'"

"With a snappy salute and a couple of 'yessirs' thrown in, I suppose?"

"If you won't learn, you won't."

"There's more going down here than I can see on the surface, that I do know. What the hell do they take Connie for? A bloody Rotarian?"

"Any reason why they shouldn't? Sadler talks very highly of your brother. Almost too effusively at times. You're seeing shadows where there aren't any."

"And you weren't shaking my bed apart this morning for fear of De Wit, eh?"

"Take me home."

"And what about this Spring character? This rabbit who spouts poetry and reckons he can sneer at the likes of me?"

"Then will you take me home?"

"I'm listening, lady."

"Clive Spring is in public relations, and something of a features writer. He can get Conrad a lot of good column inches here. We like to see a new millionaire flaunt the fact. Otherwise, how is society to know he is one? Clive can build Conrad into a public figure in a matter of months. Weeks."

"And what have they got on you, girl?"

"What *could* they 'have' on me?" Naomi almost met Wally's eyes.

"Maybe phony headaches are a capital offense."

"Take me home. Now."

"You're not bedding me for fun or profit. Even if you do like it."

"Take me home, you bastard."

"Yeah. End of a perfect day."

Wally turned the car in a veil of dust and sideslipped onto the highway. Pushed the pedal to the floor and hit 120 miles per hour until Naomi killed the ignition and the Mercedes coasted to a halt on the hard shoulder.

"Thought you was in a hurry."

"Not enough to get myself a traffic ticket with you in my car. I'll drive."

Wally still puzzled over that remark when Naomi stopped to drop him outside the Langham Hotel.

"I won't embarrass you by asking you inside in daylight."

Naomi stared over the wheel.

"Then I shan't have to embarrass you by refusing."

Wally got out and held the door.

"Why do I get the feeling I'll see you again? And not just because we both want it?"

"Wouldn't you *love* to be right about that?"

"Better than being wrong. And better than you getting tight-arsed because your Alicia's followed your road too close. Live honest with yourself and stop pretending. Christ, you'd think she'd taken De Wit away from *you.*"

Naomi's sudden look at Wally was white bone.

"Christ," said Wally. "She did."

"Goodbye, my brutish friend."

Naomi left tire stripes and a curl of vapor behind. Her brakelights flared and she was gone in traffic.

Wally went into the Langham gnawing his lip.

The telephone in his room rang with the weary insistence of a machine that had repeated itself for far too long.

"Hello."

Wally jerked his ear away from static and bad temper.

"Calm down, Con. All I'm getting is snap, crackle, and fucking pop."

He realized that apart from the odd "bloody" he hadn't sworn in Naomi's company.

Connie said "Vic Dakin" as all the sirens of all the fleets of the world whooped in the background.

"What about him?"

There was something about bank drafts. Post-dated checks. Bad wallpaper from Brussels to Florence and on to Malta. All signed by Vic Dakin on irrevocable transfers. Connie's wallet had been sliced thin by a dead man.

"How thin, Connie?"

"Seen thinner . . ." Connie faded again.

"What does Kelly say?"

"Fucking unprintable . . . next flight home . . . *You* sort it . . . You . . ."

The line degenerated into electronic birdsong and the

turkey-gobble of interference. Died completely and left Wally with Vic Dakin somehow being alive.

Wally jiggled the tines. Asked for flight details at the desk.

Knew he'd be home for Christmas and didn't know Naomi's last name.

Shame, he thought. Distracted.

Charlie hit the water clean.

The bottom came up as a surge of dappled concrete. He touched and stayed under. Dribbled air as he swam under the Chinese bridge Queenie had commissioned, and made for the shallows, where Ingrid turned brown in the shade of banana trees. Queenie, a bright turban over her white hair, glasses on the end of her nose, knitted something Archie would never wear.

Charlie floated on his back.

Geckos sunned themselves on the hot castellations of the boundary wall and early finches arrowed into the big palms to spend the night, safe from Maltese hunters who blew them apart with grapeshot.

Queenie's needles clacked as she purled and plained.

"You'll go all pruny if you stay in much longer."

"Yes, Queenie."

Charlie basked where he was.

Archie sat in a wheelchair at the far end of the pool. He wore sunhat and shorts, and his big belly was as brown as a Mexican pot. He leaned on a walking stick and stared at the pool as if daring the waters to lap his feet.

An embolism had formed below his right knee ten days before, and he had known nothing for over a week. A naval surgeon saved him before the clots reached his heart; and now, speechless and forbidden to walk, he mended slowly, his brain alive behind silent lips.

Charlie watched the shadows move with the sun, listened to a celluloid ball chase its own echoes around the high boundary walls. Archie's Maltese minders played table tennis in the sunroom, cutting shots like fencers. Charlie had checked them out with the Tonna brothers in Toronto and received a telexed testimonial.

"Time you girls changed for dinner."

"Don't tire him, Charlie."

Queenie's needles went quiet.

"I won't."

The orange trees released their bouquet with the setting sun as Queenie and Ingrid went into the villa. Charlie swam through pink light and leaned below the wheelchair to look up into faded green eyes.

"You scared me, old man."

Eyes the color of money said they knew.

"The mail train trial's over, Arch. Brixton, Alfie, and the lads drew thirty years apiece. They're all willing to pay the price to be sprung. Except that moron Popeye. He's playing the amnesiac over Ollie and Pim, but the sorry bastard's sent word that his memory'll come back if he ain't sprung from Wandsworth Prison for free. But, knowing Popeye, he'd hold a press conference the moment he hit Rio, and blow the whistle on everybody. Don't see how that leaves us much choice."

The green eyes agreed.

"Bonar votes for hitting him inside. It's that or spring him."

Archie's cane rapped twice.

"Then we hit him."

Charlie wished Ingrid had left her cigarettes behind.

"A body that could have been Buster's turned up headless in Rotherhithe. Knowing Popeye gave Buster to the Troys, there won't be a shortage of volunteers to snuff Popeye."

The eyes blinked and narrowed.

"The Harolds are in Jo'burg with Sadler. Vic Dakin got away with a whole bundle of Connie's dough, and Pim got me the word that Connie's sent Wally home to sort it. Pim's still hot as a pistol over Wally staying away so long, so theirs should be a reunion with a difference, eh?" Charlie grinned and sobered.

"Connie can't clear his stolen earth-moving equipment through South African Customs. He lacks the finance to bribe the bribable officials, and he can't produce the proper documentation to do it legally. Now, with Connie needing heavy funds fast, it could be he might just get Wally to start some cowboy action to get it for him. Question is, which way will he jump? East or west?"

The faded eyes became distant.

The sky had darkened to a royal purple, and a rare owl hooted from the bowers above the north tower.

Archie's cane pointed south.

"Brighton? Connie won't find that an easy patch. That's where you let the dregs of the old firms melt away. And like you said, 'Always leave a man somewhere to run, or he'll have no choice but to come back at you.'"

I did, said the eyes.

"There's still a lot of mail train money waiting to come on to the streets, and we don't want it on our turf. How about we see it gets nudged towards Connie? No reason why the chaps who want an early release from their thirty-year sentences shouldn't end up in sunny South Africa with their pots of gold. Better it ends up out there than burning holes in our turf."

Work on it, said the eyes.

"I'll have to divert Wally somehow. Give me time to get things rolling. Jesse's taken our fairy back into the Fortress, so the information's coming out of there all right. Limehouse Lou's a loaded gun ready to be pointed, but I'll keep him in my pocket for a bit. You agree?"

Archie's cane rapped yes.

"I've done nothing about Kosher Kramer. Nor about Manchester Freddy and Maltese Maurice. Gloves on or off, Archie?"

Patience, said the eyes.

"I don't like leaving it lie, Arch."

The eyes understood. Said: *Patience, Charlie. Hold water.*

"I'm gonna be busy when I fly home, eh?"

You are.

"Shall we join the ladies?"

Why not?

Charlie wheeled Archie through the fragrant garden as the rising moon took on brilliance. The board meeting was over.

Ingrid wondered how she could feel sick and ravenous at the same time. Nausea bumped the back of her throat when she found Queenie admiring the dress she had laid out on the bed in her room.

"You were sick, sweetheart?"

"Too much sun."

"The water's different here, too."

"Yes."

"And you should wash the fruit before you eat it."

Sequins gleamed on black taffeta when Queenie turned the dress on its hanger.

"May I have that?" Ingrid smoothed her slip.

"I'll button you." Queenie hooked hooks. "A bit snug around your sit-upon."

Ingrid twirled to check her stocking seams.

"Too much of your good cooking."

"And it's too early to show."

"What?"

Queenie's hand rose and fell in dismissal.

"I'm an old woman who's seen the elephant too many times. Charlie hasn't noticed, but what man does?"

Ingrid flushed and frowned.

"Queenie Ogle, if you say one single word—"

"You haven't told him. I thought not."

"This may be the permissive society, but not in my heart of hearts. No, I haven't told him."

"Maybe you should before he sees for himself."

"And lose him? Have him get that cold look in his oh-so-cold grey eyes and say, 'Wham-bam-thank-you-ma'am, there's the door'?"

"How d'you know he'll take it like that?"

"How? Would he be who he is, do what he does for Archie, if he wasn't *just* like that?"

"But how d'you *know?"*

"You're a stuck gramophone needle. Would you have told Archie if it had been you?"

"With brass bands and flying flags I would, you silly bitch. A kid's what we always wanted and never had. The closest we've got to a son is Charlie. Your Charlie. If a baby don't bring you together, nothing will. And if it pushes you apart? It was happening anyway. You can't hold on to what you haven't got, sweetheart. But you have to know either way, right?"

"I suppose . . ."

"Will you tell him, then?"

"I'd have to be good and tiddly."

"Whatever. But remember the baby eats and drinks what you eat and drink." Queenie's look was bittersweet. "I'm an expert on other people's babies."

"You can be any kind of mother to this one. If you want . . ."

Ingrid kissed Queenie's seamed cheek.

"You'll keep it, Ing?"

"Yes."

"Whatever he says?"

"Whatever he says. Of course."

"No 'of course' about it. And now we're both crying. Wash your face and we'll open a bottle. To celebrate what I don't know."

"Life?"

"Corny. Even for a mother-to-be. But we'll drink to it." Queenie opened the door for Ingrid, and neither of them saw Charlie flattened against the wall as they headed for the stairs.

Charlie found himself looking at a man in swimming shorts with a comical look on his face. It was a reverse image of himself in the mirrored niche across the landing.

Charlie stared at Charlie, and the reflected one seemed to have all the answers.

Wally cleared Customs with a sick migraine a week later than he had planned. In Pimlico's Jaguar he said, "Straight to Camberwell, son. No messing."

Pimlico turned through Longford, away from the M4 to London as Wally talked angrily.

"Connie got back two days ago. And where have I been? Twiddling my thumbs in a cell, that's where. And why? Interpol and the Fraud Squad are investigating thousands of naughty airline tickets, and picked me out at random. Turns out I was traveling on an excess-baggage ticket issued by Vic

Dakin's old travel agency. Can you beat that? Connie's flying about first class, and has *me* traveling on a bloody excess-baggage ticket."

Wally blew smoke. Blind to Pimlico's silent disapproval.

"And now I've got to have Kelly bend my ear about all that earth-moving equipment she's shipped to Durban and can't pay duty on 'cause tricky Vicky Dakin came back from the dead to clear out Connie's piggy bank. And all that plant she's had swiped from motorway construction sites she *can't* ship because South African Customs want documents of origination and ownership she plain *can't* supply. It's just as well the insurance money from the warehouse fires went into a different account, or Connie'd be up the bloody Mississippi without a banjo."

There was more of the same before Pimlico pulled off onto the common land beyond Poyle. Wally followed Pimlico across grass stiff with frost.

"Couldn't you take a leak in the terminal, Pim?"

Distant cows huffed white breath and a colt skipped about a mare.

"This is igloo-land after the jungle I've—"

Wally sat down and skidded on his buttocks. Pimlico's fist had taken him in the mouth. He stared at the green trail he'd blazed, and cold struck up through his rimed trousers.

"What's your game? I ought to—"

Pimlico kicked the wind from Wally's lungs. Crouched on his hams to watch Wally sit up and hold himself.

"You want some more? Or you want to listen?"

Wally touched a swelling lip.

"I'll listen. One-sided chat anyway."

"Okay. So don't thank me for climbing out of bed at five this morning. Or for driving all the way up from Brighton. Don't *once* ask how business has been since you've been playing Tarzan in wogland. And don't, just *don't* expect me to drop my marbles every time your brother gets his arse in a sling. We've got our own problems to fret over."

"Who said . . . ?"

Pimlico ripped a frozen stalk of cow parsley from the turf and slashed the air with it.

"I'll take you to Camberwell to see Connie's Kelly. I'll

even hold your coat when you pat her head and tell her, 'Shame, darling.' But for that you get just five short minutes, right? Then you and me are going to a meet I made with Charlie. Any arguments about it and you and me are history, *right?*"

"But there's millions at stake . . ."

"Ain't my millions. Nor yours."

"But, Pim . . ."

"And if this mining lark is so lucrative, how is it the South Africans are handing it over on a plate? To a foreigner?"

"Connie knows . . ."

"Connie knows nothing."

Wally pointed a heavy finger.

"He's my brother, Pim. Like you and me are brothers. The only difference is you and me chose each other. I got born alongside Con. You've got a punch, you know that?"

"So long as you do."

"You're taking a lot for granted I won't belt you back."

"You can try."

Wally offered his hand for a lift.

"Hell, no. But I'd like to sell tickets if you and Charlie ever squared off. Can I get up, or are you planning to kick my legs away?"

Pimlico stepped off a few paces.

"You can make it to your feet without me. And I saw that move in ten old John Wayne movies."

Wally slapped his soaked backside.

"I can sort this Vic Dakin business *and* take care of us."

"Not if Brighton goes sour you can't. Kosher's crowd don't want our machines—say they're dealing with Tommy Troy, which is a field of cowcake. And Charlie wants it sorted. Yesterday."

Wally retucked his scarf and found his hat.

"Hitting me won't sort nothing."

"Had to make you listen."

"To what? Charlie comes first?"

"That and the fact that the Troys have laid a carpet of dough in Brighton to keep us out. And sent a message to say it's their turf now they've cozied up with Kosher Kramer."

"You could have got that said without whacking me in the

mouth." Wally stared into the neutral haze. "So that's how they figure to make happy with Sadler. Get strong with the old firms before moving into the Smoke. Connie said they'd try something like that without the chance of screwing up."

"What are you wittering on about?"

Wally saw bands of color as migraine clamped his head.

"Troy figures to get at Connie through us, that's all. And get at your precious Charlie the same way. They've chosen the turf, and figure we'll pile into Brighton with our soldiers and get a bad licking. Unless we box clever."

"That's why Charlie wants to see us, Wal. He's too smart to get caught with his pants down in Brighton."

"So Charlie's smart. Is there anything else on your tiny mind, O Master of the Magic-flaming-Ring?"

"Yeah, don't smoke in my car."

"And welcome home, Wally," Wally sneered.

"Welcome home, you fart. I've missed your ugly face."

"Stands out a sea mile, does that."

"And congratulate me. I got married."

"Now, that"—Wally sat in the car—"is real trouble."

The stage at Mother's Club had new curtains.

The flats and backdrop of Highgate Hill where Dick Whittington turned again for fame and fortune in the City of London needed six feet of sky, a door for the medieval pub, and numerals for the milestone. Electric Raymond sewed a tail onto a cat costume, and Kensington Kate sat in muted light from a niggered-pup with the white-haired boy. The same nude reclined on his painted pillows, and the same incense tickled Charlie's nose as he helped himself to coffee from the Cona.

Penny opened his silk blouse to show weals and scratches, the big blue pigeon's egg under his long white fringe.

Kate's nostrils pinched.

"Sorry in triplicate won't make this right, Charles."

Charlie blew on his scalding drink.

"You're always formal when you chide me. Jesse's handiwork, Penny?"

"His brother, Tommy's. It was just after Helen's memorial service. I was upstairs. Changing for Jesse. He likes me in lingerie. They were things Helen gave me before she—"

"Slowly, son," Charlie soothed.

"—killed herself. Tommy came into the bedroom. Just came in and went berserk. Screamed her name over and over again with spit jumping out of his mouth. Tore my clothes off. Tore everything away, looking . . . for her. And when he saw there was only me he started punching and punching. Ripping at me with his nails . . ."

Penny gagged, clicked his teeth.

". . . Then Jesse came in at a run. Jumped at his brother. Trampled all over me like madmen. With Jesse holding Tommy around the chest. And Tommy hitting down anywhere he could. Head. Face. Shoulders. Kicking, too. The mirrors smashed. They fell over the bed, and the pillows burst. Feathers went everywhere. All over them. In their eyes. In their hair. Then Jesse hit Tommy with something hard. Tommy went down and went to pieces. Just sobbed and punched the bed. And Jesse held him like a little boy. Ida screamed for the others to do something. But nobody would come in. Not even Gordon. Then it got quiet. Like they were asleep. But they weren't. They were whispering as if they'd hidden something. Something only they knew about. Not Ida. Not me. Not anybody . . ."

Penny sipped Charlie's coffee.

"Take your time, son."

"And . . . when I looked they were holding something. A cigar box, with rings and pieces of gold. Shiny things like that in it. Turning them. And touching them. Nodding and smiling. They were in another world. Like bad children . . ."

Kate glanced at Charlie. Rubbed his neck as if bristle grew back into his skull.

Charlie drank coffee, but his mouth wouldn't moisten.

"And then . . . slowly, and then all at once, they grew up. Were men again. But private. Touching the things in the box as if they were . . . magic. It was . . . I don't know. Just nasty."

Charlie's "uh-uh" was taut.

"And they stayed on the bed with their foreheads touching. With white down drifting down all around them. And they made plans. Sometimes there were words. Mostly they sort of knew what the other brother was thinking. They mentioned Brighton and how many soldiers they needed to make a war, and talked about this man Sadler in mumbly voices. Too mumbly for me to hear. And Archie Ogle was dead. Finished because of the contract on him. Who are Sadler and Archie Ogle, Charlie?"

"Nobody. What else?"

"And when they said your name, Charlie, they made a circle with their hands and . . . spat through it. Three times."

"Romany rubbish," said Kate. "You'll have them burning feathers next."

"They did."

Kate rubbed his neck some more.

"And lit candles. And let the wax drip on something I couldn't see. Said a name and said he was dead. Said other names and said they were dead."

Penny drank coffee and shuddered.

"What names?"

"Yours. An Irish name. Who missed an old lady and you and shot . . . a horse . . ." Penny touched his bruised forehead. "Does that make . . . sense?"

"Dublin Gerry? Was that the name?"

"But he's one of—" Kate started.

"Shut it, Kate. Was that the name?"

"I . . . think so."

Charlie's smile was a fleeting thing.

"Dublin pulled the trigger without triggering the target. Makes sense. If you're Irish." He nudged Kate. "And talking of Irish."

"I've gone." Electric dropped his sewing and poured Jamieson's over ice in a tall glass.

Penny shook like paper in the wind.

"I'm not going back. Money or no money."

"No, son, you and Shane are going on holiday."

Penny's smile was beatific.

"They also mentioned Manchester."

"Manchester?" said Kate. "They're bringing provincial villains in the Smoke?"

Charlie shook his head.

"Not the town, Kate. The man. Wheel Penny away, old son. Pim and Wally are due here for a meet."

Kate stood.

"Good. They can fix that bandit of theirs to pay out more generously. My fairies aren't made of money." The snap in Kate's voice almost masked his pleasure. He rounded on Electric Raymond with, "And if that cat's tail is on straight I'm Rita Hayworth."

"Don't you wish, dearie."

Electric handed Charlie his long Irish as Kate took Penny away up the stairs.

"You've pleased the old dear."

"Fair exchange, Electric."

Charlie toasted Dublin Gerry on a job badly done.

Connie glared at Wally, nodded at Pimlico, stuffed geological surveys into his briefcase, and gave Kelly something to file. Harry the Crack and Sailor Mailer loaded perlite samples into a van in the yard.

"You've missed the fatted calf, prodigal."

"And who left me at Jan Smuts Airport as excess baggage without a dildo to dangle, eh? My bloody brother, that's who."

Wally's head was a ballroom of angry echoes.

"You had Naomi Leathers to ease the wait."

So that's her surname. "Yeah, she was allowed to look through a grill at me while you was playing footsie with her daughter, Alicia."

Kelly spiked a docket.

"Sounds *fun.* Do tell."

Connie's eyes marbled.

"He's throwing dust to cover his own naughties. Alicia's only a kid."

"Nineteen going on a thousand. You'd clean her clock in a hot minute if you wasn't so scared Uncle De Wit would clean yours first."

"Well, tick-tock."

Kelly answered the phone with a stiff back, and Connie stabbed his blotter with a stiffer finger.

"I wasn't back in this office five minutes before I had West End Central on my back for a sweetener. You boys want to operate in Soho you have to pay off the law. You've forgotten that drinks for the boys in blue is the first order of business."

"We don't backhand the filth," Pimlico said.

"Crap. First law of villainy: buy the right copper."

Wally's neck and earlobes flushed.

"Come off it, Con. Wasn't me who got taken by Vic Dakin, was it? And buying coppers ain't where it stops for you, is it? No, you want to buy whole governments. Let me off your carousel. I'm riding the dead horse."

Connie pointed over both fists.

"And Charlie Dance ain't deader? Why don't you shake hands with the Troys and really cut my throat?"

"You don't need me to cut your throat, you're doing it all by yourself. You brought Dakin back and crowed on about how you had him well under the thumb. Then he was dead except he wasn't, and a lot of *our* dough went walkies when he did his Jesus Christ trick and rose again. Get your feet back on the cobbles where they belong, brother. Me and Pim have got the Troys on our backs because they won't come after you straight. Well, thanks a bunch. We'll wash your shitty socks for you, you get back to your big-deal scheming."

Connie looked and sounded strangled.

"Hold it. No cowboy action. No Mickey Mouse. After Christmas maybe . . ."

Pimlico snorted softly.

"You clown. It's never *now* with you, is it, eh? Always later. When later, Connie? Easter? Whitsuntide? All Hallows? Never?"

"I need dough, not aggravation."

"Then earn it. On the cobbles, where you belong."

"You'd choke if I didn't swallow for you," Connie said.

"Don't big-brother me," Wally told him.

Pimlico got his back against the wall as Harry and Sailor

came in to block the door. Connie looked wild enough to try something violent.

"You two take on the Troys? You ain't got the spit to lick a postage stamp. Charlie's got you both tamed, hasn't he? Go away and be unlucky."

"That's what Charlie said you'd say," said Pimlico.

"Said I'd say what?"

"Said you wanted a big earner and no trouble. Said there's one if you want it."

"That's a message, is it? A message from the throne of the divine Charlie?" Connie sneered, his eyes marbled and his face mottled. "So? What is it, this earner?"

"Some boarders in one of Her Majesty's penal hotels want to go on holiday before they come up for parole in fifteen years. They want a foreign holiday, you want dough in wogland. Put the two together and what have you got?"

Connie just stared, thinking hard. Blinked and leaned on his fists. "Charlie said, eh? You two give me the dry heaves."

Pimlico barely smiled. He rolled his shoulders and said, "And I had you pegged higher than the Troys. Wrong, wasn't I? You all came out of the same cracked mold. Ain't enough money in the world to make you happy. No highs. No lows. Just grab every penny because it's there and you want it. Unhappy on top. Unhappy anywhere. No joy or sorrow, just grab and grab and grab some more. You through here, Wally?"

"Except I ain't walking around them two bookends in the door," Wally said.

Kelly glared at Wally over Connie's shoulder.

"Ask them to curtsy. Curtsy and stand aside. Go ahead."

Mad lights stung Wally's eyes.

"She gives the orders; you wear the dress. That it, Con?"

Connie's fists shook on his blotter.

"Easy, Greasy. You got a long way to slide."

Wally stared at the men in the doorway. Harry the Crack showed his palms and edged aside. He wanted Wally off the firm without any trouble. Wanted the top slot in South Africa keeping Dirk Jorgesson in line. Seeing that Alicia played footsie with nobody but Connie, and keeping an eye on Spring and Colonel De Wit. Harry liked the life out there. Liked teaching the Kaffirs to play darts and to bawl ribald cockney songs as they sank their pots of frothy Kaffir beer.

Sailor stayed mute, eyes mean in his tanned face. He wanted to show Connie how good he was.

Connie may have given a sign. Kelly hissed as Sailor turned reluctantly away to stare at nothing through the grimed windows. Harry opened the door and stood aside, and the tension died like a spent candle.

Wally followed Pimlico into the yard.

"You'll come crawling back," Connie yelled.

Pimlico bundled Wally into the Jaguar and drove away fast. They were fifteen minutes behind schedule when they parked in Soho Square in plain view of Quill's vantage point above the massage parlor south of the Fox building.

Quill lowered his binoculars.

"They're going to Mother's, Buller."

"Five minutes behind the Troys. Do we steam in now, or let them all sweat for a bit?"

Quill's eyes shone like wet tarmac.

"If there's an affray, we won't need a warrant. Have the squad on stand-by."

Electric Raymond flipped coasters onto the bar and wiped the mahogany with a bar towel as Jesse came through the tables with Tommy, Gordon, and three of their heavy villains.

Kensington Kate ran scalding water into a pitcher and held it below the counter.

Jesse's face was as yellow as old ivory and wouldn't hold still. He seemed to be shaking apart from within.

"A round of mixed drinks here, Electric."

"Jesse, dear. Haven't seen you since my party three months back. How's our Penny?"

The barb went deep, and Electric didn't seem to notice the harm he'd caused. Kate worried a lip. Charlie sat in a spotlight and made no move to leave.

Tommy tapped the bar with a manicured nail.

"Still the comedians, eh?"

Kate didn't bother with a smile of greeting.

"Only in the right company, Mr. Troy, dear. Five small iced pigeon's milks? Or manly pints of bitter with lipstick smears around the rims?"

"Large vodkas," said Electric. "Don't mind Kate, boys. That time of the month."

"Large *free* vodkas," said Tommy.

"And you can get Penny out here as quick as you like."

Jesse's face wouldn't compose itself. He sneer-smile-frowned with damp lips. His heavy eyebrows jumped like caterpillars with a multiple hotfoot.

Kate sighed and let more water into the pitcher.

"A refusal often offends, but we haven't seen the little love. Not since—when was it, Electric?"

"My party in Manor House."

"Her party in Manor House."

"That right?"

Tommy emptied his glass and turned it in his hand.

"Right," Kate affirmed. "Not since Jesse abducted Penny and left us without a raffle prize."

Tommy's smile had malice.

"I drink vodka in the Russian style. Means you don't get to use the same glass twice. Fredric March done it in a Garbo movie. All these army officers had one swallow and whacked their glasses into the fireplace."

Jesse swilled his drink.

"Penny was *seen.* Coming in here."

Kate's sarcasm deepened his baritone.

"Leading a pink elephant by the trunk? Dancing on points in a tutu woven from moonbeams?"

"You've been told naughties, Jessie," said Electric. "Wicked how some people just can't help lying."

A villain said, "Anywhere on the top shelf, Tommy? Knock 'em down and win a prize?"

Gordon liked that remark.

"If we play Russians, your backbar's gonna be a disaster, Kate. All those wee glass animals, ballerinas, and Guinness toucans. Your Johnnie Walkers. All gone with the wind, just like Ida's did."

"Last chance, Kate," said Tommy.

Kate held the pitcher of scalding water at his side. Looked Tommy in the eye and said, "We both know it won't make a jot of difference what I say or do, don't we? You'd still have to make your mark. I'm too old and fey to spit into the wind or fart in the face of the inevitable. You smash away, dear heart. My glass salesman's sitting right behind you, and he gives me lovely rates for breakages. Don't you, Charles?"

"Oh, blimey, yeah."

Charlie was a severed head in the spotlight.

Tommy turned easily, and short staves slid from overcoat sleeves into ready palms. Kate showed Jesse the pitcher of scalding water when he started across the bar, and Electric Raymond's kitchen knife was as long as a moonlit road.

Tommy wished he could see more than shadows around Charlie's smile.

"That can't be you, Charlie?"

"Run out of bars to smash in Bethnal Green, Tom?"

"Somebody upset the brother."

"Not difficult, the way I hear it."

"That's as may be. Question is: why are you cozied up in this poofs' parlor at the exact moment Jesse's favorite fairy goes missing? A nasty thought occurs right away. Was that Penny whispering our secrets into your ear?"

"Lively imagination you've got there, Tom. You should write gags for Kate's Christmas show."

Tommy looked at a fist. Opened it and put it in his pocket.

"Flying glass gets everywhere, Charlie. Kate won't get no damages from the Arts Council. Just the paper hat from us."

"Like a certain punter of yours? Threw himself through his own plate-glass window to save you the bother? Twice? I heard they had to number his parts to put him back together again. Just like poor old Popeye Greenland."

Tommy edged towards Charlie's table.

"What about Popeye?"

"Happened in Cardiff Prison. There was Popeye carrying his pot to the sluice. Minding his own business and looking forward to his breakfast. Took a sharpened spoon through the kidneys. Touch and go in surgery, I heard. And all because somebody had the quaint idea Popeye had given Buster Barnes and his mail train money away to somebody in Bethnal Green. And that Popeye was willing to give up two other chaps to the law if he wasn't sprung from prison for free. Popeye's given up the idea of getting out for nothing, and he's got total amnesia about who was with him on the train. Got the word out through his sister Elsie. You know Elsie, Tommy. She's the one who's susceptible to burns in the kitchen."

Tommy rubbed his jaw.

"Tell the chap with the spoon I'll buy him a good drink if he does better next time."

"He wouldn't drink with you. But I'll buy you one if Electric saves that pig-sticker for cutting sandwiches."

Jesse shook his head and found his voice.

"I'll shove it up sodomite valley if I don't get my Penny right now."

Tommy wore conceit like a cheap overcoat.

"Jesse's too upset for the silly sociables, Charlie. You and the Dolly Sisters are overdue for a heavy spanking. Now's the time, and here's the place."

Charlie said nothing and his face remained pleasant.

A silence gathered all by itself and the Cona bubbled like an upset stomach. The ceiling stayed where it was and the floor didn't quake.

Tommy's contracted pupils were as hard as the ends of freshly snapped pencils.

"Heart holding up, is it, Charlie?"

Charlie's head shrugged into unlit shoulders.

"Bumping along nicely. Penny not being here shouldn't bother anyone but Jesse."

"I'll show you bother, Dance."

Jesse shook with emotional ague. His pink eyes snapped at nothing and his hands washed themselves sweaty. He looked ready to fall a long way into somewhere dark and unpleasant.

Charlie wondered how he could nudge him over the edge.

"Love never runs smooth," he said.

Tommy pointed a finger.

"It's you who's sweating."

"You haven't looked in the doorway."

"At what? I've got the front covered."

"*Had* it covered, Troy." Wally stepped out from the stairwell.

"You never said truer, Wal. Morning, Chas." Pimlico nodded at Charlie and inspected Tommy as if he posed in a tailor's window.

"Does that coat come in bigger colors? Are them padded shoulders an optional extra? And, hello, here's some faces we usually only see the back of. Where'd you get this lot of rough, Tommy? A job lot from Mothercare?"

Fury paled Tommy's face.

"Don't prod your old friends, Pim. You still owe us for putting rent money on your Miriam's table."

"You was the one doing the prodding, Tommy. Miriam welcomed you with open legs. So who owes who?"

Tommy bit into his half-smile. Stared at Pimlico with raw hatred.

Jesse said, "Penny" and sighed.

"You still owe us, Pim. Jesse, get your mind out of your underwear."

Pimlico leaned against the bar.

"So the husband gets to pay for you shafting his wife? Like how, Troy? By not putting our machines in Brighton?"

"That for openers. And standing aside now."

Pimlico let a stave drop from his sleeve. Rolled it down the bar towards Jesse and tutted.

"Bit late for standing aside. Your face on the door handed me this when I hooked him. How'd you want to play this, Chas?"

Charlie remained still. "A good host lets his guests choose the party games. What's it to be, Tommy? Musical headaches? Pin the paper hat to the moron?"

Tommy's sneer almost came off.

"Comedian."

Jesse kicked his bar stool away and grey tears trailed his face. "You've got my Penny, you bastards . . ." His face caved in on itself and he sobbed as though he were alone.

"What *have* you girls said?" Pimlico asked Kate.

"This is a stand-off, Tommy," Charlie said. "Pick up your marbles and go home."

Kate stabbed his glass at the Pernod optic, and his hands shook as he added ice.

"Nine butch straights and not a fairy in sight? What sort of a name will poor old Mother's get now?"

"Thirteen," said Electric. "The law's in."

Quill's squad milled about on the stairs, and Bulstrode was saved from falling by Wally's stiff forearm.

"Nobody move," Quill bawled. "I have reason to believe—"

"Are you gentlemen members?" Kate asked.

"—there has been an affray in contravention and in breach of—"

Bustrode straightened his necktie.

"Hold it, Prophet."

Kate insisted on seeing the gentlemen's cards.

"Not warrant cards," Electric told Payne as he flashed his wallet.

Kate sighed at the ceiling.

"Fourteen straights and nobody drinking."

"You!" Quill poked a hole in the air near Charlie's face. "Stand up. You're carrying a concealed weapon."

Payne seared the bar with his flashgun, and light slicked the staves Tommy's men held.

"What the hell are they?" Charlie asked. "Lollipops?"

"Stand up."

Charlie's head rose into shadow, and Quill's hand was spotlit as he took Charlie's wallet.

Payne asked Tommy his name.

"Count Basie. This is my orchestra."

"Your what?"

"It's an audition, you soppy copper," said Electric.

Tommy found Pimlico over Payne's head.

"Just you and me, you disloyal bastard. No lawyers."

Pimlico bared teeth.

"Pick your turf."

Wally wandered to the bar and asked for a vodka to wash down a soluble aspirin.

"Get names and addresses," Quill told Dillman.

Wally gargled vodka.

"Duke Ellington, Hollywood. Never black up for rehearsals."

"Barbara Stanwyck," said Electric. "And she's Rita Hayworth this week, aren't you, petal?"

"Autograph, handsome?" Kate offered.

Jesse buried his nose in a handkerchief and snorted long and loud.

"Stage fright," said Electric.

"You know who I am," said Pimlico.

Paper bands fluttered to the carpet when Quill fumbled with notes and credit cards.

"What would you say they were, Buller?"

Bulstrode knelt beside the paper bands. Recognized the colophon of a Scottish bank. Looked up at Charlie and said, "Mr. Dance has some explaining to do."

"What a turn-up!" Quill crowed.

Bulstrode couldn't look at Quill. He blinked up at Charlie.

"He'd starve as a cardsharp," Charlie said softly.

"We'll have to take you in, Charlie."

"Suits me, as it happens," said Charlie.

Bulstrode used tweezers to put the bands into an envelope.

"This don't feel right to me, Chas," he said.

Quill found his handcuffs and a printed caution.

"Turn around, Dance. Hands behind your back."

"Out of order, Prophet," said Bulstrode.

Quill just read from his card with his face lit from within.

Dillman fumbled with notebook and pencil.

"What do I write as the accused reply?"

"Write nothing," Bulstrode said as Quill's handcuffs snarled around Charlie's wrists.

"Write the Lord's Prayer for all I care," said Quill. "He's pinched, and that's that. Job jobbed."

"What are all these wooden clubs for?" asked Payne.

Kate swept from behind the bar to tweak Payne's cheek.

"Props, you sweet thing. Hand them in, boys. You know I don't like you playing with them. We're closed for rehearsals, but you can stay. That camera looks so professional."

Payne colored and went behind Bulstrode.

"You're swallowing this, Chas?" Pimlico asked.

"Why not?"

"Don't talk to the prisoner," said Quill.

In the street Charlie sniffed the early evening air. Smelled frost in the lowering scud of mist and chimney smoke.

"Breathe deep, Dance. That's the last free air you'll know for two or three decades."

Charlie was ducked into a police car and sandwiched between Bulstrode and Dillman. He played a mental game of poker to pass the time and smooth his face, and didn't react to Quill's taunts.

CHAPTER 2

THE CELL WAS JUST OBLONG OF SQUARE AND THE LIGHT stayed on all night. It had a grey steel door with rounded bolts and a fisheye lens set in a concave oval viewing port. The floor was brown composition with faint red figuring, and rolled up to make a hard sanitary skirting to the base of the tiled walls. The wooden bunk was three inches too short for Charlie and was deadbolted to the left-hand wall.

A fumigated mattress the thickness of an arrowroot biscuit and the brown of old feces was tightly rolled beside a small rubberoid pillow with an off-white slip that also smelled of treated sewage.

The corner sink was stainless steel, and the button taps dribbled lukewarm chlorinated water when leaned against. There was no mirror, no razor, and the soap was a hard slab of yellow sawdust that gave grudging lather and a swale that refused to wash away.

The toilet bowl was cantilevered white ceramic crazed by age and use. There had once been a window, but now there was raw brick beyond the thick steel bars.

The towel Charlie had been issued was the size of a large facecloth and its nap was as abrasive as a Brillo pad. He had shaved, watched by a warder who took the razor away when he was finished. They had also taken his tie and belt and shoelaces.

Breakfast had been a compound of eggs, a sliver of fatty bacon, a cob of bread, and a mug of dark tea sweetened with evaporated milk.

Somebody had cried during the night. The sobs had become long withdrawal moans. Then screams. Doors had clanged, a doctor called, and the weeping addict sedated enough not to dream vampires ate through his rib cage.

All Charlie needed was a Negro singing the blues and he could have believed Burt Lancaster reared canaries in an adjoining cell.

Charlie no longer cared what day it was.

He lay on the bunk and calculated complicated bets to keep his mind sharp.

A uniformed policeman slammed the door open and poked his head inside. It was a hard, shaven head and the eyes were tougher than nailheads. The jaw said: *Don't look sideways at me. Don't even look at your own shoes. Look nowhere. Look smart. And jump when I say jump. I'm the man, and you're nothing but grist to my mill. Move when I say and not before. Wait for the command.*

"Out," he said, crashing a heel against the door.

Charlie was walked along a corridor of the same white tile and the same flooring. The stairs were spiraled and rang under his feet as he climbed two stories to another door.

"Stand *still!*"

The screw opened the door with the right key on his jangling ring and hustled Charlie through, locking it with a deft twist.

This corridor was green and dull cream, and there was glass in some of the doors. Charlie glimpsed a pigeon on a sill beyond bars before he was sent into a room with two chairs and a wooden table. The tall window looked out on to a tiled light-well through more bars.

"Wait," said the screw, and went away.

Charlie waited.

High heels walked across the ceiling on linoleum and a

filing cabinet drawer slid on steel runners. Two fingers stabbed at a typewriter, and keys jangled as policemen in shirtsleeves strolled down the passage. A late bluebottle blundered against the window and flew away up the light-well. A light switch clicked inside the cavity wall and a floor joist creaked. Then nothing happened for a long time, and there was no clock to record the wasted minutes.

Then two men came in.

The tall one with a long face and grey receding hair took the chair in front of the window and the stout younger one stood at his side with a buff file and a large notebook. The tall one scraped his chair. Scratched an eyebrow and the bridge of his bony nose. Looked at the file the stout one placed on the table in front of him. He did not look at Charlie when he said, "Sit down, Mr. Dance. You may smoke."

The stout one watched Charlie stay where he was through large tinted glasses with lenses the size of apples. His chubby leer let Charlie know they meant business—knew his hat size and his laundry number, how many fish were in his aquarium and the titles of the books on his library shelf. He said, "You heard the Detective Chief Superintendent, Dance. Sit."

"Please," said the long-faced D.C.S.

"Please?" said the stout one.

Charlie sat in a hard chair and watched for more bluebottles.

He was asked his full name, address, height, age, date of birth, even though it was all typed neatly on the form in front of them. He was told he was a remand prisoner, could wear his own clothes and order meals from outside. Was allowed visitors and had visiting rights.

"Can you account for your movements between 5 August and 9 August?"

"This year?"

"This year."

"If I thought about it."

"Do so."

"Okay."

"Well?"
"Well, what?"
"The dates, Dance."
"I'm thinking about it."
"Slow, aren't we?" said the stout one.
"Slow enough to fall for the three-card trick. Slow enough to know you've got my passport and would oppose bail if I asked for it. Slow enough to know you two would like to play 'nice' and 'nasty' with me. The old Mutt and Jeff. Chubby there gets to be nasty. You get to be the placatory, avuncular one. Chubby yells and gets red in the face. You offer me a cigarette and fatherly advice. And tell me how hard you'll fight to get me a fair shake. I play the dumb yo-yo and end up wearing the paper hat. That act should have gone out with high-button shoes and 'Vote for Disraeli' posters, Mr. Cotton."
"You're not so slow you don't know who I am."
The one with the long face found crumpled Gauloises and matches and offered them to Charlie.
"Here's the smoke. D'you want the avuncular advice?"
"Neither, thanks."
"Independent, isn't he?" said the stout one. "Hasn't even yelled for a brief. Don't you know a bent solicitor?"
Charlie folded his arms. "Is there a straight one?"
"You sound like a couple of coppers I know."
Cotton straightened a Gauloise and rolled it into his mouth without lighting it.
"Straight are they, these coppers?" said Charlie.
The stout one frowned and said nothing.
Cotton just looked at the file and said, "Suppose I tell you you've been named as the laundry for the mail train money? All signed, sealed, and delivered. Sworn depositions and everything. You'd want to make a statement then. Get yourself a silk with a long line of legal objections."
"No."
"No?"
Charlie watched moisture darken the cigarette in Cotton's mouth.
"No. I like the quiet life. You have to prove I've done what

you allege. Establish guilt without a shadow of doubt. Not just to your satisfaction. To the court's. I don't have to prove anything. Now or ever. And I don't need legal advice. Only the guilty or the innocent need all that nonsense. Remand way. Postpone. Adjourn. Do it up brown. Pleas of mitigation and cross-petitions are a pain. Me, I'll sit here with a paperback, three meals a day, lots of uniformed protection, solitude. And, more important, peace of mind."

"Confident as well," said the stout one. He leered and jabbed thick thumbs into his waistcoat pockets. "You want the country drive, do you? The scenic tour of British penal institutions?"

Charlie shrugged at him.

"Sounds different."

"You'll change your tune after a week in Brixton. Another in Maidstone. A third in Durham or Swansea or Newcastle. We can yo-yo you up and down the country from prison to prison until you think your head's twisting off at the shoulders."

Charlie did not respond.

The stout one leaned forward from the waist.

"And during the tour you have to meet up with some chummies who owe you more than a moody dig. Plenty of cons with sharpened spoons. A razor blade in a potato. They'll carve on you just to say they carved on the famous Charlie Dance. And if you live to go to trial, you won't draw Number One Court at the Old Bailey, Mister. You'll get shuffled into the crown court at Aylesbury. A nowhere place for a nowhere face. You could be on remand for a full calendar year. And there's no remission for that."

"Want to reconsider, Dance?" Cotton asked.

Charlie uncoiled from his chair. Stared through the barred window. Watery light formed silent patterns on the white tiles. The bluebottle made a final circuit and went away in an upward spiral.

"Well, Dance?"

Cotton was ready to call a constable with shorthand.

"Who do I see about buying some decent Christmas cards?" Charlie said.

The stout one showed disappointment.

Cotton closed his files and shook his head.

"Hard-nosed and very, very stupid," he said.

"With robins on logs." Charlie smiled.

Silversleeves Sutton bought plaice and chips in Catford High Street. The headlines on the newspaper wrapping was five days old and read: KENNEDY SHOT IN DALLAS.

Silversleeves wished the fish were as fresh.

He wove through the market in a bitter wind. Soho had been alive with advertising agencies starting their Christmas jollies early. Silversleeves had been punched by a model who shot arrows between cider bottles in television commercials. How Silversleeves had earned a split lip was lost in alcoholic haze, but he knew the archer's muscles weren't painted on by Special Effects.

He pushed into the snug bar of the Minstrel Boy and got himself a pint of Younger's. Nobody bought him a gargle anymore, and getting hold of decent warehouse oddments to sell from a suitcase in Oxford Street was impossible now he had been marked as a Troy snitch. When he'd laid out cash for information on the mail train he'd had friends coming out of his ears, but after the money was gone and Popeye got stabbed in prison, Silversleeves's face no longer fitted.

"Silver," he told himself, "you need another drink and a change of luck."

Tommy and Jesse Troy had changed for the worst. They talked about tackling Pimlico face-to-face on neutral turf, but that wasn't how it would happen. They would be six to one when they finally caught him alone in some dark alley with his back turned. The word had gone round and nobody wanted to know the Troys anymore. Or anybody on their firm, including Silversleeves. Even Barry the Blag and Johnny the Builder turned their backs when they saw him. The only way Silversleeves could earn a few shillings was by finding Limehouse Lou or anybody on Pim's firm.

Silversleeves flagged the barman in the saloon bar, where the dart players drank more doubles than they hit. Then he checked the public bar, where a barmaid with a rear like a full moon watched two men check the coin-drop on a one-armed bandit.

Silversleeves knew his luck had changed.

Wally Harold lifted the machine back into place, and Vinnie Castle gave the barmaid some free discs.

"Have some free pulls, Maisie. You could even win."

Maisie laughed like a throttled goat.

"And porkers might levitate, Vinnie Castle. I knew you when you had nothing but mischief in your pockets to get girls like me in trouble. Time was, I might have let you."

"Time was, you should have."

Maisie said something lost in the racket from the saloon bar, and Silversleeves dialed the Vallance Street number. Ida passed him to Gordon, who finally handed him to Tommy.

"See they stay there," Tommy ordered, and the phone went dead.

Sweating in anticipation, Silversleeves broke the back of his last pound to send doubles across for Wally and Vinnie, and ducked outside before they saw where the drinks had come from. It was much colder, and a parked Bedford with IMPERIAL MACHINES lettered on the side ticked as it lost engine heat. Silversleeves sheltered in the doorway of a furniture store to watch all three entrances of the Minstrel Boy. Vinnie and Wally were misty patches beyond acid-etched glass.

Christmas lights flicked on and off in the store window, and a plastic Santa smiled beside cheap chairs that might hold together if they were sat in by a dwarf with no small change in his pocket.

Silversleeves sneered at the furniture.

And waited.

J. C. Hatton got Charlie's signature on the last document and closed his briefcase with a loud double snap.

"You look—and I don't wish to strike a dismal note—distinctly jaded, Charles."

"Then don't."

Charlie dredged up a wink for Ingrid, who suppressed tears.

"They only moved me from Maidstone last night. How did you find me so fast?"

"We're not entirely without influence, Charles. A chum of mine flew us down from London. Swansea has quite a decent airfield."

"No problems running the firm?"

"The casinos take care of themselves as ever. The betting shops were marginally more profitable than during the summer quarter. We've added yet another branch to our meat distributors. Nothing else bothers me overmuch."

"Nothing from Toronto?"

"Golden silence, which is as it should be."

"Keep tabs on the Tonnas, J.C. Don't want any surprises."

Hatton's wink barely fluttered his lashes. He patted Ingrid's hand and went into the passage.

"Hello, Funny Face."

Charlie's hair was badly cropped, and his face was chapped from cold-shaving with a dull razor. His eyes were as vague as scraps of fog.

"Why wouldn't you let me come before?"

Ingrid's eyes brimmed without overflowing.

"You would have cried. Like now."

"That's just me. Means nothing."

"That kind of nothing sticks." Charlie touched his temple. "Here. After I've counted all the tiles in the cell, the lights are out, and I can't even read the graffiti on the ceiling. I still can't figure out how the fellows get up there with their crayons. Must be ten or twelve feet or—"

"In heaven's name, Charlie. Can't you—"

"No, I can't. Nor can you. You've got two to look after now, and I can't be there to see things are as they should be."

Ingrid blinked.

"Yes, love. I know about the bundle of fun. I listen at doors. My Aunt Maud could never break me of the habit."

Ingrid turned shy and rewrapped her duster coat.

"It's beginning to show. I'm not holding you to anything. I wouldn't, even if—"

"Even if you could?"

"I suppose."

"You're on the next flight to Malta. J.C. will fix it. There you'll be safe. And old Queenie'll have a fit if you don't pull a Christmas cracker with her. There's no choice, right?"

"That's what you want?"

"That's what I want."

"But you here for Christmas, Charlie. I feel so inadequate."

"Don't. Going without an apple, orange, a new penny, and a piece of coal in my stocking won't hurt me. I'm in the best place, believe me."

"Dotty says she'll swear on a stack of Bibles you were—"

"Never heard of her. Go away now, Ing."

"Mr. Self-contained."

Ingrid showed bitter need.

"Go away. Go away now."

"Yes, Mein Führer. I always follow orders. Anything else I have to do?"

"Take care of you and my kid."

"Anything else?"

"Yeah."

Charlie stood and rapped on the door to the cells.

"I love you, you silly cow."

"You . . . what?"

But Charlie had gone.

The screw watched Ingrid get hysterical, his face a blank as he carefully closed and locked the door.

Cars and vans passed and kept going.

A mongrel with a bad hind leg dampened a lamppost, sniffed at the meager mist he had raised, and trotted off as if he knew where he was going.

Silversleeves leered at the dog.

A dark saloon coasted past, slowed almost to a standstill, gathered speed, and lost itself down the street.

Silversleeves warmed himself with thoughts of money. Of the drinks money would buy. Rows and rows of bottles with the right labels. The best bonding. All his alone. In a darkened room where there were women who poured for him without drinking themselves. Who patted his hand and left fragrance close to his face without speaking or wanting him to talk. The dream had recurred all his life since puberty. When pathological shyness clamped him in a sure grip. Made him inarticulate and impotent around *them.*

Women.

In the street it was different.

There he was in charge.

He could silver-tongue them into passing the half-crowns at will, whatever he sold: stockings with crooked seams or legs of differing lengths, blades that fitted no known razor, after shave that smelled of goat curds—anything at all.

Silver-tongued Silversleeves, who could sell sand to Arabs and junk to women with locked purses.

The alcohol died, and Silversleeves knew he had caught cold. He shivered violently when Vinnie and Wally came out to laugh in the glow of the mongrel's lamppost. Wally dropped a toolbox into the Bedford, making it bounce on its suspension. They laughed at that and did not look up when the dark saloon reversed to a halt beside them, white smoke popping from the exhaust.

Something dark and metallic slid through the open rear window and all the flashguns in the world went off in a searing clap of white light. The concussion flattened Silversleeves's clothes against his chest, flexed the plate-glass window, and rang in his ears like a million untuned bells.

Vinnie was lifted, hurled against the pub door. Small coins chimed on the pavement as the skirts of his topcoat blew into tatters along with gobbets of flesh from his thighs. The whole of his left leg showed through ruined trousers before he flopped onto his haunches with his hands above his head.

Then he said, "Oh," as if somebody had stolen his last boiled sweet and became a bundle of discarded clothing on a discarded dummy.

Wally had not moved.

There were blood spots all over him. He swung a fist at the car roof. Dented the metal skin. But the saloon was already gathering speed. Slid away leaving a last coil of exhaust in the cold air. Then that was blown to nothing and the normal sounds of the night came back. Creeping like thieves.

Silversleeves found himself moving away.

Going anywhere.

Telling himself he was nothing to do with what happened.

They was just gonna rough him up, wasn't they? Cut him a bit. Razor him. Mark his face. Break his legs like usual. Not put a bloody shooter to him. Not a shooter . . .

Silversleeves ran blindly. Did not see Wally try to staunch the wound in Vinnie's groin with a red rag of shirttail. Or Maisie holding the head in her ample lap. Crying for the boy she had known all her life.

Pimlico just held the wheel.

The telephone was still a presence against his face.

Dotty's Mini found the green lights and the fast lanes without him. He could still see Dotty with street cold coming off her coat as the telephone told him about Vinnie in Wally's broken voice.

His belly just spilled out over his belt buckle, Pim. His legs were just meat open to the bone. . . .

Pimlico blinked to change the picture in his head.

Blink. Vinnie aged eleven outside Southend Kursaal with a parakeet on each shoulder and a sock down around his ankle. Another Vinnie nine years on, grinning in RAF blue. Both Vinnies framed in silver on his mother's mantelshelf.

Blink. Vinnie with last month's receipts from Imperial Machines. All ice cream smiles because they were in profit.

Wally had groaned. *His kneebone was on the pavement by his foot . . . like a bloody piece of cuttlefish. . . .*

Blink. Vinnie kissing the bride outside Caxton Hall for the photographer. Dotty kissing him back with her skirt hiked to show her lucky blue garter.

"Who? Who did it?" Pimlico asked again in the speeding Mini.

Wally had choked with frustration.

The Troys, who else . . . plain as day and as nasty as ninepence . . . I was too slow. . . .

"Against a sawn-off?" Pimlico asked the streaming sodium lights of the somnolent City. Racing into Aldgate's cheerless glare of whelk- and coffee-stalls, Jewish and Chinese restaurants, Seamen's Missions, churches darkened by television and apathy.

At the City Hospital he abandoned the Mini in a surgeon's reserved space with the indicators blinking life from the battery. Ran up stone steps into the wet-blanket smell of steam central heating. The hushed sounds of a hospital putting itself to sleep for the night.

A black student nurse pointed him toward the casualty ward, and he tried to slow to a walk. To show nothing in his face or manner to anyone. To himself.

Vinnie's mother was dwarfed by a brace of doctors and a young beat constable.

Pimlico reached for the double doors, was pulled into an alcove by Wally.

"Too much law for us, son. They're all round Vinnie's bed."

"I'm going—"

"Nowhere but out of here."

"Don't stick your oar—"

"Arthur Ax has charge of the case, you moron. He's the Troys' own tame copper. Bought and paid for. Away, come on."

Wally drew Pimlico down a metal staircase into the basement. Laundry made soiled white mountains, and dim service lights formed dark grottoes in the vaulted ceilings. Pimlico dragged his feet. Took a meaty slap across the face when Wally wheeled him about in the freezing car park.

White breath gusted as Wally said, "You'd only get collared by the local CID. End up at Leman Street copshop. Vinnie's close to had it. Sweating under Arthur Ax's lights won't help him. Right?"

Blink. "You've seen Vinnie?"

"Told the nurse I was a reporter on the local rag. Even got a date for Thursday night if I want it."

"You're chatting up nurses when—"

"With them ankles and a bum as big as all outdoors? Earned me the inside dope, that's all. Vinnie won't never walk straight again. Even if they save the one leg and his heart gets him through surgery."

Pimlico could not stop blinking. The lights were crazy smears in the night. Glaring softly.

"You want back at them, Pim? Hard?"

Blink,

"You listening, or do I have to whack you again?"

Blink. "I hear you."

"In the car. Move."

Pimlico shrank into the Mini, and Wally drove to a lockup garage off Roman Road. He closed and locked the doors and laid a heavy fishing bag on the front seat of the Mini. Patted it and said, "We can start a war with this."

Pimlico's face was all hard planes in the spill of dipped heads. "Just the two of us? I'm livid, not stupid."

"I've been on the phone. Got us a team."

"Who?"

"Trust Uncle Wal." Wally unzipped the fishing bag to show Pimlico a pair of sawn-off .410s, restocked and shortened twelve-gauge shotguns, a .38 Smith & Wesson on a .45 frame, ammunition as red as blood.

Pimlico worked the pump-action of a Remington. Wally filled his pockets with cartridges and said, "We don't touch Brighton or the Fortress. We hit them in Catford. There's a club crying out for our machines and some heavy crowd control. The Bellavers have got their pinkies in the cash register, creaming off the profits for the Troys. It's perfect, Pim. They won't expect us tonight of all nights. The Troys will be nowhere near the Fortress."

"But Arthur Ax will be, right?"

"That's my old Pim. Thinking straight."

Wally plumped shells into a twelve-gauge and snapped it closed.

"Tell me about this club, Wal."

"Called Captain Jones and the Ju-Ju Men."

Pimlico blinked. Saw Vinnie on crutches. In a wheelchair. No more fast swerves in front of the goalmouth at Highbury Fields.

"Pinky and Red Bellaver, huh?" he said.

"The same."

Pimlico stopped blinking, and his vision was very clear indeed.

"Let's go."

The sign was as vulgar as the club.

White bulbs chased themselves around a red neon monkey in a green palm on the illuminated fascia. Discouraged brown rubber plants nodded sagely from brassbound tubs on either side of an entrance tricked out in painted concrete bamboo. Woven bamboo trellised the lobby carpet, and the reception desk was faced with dyed reed. A black girl in a glitter-dust sarong took entrance fees without losing the basket of fruit she wore as a hat. Split bamboo covered the walls except where inset squares of rattan cane framed enlarged jungle-movie stills.

Hope grinned at Crosby in Bali, Sabu waved his steel tooth at Sheer Khan, Fay Wray screamed from Kong's fist, Bogart hauled *African Queen* through Hollywood reeds and Johnny Weismuller called elephants from the Universal City waterfall.

Pinhole lights were stars in the black ceiling above palm leaves on wooden poles. A poster advertised "Jungle Jim's Bingo" on Tuesdays and listed forthcoming attractions in Day-Glo.

Wally and Pimlico drank at a bar where vines twined, grapes hung in plastic clusters, and the barmen wore boleros and bow ties over bare chests, and waitresses in grass skirts flitted through the tables as a trio played sugary numbers for the couples eating each other's faces on the dance floor. A planter's veranda overlooked the dance floor and a jungle battered by mechanical storms every hour on the hour.

Red and Pinky Bellaver drank at a long table on the veranda with a crowd of noisy friends. Pimlico spotted Kosher Kramer and three Maltese pimps in the company. One was Manchester Freddy, and Pimlico wondered why he was drinking with a rival firm.

Wally downed a third vodka.

"Freddy's a fader. He won't trade punches."

Pimlico swallowed Scotch and water.

"That's as may be, but he's married into the Tonna

family. He got their sister Fat Maria pregnant and married her before Roger and Jesus shortened him by a couple of yards. They had to take him into the family and give him a living. Before that he was a small-time pimp who did most of a five stretch for torching his ex-girl friend's flat with her still inside it. Scarred her for life. He's garbage, Wally, and him being in that company is out of order."

"Then, he takes his chances like the rest of them," said Wally.

Pimlico worried a knuckle between his teeth and took comfort from the shotgun under his coat. Harry the Crack and Sailor Mailer drifted to a side table and were joined by Froggy Farrell and Nasty Nostrils.

Wally jerked a thumb. "There's a sight you never thought you'd see, eh? Those faces drinking together? Have you seen Harry use six-inch nails at a dart match? He can take a cigarette out of your mouth at thirty feet with a nail."

Pimlico rolled cartridges in his pocket.

"That right?" he said for something to say.

"Yeah. Harry's dead keen on South Africa. Hot to live there. Figures tonight as a favor that'll keep me off Connie's firm and put him on an airplane to Cape Town. Sailor sees himself as Connie's right hand in the Smoke with me gone, so everybody's happy. That's how to work the oracle, Pim. Dangle the right carrots."

"And Nasty and Froggy?"

"Vinnie has friends, Pim. And maybe Charlie figures you ain't allowed out alone after dark." Wally looked amused.

"There are still eight to our six."

"Scrub round Freddy, Maltese Maurice and Johnny Valletta. You don't count *pimps* as opposition. They're just three brass monkeys in need of a good polish."

"You got a carrot for Kosher?"

"Yeah, double-barreled."

Wally smoothed a bulging lapel.

"It's time, Pim."

The restaurant was closed. The trio finished their last set and dancers drifted towards the exits. Wally sauntered across the sprung floor and stepped onto the veranda.

"Thought I'd buy you chaps a gargle."

Pinky was owlish with drink. His pocked face was flushed and he grinned with grey teeth.

"On our own turf, you cheeky Arab? This ain't the Brighton Belle, right, Red?"

"Seems we owe you something, Harold. You and that Pimlico bastard behind you. Maybe a drink with lumps in it."

Wally smiled at that.

"Not just me and Pim, is it? We're in company, and we couldn't take a solitary drink without the chaps got one too."

Red's eyes flicked at Pimlico. Swiveled to take in Harry, Froggy, Sailor, and Nasty. Hovered there and came back to Wally.

"A drink for them won't break us. Part of our expenses for special services to the management."

"How special would they be, Red?" Wally nodded at Kosher, who held a goblet of champagne in a hand covered in rings. The scarred face stayed neutral and the eyes could have been lead slugs.

"Can't say," said Red. "Nobody ever put us to the test."

"All little boys in this manor," said Kosher.

Manchester Freddy liked that enough to repeat it. The two Maltese smiled in waxy silence.

Wally stabbed a finger at Harry's table.

"You think they're little boys?"

Red Bellaver leaned back in his chair, and the butt of a gun showed against his shirt.

"Look like choirboys from here. Have 'em sing us a song."

Wally wagged a finger. "You wouldn't like the tune."

"Thought we were drinking." Freddy wiped his pencil moustache with a damp finger. Called for a tray of pint glasses, upended a bottle of Stolichnaya over a glass and slammed it down in front of Wally. "Have some of that."

"Don't leave me out." Pimlico emptied most of a bottle of Scotch into a straight glass and filled another for Freddy. His hand had lost its shake when he pushed it forward. "Get that down you, *pimp.*"

Freddy's bow tie bobbed. His eyes turned sullen as his hand twitched beside the huge Scotch. Unwilling to pick it up.

Wally chuckled.

"You're the host, Red. Do we all drink, or is this a little boys' bluff I'm calling?"

Kosher shifted in his seat.

"Call the drinks in, Red. No room for bluff here."

"We know that," Pinky snapped. "You want drink for drink, you got drink for fucking drink."

Freddy sniggered and earned a hot look from Pinky, a cool one from Kosher.

"Gin, is it, Harry?" Wally called.

"Very, very dry."

Harry looked huge in a camel's hair coat. Dwarfed everyone at the long table. He draped an arm around Sailor's shoulder and laid a hand on Nasty's elbow. Jerked his head at Froggy.

"Shampoo for Nasty and Sailor."

Red Bellaver widened his eyes in mock astonishment.

"Champagne, Harry? In fairy-sized glasses—sipped like some old duchess with the colic?"

Pinky leered at his brother. "They are choirboys."

Harry just smiled.

"A bottle each, drunk down in one go. And Froggy'll take a bottle of Canadian Club. And while that's coming from the bar we'll watch Freddy and Pim drink theirs. Or is the pimp's mouth the biggest thing about him?"

"I'll show you mouth." Freddy took a long draught of Johnnie Walker. Choked and held the alcohol in his throat until he got it down. Eyes watering, he sat heavily. Gasped, "How's . . . that?"

"Pitiful," said Wally. "You wanna show him how it's done, Pim?"

Pimlico's spine was ice, and great balls of sweat ran down his back. Vinnie haunted him as he emptied his lungs, opened his throat, and drained off the pint of whiskey without a blink. Set the glass down without a tremor.

"Fucking Christ," said Morrie Torrance.

"And his sister from Cairo," Kosher added.

Wally banged the table.

"A pint here for Pim. Must need a beer chaser for that."

Pimlico stayed upright without weaving.

"But not without a toast," he said.

A pale waitress brought a tray of bottles and a pint of lager and lost herself in plastic greenery. The bar staff had melted away. Red leered at his brother.

"What's the toast? His grey-haired old mother?"

Wally rapped the table again, and Froggy stripped foil caps from bottles, popped champagne corks.

"No," said Wally. "Nor slow greyhounds nor the price of penny buns. Let's have all of you with a bottle in your fist. Malt whiskey here for the Malts, Frog."

"Don't take the piss," Freddy mumbled.

"I want that drink gone in one this time, Manchester. You offered the gargle, only fair you should match drinks with us."

Red filled glasses for Pinky and himself.

"That much is right. But it's *our* firm you're drinking with."

Pimlico held his glass up to the light.

"To your firm, Red. And to a face you'd have been proud to drink with. If he wasn't in surgery losing a leg. To Vinnie Castle, who got triggered tonight. From a moving car by animals who should rot in hell. Vinnie Castle."

Red spilled ash down himself.

"Red's firm and Vinnie Castle," Wally said, drinking.

"Seconded."

Red nuzzled his drink, seeing everybody did the same. Three gulps and he gaped and stopped swallowing. Pinky did much the same. Freddy and the Maltese took less than a solid mouthful. Morrie Torrance made frogmouths into his lap, and Sailor coughed champagne on the floor. Harry turned away with puffed cheeks, and Froggy sneezed Canadian Club down his waistcoat. Kosher kept drinking until Pimlico finished his lager, upended his glass on the table, and sat back in his chair with a long belch and a look of admiration for Pimlico's capacity.

"To Red, Vinnie, and a change of management," Pimlico said.

There was a silence that Red broke with a fulsome belch and "Is that your idea of ho-flaming-ho, mister?"

"Ain't a laugh left in the world," said Harry the Crack.

Wally took a bottle of Stolichnaya by the neck and slammed it down in front of the Bellavers.

"That's your last free gargle in Catford, boys. Take it and don't come back. Ever."

Pinky scraped his chair back a millimeter. Harry leaned on the chairback and ground him to a halt.

Freddy waved a sloppy hand.

"Hard talk never bought baby a new bonnet. I drink what I like, where I like, when I like. I'm not just some two-penny—"

"You're nothing."

Pimlico swept Freddy's drink into his lap and slapped his face with a return swing. The slap lost itself in the palms and bamboo before anybody reacted.

"Out of order."

Pinky threw himself into the bottle Wally swung at him. Hit across the throat, Pinky slammed an arm into his brother's face and made sounds in his chest like glass grating under a heel.

"My suit," Freddy wailed. "Thirty guineas of threads . . ."

Wally threw Pinky from the veranda and hurled the chair after him. Pinky hit the polished floor and was still skidding when he fired his sawn-off .410 without bothering to aim. The chair still bounced when pellets sprayed the table. Morrie Torrance clapped a hand to his torn neck and looked stupefied.

Harry the Crack's left drove Red Bellaver into Wally's arms and they fell together in a thrash of legs and tumbling bottles. Kosher came out of his chair heaving the table over. He was no longer a slow and heavy middle-aged man. He head-butted Sailor, and cutthroat razors came out from behind his lapels.

Sailor turned to vomit champagne over Morrie Torrance.

Morrie reared away to save his suit, blood spitting through the fingers he held to his neck. He tripped over Wally and Red, crashed down beside them, and kicked Sailor's feet from under him.

Pinky's shotgun tore holes in the air where they had all been a moment before.

Pimlico mashed Maltese Maurice's nose with an upswinging right. Maurice flailed away as Johnny Valletta slashed at the air with a switchblade, trying for Pimlico's jugular. Pimlico decked him with his shotgun butt. Johnny flopped in a cascade of glassware and a sudden swill of spilled alcohol, squealed as he ground glass into his buttocks.

Freddy fell behind the overturned table where Froggy caught at his ankle. Hauled himself up Freddy's body. Biting where he couldn't punch. Freddy used his nails like a hysterical woman, gouged Froggy's wrists and face.

Pimlico pointed the shotgun at Kosher to keep him away. Watched Wally punish Red's head against the floor. Saw Morrie and Sailor fight in their own puke. Let Johnny Valletta crawl for the exit trailing blood from a badly slashed buttock.

Harry the Crack had vaulted the rail and made a running kick at Pinky's head. His leg was in midair when Pinky fired one-handed. Hit in the thigh, Harry spiraled to the floor and took a second charge in the lower back.

Distracted, Pimlico barely dodged the cutthroats darting in crisscross near his face. One slashed through his lapel. The second blade nicked his shoulder. Kosher's bulk drove him back a step. The razors slashed again, parting his hair.

Pimlico stabbed the shotgun into the big belly. Brought it up across Kosher's nose in a savage arc. Spattered himself with blood and phlegm from Kosher's nostrils. Kosher still came on, the razors out ahead of him. Pimlico felt the Remington buck. Pumped the action automatically and fired again. Kosher stood still and shook his head. The front of his suit was peppered and blackened, and spurts of carmine ruined what was left of his white dress shirt. His jowls shook and turned grey under the dark beard stubble and white scar tissue.

"Now ain't that a bastard," he said dreamily.

Pimlico racked a third cartridge into the chamber, and the sound brought Kosher's eyes up.

"You won't need that one, son," Kosher said. "You've done me handsome. Can I go home now?"

Pimlico nodded. At a loss to know what else to do.

Kosher held his belly and turned away very slowly. Winked at Pimlico and followed Johnny Valletta's red trail through the kitchen to the emergency exit. A leg went rubbery, and he saved himself with a monumental effort of will. Leaned into a crouch and kept walking until he turned from sight behind the plastic jungle where lightning flashed and rain hammered rock and palm and a volcano smoked sullenly.

Pimlico swung the shotgun to cover Wally. Sailor and Morrie were tumbling chairs about at the far end of the veranda, and Froggy was getting the best of Freddy. Maltese Maurice had disappeared, and Harry still lay on the dance floor, searching for something inside his coat as Pinky reloaded and grinned his grey grin, deciding where to shoot Harry next.

Pimlico felt the Scotch and lager hit him harder than the cold fact that he had finished Kosher Kramer. He saw Pinky as a blur of menace. Raised his Remington and shouted Pinky's name. It came out as a muddy croak.

Pinky ignored the shout. Took a step closer to Harry and brought his shotgun up to his shoulder.

Harry found what he was looking for, and his right hand darted forward with a delicate flick of the wrist. There was a silver blur and a light tick of impact, and Pinky looked surprised. An inch of polished metal grew out of his button-down collar. He tried to look at it. Was still trying to look at it when a second six-inch nail went into his cheek below his right eye. He took a step away from the pain, thought better of it, and made for Harry, the .410 out ahead of him.

Pimlico sighted along his Remington, blinked uncontrollably again, sweat in his sockets stinging his eyes.

A third nail hit Pinky in the heart. He let go a long breath and pitched onto his face. The shotgun skittered away and came to rest against Harry's foot. Harry bowed over himself and muttered an obscene prayer.

Pimlico slumped, remembered Wally, and turned to cover him again. Wally had lost the bottle he'd used to punish Red's face, and both men had their hands around Red's sawn-off. Wally jerked it away from his face and Pimlico saw both bores flash in concert, throwing flame at him.

Then he was reeled away. Found himself bowed over the overturned table. Deafened by shock and concussion, he took a long time to move. His teeth ached from grinding together, and whatever he looked at swam too close to his eyes. He levered himself upright using the shotgun, and the nightclub came back on a dark wave of nausea as he tried to remember who Vinnie was.

The breast of his topcoat was black with powder burns, and his raked ribs stung and pounded. More than sweat ran down his chest as somebody used his voice to tell him to finish something.

He shook sweat from his face in a fine spray, and the shotgun was too long and too heavy to lift. He let it drop and felt better about something.

Pimlico sagged against a bamboo upright, and plastic vine leaves caressed his face. He hadn't the breath to blow them away.

Sailor kicked Morrie Torrance in the ribs like a robot footballer.

Froggy and Manchester Freddy still made shrill noises as they fought like old women.

Wally bounced Red Bellaver's head off the floor and kneed him in the crotch at the same time, his face manic. A cold breeze came through the emergency doors, snapped paper napkins from their holders, and drifted them about the club like ghostly moths.

Pimlico was colder than he'd ever been in his life. His lower gut burned like dry ice. He wished Dotty was there to warm him with her body and hot drinking chocolate. He walked and walked and walked with small pecking steps, leaned against glass doors until they parted for him. The rubber plants nodded, and the neon monkey was monochrome on the unlit sign.

Something that could have been a man lay on the driveway, and the sideburns and scars could have been Kosher's. The low bubbling voice that could have been Kosher's talked in soft monotone to an uncaring sky.

". . . Should've stayed in Brighton where it was . . . safe . . . not listened to all that shit and glory crap from Tommy and Pinky and Red . . . All them miles and miles of talk with no mileage . . ."

Pimlico heard without listening as he walked and walked and walked.

In the main road a Belisha beacon blinked at him.

A car at the curb called his name.

He dared not look for fear of being seen.

So he walked and walked and tried to walk until he was herded into a saloon by a redhead who said not to struggle or the hole in Pimlico would tear him apart. He fell into a leather seat, and the world rolled on without any help from him. The redhead driving talked about phone calls to Dotty and being at Charlie's flat when the news about Vinnie came in. How Wally had told Dotty and Dotty had called Charlie's flat and told Lou what had happened and how he had come out to search . . .

Pimlico saw the driver would have real red hair and freckles in proper light. Sodium wasn't real light at all.

"You'relimehouselouandtheykilledvinnie . . ." Pimlico mumbled.

"Chas said this would happen." Lou worried a lip with uneven teeth and tooled the saloon towards Spitalfields.

"Charliedunnoeverything."

"Don't talk, Pim."

The handbrake ripped on, and Pimlico found oblivion as he was lifted. The floor jogged under his face and an old voice told Lou to lay someone on a table in a searing white room.

"How can I use anaesthetic with all that alcohol in him? He'd drown in his own vomit if his heart didn't explode. Maybe Novocain locally. That's all. I don't even know his blood type to make a cross-match. He needs a proper hospital."

"Taking him to a hospital would be giving him to the law, doc. Arthur Ax would get him thirty years."

"He'd be alive."

"And captured. That'd kill Pim."

Breath smelling of old library books gusted as Pimlico's eyelids were peeled for a penlight. The sweet odor of final corruption coming from the gentle old hands.

"I can only try."

A metal probe went into Pimlico's groin, and he followed Vinnie down a long arcade where parakeets the color of agony beat their wings at his nerve endings and cracked lead pellets in beaks like bullet probes. Then he flew with them into a night without end. Was an Icarus falling into a dark sun where all the hues were black.

Black nothing.

Blink.

Gone.

Connie Harold stood at the window in shock.

The tall American from Florida had sipped iced water at the head of a teak conference table and said, "Our offer is one million dead."

Dirk Jorgesson had doodled on his pad, and Kelly sat in her white dress contemplating her own cleavage. The other executives of the mining company were just a row of men in leather chairs with well-groomed faces and lightweight suits.

One million.

Connie used two fingers to open the slats of a fabric blind. Bleached his face with hard sunlight bounced from cement paths between landscaped palms and bird-of-paradise plants. The tomcat smell of ground ivy blended with the bitter tang of flaking gum trees. Flags of all nations batted on the poles facing the white sand beach. Sprinklers chattered arcs of spray over a brown lawn. A girl in Bermuda shorts carried a toy dog the color of ivory. Her cinnamon hair streamed in the salt breeze. Connie watched her cross the manicured courtyard, sit in a tiny red car, and drive herself out of his life.

His mouth was as dry as a stale crust.

"Dollars or sterling?"

Connie wondered if the girl would have thrown him a brilliant smile if she knew he was a millionaire for the want of a simple "Yes."

There was only vague shadow and an oil spot where her car had been.

"Your national currency, of course."

The man from Florida drew smiles from his board.

Connie closed the light out with slow fingers.

Part of him wanted the soft option with six zeroes. A certified check small enough to fold into his wallet and sit against his chest when he walked out into the Nassau sunlight. Tiny beads of sweat pricked his eye sockets, drying almost before they'd formed in the arid conditioned air. Air without taste or smell. Filtered for the corporate nostrils of men used to buying what they wanted with signatures on oblongs of engraved paper. Thinking no more of a million than a coin flipped at a news vendor.

Connie had thought money had a smell. Like the London cobbles or Namaqualand when he first walked there, the smell of wealth locked in the ground since it had been closed to prospectors in 1928. And Connie had opened it up. The question was, for whom? For himself? Or these smooth corporate men breathing their dead air in a deader building?

Six zeroes backing a lonely number one.

Why shouldn't a three or a five front those six zeros?

Connie went back to his chair and ran a thumb over brass nails and leather. Decided white was not Kelly's color. It was too bleached for her dull olive skin. And Jorgesson looked like a reformed drunk in a borrowed suit. It was almost time for Connie to make the last few rungs to the top alone. To discard the passengers riding on his coattails. The cautious part of his mind winced when he said, "Thank you, gentlemen. We'll consider your offer."

Connie shook hands all around the table, and the man from Florida looked impressed as he scribbled on a business card and tucked it into Connie's top pocket.

"A little reminder," he drawled as he walked Connie's party through a marbled hall of sober greys and golden hardwoods, waved their taxi from the compound with a reflective smile.

"A million, Conrad. One thousand thousands," Jorgesson said. "That calls for a methuselah of champagne, by damn."

"Don't spend what you ain't got, Dirk."

Connie watched a shopping mall glide past. The Christmas decorations tawdry in the tropical sunlight. As tawdry as Kelly was beside Alicia Jorgesson. Alicia belonged in boardrooms and on elevated terraces above the city skyline. She and Naomi Leathers had that elusive quality Connie needed to own for himself.

Kelly yelped and snatched her hand from Connie's fist.

"Down, Tiger. Enough time for rough stuff later."

She blew on small knuckles and dug a finger into Dirk's midriff.

"And who didn't want to fly out here to hear what the Americans had to say, eh? Wait until I tell Alicia what a *dassie* you are."

"What my wife thinks is of little moment," Jorgesson said.

Connie made fists in his lap.

Maybe Jorgesson didn't care what Alicia thought, but Connie did. He wanted to see her eyes shine when he doubled and trebled millions. Wanted her admiration in the boardroom and in bed. Dirk saw nothing when Connie looked at Alicia, but De Wit did. And so did Clive Spring. Wally thinking that Spring was nothing but a peeping-tom reporter who took photographs when people weren't looking, but Spring admitted he'd done time for a Mayfair jewel heist back in the fifties. Had started over fresh in South Africa after a five stretch in Maidstone Prison. And if De Wit trusted Spring, Connie had no option but to go along . . .

"You ain't listening, Con."

"I heard. But so what if the Yanks double their offer, Kel?"

"Two million ain't a 'so what,' Connie Harold."

Kelly fanned her cleavage for Jorgesson's benefit.

"I'm sweating hot, ain't you?"

Connie knew Alicia wouldn't have said that if her panties were alight. She'd have borne the discomfort with a sweet smile.

"Ain't you hot, Con?"

"No. And stop showing Dirk next week's washing."

Connie threw money at the black driver and made for the hotel elevator. In their suite he made a Tom Collins the way Naomi had taught him and told Kelly to come out of the shower to answer the phone.

"It's London. For you."

Kelly was a bedraggled urchin in a huge bathtowel, and her thin wrist shook as she offered the receiver.

Connie stared at her.

"Well?"

"Wally's been arrested. For murder."

Connie took the phone and turned the card the man from Florida had given him. It read: *You'll never forget the day you turned down a million.*

That was for certain, Connie thought as he listened to Sailor talk him through the details of Wally's arrest.

CHAPTER 3

Detective Inspector Lemmon winced when the grey steel door closed him inside the grey windowless room. Claustrophobia was a second overcoat for the long, dreadful moment it took to shrug the fear of confinement away. The grey electric clock on the grey wall ticked off seconds. The grey heating vents hummed as far doors slid and clanged and screws walked with measured tread.

"One away to you, mister," somebody yelled.

"One away to me. Step it out there, mister."

Lemmon laid his trilby on the grey steel table and found himself rolling a Player between his fingers. He laid the cigarette on the crown of his hat. Pulled a grey metal chair out from the table and didn't sit on it. Felt he would take root if he sat in the empty room alone. Trapped in the greyness for as long as his heart held out in the featureless monochrome.

Even the tin ashtray had been painted grey.

He laid his cigarettes and matches beside the ashtray. The sailor with his HMS *Hero* hat in the roundel on the Player's pack took on a prison pallor. His scrap of green sea was frozen, and the lighthouse in the background seemed to gather grey fog. His neat naval beard became unkempt, and the blue eyes lost their keenness. Lemmon lit the cigarette on his hat and watched the grey smoke lose itself in the greater greyness of the ceiling.

A prison officer opened the door, said, "Remand prisoner Dance," and made a deal of rattling the lock before going away like a toy soldier with a steel spine.

Charlie's slate eyes were holes in his face. The same colorless nothing of the interview room. He sat opposite Lemmon and said, "Welcome to Auschwitz on the Congo. Capital of the West Indies and the armpit of noplace. Brixton Prison."

"I'm glad you decided to see me."

Charlie's almost-smile was as shallow as the chrome on a Ford hubcap.

"You didn't have to dress. We're very informal here."

Lemmon touched his black tie and starched collar.

"Formal dinner tonight. Smoke?"

Charlie lit a Player with a Swan Vesta that refused to snarl. When he broke the match it sighed apart instead of snapping.

"Everything rots in here. Given time."

"A smart lawyer could have bailed you."

"Is that right?"

"You chose this road, Charlie. Why?"

Charlie leaked smoke with a shrug.

Lemmon leaned forward.

"Just the two of us here, so let's play the truth game."

"It's your twopence."

"Buller talked to me after he heard about Vinnie Castle. In confidence. He talked about Quill. At Mother's Club."

"And?"

"Cotton's pirates and the Bucks CID presented seventeen hundred pieces of evidence at the mail train trials at Aylesbury crown court. Those prosecuted went down for thirty years apiece, including a couple of villains *in absentia.* Now it could be that a small item marked 1693 is surplus to requirements. Could go missing. Which means a certain somebody not an arm's length from me could be home and free in no time at all. For a certain consideration, that is."

"Mr. Clean offers a deal?"

"Gloves off, Charlie. I want your collar. But I want it straight."

"What difference would it make?"

"To me? All the difference in the world."

Charlie sighed smoke.

"What *do* you want?"

"Apart from you in here for the right reasons?" Lemmon came close to a smile and rubbed it out with a brown hand.

"Apart from that, yes."

"Clever old Charlie Dance who knew the bloodbath was coming and took a rigged fall to keep his firm's nose clean. Eating his porridge in the choky whilst the rubbish leaves its claret on the cobbles. Killing each other off with you safe behind bars. Leaving you and Archie to pick up the pieces when it's all over. It's as clear as your barber's rash."

Charlie did not touch his face.

"That'll go with a change of diet."

"Only if you deal."

"With you."

"With me."

Charlie's eyes could have been shards of grey ice.

"You're a still, small voice in the wilderness, Mr. Lemmon. Just how do you figure to climb the wall between you and me when your own patch of copperdom is a mud wallow? You can't kick Quill out to pasture without a nasty internal song and dance. Or the Sunday tabloids printing fat headlines about police corruption. I've got more chance of spanking Prophet soundly than you'll ever have."

"You lay a glove there . . ."

"Me? Lay a glove on my old mate Prophet? Why should I, when he'll fall apart like the house-of-cards of a case you've got against me. Your forensic wizards can't place me at that farm; I was never there. Nor on the viaduct or the train itself. And if I laundered the dough, how come Cotton's pirates have recovered so much of it? And you won't find my dabs on the stuff that 'fell' out of my wallet, neither. Some deal you're offering. You're as much in prison as I am. Only diff is *I'll* get out. You're a lifer with no chance of remission."

Lemmon's breath whistled in his nostrils. Spots of heat burned his cheeks. His brown fists came together at the knuckles and squeezed his Player flat as they softly pounded the grey table. His shoulders spread inside his coat and a flush stained his thick neck. His lips parted from his teeth with a tiny pop of air.

"And you're so innocent, eh, Dance? Vinnie Castle's on the critical list. And you let it happen. Pimlico Johnny Parsons is missing with some serious holes in him, his dabs and blood type all over the sawn-off he dropped. Harry the Crack and Froggy Farrell are on the run for the same affray, except it isn't that anymore. It's a capital charge. Pinky Bellaver's on a slab with some strange holes in him, and Kosher Kramer's wearing a tag on his big toe. All due to your cleverness, Charlie. With Kosher gone Brighton's a walkover, and Bethnal Green and Camberwell are at each other's throat over that lucrative territory. Just like you planned."

"You're right. If my homing pigeons let me down, I write my instructions in blood on paper airplanes. Fly them out through the bars. And a zephyr of wind comes out of the west and blows them straight into the right letter boxes. Simple."

"Play the simpleton. But you'll dance to another tune before you're much older, Charlie."

Charlie's eyes went behind his lids and came back flinty.

"Nobody cares if Bethnal Green and Camberwell kill each other off. Let them. Save you coppers a lot of headaches, save the taxpayers a fortune in legal fees. The only people weeping would be the lawyers who lost out on a lot of fat briefs. You and the other straight cops can go back to sleeping nights and worrying about jaywalking and motorists who use Guinness labels as tax discs."

"I'd still have your firm to dismantle."

"If you want that, you'd best leave me in here."

Lemmon picked up his hat, turned it, and laid it back where it had been.

"Full circle. I'll have you straight, Charlie. No other way."
"You're here to salve *your* conscience, not mine."
"A psychoanalyst with wide lapels, well, well."
Charlie plumed lazy smoke.
"Nobody's goading you, mister. Except the little man in the back of your head who comes out in your dreams. Tells you all the rotten things you push aside in daylight. He's the one who's looking at me through your eyes now. Not the career copper who goes by the book and doesn't dare see his face in his shiny toecaps when he laces his boots in the morning. And the funny-sad thing is, if you'd learned to bend the rules, you'd have your commander's pips by now. And just maybe have the clout to make your patch of copperdom as squeaky-clean as you'd like it."
Lemmon paled and lit a Player from his stub. Charlie took it without thanks and said, "Don't lose Quill's 'evidence' on my account. It's your lily-white integrity that's in jeopardy here whatever you do. And that's your dilemma, isn't it? Lose it or use it, that junk of Quill's has compromised you right where you live. In your honorable heart. You're in a no-win all-lose cleft stick, you poor bastard."
Lemmon had Charlie's shirtfront gripped, a ham of a fist hovering mid-punch.
Charlie blew smoke at it.
"Go ahead. Compromise yourself a little more. The screws will back your story. Prisoners fall and hurt themselves here all the time. It's just part of the system. Hit me and join them all the way."
Lemmon opened his fist and buried fingers in his hair.
"You cynical bastard. I almost . . ."
"But not quite, Theo. Not quite. Like it or not, we're of a kind, you and I. I've learned to live in my mud wallow, that's all. I police my animals as best I can, but I let the rabid ones go to the dog pound for the big chop."
Lemmon tidied his hair with a steel comb.
"And you'd have made a good-bad copper like Prophet Quill? If that's your contention, it stinks."
Charlie killed a long stub and took three cigarettes from Lemmon's pack with one fluid movement. Uncoiled from his chair, tucking them in his shirt pocket.

"For later," he said. "All democracy is a compromise, Theo. Live with it."

"Not your sick view of it."

"Nobody cried for Stephen Ward when he suicided over the Christine Keeler case, but they hated Jack Profumo. Not because he compromised state security by sleeping with whores who also bedded a Russian, but because he got caught out in a lie. Didn't do the honorable thing like putting a revolver in his mouth and kissing his brain goodbye. Before Cromwell and the Long Parliament *all* the kings of England ran police states. Only *they* called it Grace and Favor when they bribed rich allies with earldoms and changed the rules to suit themselves. Now we have elected governments and the Queen is titular head of state. But all that means is she controls the armed forces. Means *they* can't use the military to declare a republic or a dictatorship. It doesn't mean *they* can't grab off the gravy. It's still jobs for the boys and knighthoods for the self-servers. And you never hear of a judge or a politician dying in penury, right? You take a leaf out of your chum's book—Bunny Halliday. He used you, didn't he? Maybe he owes you one or several favors back."

Lemmon could have been a stone man in the grey room.

"You're playing marked cards, Charlie."

"They ain't coming from the bottom of the deck. I'm a villain. I can afford to be honest."

"You've got a sick view of the world."

"It's a sick old world. And like Archie says, 'I didn't make the times, but I take my profits from them.'"

Something glowed deep in Lemmon's eyes.

Twilight lit by inner lightning.

"Thanks, that makes it easier. You think Toronto's far enough away from Malta, Charlie? You think that maybe, just maybe, old man Ogle can cut the mustard without you? I mean, what's another dead Maltese pimp to a man like Charlie Dance? Nothing."

"I'm listening."

"Got your attention, have I?"

A line as fine as the print on an insurance waiver creased Charlie's forehead before he smoothed it away.

"For the moment."

"Johnny Valletta is some sort of relative to Roger and Jesus Tonna, isn't he? That's it, he's a cousin. Or more precisely, *was*. I must get the tense right. *Was* a cousin."

Charlie reached a cigarette from his pocket and held it like a pencil.

"So he's past tense. So what?"

"He bled to death in the same affray as Kosher and Pinky. Manchester Freddy was very upset about it. Talked nineteen to the dozen when we pulled him into Catford Police Station. Freddy figured Pimlico and Froggy were on your payroll. That you had Freddy and his unlovely friends hit on account of what happened to Vinnie Castle. And our Freddy only an innocent pimp out for a drink, too? I'd describe his mood as outraged. And, Charlie, that outrage has to get passed on to Toronto, wouldn't you say?"

"I wouldn't say anything."

"And you so full of words a moment ago."

"That was then."

"And this is now. Freddy's a talker, Charlie. A loudmouth. And who else has he tell his troubles to than his in-laws out in Toronto? Tell them how Charlie Dance almost had Freddy killed alongside his prince of a cousin Johnny? And for no good reason Freddy can see. Spiteful little shit is Freddy."

"Keep talking."

"We let Freddy go on his own recognizance with a few oblique pointers to help him on his way. Now, if you wanted to forestall him, give me a signed statement I could use, I could have you on a plane for Malta by . . . when? Christmas Eve tomorrow? Let's say, Boxing Day?"

Charlie mashed the unlit Player and wiped tobacco from his palm.

"Ring off, Mr. Lemmon. Wrong number."

Lemmon's fist made the steel door boom.

"One away to you, mister."

An hour later he was parking in Esher, and Charlie had begun to break up his cell.

* * *

There was snow in the fog.

Lemmon stamped slush from his galoshes as the bellpull chimed the first coda of a carol. Wishing he was home.

Elizabeth had insisted: "Of course we must go. If Bunny Halliday wants you in your penguin suit and me in my best black, then so be it. There are worse things than dull company and indifferent sherries, you know. Like being married to an able and lovable inspector who ought to be a commander. I'm tired of your being passed over for promotion."

"Sucking up to the After Eight set won't change that."

"Good. I'll write a bread-and-butter acceptance," and Elizabeth had confined herself to bed with a viral temperature of 102°.

A svelte young man in maroon and black took Lemmon's coat, hat, and scarf, and left him in a library of rosewood, brass, and leather bindings. Apple logs snapped in a mock-Tudor chimney and marble knights supported a huge overmantel of swashes and armorials. Low chairs with carved backs crouched in dim corners and good period furniture stood about on Chinese carpets that were new when Richard Coeur de Lion romanced Blondin to the sound of lutes.

Conversation drifted through the paneling like surf on a distant short as Lemmon warmed his hands and found Charlie's face in the leaping flames. Quill's eyes were in the hot motes spiraling past the blackened fireback, and Bulstrode's voice whispered with the crackling wood. The wail of a dryad in a haunted tree.

"Glenlivet and Malvern water." Bunny held identical drinks, his silver hair platinum in the firelight. "I thought a quiet word before you met your host and hostess." He sat and waved Lemmon into a facing chair. "I can make amends without apologizing, I think, Theo."

"I'll take the drink. That's real."

Lemmon eased his jacket open, and a button bit his lower back.

"Cheers, then." Bunny sipped delicately and said, "Yummy."

Lemmon looked attentive and thought: *Here it comes.*

"There's no shadow of a doubt that your help over that small matter of the train robbery was invaluable, Theo. Saul Cotton's praise was fulsome. But naughty old political expedients do have a way of muddying the water. Whatever one's best intentions may be. Your reward will come, but not quite in the way you or I may have envisaged. I should have broken silence earlier, but . . ."

Bunny fluttered pink fingers and looked solemn in the uncertain light.

"You do understand, I'm sure."

Grace and Favor, Charlie said from the fire.

What's changed?

"You'll make it clear, Bunny."

Bunny offered cigars with a neat skim of the wrist.

"No? Pity, they're rather fine. It will, of course, mean you'll have to tread a very familiar path just *once* more."

"Lousy with primroses and mud."

"Pardon, old man?"

"Just something a villain told me not ninety minutes ago. You reminded me, that's all."

Lemmon watched Bunny trim and light his cigar with the care of a neurosurgeon snipping a frontal lobe. Found himself prowling the carpet trailing monstrous and shifting shadows across the shelves of old volumes.

"That's very distracting, old man."

Lemmon sat with a "Sorry" and: "What *do* you want, Bunny?"

Christ, Dance again. But there was nothing grey about this rich room. Nothing at all.

"We have most of the train bandits behind bars. And Cotton's confident he'll collar the rest. But there are some rather shadowy loose ends. The money, Theo. Seems much of it *has* gone missing somewhere. And we—that is, our masters in Whitehall—have the quaint but implacable notion we should recover it. One way . . . or the other. That seems to require the collaring of some very heavy gentlemen indeed. And not just the heavy sort of gentleman you are familiar with in your line of business."

Lemmon's knees ached from his clamped hands. He stamped a foot and felt pins and needles.

"Quite another league entirely," said Bunny.

Lemmon rolled malt on his tongue and looked awake.

"We have a clandestine task force in mind. All low-key. And answerable to the Home Office only. You and your squad will remain what you seem as far as the lower echelons of the Metropolitan Police Force are concerned. But through me you will report directly to one other in Whitehall. He'll be a simple report-gatherer as far as you are concerned; anything more about him is of no interest to you. And the collars, should they come, will, in all probability, not be yours."

Lemmon thought of acres of primroses and said nothing.

Bunny stood to spread his coattails before the fire.

"There is much at stake here, Theo. More than you can probably imagine. This has been a terrible year for the country. One administration has revamped itself because of the Profumo affair. A third man has been named in the Burgess–Maclean ménage. We've lost a good friend in the White House and now have to come to terms with his successor. And to go into the New Year with a police corruption scandal would change the face of British politics too rapidly for both sides of the House. Changes will come, Theo. Radical changes. But they must come by evolution and not by revolution. Given time, there will be an enormous shake-up. Stories of graft and corruption are leaking out to my peers in the county constabularies. Too many stories. But before we clean house we have to strike at the root cause of that corruption. Outside the police force. You must help us to present an untarnished image to the great unwashed masses, the man in the street, the voter."

Lemmon rolled his eyes. Looked coy. Shuffled his feet and said, "What, little old me? Shucks, Mizz Scarlett."

"By God, I could strike you."

Bunny was no longer a bland pink fat cat. His decorations no longer baubles on a baby-pink sash. There was a patina of blood on their gleaming faceted surfaces. The flushed jowls could have been carved from red hardwood. The moist eyes were crumbs of raw gypsum.

Lemmon swallowed whiskey and tried not to stare, smoked a Player he didn't remember lighting.

"Easy, old friend."

Bunny's face changed without altering expression.

"What is so bloody difficult about making common cause with our masters, Theo? They want what we want: the heavy villains off the street. Whatever it takes. Just so long as there is no chance of them using legal technicalities or tales of dishonest coppers to set themselves free. Is that so very hard for you to comprehend? Am I talking to an honest fool or, as I had hoped, a man who loves truth enough to lie, cheat, and perjure himself to maintain the greater truths at the cost of a few of the lesser ones?"

A lie is a lie is a lie . . .

Bulstrode whispered in the chimney, and Charlie laughed with the jumping flames.

Democracy is a compromise. The old Grace and Favor. Jobs for the boys. Say yes and be a commander, son. . . .

Bunny's smile grew dimples.

"No buts, or back into obscurity you go, Theo."

Lemmon heard himself say, "And you believe this, my achieving friend. I've taken a good long look at myself tonight. Helped by you and another achieving bastard very like you. And that clever wife of mine with her suddenly convenient headache. You did get her to take to her bed so that us lads could chat in private, didn't you? Don't answer; it doesn't matter. What does matter is that I'll make common cause with you, Halliday. I'll earn my fatter pension through your gilded back door. But—and it's a big but—you drop me halfway, leave me out in the cold for your political expedience, and I'll make you eat my whistle, badge, and truncheon before I pull your plug."

Bunny dimpled again.

"Applause, applause. I'll remember that little speech."

Lemmon was suddenly jaded.

"When do I start as the Masked Avenger?"

"Now. Tonight. That's why you're here in this house. Thought you'd like a close look at someone you could well be netting for us. Your host."

"Why? Is he an independent voter? Or a card-carrying commie who walks backwards with a sword for the Queen?"

Bunny linked arms with Lemmon and opened the library door.

"Our host's name is Malcolm Sadler. And I rather suspect he's sailing close to the legal wind in several financial seas. And because of him you could well earn a flight to South Africa."

They walked into soft gales of polite laughter and the softer glow of chandeliers.

Charlie threw the second screw into the wall of his cell. Faked a trip and turned his head away from a rabbit punch aimed at the base of his skull. It took him high on the shoulder, and he was woozier than he expected when he flopped across his ripped mattress. Knees dug into his back, and the third screw kicked a rib before helping the first screw to handcuff Charlie's arms behind his back. They dragged him down to the infirmary and were waiting for the prison doctor to sedate Charlie when two escort officers came in behind the screw in charge of reception.

"What happened to him?"

"Went bananas. Right after that CID man interviewed him."

The third screw rubbed a raw shoulder.

"Threw me about like a packet of cornflakes."

"Caught me close to the family jewels. Can't rub that in public."

The reception screw shook his head at the escort officers.

"I'd leave him here overnight if I was you, lads. Let the M.O. give him a sleepy-byes shot. Nobody wants a raver in the Maria, do they?"

"He don't look nothing special," said the escort officer with acne. "Anyway, they want him down at Maidstone chop-chop."

"Waffor?" said the first screw.

The second escort officer looked at his clipboard, chewed a match at it, and said, "He's down for the yo-yo treatment. If they want him, we take him. There's the bloody roster if you want to see it. I ain't the Home Secretary, am I?"

"Who is? But you ought to let the M.O. see him before you cart him off."

"He won't give us no bother, will you, sunshine?"

The first escort officer ruffled Charlie's hair, and the head lolled under his callused palm.

"They don't none of them give *us* bother."

The reception screw sighed and scratched the bald spot under his cap.

"Sign for him downstairs and he's yours. And don't bring him back. We got enough nutters who break up their cells this time of the year. Christmas is always a bastard."

They talked about lunatics on three staircases and when the paperwork was completed Charlie felt night air in his face. The rear doors of a Black Maria opened and he was pushed up the steps. The yard was dusted with snow, and more flurried in the cold wind. Then the Medical Officer was there wanting to check Charlie out before he went into transit, talking down to the reception screw with an Oxford accent.

"Up you go, Charlie. Move your sodding legs."

Charlie's head snapped up and he saw sweat on the first escort officer's lip. The sheen of spirit gum under his stage moustache.

"Move. Or I'll shiv you here."

The second escort officer hacked Charlie's ankles.

Charlie let himself fall on his back. Braced his shoulders and threw both feet into the first escort officer's face. His wrists screamed inside the handcuffs and a cap sailed into the darkness. Charlie enjoyed the shock of his heel snapping a chin back. Scrabbled away from the Black Maria on elbows and heels.

The Oxford accent had risen in pitch, and the reception screw was following the M.O. out into the yard.

Something long and sharp flashed between Charlie's side and his right arm. A blade nipped his bicep and skidded across his ribs before skittering away to lose itself under the vehicle.

Charlie used the pain to summon everything he had.

Hoped it was enough.

Arched his spine and came up onto the balls of his feet.

Rolled into the second escort officer as he made for the cab of the Black Maria. Brought him down with a leg scissors and kicked him twice in the crotch. Dropped on the gaping mouth with all his weight behind his bent knees. Jumped away to get his back firmly against the side of the phony prison vehicle to dodge a lunge from the reception screw.

"They ain't real filth, you prune. I'm shivved."

"You're a flaming nutter."

Charlie head-butted the reception screw in the face. The screw went down spitting out a broken dental plate and the M.O. with the Oxford accent had Charlie all to himself.

"You're disturbed, old chap."

"I'm stabbed, you medical moron."

The M.O. watched Charlie slide down the side of the Black Maria, leaving a snail's trail of crimson on the paintwork.

"Is that claret, or is that claret?"

Charlie's grin was lopsided.

"I'd call help if I was you, my old quack. . . . Thass Red Bellaver lying there. . . . The other one's Morrie Torrance. . . . They won't be out for long. . . . Tough bastards . . . I could make them talk for you . . . for me actually . . . but there just ain't . . . the time. . . ."

The M.O. yelled inside the prison. Rang an alarm bell.

". . . Merry Chrissmasssss . . ."

Charlie passed out with snow falling on his face.

Valletta simmered.

A furnace of marzipan buildings under a hot and white Sahara sky. Whiter than snow and hotter than sand. The noonday promenade in Kingsway had been a listless mill of bored soldiery and young Maltese, all too jaded to flirt or exchange the usual ribald banter.

Ingrid sat in Queen Victoria's shadow with iced coffee and *gâteau,* resting before the drive back to Tarxien. She had bought silly, frivolous presents to amuse rather than impress.

A pair of wind-up tin mobsters that fired bubbles from tin machine guns for Archie. Candy jewelry and home-baked gingerbread men decorated with Edwardian lithographs for Queenie. Silly things to match her mood of gay optimism. She turned the gold band on the third finger of her left hand. Pretended she had not bought it herself. Polished it slowly on her rising belly, enjoying the hot metal against the silk of her dress. The fine material against her skin.

The roly-poly doctor from Bugibba had told her she would carry the child well so long as she gave tennis up for swimming.

"And not too much love-making."

He had looked over his half-glasses and wagged a finger.

"And not too little. A father needs his love, too, eh?"

His chocolate eyes and Hitler moustache had glistened with moisture as he closed his black bag.

"And you a Catholic, Dr. Micalef," Ingrid had teased.

"But a man first. God would see it my way. We talk all the time. Mostly I talk. He listens. And not always in church, eh?"

Then he had patted her head and left through Archie's rose bower.

Another month and the baby would stir.

Ingrid longed to snuggle against Charlie's back so that he could share the kicks he had helped to create. And make love without pressing on her swelling belly.

Gently, gently . . .

Ingrid blushed crimson. Watched by two young sappers with their soldier's haircuts and boyish faces. She poked her tongue at them and took her packages to her car.

Ingrid drove carefully. Avoided the many potholes and the carefree Maltese drivers who obeyed no rules. As if their battered Fords and Mercedes had one fast forward speed and brakes were an extra.

She parked in the meager shade of the dusty orange trees and prickly pear below the old rampart wall and toiled up the steep stone steps to a walled garden with the arms of the last Grand Master of Malta carved over the gate.

A fallen banana frond had drowned in the shallows. The rest of the pool was an angry glitter spiked by dancing light. The honey walls shed heat into the fruit trees Queenie had hung with colored lights, and the statues in their niches wore bright party hats and sprigs of mistletoe. The fairy at the top of the twenty-foot Canadian pine spread her wings against the brazen sky, and her chintz skirt stirred in the molten breeze.

Missing Charlie, Ingrid walked through the games room. Walked softly in case Archie enjoyed an afternoon siesta on his fourposter. His speech improved slowly, and he made himself understood when he spoke with care. Queenie avoided sharp and angry raps of his cane by curbing her inclination to finish sentences for him.

Ingrid laid her packages on the kitchen table, filled the kettle for a cup of tea, and listened for the clack of Queenie's needles.

The bougainvillaea tapped the kitchen wall, and a car with a riddled muffler chugged along the lower road near the megalithic temple. The ceiling fan beat the air as though it stirred syrup, and a pair of finches chirped in the red bracts outside the window. Ingrid decided that Queenie dozed and made tea through the strainer, practicing the austerity of her childhood. Waste was a crime no matter what could be afforded.

She sliced a lemon, when a brown hand clamped her mouth and an arm circled her waist.

Without thinking, and scalded by shock, Ingrid drove the paring knife over her shoulder. Felt it strike muscle.

Garlic breath made a hot, moist explosion against her neck as it was twisted aside. Grated bones against the base of her skull. Tears popped from her eyes. She bit her tongue and hacked back with her heels.

They drummed uselessly against a man's legs, and her flip-flops dropped to the floor as she was lifted and thrown. A stream of hot Maltese followed her sprawl, and her head hit the limewashed wall a moment before the rest of her limbs caught up with her.

Ingrid curled over herself, protected her belly, but her head was lifted by the hair and a horny palm beat her face from side to side.

Red centipedes wriggled behind her eyelids amid bursting

grey balloons of nausea. She went limp and was lifted by elbow and throat and dragged along the cool marble passage to the drawing room, where she was dumped in a heap on a scatter rug. Again she wrapped herself in a fetal curl and sobbed for breath, her eyes squeezed closed against the woolly nap of locally woven thread. Breathed for the baby and thought of rape.

"Bitch cut me good."

Ingrid edged away from the voice, and her hand found the edge of an overstuffed chair. A shoe and a heavy cane.

"A flea bite."

The second voice was unruffled and cold, a scratch of a voice in a deformed throat. Dry leaves rattling in a tomb.

A fruit bowl hit the carpet with a roll of apples as the antimacassar was pulled from the coffee table.

"Use this."

Archie's hand squeezed Ingrid's shoulder and she laid her face against his leg, looked into his strong and tanned face for comfort. His eyes were pools of angry russet. A nerve ticked in the flap of skin under his right eyebrow. He stroked Ingrid's hair, his entire attention on the men in the middle of the long vaulted room.

"Sit . . . tight . . . ," he said slowly and quietly.

"Sound advice," the dead voice scratched.

Ingrid cuddled her legs under her chin and looked without wanting to.

A young Maltese with hot black eyes stuffed the wadded antimacassar inside a tan leather jacket. Blood was a ragged bloom on his torn lapel. He bared overwhite teeth and purple gums in a thin, smooth face. The long-barreled Savage he held on Queenie seemed too heavy for his lean olive hand.

The second man was older and taller and more olive. His face was all seams. The hollow cheeks were lightly pocked and his throat was a livid turkey wattle. His black hair had red tints and laid too close to his skull to be real hair. His sideburns were as grey as the salt-and-pepper bristle on his neck. He looked at Ingrid's legs. Smiled at them with pale brown lips. One eye blinked and the other stared as cold and as unmoving as glass. Frozen in a socket the same rough texture as his ugly throat. His teeth worried a brown lower lip.

"You're looking at my eye. They all look at my eye. You want to see it closer, girlie?"

Ingrid gulped bile. Drew strength from Archie's hand.

"Maybe I save her for last, eh, Mario?"

"Yeah, she goes last. She cut me good."

"You can have her. After me."

Queenie laughed suddenly. Just short of hysteria.

"After nobody. Somebody crossed your wires, Ugly."

Archie tapped with his cane.

"Acid . . . burns. . . ."

The man with the frozen eye almost touched his neck. Brought a revolver from somewhere instead. It blurred into his hand like an angry hummingbird. A flick of blue steel and it was there.

"You don't speak. Until it's time. The old lady shut up good, too. And girlie. Stay quiet until it's time."

"Time . . . for what?"

Archie's cane went quiet.

"M-my M-malts didn't just take off . . . for no good *reason.*"

"Slowly, Arch," Queenie warned.

"Old lady don't say nothing," said Frozen Eye.

Archie breathed carefully, his big hand a clamp on Ingrid's shoulder.

"I get it. . . . Toronto sent these two . . . Queenie. . . . Crossed wires is right. . . . They're on contract for . . . Roger and Jesus. . . ."

Mario shrugged and made himself wince.

"You can talk when they come."

"How m-much to do a deal . . . ?"

"No more talk."

"Money always talks, Ugly." Queenie reached for her knitting bag. "Mind if I busy my hands since I ain't allowed to talk?"

"Old lady, stay quiet and make things."

Frozen Eye's gun swung at Archie, down at Ingrid, and

across to Queenie. The fast, practiced move of a man who hated wasted motion. Making shots. His hand flexed and the revolver spun and was gone. The good eye fixed on Ingrid's legs.

To divert him Archie asked for water.

"No water." The eye ran up Ingrid's body to her mouth.

"The pattern's here somewhere." Queenie rummaged in her knitting bag.

Archie licked a dry mouth. "Don't f-find it too . . . quick. She might finish that thing and I'd . . . have to wear . . . it. . . ."

"That ain't your worry, dad," said Mario.

"Cold in Toronto, is it?" Queenie asked.

"Not as cold as you're gonna be," Mario drawled.

The frozen eye looked at nothing and the blinking one moistened as Ingrid was told to stand up.

"Cold must be . . . m-murder on an acid . . . burn. Must burn colder than . . . hell. . . ."

Archie's fingers dug into Ingrid's shoulder, and he pointed his cane at Frozen Eye.

"You're Pru M-mizzi. . . . Has Roger forgotten how s-small this island is? . . . Hey . . . Mario . . . you won't make it out of the airport with that f-frozen . . . face . . . in tow. . . ."

"Shut it, dad."

Pru Mizzi's throat crackled with dry leaves of laughter.

"You want lumps, old man? First, girlie pleases me. Then you and old lady get lumps."

"You'll get my knee where it matters, you gargoyle," Ingrid said, dizzy with fear.

"That cuts it." Mario showed teeth and gum. "What now, Pru?"

"*She* comes here."

Mizzi tore Archie's cane away and it bounced off to crack a pane of window glass. He grabbed Ingrid's hair and pulled her toward him.

Ingrid buried teeth in a wiry groin.

The gun made its blur and searched for the nape of Ingrid's neck.

Archie fell forward and butted Mizzi in the abdomen.

Mizzi staggered. Kicked Ingrid off his leg as he was dragged to the floor by Archie's dead weight.

Mario was in motion. The Savage snapped out to train on Archie's scalp.

Queenie raised her knitting bag and flame cut a black hole through the embroidered side.

Mario stood very straight. Looked puzzled when his necktie jumped away from a second red bloom on his shirtfront. His white teeth snarled and ground together. Then he just stood there looking weary. A bored young man with nothing on his mind.

Mizzi rolled on a curved spine. His leg came free with a wet bite mark on the left thigh. A ribbon of spittle spun from Ingrid's mouth as she held her kicked stomach. Settled on the floor with rigid care, whitened by pain and shock.

Mizzi's fast revolver shot Admiral Byng from the wall, and the walnut frame came to pieces. Archie's hair ruffled as crimson striped his scalp. Spattered the chairback. His meaty fists beat Mizzi's face, and slow grunts came from deep within him.

Queenie got down from her chair without hurry and fired into the top of Mizzi's shoulder.

Twice with her tongue out.

The small nickel Beretta snapped in her tiny hand. No louder than a thirsty lapdog.

Mizzi's glass eye popped from the socket in a spurt of rich blood and rolled away. His head strained on his ugly neck and the wattled Adam's apple jerked aimlessly.

Queenie's next shot took him in the ear, knocked him on his side. The fast gun trembled in the olive fingers, then lay on the carpet under a slowly stilling hand.

Mario was trying to work out why his Savage pointed at his own foot. He was smiling apologetically when Queenie pumped two small-caliber bullets into his perfect teeth.

Mario coughed red bubbles. Sighed a last deep sigh of regret and fell on his face. He did not feel Queenie hit him with her embroidered bag or see hundreds of tiny beads bounce to all four corners of the room until Ingrid dragged herself across to pull her away.

Archie picked up the two revolvers and dragged himself back to his chair. And waited for the Tonna brothers.

Margot Sadler's eyes were oval, sharp, and very blue. She looked at Lemmon as if he could be valued in gossip-column inches and her handshake was manly. Her no-nonsense voice was languorous and her drop earrings could have paid off the national debt of a banana republic. Her hair and dress were black and sewn with seed pearls, her wayward nose was a marvel of unrelated curves, and she smiled with far too many teeth. She had the brittle glitter of a faded ingénue who had sailed across footlights into the arms of money before she and the bit parts dried up, and her laugh said she knew that all too well and didn't give a damn.

At first glance, her husband was just a sleek executive with tinted hair and a face as solemn as organ music. His light tan had not penetrated the crow's feet round his eyes and gave him the look of a startled somnambulist. His comfortable stomach fronted a hollow back and probably reduced his tailor to bitter tears. His nose was a careless afterthought with nostrils, and his mouth was just something he ate with. His chins were chins and his cool eyes flicked from face to face like flags in a cash register.

Margot laughed and said, "So you're Bunny's favorite copper. He dines out on your exploits all the time."

Bunny laughed back.

"Perhaps I should eat at home more often. One should not turn one's friends into anecdotes."

Margot stage-managed drinks.

"You'd starve or die of boredom. And our buffet table groans under the weight of gourmet goodies. Malcolm has decided to outdo the Guildhall yet again. Haven't you, darling?"

Sadler's eyes flicked and flicked away.

"Entertaining is an art. Like all things theatrical. One must get the props right. Mustn't one, *darling?"*

"Meeow," said Margot, her own eyes nailing Lemmon. "Are we to be riveted by tales of police deduction, Inspector dear?"

"I never tell tales out of school. *Sub judice,* you know."

"Such discretion. And such a bore. Malcolm was so looking forward to tales of thud and blunder. He eats a constant diet of *True Crime* stories. His bedside table is simply littered with the most lurid magazines."

"This whiskey sour is excellent, Mrs. Sadler." Lemmon hid a yawn in his cheek.

"Which means you won't talk about such things. Such a real disappointment for all of us. Poor, poor Malcolm," Margot said with a wide and insincere smile.

"One has to do something before dropping off to sleep."

Sadler's glance brushed Lemmon's face before settling on a tall blonde in a sheer backless gown the turquoise of tropical seawater. Her tan was as permanent as his was transitory.

"Doesn't one? Who is that attractive creature?" There was mischief in Bunny's voice. "She has the look of a wanton mermaid in that most stunning of gowns."

Sadler's mouth tasted itself and said, "Naomi Leathers. She and her daughter are here on a shopping trip. And for Christmas of course. Business acquaintances in the loosest sense of the word. More friends of friends."

"Loose, precisely," Margot muttered.

"Did you say something, darling?" Sadler asked.

"I?" said Margot.

"You," said Sadler.

"Only that you adore all things criminal, *darling*. And there is nothing drearier than corpses over the consommé; death by ligature, garotte, and hempen rope through the entrée; and gore, graves, and ghoulish practices for dessert. And it is as well English is already a bastard tongue. Some of the people Malcolm invites to the house are really beyond the pale. . . ."

"Cats," said Sadler, "should stay in their baskets with their claws sheathed. Cats should look regal and not scratch Papa's furniture or his good humor. Cats who wail on walls get snipped by vets with small sharp knives. Cats—"

"Malcolm has been drinking wine. Well if not wisely," Margot said.

"Cats," Sadler said dreamily. "Cats can use up their nine

lives so very quickly. Then it's a sack and the canal at midnight. If you gentlemen will excuse me?"

Sadler drifted away and lost himself in a knot of guests near the blonde in the seawater dress.

"You two do have the knives out tonight," Bunny said.

Margot's smile was as bright as a musical overture.

"Another Christian chauvinist, Bunny? You think Puss should play the dutiful wife as usual? Most especially on the eve before the eve of immaculate birth? Marriage is an interminable roadshow with the dullest notices, a dull script, and an even duller cast of two."

She drained her glass and whisked another from a passing tray.

"God and fishes, but I'm tired of this role."

Bunny laid a pink hand on her slender wrist.

"Now, Margot. Santa doesn't come down the chimney for naughty girls with carrying voices. And jealous green isn't your color. Sexual window-shopping is the last privilege left to the married man. And looking at the goods is so much better than the concomitant sordid scenes of an actual affair. A cat may look at a queen without designs on her crown."

"Witty and empty," said Margot. "Like your smug old face."

"Now I'm wounded," Bunny mocked.

"And I adore you, too," said Margot. "But not tonight. If I stay here a moment longer, I shall scream blue bloody murder."

"Do you have a telephone I could use?" said Lemmon.

"What? I mean . . . pardon?" said Margot.

"A telephone. Dial-dial-ring-ring-hello? Telephone? I'd like to tell my wife she's wrong. Very, very wrong. And that I'd like to come home and prove it to her with warm and clinical precision. Wrong about me and many other things. I can afford such luxuries now, and I do have the right copper coins to leave in the silver tray."

"Now, *there* speaks a truly married man."

Margot found another drink and ordered whiskey sours for Bunny and Lemmon.

"Oh, dear," Bunny said. "I shall get tight."

"Which can only improve him, eh, Inspector?" said Margot. "What's your first, Christian, or given name, Married Man?"

"Theo," said Lemmon.

"Come with me, married Theo. Then both Malcolm *and* Bunny will be free to watch the mermaid's dumplings boil out of that dress. Bunny might even give Malcolm's nervous little eyes a rest by ogling for him."

"And double meeow to you, Margot dear."

Bunny held his fresh drink and watched Margot lead Lemmon through a door that could have graced a cathedral. Then he slipped away to wake his driver and have himself driven home.

Elizabeth was snuggled up with hot milk and a paperback romance. She said fond goodnights in a yawny voice, blew a kiss, and rang off.

Lemmon redialed, and Bulstrode said, "Bulstrode."

"It's me."

Lemmon watched Margot eavesdrop as she roamed the anteroom plumping cushions. Silver gleamed in glass cabinets and the oiled paneling shone like dark waters in the dimmed light.

"There was an attempted breakout at Brixton Prison. Red Bellaver and Morrie Torrance tried to pull Dance out."

Lemmon kneaded his stomach.

"And?"

"Charlie worked them over after they put a shiv through his ribs. Then bent a couple of screws before he fell over. He's in intensive, but he'll live to annoy us another day."

Lemmon squeezed the phone, seeing grey eyes in a greyer room.

"He's all right, then?"

"Stitches and sedation. M.O. said he was lucky."

"And getting luckier."

"Eh?" Bulstrode was puzzled by Lemmon's tone.

"That package. From the mail train."

"Yessir?"

"Mark it 'Lost in the Post' and do just that."

"If you say so, Guv."

"I say so."

"And Dance himself?"

"Leave him to due process. Now lose yourself for the rest of the holiday. Merry Christmas, Buller."

"And you, Guv. And . . . thanks."

"For what? Doing what's right?"

Lemmon found Margot in the doorway beside a tapestry of medieval horsemen chasing stags through a forest of stylized trees.

"Where do I leave the gratuity?"

"Have the calls with the compliments of the season. Are you unwell? You seem very pale."

Lemmon squeezed sweating temples.

"Must be vertigo. Must be I climbed too high and too fast up the social ladder. If I have a nosebleed, I'll spill Olympian ichor, not real blood at all. And if I fall from these golden rungs, I'll leave the perfect outline of a failed copper in the gutter on my long drop into Hades. And who will pay Charon to ferry me across the River Styx to join the dead? And what would it matter anyway? The afterlife can only be a mirror image of all this. Good liquor in bad company. The same old Grace and Favor rules. That is how it works, isn't it?"

"Great good heavens. A copper with a classical bent. Yes, Married Man, those are the ground rules for the initiate."

Lemmon shook his overheated face, looked into his empty glass for clues.

"Fresh air and a fresher drink are what you need, my lad."

Margot led him down a dark passage and through glass doors into the hot smell of sweet sap and moist earth. The old-maid odors of orchids and tropical fish. Fleshy leaves dripped with moisture and fish swam in stone pools between banks of mature rare plants. Fog curled against the conservatory roof like primordial mist above a rain forest.

Lemmon slumped on a slatted bench, and Margot fixed iced drinks at a bar behind a fall of purple pitcher plants.

"Here." She handed Lemmon a frosted glass.

He savored the clean astringency of limes laced with gin and could have been alone when he said, "And they dallied by the streams of the forest until it was time to leave that enchanted place, for it is known that Man may not remain too long away from his own time, his own people, for too long."

Margot fed a carp by hand.

"That should end 'For there lies Madness and Death.' I'll raise a bumper to that merry thought."

"Maybe it does. I read it somewhere."

"And now you're going to ask me about my errant husband."

"Am I?"

"Bunny Halliday didn't bring you here for no good reason. There's a reason for everything Bunny does."

"Maybe, and maybe not. A million maybes and not a truth to hang your hat on. And what are you going to ask me for? Fix a parking fine or two? An invitation to the Black Museum?"

"Direct, aren't you, Married Man?"

"Mr. Oblique, at your service."

"Tush. It isn't me who needs information. It's the mermaid with the boiling muffins. I said I'd see what I could do."

Margot sent ripples across the pond with a flick of a silver nail.

"Shall I ask, Married Man? Or pander to your morbid mood?"

"Is the mermaid playing four legs in a bed with your husband?"

"She isn't. He'd like to. And she'd *loathe* it if she did."

"I see."

"No, married Theo. You do not see."

"All right. I don't."

"It is not all right."

Lemmon offered his glass.

"This whirligig needs refreshing. Is there more lubricant?"

"Oodles and oodles."

Margot poured from a silver thermos, compensated for Lemmon's shaking hand.

"Poor Naomi. She has the rottenest luck with her casual

consorts. If her brains were in her bra, she'd be in the genius class."

"You're not that flat-chested."

Margot's sigh could have filled a spinnaker.

"Liar."

"I'd better go back to misquoting things, look sorry for myself. Nothing else seems to please you."

Margot took a long frond and trapped it between her nose and upper lip to give herself a long green moustache.

"A bosom of gigantic proportions isn't everything. I have other attributes. Not that bastard Malcolm sees them anymore. Perhaps he never did. He prefers to saddle me with low-lifers from the East End for interminable weekends, and gloats until I could shriek. Awful people with clammy hands and eyes like boiled sweets."

"I thought we were talking about the Muffin Lady?"

Lemmon accepted a refill from the bottomless thermos.

"But we are, married Theo. I just don't like linear dialogue. What woman does?"

"No comment."

"He's the brother of this man Malcolm has been cultivating for his own curious and perverse reasons."

"Who is?"

"Naomi's bit of East End rough, darling. I'm telling you, aren't I?"

Margot released the frond and it swayed off into the humid green canopy to rattle in the shadows.

"If you say so," Lemmon said.

"The brother of the one Malcolm has so much time for. The one with a name like two given names. Walter, that's it. Walter Harold. There, I remembered."

"You certainly did."

Lemmon winked both eyes, thoroughly bemused.

"She, Naomi, met him—them—in South Africa. And had this, you know, *thing* with the brother."

"The Muffin Lady and Wally Harold had a romp in South Africa, is that it? She's a big girl, how could I help her?"

"To tell her why, you obtuse copper."

"Why what?"

"Why he's been arrested."

Lemmon tried not to stumble over words oiled by alcohol.

"Apart from telling you he's on a murder charge, I can't talk about it."

"But Malcolm said it *was,* over breakfast."

"Was *what* over breakfast?"

"Your case, darling. Or, more precisely, Bunny's chum's case is what he said. He said, 'Bunny's chum's handling that.' That's what Malcolm said."

"Bunny has dozens of chums. Bunny has chums like other people have mice."

Margot's smile-frown was slightly myopic.

"So you can't help our Muffin Lady?"

"Why would you help a woman your husband lusts after? I thought wives were territorial. I know mine is."

"Me, territorial about bastard Malcolm? My dear married Theo, bastard Malcolm could have starred in *Lawrence of Arabia.* He likes boys and women who'll act as boys. I'm just the dressing on the top of his perverted sexual sandwich, and Naomi isn't that sort of a girl."

Lemmon watched the drink soften the palms over the pool.

"Poor Muffin Lady, and poor you," he said solemnly.

Margot topped their glasses.

"Damn other people's indiscreet affairs. They so impinge on one's own. Don't they, married Theo?"

"Are you having an affair, Mrs. Sadler?"

"Only if you ask me."

"Ah."

"And it's Margot. Don't be stuffy. I mean, you're one of us now."

"I've been seduced once this evening already. Twice would be too much, thank you kindly. I like you, Margot. You're both indulging and patronizing me."

"I patronize the arts, not people. I'm drinking far too much, far too quickly, with a tarnished knight without an escutcheon and no real dragons to fight. Poor married knight, Theo. And a tipsy wife, however badly used she may be, should not go public with her soiled linen. And bastard Malcolm is not to be betrayed to . . ."

Margot swallowed the rest with her drink.

"The likes of me? Who's asking you to? I'm drinking with Solomon's wife and a lot of fish. In a jungle. Can't get drunk, though. Heat drives off the alcohol. Thiss iss juss colored water. Cannibalism. Lemmon drinking lime."

"I believe you," Margot lied.

"You're right. I'm by-God drunk and nobody's asking anybody anything. And I can't pretend to romance another man's wife for shiny pips and a bigger pension. Too stuffy and middle class. Even if I was led to it by an old school friend with a phony conscience and a pink sash. Sorry and all that, old girl."

Margot arched an eyebrow over a blue oval eye.

"Is that what you thought you were doing? Well, you're making a perfectly rotten job of it. *If* you don't mind my saying so."

"Don't if you don't. Thass fair."

Margot emptied the thermos over their glasses.

"Fine logic, Sleuth. Cheers, Sherlock."

"Chuzz."

"And now, if you'll lever your nose out of that drink, I'd like to be kissed rather firmly."

"You're . . . smart lady. Know it wouldn't mean anything."

"I shan't until I try, damn it."

"True."

"Well?"

"I'm extremely married."

"Try anyway."

Lemmon leaned into Margot's mouth. Tasted limes and Cognac and gin on her firm mouth before she ran her warm tongue against his teeth and her hard hips ground against him. They clung together in a locked sway as the humidity plopped all around them. Each salving the ache of profound solitude. Then they parted shakily and became strangers again.

Margot leaned on a long forearm and used the pond as a mirror to repair her lipstick.

Lemmon twirled his glass.

"Time for weary coppers to wend homeward."

"What? No third degree? Kiss and run and no rubber

hoses? And I was so looking forward to a ghastly experience."

"All frogs don't turn into princes. But don't stop looking, Margot."

Margot grinned at her distorted reflection.

"I just kissed a bluebottle. Are any of them princes?"

"Stony ground for nobility, the filth."

"Stony ground everywhere, Inspector Lemmon."

"And a formal goodnight to you, Mrs. Sadler."

"Goodbye, married Theo."

Out in the fog, Lemmon could just pick out the yellow glow of the conservatory above a wall and a gap between bald elms.

He drove home with his wheels close to the curb.

Asleep beside Elizabeth, he dreamed Margot Sadler hunted crowned frogs through a grey steel jungle with a golden butterfly net. Dislodged leaves like banknotes, all with Bunny's head in the Queen's roundel, and bearing the legend: *Grace and Favor.* Apes with screws' voices swung through the grey steel canopy crying, "One away to you, mister," making the steel tree trunks boom with their fists. Charlie was there, leaving a spoor of bright red blood, confusing poor Margot, who hacked about and got crosser and crosser and lonelier and lonelier in her search for a loving royal frog. And somehow Charlie had all the frogs and crowns and made Margot run in smaller and smaller circles until her unraveled hair spun itself into the cocoon of a black butterfly that flew into Lemmon's face and woke him with a monumental hangover on a disordered bed.

CHAPTER 4

JANUARY HAD COME IN HARD AND SMELLED OF SPENT CARtridges. Brixton glittered with frost under a sky greyer than his cell when Charlie heard the prison door slam him out into the real world.

There was nobody to meet him.

He took a taxi to Pimlico through silent early morning streets and took the elevator up to his flat, where he drove must and silence away by floating Vivaldi's baroque arabesques on hot conducted air.

He lit the wall-length aquarium, and his Discus sailed through slate gorges and submarine weed. Circular rainbows with sad golden eyes. He made coffee to spice the antiseptic air. Smashed ice cubes, salted a tequila glass, and built a shaker of margaritas.

He booked a call to Malta and could not settle.

He wandered from room to room. Turned on lights and wound his collection of antique clocks. Straightened perfectly hung pictures. Turned back his bed to air and laid out a new toweling robe. A stranger in his own home.

He took the coffee and cocktails into the bathroom. Ran the taps. Broke open fresh bars of soap. Sprinkled bath essence into the foam and warmed towels over the heated rail.

In the living room he stripped naked.

Slashed the clothes he had been wearing to ribbons with pinking shears and stuffed the rags into a plastic refuse sack. Padded to the refuse chute and listened to the sack slither down the shaft to boom into the basement garbage bin.

Vivaldi's *Winter* gave way to Shostakovich's *Spring* as he lowered himself into fragrant suds and methodically scrubbed five prisons away between swallows of coffee and margaritas.

He scrubbed for a very long time and through several changes of hot water. Hard-toweled off until his skin glowed crimson.

He was almost drunk enough to sleep when the telephone rang and Queenie told him Ingrid had lost the baby, crying for both of them.

Charlie just listened until she was finished.

Then looked at nothing as the day became night filled with soft flurries of snow.

And at dawn he went hunting.

BOOK II

The Smoke

CHAPTER 5

MARIA'S FAT ARM WAS ACROSS FREDDY'S FACE.

Smothering him.

He vowed to buy single beds for the trillionth time and made to shrug away. She wouldn't shrug a damn, and the backs of her hands were stiff with male hair. A pad clamped his nose and mouth. Watering his eyes. He choked on cloying sweetness as he started up from the pillow. Pressed back and down, a red pole of light grew from below his feet. Whirled him through the floor on the spokes of a nebulous ferris wheel. Spun into drugged twilight, he sneezed against a ribbed metal floor and was jogged by a van's suspension.

Stars jiggled in a swatch of night sky as he was carried across frosted rubble, down creaking stairs into darkness, and flopped into a chair in a spill of torchlight. He was grateful ropes stopped him falling. Then they constricted his chest, snagged his ankles, and brought his feet off the floor.

The pad left his face and he smelled dead air, dry rot, and the bitterness of wet coal. Ammonia seared his nostrils. Startled him fully aware.

And fear came with the snapping cold.

The flashlight showed him a cellar floor black with coal dust. Panes of grey glass lying against a bunker. A rusty gas meter and scales of fallen plaster. Fungus on the rafters and walls of crusted brick. Dusty cobwebs bellying in a draught that turned his feet to stones.

He remembered his name. Knew this was a mistake. Tried to talk. But his tongue was just a thing he swallowed around. The torch clicked off, and a voice in the darkness said, "Time to own up, Freddy."

There was no face he could match to the quiet monotone.

Own up to what? "Wrong man, mister . . ."

"Now or later. You'll tell me."

Freddy said the three foulest words he knew.

The darkness sighed.

"You hear me, mister? You ain't dealing with a little boy."

Freddy heard cracks in his bluster. The cold had cracked his lips.

"You *hear* me?"

The darkness stayed silent.

Freddy listened until his ears popped.

Nothing.

Then the saccharine-citrus stench of chloroform slammed against his face, and Manchester Freddy fell into a darker darkness in a long chime of silence.

"You'll talk."

Charlie climbed stairs into a fresh fall of snow.

The house in Esher crouched in snow with dripping eaves.

The green-tiled roof ran between dunce-cap turrets and jabbed ornate lightning conductors into snow cloud. The central mansard was bordered by finely scrolled ironwork with gilded spearheads. A weathervane pointed its flag to the east, and Father Time leaned over a scythe wearing a snow skullcap.

A dying run of red creeper shed ice-melt onto the pitched portico, and icicles dripped themselves to death over wide stone steps leading to the heavily carved front door. Swiss shutters grafted onto the Tudoresque façade were folded back from the ground-floor windows, and heraldic lozenges set in the leaded glass leaked vague patterns of color onto the snowbound lawn.

A lean-to garage of ship's timbers and more green tile housed a Porsche and a new Mercedes, and a chauffeur steamed frost from a maroon Daimler with an air hose on a flagged drive. All that could be seen of the kitchen gardens and the rear grounds was bald elms and a conservatory roof above an arched wall with rubble infills.

Mature monkey puzzle trees bordered the front garden wall and spread their spiked branches over the pavement, low enough to graze pedestrians' faces. It was a suburban street where only the postman walked.

A Post Office van nosed into the curb, off-loaded a candy-striped tent and red folding barriers, and drove away. Two men got out of an official red van, set the tent over a manhole, and disappeared inside to locate the right circuitry to cut the house off from outside contact. The one with freckles and unnaturally black hair wore earphones, and the one with slate eyes sent feedback down the wires.

Inside, Malcolm Sadler dialed 0 to clear the line, and electronic discords fought the Talking Clock for his attention. He swore, pinched his mouth bloodless, and earned a brilliant blue glare from his wife.

"Profanity changes nothing, Malcolm darling."

Margot blew on silver nails.

"Take care, Cat. This house lives by the telephone."

Sadler's mouth flushed as blood returned.

"The world's stock markets are closed on Sundays. So be grateful there's at least one day in the week when you can't sell yourself short in Tokyo or New York. What with tin on Wednesday, and magnesium on Thursday, I can hardly keep up with your countless market shortfalls. That *is* the right phrase, isn't it, darling?"

Margot pouted into her mirror with a sardonic purr. Settled a black slip over her narrow hips and recrossed her legs with a hiss of nylon.

"*Short*falls?" she repeated.

"A momentary setback. And a subject high above your avaricious whiskers, Cat."

Sadler worried a perfect knot into his shirt collar. Grunted over his folded belly when he tied his shoes.

"You *could* blame the Labor opposition, darling. You've been far too nice about them since Gaitskell died and small fat Harold became leader. And that screaming skull Lord Home makes chubby little Wilson seem quite attractive by comparison. Perhaps we shall have a socialist government after the next general election. Then you'll really be 'one of the lads' when you entertain your East End roughnecks, won't you?"

Sadler tried the phone again.

"You'll find most of them are emotional socialists and have rapidly moved to a conservatism far to the right of Genghis Khan. In their world it takes more than a cut-glass accent and a stream of friendly bank managers to prevail against the opposition. Take care you don't brush their fur the wrong way, Cat."

Margot eased into a very frilly black blouse, zipped into a charcoal grey skirt, and added four inches to her height with French heels.

"Will your robber barons require cutlery? Or will they eat their rancid faggots and pease pudding with their fingers as usual? I forget the protocol, bastard, darling, Malcolm, sweetie."

Sadler reached Margot in two strides. Moved quickly for his sleek bulk. Thick fingers twined into the hair at the back of Margot's neck. Twisted with a vicious upturn. A thick thumb and forefinger closed around her throat. Squeezed slowly, lifting her inch by inch from the floor.

"You go too far, Cat. Far too far . . ."

Margot smelled breakfast marmalade on his breath, the harsh tang of witch hazel on his shaved cheeks.

"Just wifely cat noises . . . Mal . . . colm. . . ."

Margot's pointed toes tried for the floor. She thought of driving silver nails into the whites of his eyes. But her sight was gone in mist and her heart was a slowing engine.

He swore he'd never play this foul game again. . . .

She was plunged back to Biarritz, when Malcolm and her wedding band were equally strange. Clever ingénue Margot, who had avoided bedroom scenes with shy Malcolm until after altar pledges were notarized and she had tossed orange blossom to her maids of honor. The champagne whirl into the bridal suite, where Malcolm had used her as if she were the chorus boy who had introduced them. Angry she had not embraced sapphism as he had supposed. Angrier still when she would not complete the triangle when the young man flew in the following day. The humiliation of nights on the couch as they used her bridal bed.

"Too catty to be wifely, Cat."

Margot spun on the edge of consciousness as the voice brushed her with the threat of sadism.

"The cat must lap the milk of penitence. Lap it and drink it down like a good and dutiful queen. But tree queens can have kittens. Can't they, Cat? And this queen is barren. Not a real queen at all. Just a cat who pretends she had eggs. Just to bring Malcolm into her bed for her own lascivious ends. No son for Malcolm. Just a cat. . . ."

"No . . . Malcolm . . . you swore . . ."

"But it's yes, Malcolm. It's always to be yes for Malcolm."

Agree before he peels your scalp like pith from an orange.

"Yesss . . . Malcolm. . . ."

"Again, Cat."

"Yesss. . . ."

Sadler drove Margot to her knees. Made her crawl toward the bed.

"Nothing inside my cat but avarice. And the need for punishment. Now, what should that be, I wonder? Should Malcolm buy himself a new cat? Make the eggless cat kiss the new cat's paws before the old cat laps milk from Malcolm's lap? Hmm?"

The bed and Malcolm sighed as he lowered himself onto the counterpane, Margot's face trapped between his great thighs. He released the pressure on her throat and she drank in the smell of laundered sheets, Malcolm's oversweet male perfume.

Her face was slowly raised, and Sadler was a dark buddha against the hot orange of a stained-glass lozenge.

"Well, Cat."

Feed his perverted fantasies . . . and live.

Say it and get it over with.

"Yesss . . . Malcolm. . . ."

"Only yes, Margot, cat? Barren cat?"

"Yesss, Malcolm. Please, please, Malcolm?"

"Margot cat wants to lap the milk of penitence?"

"Yes, please, Malcolm."

Margot unbuttoned the pinstripe fly with dreary care.

Freed the half-risen member and took it into her quivering mouth very slowly. Felt it become a hard pole against the roof of her mouth. And with her eyes locked on Sadler's shadowed face she lapped her milk like a good cat until he exploded against her tongue with a long guttural moan. Hammered his thighs against her face. Withdrew to glisten her cheeks with the last milky pulses from his flaccid erection. Turned Margot into a little girl being blooded by a foxtail on her first hunt in the long-gone mists of Surrey. She had cried for the red fox and a little for herself. Denied her father's need for a manly daughter.

The hands left her hair, and Margot was pushed on her side with: "Clean your whiskers, Puss."

Margot crawled to the bathroom.

Wiped tears away with the semen and did not vomit until Sadler had gone below to swear at the dead telephone.

She repaired her make-up and changed into a pale oyster trouser suit, and checked that the cold buffet had been properly laid out in the library, where Bunny and Lemmon had had their private talk. Then she rebuilt her brittle shell with Cognac and fresh limes in the conservatory, and was halfway down a bottle when the telephone engineer with slate eyes scratched at the window.

Crystal Palace was Sunday-quiet under a fresh blanket of snow.

Bulstrode was kissing a plain-clothes W.P.C. when Connie Harold parked his Vanden Plas beside the unmarked Q-car. The BBC transmitting mast cast blue shadows as Connie walked Pimlico across crackling snow and Bulstrode contacted Quill's mobile by radio. Dillman acknowledged as Connie climbed a bank to the footpath and said, "The train robbers drew thirty years apiece, and only the driver earned a cracked nut, so what chance does Wally have? You only draw fifteen for murder, and you're free after serving eight. But the law's after us in a big way. All the bloody way."

Pimlico refused Connie's arm, favored his right leg, and held his tender groin as he climbed to the footpath, feeling the cold in his newly healed stomach. Doc Rudge had worked miracles and tutted sadly when Pimlico said he had to go out in the freezing weather.

Pimlico paused to pant and pull his collar higher.

"That's why we're here. For Wally. No other reason."

"Which way?" Connie's breath was tainted by Cuban tobacco.

"Around the tennis courts and the ornamental gardens."

Pimlico kicked slush from his shoes.

The sky was a leaden sprawl of windless cloud, and the bald trees were black skeletons against the white ache of pristine snow.

Connie windmilled his arms.

"The law's as hard as the weather. Information from my bought-and-paid-for coppers is rarer than Russian Studebakers since Wally was collared. It's as well I squared that truce with the Troys, and with Charlie Dance nursing his stab wounds in prison, I'm free to take care of Wally's problem before I go back to sunny South Africa."

Pimlico spat a hole in the snow.

"Handshaking with the Troys? That'll buy you less than nothing."

"Buys me time. All your hardnosing bought you is trouble from the heavy filth, Harry limping from shotgun wounds and pining for Jo'burg, you hiding out in Spitalfields, Sailor on the wanted list, and my brother sweating on a murder charge. You can't even keep your Soho patch going, let alone moving in on Brighton."

"We'll sort Imperial Machines when Wally's back on the cobbles."

"Only if Charlie Dance lives long enough to hold the Ogle firm together. The man's running out of shadows to hide in, and he can't watch your backs as well as his own. Come over to Uncle Con while he can still use you."

Pimlico sniffed the chill overcast.

"You'd love that, wouldn't you? Me and Wally handling Kelly and the London end of your firm? Knocking heads with the Troys with you out in South Africa with clean hands—making money and making Jorgesson's wife? Highly lovely, for *you.*"

"Ain't your fish to fry, Parsons."

"Ain't that what I've been saying?"

"All *right.*"

Connie halted near the running track. Pointed at a man in orange strip padding around the invisible perimeter timing his run with a stopwatch.

"That's you and Wally. Running going nowhere. I've handed the Troys my share of Petticoat Lane. Given them a free road to Malcolm Sadler by elbowing him out of my mining deal. Two lovely sweeteners they couldn't resist. But it does mean I need dough from other sources. Springing Brixton Billy and Bonar's boy Smiler is a good earner, and puts their mail train money in South Africa where I need it. And there's a regular earner out at National Car Parks, Heathrow Airport. The guys on the barriers charge the motorists the full parking fee and pocket half. They're splitting two thousand a week between six of them, and I want half. You can have a quarter of that for collecting once a week."

"Why so generous?"

"Because I *know* you'd collect. And if you come in on springing Smiler and Brixton—"

"Suddenly that's *your* idea, and didn't come from Charlie? You don't just hook them over the wall, you know. I've got the neck, but not the know-how. You need—"

Connie laughed smoke.

"Dublin Gerry. He's in."

Pimlico stared and held his gut.

"Gerry ain't fond of me, and if you're dealing with the Troys, there's a lot you just ain't saying here."

"Ain't you the clever one?"

"Clever enough to know you've offered the Troys more than a few market-traders subs and this Sadler."

"So hurt your brain and tell me."

"A share of South Africa. Got to be."

"That's about it."

"Ain't enough. They'll want more, whatever you've offered."

"But they'll take *time* wanting more."

"As long as it took to shake on it, Con."

Connie shook his head. Flipped his cigar butt into a hedge fat with snow, and blue smoke curled from the crater.

Pimlico watched for shock as he said, "Gerry's strictly cash; he won't take shares in a mine. He don't like me, and he hates the Troys. Does he know you're handshaking with them?"

"He knows."

"Does he know the Troys have a wreath with his name on for not triggering Charlie and Queenie?"

Connie's face almost stayed calm, and Pimlico nodded.

"You *didn't* know that."

"So what? It's only a detail."

"More like the main event."

Connie snarled white breath and: "Always the bloody Jeremiah. Gerry earns where Gerry can. Business is business."

"And dying is dying, for Chrissakes," Pimlico said.

Connie looked out over the frozen ponds and the prehistoric lizards on their islands. Hoary with frost, the silent saurians raked the sky with fretted backs, ugly with menace under scales of peeling brown paint.

"Who put them things there?"

"They're Victorian. Something to do with the Great Exhibition of 1851." Pimlico huffed breath over the crusted ice. "I used to bring sandwiches and a bottle of pop here when I was a kid. Get in amongst them and pretend I was Stanley or Livingstone finding them for the first time."

"Who'd *want* to find the buggers?"

"Weren't you *ever* a kid, Connie?"

"Too busy earning a crust for kids' stuff." Connie clapped his gloves together. "Where's this face we're waylaying?"

"He'll be along. Walks his dog here every morning."

Connie dribbled white breath.

"Are you in or out, Pim?"

"Heathrow, yeah. But forget me ducking in and out of maximum-security prisons."

"Mr. Hard goes soft." Connie cracked a puddle with his heel.

"Sensible ain't soft. You could find that out sudden."

Connie almost grinned. "Yeah. This him?"

Pimlico watched a man plod round the bend after a dog snapping at the snow. The bushes of rhododendron were fat white bouquets hung with icicles. The setter barked fearlessly at nothing and ignored a call to heel. The man snapped a leash at the setter and it bounded off a few steps, full of mischief.

"Nice dog."

Connie blocked the path.

"A complete fool. But he makes me take my regular constitutional," said the middle-aged man. Eyes friendly in a windburned face.

"Just a pup, eh?"

Connie saw Pimlico catch the setter by the collar.

"My previous old friend died after thirteen years. I got this scamp to take his place."

"Dogs do get to you, Mr. Dalgliesh."

The man looked puzzled.

"You know me?"

"A friend of mine does. You and eleven other citizens will be looking at him from the jury bench soon. And you could turn his misfortune to your advantage. A thousand favors, all green with the queen's head in the corner. Lovely used notes. Yours. All my friend wants is a quick 'Not Guilty' at Kingston crown court. He goes his way, and you go back to walking your dog with a thousand new friends crackling in your wallet. How bad?"

"I have been called for jury service . . . ?"

Dalgliesh paled under his windburn and cast about for other people. There were only white hedges and giant concrete lizards.

"Let me pass."

Connie put his face close to Dalgliesh, and his voice was low and confidential.

"I know of a dog. Got trapped under the ice. Couldn't get him out before he went down for the third time."

"Happens to people just as easy," said Pimlico.

"Hear your wife Florence is a bit frail these days. A fall at this time of the year, broken hip, nasty."

"Fatal," said Pimlico.

Dalgliesh looked jaundiced.

"We don't want to see Towser fall in, do we? Or your wife fall downstairs while you're out of the house trying to save your drowning mutt? Course we don't," Connie said.

"Ice looks thin here." Pimlico stroked the puppy. "Wouldn't hold his weight."

Dalgliesh shrank inside his tweed coat as Connie's breath curled around his face.

"And you'd be alone if you went for a 'Guilty.' We've taken care of that. One lady almost went under an Underground train before she wised up. Had her nose right on the rails. Electric sparks and the last goodbye just inches away. You don't go out with a bang, you know. You burn long and slow on electrified lines. A fact."

Dalgliesh couldn't talk.

"You wanna know about the rest of the jury?"

"I . . . No, I'm convinced. . . ."

Connie tucked Dalgliesh inside his collar.

"Well, that's nice. Ain't that nice?"

"Nice." Pimlico tested the ice with a toe.

"But, to make sure there's no accidents, somebody'll cruise past your house every night. Number 41, right?"

"Oh . . . God. . . ."

"He's out to lunch with his Uncle Jack and the Holy Ghost. You take your dog straight home now. And walk careful. Treacherous, these paths."

"Yes, yes, I'll . . ."

"And keep an ear open for passing cars."

"And hope they keep passing." Pimlico let the setter skid away, wagging a stump of a tail.

Dalgliesh leashed the dog and broke into a trot at the first bend. Left a coil of white breath in the still grey air.

The park crackled and plopped in hard silence.

"Nice man."

Connie's laugh found Dillman crouched beside a Saropoda with young. Out of earshot of the preceding threats.

"Coming your way, Mobile 1," he told Bulstrode.

"Snow's played havoc with the overhead wires."

Charlie watched Margot Sadler take that in with slow blue myopic blinks. She wagged a finger beside her drink.

"Snow always brings this benighted country to a halt. And unions keep us stationary. Snow and unions. The British diseases. Come in, come in."

Charlie edged into the subtropical cloy of damp humus and orchids.

"Come along, Working Man."

Margot wove through fleshy bowers and along a passage to the library. Waved her glass at a telephone on an escritoire.

"That's the one for His Master's Voice. There are six or seven others dotted around. And oodles of those jack-plug thingies. This house *lives* by the telephone."

She crossed a leg to watch Charlie unscrew the mouthpiece and thumb a bug into place. He added a miniature microphone to the skirting junction box and asked where the other instruments were.

In the Chinese room she learned he was unmarried. In the master bedroom they were on first-name terms. In the paneled anteroom he admitted preferring whiskey to gin, and back in the conservatory he accepted a small Irish to keep out the cold. Margot by that time held a longer drink and listened for sibilance in her speech with alcoholic care.

Charlie dialed a phony service call to activate the bugs and Limehouse rang back to say a pink Cadillac had drawn up outside.

"Thanks, Exchange. Keep me posted."

Charlie smiled at Margot Sadler.

"They're checking the circuits now. It could be an hour or so, so I'll get out from under your feet and wait in the van."

"In this weather?"

A doorbell chimed, and Sadler let the Troys into the house. Their voices were dulled to baritone fuzz by the massed foliage and double glazing.

"You've got guests to look after."

Charlie took a Perfectos Finos and held Margot's wrist to steady the lighter flame. Her cornflower eyes darkened as she blew smoke, and the voices died behind the library door.

"I'd rather die of leprosy." Margot shivered and held herself. "Ignore them, they're an illusion."

"I've got in-laws I can't stand myself."

"Even yours can't be as Neanderthal as those people. I told you, they're but an illusion."

Charlie pinged a nail against her glass.

"And this is reality?"

A carp cut a chevron as it arrowed between water lilies, and Margot laughed without expression.

"There are two undeniable forces in my universe, Charlie. Age and gravity. They both pull you down in the end."

"Black coffee won't change that, lady. But it might give your liver—"

"A fallacious concept, Telephone Charlie. Watered drinks mean the alcohol assimilates in your bloodstream that much faster, that's all. Doesn't hit your liver in one great lump."

Charlie heard the doorbell and transatlantic accents.

"No jollying you along, is there, lady?"

He lifted the wall phone.

"Exchange?"

"Strangers to me, Chas. Came in a taxi and didn't get change of a five. Italians or Yanks maybe?"

"Out, Exchange."

"And don't call me 'lady.' Makes me feel like a chipped remnant on a cheap market stall."

"All right."

Margot spilled amber liquid near her glass and across an oyster thigh.

"Damn. I should rinse this at once."

Charlie damped a bar towel and offered it. Margot grabbed Charlie's bicep, and her shakes jogged up into his shoulder. A nerve ticked near the bridge of her wayward nose, and her eyes swam with unshed tears.

Charlie heard forced laughter from the hall.

"Americans?"

"Canadians," said Margot. "Let it stain."

Charlie got his hand back and dabbed the alcohol away.

"Nice things deserve nice treatment."

"Frugal little soldier, aren't you?"

"Mother's little helper."

"You're no telephone engineer," Margot accused, her face chalky.

"No?" Charlie's neck bristled.

"No. Malcolm's put you up to this. You're one of his bleeding hearts who use their wiles to get him grounds for divorce."

"Oh, blimey, yeah. It's the GPO's latest sales gimmick. A free divorce with every extension phone. Leave it out, lady."

Charlie watched the sorrowing face flit through half-formed expressions. None stable, none attractive, and they reminded him of Jesse looking for Penny at Mother's.

"It's Margot, Working Man. And when did you last help a woman sleep without the need of that last little drink to find blessed oblivion?"

"Not this year, lady."

"Don't call me—"

"Act the lady you are, then. Then maybe I'll call you bloody Margot."

Charlie held the moist blue eyes and plumed smoke from the side of his mouth.

"More than one of my workmates has lost his job because some frustrated hausfrau wanted some slap and tickle and yelled rape when she didn't get it. Are you going to scream me out of a job?" Charlie was ready to choke Margot unconscious.

"Perhaps I was thinking along those lines. The reasons—"

"Are none of Charlie's business."

Margot pinned a fleeting smile to her lips.

"And I thought one could be brutally frank with strangers."

"Don't mean they won't lie to you."

"Or I to them. So where's the harm?"

"In how many lies you don't admit to yourself."

"Well, bravo with brass knobs." Margot tried to sneer and

Charlie grinned. "What's the Cheshire Cat for, Working Man?"

"For you. You'd run a mile if I laid a glove on you."

"So that's what's at the back of your seedy little mind."

"Nope. But it's at the front of yours."

"Poo," said Margot.

Charlie leaned a hip against the bar.

"Why is it rich women don't seem to have fun? You laugh, but it's just a sound. And your clothes are just clothes. You didn't have to save your pennies for them, so why take pride in what comes for free? The shops are full of nifty little numbers you can charge to the old man's account."

Margot's eyes snapped. Roundels of anger burned the chalky cheeks.

"That's brutal, smug, and bloody inaccurate. I've been down to my last pair of gloves and washed my dainties out in roominghouse sinks, you moron. Begged lifts in transport cafés when the entire cast has been abandoned without train fare home. Squalid theaters and dirtier digs. Leading men who wiped their personality off with their make-up. Managers with minds grubbier than their fingernails. You can't eat the tinsel dream when you're hungry, dirty, and friendless. So stuff your inverted snobbery, Telephone Charlie."

Charlie found himself grinning again.

"There's always hope for somebody who can get that cross with herself. Means you still have some self-respect."

"I'm cross with your impertinence. Not with me."

"Not true. I'll soon be gone and forgotten. You'll still have to live with you."

"A nice convolution, you viper."

"Yes, ma'am."

Margot cocked an eyebrow.

"And now I'm supposed to kick you out. Let the silence come back and drown myself in this stuff. Pretend that rabble in the library isn't there. That my bastard husband didn't make me take his filthy . . ."

Margot's shudder almost emptied her glass, and her high heels grated on the stone flags. Her somber eyes darkened to match the witches'-butter algae on the side of the pool.

"None of your business, though, eh, Telephone Charlie?"
"No, ma'am."
Charlie held the wall phone to his ear. Heard Limehouse tell Sadler he'd be called when the circuits were restored. Added a "sir" colder than the snow he crouched in.
"How's the front, Exchange?"
Lou described the minders outside as four broken circuits.
"Best stay where you are inside, Service."
"Stay inside, the man says."
Charlie gnawed a thumb at the spot where Margot had sat. Her trousers were flung over the spikes of a yucca, and a damp ring marked the stone where her drink had rested. She waded across the central pool with a tray of drinks, four inches of white thigh showing above black stocking tops.
"Paddling in high heels?"
Charlie shook his head. Reminded of another stretch of water. Black faces and the bore of a gun in moonlight.
Margot said "Uh-uh" and went through a thick fan of palm, green spears brushing the greener water.
"Mind the alligators, Charlie."
Charlie took off his boots and socks, rolled up his trousers, and followed her through the thick bower of fronds into a cocoon of *eau-de-nil* light and cool russet shadows.
Margot was a little girl playing tea party.
Mixing drinks on a long tongue of rock carpeted with Korean moss. A dim yellow canebrake rustled in the windless air, and elephant-grey trunks with boles like ancient kneecaps twined and crooked into the dark canopy of varicolored leaves. Irregular spills of water formed a small waterfall and drummed amongst glossy lily pads, running off as fast marbles of mercury.
Charlie hauled himself onto springy moss, and his face brushed Margot's cleavage as she moved in against him, her voice muffled in his hair.
"Do I need this drink, Telephone Charlie?"
Margot cringed from her childish question. Feared scorn in her private everglade.
Instead, her hair was tumbled into soft falls around her face. A thumb ran down her nose to part her lips for a cool

mouth tasting of peat fires. She leaned in to twine tongues as her back was bared and arched by a firm palm. Hard shoulder muscles bunched under her gently biting nails.

She rolled her head as the mouth enclosed an aching breast, once more panicked by the head prefect who sucked her budding mammaries after lights out, the Oxford graduate who knuckled her labia in the back seat of a rented tourer, the understudy who relieved her of innocence in the wings whilst the second lead was accused of murder most foul by a theatrical barrister, a last meaningless encounter before Malcolm turned her into a shrewish sophisticate who found oblivion and numbed peace with a cocktail shaker.

Margot was lost in a thousand places and nowhere.

Her slip was a wisp of black silence beside her overturned drink, and sure stranger's hands kneaded the soft swells below her damp spine, brought her closer and closer to the erect man in a long upsurge of need, a need maddeningly tempered by the timeless dread of male invasion.

She drowned in her own hair and had visions of a rampant snake in a dark and liquid purse as she made a great salmon leap across an infinite weir, fell ever upward to embrace a massive full stop to seven lean and celibate years.

Mounted on a great spur of rock she both rode and surrounded, she spiraled through the veridian canopy into the primordial boil of her own inner seas, where a great rolling scald left her beached on the island moss. The incoming spasms died, and the locked loins pulsed to a halt as her fists opened like tired flowers and lay quietly beside her.

Then shyness came and she wanted to press her face into the ground, hidden in her tent of hair. But firm hands and slate eyes pinned her where she lay. Forced her to enjoy the last long quivers of a marvel forbidden her save in lonely orgasmic dreams.

Her need to say something tart emerged as a yawning sigh. As warm as her snuggle of contentment. As pneumatic as the opening conservatory door.

Sadler was a shadow through leaves. An indistinct reflection in the pool.

"Margot? Damn the woman, where are you?"

Margot laid a finger to Charlie's lips and deliberately slurred her words.

"Lying here with my lover, darling, bastard, Malcolm, sweetie."

"The bitch is drunk," Sadler said without surprise. "Well, Cat, and where does your master find more ice? That moronic cook of yours has gone heaven knows where."

"In the freezer, bastard, love. Surely that fool of a chauffeur can put his hands on it. He finds the cooking brandy readily enough."

Margot belched lightly for effect. Flicked a nail against Charlie's pectoral and curled her stockinged heels against his buttocks. Enjoyed his flinch and the inadvertent buck between her thighs.

Sadler oiled his voice.

"Damn you, Puss. We have guests and my cat thinks herself safe."

"Perfectly safe."

Margot crossed her eyes, extended her tongue, and grinned like a twelve-year-old.

"But guests go home, Puss. And then we shall see just how safe my cat is."

The door hissed closed, and Sadler was gone.

Margot began to shake violently.

"Put me in your pocket, Telephone Charlie," she whispered. "Let me curl up like a dormouse in your teapot. I don't want to be a cat anymore."

Charlie held her until her face slept in the green twilight, shedding years as her eyes closed and her mouth slackened, seeing another more oval face, fuller breasts that had lactated in early pregnancy, longer legs with narrower feet without silver nail gloss.

Until Mario and Pru Mizzi and the kick that miscarried his son. Turned him into just another crimson smear on that stone villa floor.

The whirling tapes in Limehouse Lou's van recorded the Troys and Tonnas in Sadler's library. Another nail in their collective coffin, courtesy of Charlie Dance.

But that cold comfort did not stop Charlie from feeling he

had contracted a disease that made his neck permanently dirty.

Black ice was a hazard on the road to Stoke Mandeville.

Bulstrode walked the length of an airy ward of limbless ex-servicemen and found Vinnie Castle in an observation room overlooking a frozen valley six miles from Bridego railway viaduct.

A cold afternoon sun set fire to the sky behind purple hills. Gilded the naked elms and pasteled the snowscape with sage and violet.

Vinnie came out of a doze to thumb the magazines Bulstrode dropped into his lap. He had lost weight, but his smile was still brilliant.

"Nice of you to come in this weather, Buller."

"You're worth it, Ugly. When d'you get your tin leg?"

Vinnie's teeth were too white in his gaunt face.

"When the skin grafts take. The limbs are plastic nowadays. The doc figures he can fit a rubber lining so I can fill it with gin and be a walking distillery. And make me taller if I do lose the other leg."

Bulstrode wiped his mouth.

"How d'you stay cheerful, son?"

A legless man with a mutilated face whined past in an electric wheelchair, working the controls with a three-fingered hand.

"That's how. Funny how it's the patients who cheer up the visitors."

Vinnie peeled an orange, and Bulstrode refused a wedge.

"And I throw a wobbly if the gas bill's too high."

"And more wobblies when you and Lemmon realize how bad you are at capturing villains, eh?"

Bulstrode touched his cigarettes and left them in his pocket.

"Charlie's out," he said.

"Is that so?"

"You know," said Bulstrode.

"Yeah," said Vinnie. "Now you'll see some unhappy faces."

"Tell him to hold off, Vin. We're getting there with Bethnal Green and Camberwell. And you could drive a coffin nail by fingering who triggered you."

Vinnie dribbled juice and snorted through orange pith.

"Then I'd really be the one-legged man in that famous arse-kicking contest. The word of one man against half of Bethnal Green? The Troys would have rigged the jury and be back on the streets before the judge disrobed and reached for a glass of Amontillado. Just like Connie's doing for Wally right now. Scaring off them he can't buy, and that's with your law firm on his tail for breakfast, dinner, and tea. Don't kid a kidder, Buller."

"Take the stand. We'll ring you with more blue uniforms than you'd see at three Hendon Reviews."

"And if I lived to make the witness-box, what then? Vinnie Castle, the gimp who snitched. I'd be spat on and end up in some ditch. And deserve it. You want Bethnal Green and Camberwell, deal with the Man."

"Archie?"

Vinnie wiped juice from his smile with a pale hand.

"Charlie."

Bulstrode stared. Washed his hands between his thighs and turned his signet ring.

"And when did Dance earn that specious accolade?"

"He's out earning it now."

"I heard there was a double hit. In Malta."

"Is that right?" said Vinnie.

"Give me something upright and breathing, Vinnie. No more bodies with toe tags."

"Talk to the Man."

"Exchanging one of ours for the Troys? Quill's head on a plate like they served John the Baptist to Salome?"

"Chas might listen to that."

"I'll bet."

Bulstrode stood at the window, where early stars faded into dull, glittering strands in the upper darkness. His breath formed a patch of vapor on the glass and he drew a swastika in it without knowing why. Thought of cabbing or tending bar as an alternative lifestyle.

Vinnie said, "You'd need the Troys standing over a fresh

corpse with shooters in their hands to nail them. Unless you wanna give Charlie . . ."

Bulstrode bowed over Vinnie's wheelchair, his hands clamped around the padded arms. Squeezing hard.

"I ought to drop you back in the sewer where I found you. A bad copper for two gobs of slime? Quill's rubbish, but up for grabs he ain't. What would Charlie want for Connie Harold? The Home Secretary on pederasty charges citing all the orphans from Dr. Bernardo's Homes? How d'you sleep nights, Castle? How many pink pills does it take to turn your rotten brain off until breakfast?"

Vinnie's face was a blank with hard eyes.

"I sleep just fine. Unless the pain has me ringing for the night nurse. Or I get to thinking about the twenty more ops I've got coming. Or wondering if my heart'll stand up to it all. Or watching my old mother going grey with worry over me. Missing the grandkids I'll never give her now I piss through a plastic pipe. Try living without an honest erection, Buller. Or knowing you'll never make a woman, any woman, go misty for your touch, you up inside her making love or babies. Ask yourself how you'd see the world with your manhood blown away. All I've got is what you see. It's me who has to live with what I ain't got anymore. One leg a memory, and the other one coming off below the knee in all probability. You man enough to swallow that? I am. But I'll never eat shit again. How about you?"

Bulstrode's knuckles cracked when he let go of the chair. His heart filled his chest and his stimulated groin fluttered. The vague brush of unbidden sexual need. Made worse because Vinnie saw it in his flushed face. His breath whistled as he said, "You bitter, bitter bastard."

Vinnie's grin was thinner than bookbinder's leather.

"Surprised?"

"You think I like seeing you like this? Like the idea of the others who've been chopped into raw liver like you? I'm a copper. A badge with a heart pinned to it. I want real justice, not the perverted crap you and yours go in for. You can't see how wrong you are. I pity you."

"Pity I can live without. Or you bleeding reason all over

me. I'm a man, not a chunk of meat for you to patronize with your Boy Scout platitudes. You wouldn't understand street justice if it bit your back pocket. Deal or don't, I should care less."

Vinnie turned his wheelchair full circle before spinning himself back to his ward.

Bulstrode wiped the swastika out with his sleeve and watched the sun die with a crimson flourish.

Needing a woman very badly.

Jutting his plump lower lip, Malcolm Sadler drew the library curtains when the pink Cadillac followed the Tonnas' taxi out of the street. Toasted himself in five-star brandy. Celebrated the culmination of three long years of planning at the cost of several thousand grey cells and very little financial outlay.

For all their vicious armory, his departed guests lacked protection from their one vulnerable spot. Their own monumental greed.

Once he had lured them out to the arid wasteland of international finance, where the solid gold-blocked assets of bona fide companies funded by their unlaundered money became ephemeral stock quotations in shadowy paper companies, then he would have them. Then the stocks could convert to yen in Brazil. Become steel shares in Pensacola. Transform themselves to American dollars in Sydney, to Swiss francs in the Cayman Islands. Spinning from there into a flurry of numbered accounts spread between Cadiz and Rio de Janeiro. Lost to sight to all save the single responsible signatory. Himself.

Then, with split-second timing, he could pauper them—could control their various enterprises by using their own capital against them.

Sadler had the details down to the last decimal place committed to memory. Calculated it would take a single calendar year to bring his plans to fruition. Until then he would dangle golden carrots in front of the donkeys on his long, long line.

The Troys had wanted a club in the West End, so Sadler had given them the keys to Titania's Castle in Bond Street.

The Tonnas had wanted the lion's share of Archie Ogle's casinos and the control of their new drug network between the Philippines and Hong Kong. Sadler had agreed. Allowed them to front him like so many dangerous puppets, grateful their massing assets were in his capable hands. Sadler let them paw over their paper profits and glory in their newfound respectability. Allowed them to strut and boast and think him the fool.

The brandy was golden fire on Sadler's tongue. Helped his heart to bump with controlled excitement.

Connie Harold's shambolic attempts to build an empire in South Africa would come to nothing without Sadler's expert hand on his shoulder, although Sadler knew he should have foreseen Conrad trying to go it alone—offering Sadler the Troys like bargain packets of soap powder. Conrad had learned to handle Dirk Jorgesson very well, and turning down the American offer of a million sterling said much for his doggedness. But his feelings for Alicia had caused some tension with De Wit.

Sadler's own respect for De Wit was based on fear.

De Wit had a very long arm indeed. Not only in Africa but also throughout South America, where his Broederbond contacts were amongst the German expatriate elite of Paraguay and Brazil. Powerful men not to be dismissed lightly.

De Wit was Sadler's way of bringing Connie Harold to his knees when he had finally overextended himself. Then there would be all the time in the world to pick up the pieces of his embryonic but lucrative holdings.

Whistling tunelessly, Sadler went to bathe and change. The reckoning with Margot was still to come, and he wanted to be clean and rested for that pleasure.

The Barren Cat should have given Sadler grounds for a simple and inexpensive divorce and not wittered on about how devoted she was to Chartings Hall. It was just a house like any other. Sadler knew he could call upon the Troys to dispose of Margot for him, but he would rather find a way without being beholden to them.

Sadler frowned and scrubbed, and thought the problem through.

Then he went down into the hot odors of the conservatory to find the drunken bitch.

He laid his dressing gown beside Margot's oyster trousers and took a long moment to enjoy his naked reflection before stepping into the warm water.

The stone floor was slick with silt, and he reminded himself to have the gardener syphon it out in the morning. Sadler would brook nothing less than perfection, and in that single regard Margot was an excellent housekeeper. It was such a pity she failed in so many other areas.

Sadler parted hanging fronds and skirted the rock where Margot lay curled up, breathing through her mouth, hair a black fan around her supine face.

Sadler breathed quietly, bit on pleased laughter as he moved silently through the water. The bruise on Margot's throat was just beginning to show, and he meant to kiss her there before strangling her awake.

Sadler sniffed the air. Caught the elusive musk of Margot and something other. A man smell not his. He froze reaching for Margot's neck. Was thinking about telephone engineers when the back of his head exploded into a million disparate colors, each color a different wavelength of pain.

His gasp did not reach the back of his teeth. Was a hard bubble at the base of his tongue locked there by muscular spasm.

He tried to turn his head as chest hair brushed his shoulders and a great clamp at the base of his skull drove his face into the moss beside Margot's silver toes. A knee ground into the base of his spine and livid primaries burst around his fluttering eyeballs. Chopped behind both knees, his legs turned to numbed flab.

He threw a wild backhand. Tried to gouge an eye or grasp hair. The arm was caught and turned against the joint. His elbow grated, stung his mind with the flare of pinched nerves and torn muscle, and hung in numbness.

Sadler's cry was as liquid as the slap of carp on still water.

His teeth scraped rock as his head was plunged into the pool. His ears sang with pressure and his world turned green. He saw his own toes flex in silt between another man's feet. A gout of air from his mouth boiled up around his face. Took sound to the surface and left him behind. His eyes bulged and tried to follow the bubbles, so Malcolm would drown in blindness. His nose smashed against the bottom, then he was back in tropical smells, breathing raggedly through his own blood. Angry enough to weep before he was plunged back into brackish water.

Part of the pool now, he was without substance, and living meant nothing. There was only the need to float deeper and deeper in submarine weed, where calm and sleep were down and down . . .

Knuckles bruised his scalp. A hard palm slammed his face from side to side. Brought him back from his drowned paradise. Made him taste salt blood in his mouth, running warm in his mashed nose. Made him fill his ironbound chest with precious oxygen, and sob. Small tearing sounds smacking of humiliation profound enough to share with . . . Margot.

Sadler came out of mist to see his belly rise and fall with droplets running from it in thin streams. His useless legs hung from his hips as he lay arched over the edge of the pool.

The hand in his hair made him see his swollen genitals, puffing grotesquely from a hard downward pull that had driven him into limbo.

Then the hand released his hair. His head cracked against the hot flags and his useless hands were unable to cover his hurt. He could only breathe, see, and hear.

Somebody said the bugs were cleared.

But that made no sense because they wriggled under Sadler's drooping lids.

"Can you hear me, animal?"

Sadler said he could hear perfectly well, being polite to avoid further pain.

"Don't make me come back," said the quiet voice.

Sadler affirmed with nods. Was still nodding vigorously when the pneumatic door hissed closed on his uncontrolled weeping.

He called for a long time before he made Margot hear.

Lemmon sat Bulstrode beside his living room fire with a stiff vodka and tonic while Elizabeth made coffee and Tony

Bennett left his heart in San Francisco. When Elizabeth had brought them the Cona and cups on a tray, kissed Lemmon good night, and gone to bed with a paperback romance, Bulstrode talked about Crystal Palace and Stoke Mandeville Hospital.

Lemmon smoked through it all in silence, nodded here and there, and said, "We've got everything and nothing. We know a great deal and can prove nothing in a court of law. Doesn't mean we aren't winning, and we aren't losing, either. The breaks will come and then landslide."

Bulstrode chewed a moody Player.

"When? The jury members Connie Harold threatened or bribed won't even talk to us. Let alone bring charges of attempted bribery with threats of violence against him. We're supposed to be the good guys in white hats. It's a bloody nightmare."

"And will get worse before getting better, Buller, my son. The law's lost the respect of the man in the street. Even the law-abiding ones who work eight-hour shifts, pay taxes, and hand lost property in at the local cop shop. The tragedy is you aren't old enough to remember how it used to be. When the local beat copper knew everybody in his manor, and a clipped ear stopped more than one baby bandit in short trousers from turning villain.

"When the villains themselves turned in the heavy sods who used shooters on a robbery or turned one on a copper. When the whores told us about their dodgy tricks. Gave us the nod if there was a sexual pervert on their patch who might interfere with a decent girl. Or molest a child.

"You either get crazy-angry about it, or become philosophical. Or do what Prophet did to Charlie Dance: plant evidence to nail him on a charge, any damned charge, rather than wait and get him straight. Or do what many do: shrug and take all the bribes offered."

"That's for the Arthur Axes of the world. Not us."

"You say."

Lemmon hid himself in a last gout of smoke and tossed the butt into the fire.

"This ain't helping, guv."

"You want advice, you'll get it. You make out your report on jury nobbling and hang fire. Let Wally Harold walk free."

Bulstrode stared and lit a second Player.

"I'll say this once, Buller. That's all. As soon as that jury brings in a 'Not Guilty' and Wally's back on the cobbles, all the jurors will talk—not to us directly, but to their friends and friends of friends. Shouldn't be surprised if there wasn't a reporter or two in earshot, either. And the judiciary aren't stupid. Judges talk to each other, and their opinions reach ears in rarified places, ears deaf to the likes of us. The ears of power, Buller. You and I'd get slapped down if we made noises too soon. We just collate our facts in neatly labeled files and trot them out when the Queen's Bench prepares itself for the next big case. You want a prediction from Uncle Theo?"

"Yes, I would."

"The bench itself will order us to protect the next jury. They'll order us to provide telephones in their homes, protect their children at school. *And* make damned certain their family doctors know the stress they're under. We'll lose this one, Buller, but not the next big one. Or the next or the one after that. You've got my word on that."

"And Quill?"

"If Charlie wants Quill, he'll have him. He doesn't need our tacit consent. Charlie's trying us out, that's all."

"So I say what to Vinnie Castle?"

Lemmon tapped a Player against a nail.

"You say, 'yes,' without actually saying 'yes.'"

"A 'yes' except it ain't?"

"That's the kind of thing."

Bulstrode shrugged. "I can try."

"No, son. You can do it. Quill would make a pretty stringy Judas goat for Dance to chew on anyway. If Charlie means to give us the Troys on a plate, I won't say no. Anyway, I want to see how he plans to do it."

"You've gotta be more than just curious, guv."

"Why must I?"

"You must, that's all."

Lemmon shook his head.

"The Troys won't come down alone. I want to see a certain dirty copper come tumbling out of Leman Street cop shop. I was ordered to play the white man within the force by Whitehall, but Charlie Dance wasn't, was he?"

"Arthur Ax and the Troys wrapped up in the same pink ribbon? You play a deep game, guv, and it makes my anus whistle just to think about it."

"Coffee?" Lemmon said comfortably.

The bitterly cold darkness had a sweet smell.

Children scuttled past his bed towards the suit draped over a chairback, and Freddy waited for the chink of pilfered small change.

I'll cure them where soft-hearted Maria failed. Stealing from their father indeed. A few cracked bottoms would have them wailing Daddy has hard hands.

Maria would get that sloe-eyed look and gather them to her big belly. All suffering and reproach.

Well, let her.

They were close enough now.

And Freddy swung. . . . Nothing.

His neck cracked with whiplash.

Rope sawed his throat and suspended his cold bare feet.

The darkness whirled black on black, and the puzzle he had to solve was lost in obsidian. Returning circulation reared him against a hard chairback, and the children scampered from his squall of terror with scratching nails and tiny feral squeaks.

If only he could touch the floor, he could grow back into a man. Stop being a helpless boy in a cat's cradle of knotted hemp. The knots tightened when he struggled. Hurt his constricted bladder. Another humiliation.

Another childhood fear.

Freddy-wet-the-bed earning a whipping for nocturnal incontinence, peeling another layer of manhood away.

Poor Freddy wept for poor Freddy.

He caught the flick of a small yellow eye. Whiskers and a damp questing nose touched his foot. Distant artillery shook mortar from unseen walls. The rats went away, and the cellar was lit by dim torchlight. Fragrant Virginia bloomed in his nose, and a series of clicks wound voices into the cellar. Sadler said something about drinks, and Tommy Troy said it was about bloody time he met Roger and Jesus Tonna.

Freddy heard Roger sit in a chair and click a lighter at a cigar. Say, "I'll shake hands when there's something to shake on. I just had to shake Archie Ogle's hand. With two of my best torpedoes wasted right there on the rug. In the same goddamned room. Me and Jesus standing there like dummies with that hoary old bastard holding a goddamned Savage on us. Made us grovel and eat crow. And swear to Christ we had our wires crossed about Johnny Valletta. That we were there to *talk,* not have him blown away. And Queenie knitting and sneering. Like we still hustled whores in Charing Cross. Man, he *knew* about our drug contacts in the Philippines. The mother knew. So put your hand back on your pecker until me and Jesus hear some news worth more than ten cents on the dollar."

Jesus said, "Me and Roger ain't just birds aturding, guys. Forget 'How's the wife and the family cow' shoot. All we can see is a gaggle of Limey nebishes wanting to dip their beaks in *our* birdbath. And, guys, Archie Ogle ain't finished until he's *finished.* Like *finito."*

Roger snapped fingers.

"Which of you guys has the brass balls to cut Archie down? Him and Dance. That guy has to *go."*

Jesse Troy said something lost in babble, and Sadler emerged from hard asides with: "Details later, gentlemen. You didn't fly three thousand miles with closed minds. Archie Ogle bled you white for twenty years. And quite rightly you resent the fact. Our terms will be infinitely more advantageous, and you both know it. The world has shrunk too far and too fast for any of you to sit in your own small—"

"Small?" Tommy snarled.

"—small territories, and think Jimmy-be-damned to my proposal to cooperating internationally. We can fly to New York more readily than drive to Aberdeen, Scotland. Gems stolen in Amsterdam can be fenced just as readily in Toronto or Karachi as they can in London. Bullion from

Boston can reach here and be sold off in Pakistan before the American federal authorities have fed the details to Interpol. And hot money here is ice cold in Johannesburg. We know that for a fact. We are negotiating such a transfer at present."

"Train robbery money, huh?" said Roger Tonna.

"The very same."

"You think we didn't have the same deal with Ogle?"

Sadler cleared his throat.

"I note the use of past tense there, Mr. Tonna."

"That's still negotiable."

"And you paid seventy cents on the dollar."

"Sure we did, smart ass," Jesus said. "But once we tied in with you—if we tied in with you—the rate would climb right back up again. And we'd do the same to you guys. That's both of us between a rock and a hard place. Back to square-goddamned-one."

"I have a solution. . . ."

The tape squabbled into high register as it was wound on to Roger saying, "Okay. But we get the whole skim from the London casinos. We know what they're grossing, pal. Freddy and Maurice have fed us the receipts for the last six months. You ain't the only one don't leave squat to chance, big brain. But you guys get to handle Ogle's wooden overcoat. I'm real sentimental about that hit. His thumb up my ass once is enough. Maybe if I'd come to you guys earlier . . ."

Tommy's laugh was a hard bark.

"Him and Charlie wouldn't have walked away from that café in Mafeking Street. You've listened to Manchester Freddy and Maltese Maurice for too long, Tonna. You and Jesus both. Pimps are just that—pimps. And Freddy clawing up some opposition for you over fifteen years ago don't cut no mustard now. If his mouth was a shooter, Freddy could blow us all to shit and gone. But he ain't nothing but a whore peddler. Didn't take us five seconds to figure it was him screwed up dropping bricks on the Ogle firm."

Jesse butted in with: "And you let Maurice send his baby coons after Pimlico Johnny Parsons. They met Charlie Dance instead, and that makes them history. One man ain't enough to drop that bastard. It'll take *us* to turn him into hung meat. Me and Tom. *After* we've ground Connie Harold into liver and lights."

Roger spoke in a rush.

"You gotta waste Dance now. The guy's begging for a concrete-kimono bye-bye. . . ."

"Otherwise, no deal," Jesus added.

"So get Manchester Freddy," Jesse hissed.

"But, gentlemen, we have to consolidate our South African dealings first. If we're to launder our money through Harold's mining . . ."

Sadler's voice died in mid-sentence.

Freddy heard it keen into rewind. Winter wind in haunted eaves. A warm spurt of urine soaked his lap as he forced himself to look up into cold slate eyes.

"It wasn't that way at all, Charlie. . . ." The torch glared in Freddy's face. "I had to do it for Maria . . . for the kids. . . . You don't know them, Charlie. . . . They'd have . . ."

The stale air vibrated to the dull thump of a pile driver, and the cellar shook with the rumble of earth movers. Mortar dribbled in cavity walls and dust drifted from the rafters.

The damp patch between Freddy's thighs spread and chilled.

He knew with dread certainty where he was.

"You ain't brought me to Mafeking Street, Chas? You can't. Not leave poor old Freddy here to be . . . buried?"

Charlie let Freddy babble.

"Blame them, Charlie. Not little Freddy . . . not me . . . not meeeeeeeeeeeeeeee . . ."

A wall thundered apart, overhead timbers began to grind, and Freddy used all his breath in a long, ululating scream.

When the torch clicked off, terror shattered his sanity like a dropped dish.

After a time the machines went quiet and the rats came back. By then Freddy was a catatonic with nothing behind his eyes but empty shadows, beyond recall when Charlie threw him into a black panel truck and drove east.

Feeling cheated.

CHAPTER 6

THREE MONTHS INTO HIS THIRTY-YEAR SENTENCE, BRIXTON Billy sewed ten stitches to the regulation inch in hemp and watched the fat screw the inmates called Kaiser Bill reach out his watch to tick off the final seconds of the work period in the mailbag room.

Kaiser Bill counted silently as he habitually did, sitting in the oak chair on the dais like an overripe serge pear, walrus moustache moving with his lips. Kaiser Bill had greeted Brixton each afternoon for sixty-two days with: "Try nicking these mailbags, son. See where it gets you," adding a look of amused surprise as though taken unawares by his own ready wit.

Kaiser Bill ignored the accurate wall clock above his head even though it kept scrupulous time. His father's watch was his pride and joy, and Brixton's offer of a full ounce of prison shag to the man who dipped it was unclaimed as yet. Another week and Brixton would double the prize. Anything to see the fat screw change his boring mannerisms.

Ninety days from thirty years left ten thousand and fifty days to serve. One thousand and forty-seven of those being

Sundays. All those compulsory church services where news from the outside world was exchanged to the sound of hymns.

And 4 ounces of breakfast porridge a day meant Brixton would eat 115 pounds, 4 ounces of oats a year, a staggering 3,457 pounds, 8 ounces before he saw the outside world again. In excess of sixteen times his own body weight.

Brixton amused himself with such numerical games to pass the time, despite warnings from the older cons who knew such useless exercises led to mental disorder in a very short time.

Their sage advice was to do your sentence one day at a time. Go in for running gags rather than dreams of release. Brixton ignored them. Thought of nothing else. Thought of exactly that as he watched Kaiser Bill mouth the last second and start to stand.

Brixton drove the big sewing needle into his left palm with his leather pad. Spattered his work with sudden blood. Broke the Silence Rule with a yell of pain. Tucked the paper twist of waterproofing grease into his cuff next to the twist of granulated sugar he had lifted from the canteen.

Twenty minutes later, his prizes tucked inside a fresh bandage, he was marched back to his high-security cell in C wing, Winsom Green Prison. Subjected to a complete body search, stripped, and sent into his cell wearing nothing but a vest, Brixton lay on his bunk and counted off the fifteen minutes to the next visual check on him. His eyes lidded, he saw the screw's eye in the observation port before it went away. Brixton gave the screw enough time to get back to his chair at the end of the corridor, then blew the sugar under the cell door into the passage beyond. His early-warning system against surprise changes in schedule. He would hear the screws' boots crunch when they came to his door.

He spent the next several minutes smearing the ceiling light with the waterproofing grease. Dimming the light a little more with each application. The light stayed on twenty-four hours a day, and the cell had previously held Gordon Lonsdale, convicted of spying for the Russians.

A fervent patriot, Brixton was disgusted to be treated the same as a bloody traitor to his country, and saw no irony in his deep outrage. Thieving a few million banknotes destined for the official incinerator in no way compared with some bastard jeopardizing national security in Brixton's book, and made him sulky in rare depressed moments.

That and not seeing Smiler Tree, even though he was only four cells down on the opposite side of the corridor.

Smiler had had the horrors a couple of times during the early days, but there had been no sound out of him for weeks, and Brixton was not even certain he was still over there. Though somebody was. He heard the cell open and close at regular times, and he was sure the screws would not go to such lengths just for his benefit.

Brixton logged the passing hours by the crunch of sugar every quarter hour. Thought of escape to fill the time until nightfall. He had long ago realized that mid-week would be the best time. Security was almost doubled at weekends, and the screws were younger and tougher. And less friendly. Getting out of C wing itself was the biggest problem, and he had yet to solve it. Unless he had a shooter smuggled in. Shot his way out like Tom Mix. Something Brixton discounted out of hand.

He wanted *them* to find his locked cell empty and him long gone without a clue as to how he had achieved the miracle. Until he wrote his memoirs from some distant sunny land, where he could spend his mail train money in secure luxury. One of the reasons Connie Harold's South African firm sounded such a tempting investment. Put his dough in Connie's business and skim profit without moving from his deckchair under some shady fig tree. If that kind of a deal had come through Archie or Charlie, Brixton knew as much about sunny South Africa as he did about the dark side of the moon. Maybe less.

Brixton dozed.

Going abroad had a temporary feel to it. He'd have to come home someday when the fuss died down. There were always coppers in the Flying Squad willing to turn a blind eye for a big enough "drink." Just Brixton's luck to have had his collar felt by bloody Theodore "Mr. Clean" Lemmon, and get taken by D.S.C. Cotton himself without the chance of bribing one of his more reasonable pirates.

Brixton sleepily broke the days down into minutes and seconds, when a key turned in the cell door.

Another bloody surprise search.

Except they ain't a surprise to anyone.

Brixton rolled from his bunk and broke wind noisily—the only antisocial protest he could come up with on the spur of the moment—and stared into masked faces and a leveled gun.

"You're coming out."

The strange voice was muffled by a woolen ski mask.

Brixton's foul reply earned him a knee to the center of equilibrium.

After that he had no breath to argue.

Wally saw Naomi Leathers walk in and forgot about drinking himself stupid.

The WELCOME HOME, WALLY banner stretched the length of the prestige office suite overlooking Berkeley Square and billowed in hot convected air. Wally raised his glass to it and thought that the party was more of a puff for Connie's moving into the West End than a coming-out party for himself. Where, he wondered, were the reliable faces from the old days? The Pims and Dottys. Wally didn't know half the faces surrounding him and didn't want to.

An alcoholic peer of the realm who "guinea-pigged" for the new companies had his photograph taken with Connie and a cockney actress with a smile as wide as her famous bosom. Motor traders and accountants mixed with local councillors angling for funds for the coming general election. Three CID men from the City of London police chatted with a supermarket magnate and a sprinkling of minor celebrities from the British film industry.

A Welsh actor in a beautifully engineered toupee who played screen heavies and reveled in rubbing shoulders with the real thing had already invited Connie and Wally to a location shoot later in the year. The screenplay was about an air crash survivor who becomes the leader of a pack of ferocious baboons, and sounded about as believable as a nun becoming mother of the year.

Wally had said it sounded "ace," winked into Kelly's

cleavage to cheer her up, and found himself in a corner with Harry the Crack, who was owlish with drink.

"Sorry you had to be the one who got his collar felt over that run in with the Bellavers and Kramer, Wal. Still, all inna past now, ain't it? Welcome back."

Wally nodded, thought *Prick,* and watched Naomi. She and Margot Sadler stood apart with Dirk and Alicia Jorgesson. Hard put to understand much of the vulgar South London chirpiness surrounding them. Alicia was fragile, elfin beside Dirk's bulk, and Margot's slim severity enhanced Naomi's dress of white scalloped silk.

"Can't wait to get back to Jo'burg, Wally. Had this town up to my collar stud. I still got shotgun pellets coming out of my poor old body. Bloody lucky dip some mornings. Need some of that African sun to cheer me up."

"That right?" Wally continued to watch Naomi. Saw her flush when she caught his eye, and grinned into his drink.

"Con squared the law so I could come out of hiding for your coming home, Wal. Says the cops are well asleep now you've earned a 'Not Guilty.' I hated being cooped up in that safe house over in Tooting. Not going out for a pint or a paper. Watching the wallpaper peel and kids' television."

"My heart bleeds, Harry."

"I know it was worse for you behind real bars, Wal. I just can't stand being inside. That's why South Africa suits me so well. All those miles of outside they got over there. Handsome."

"When d'you go back?" Wally asked without interest. Connie had edged close to Alicia. Had his arm round Dirk's shoulder.

Harry grabbed another pink champagne.

"Just fizzy pop, this stuff. How'd they make it pink?"

"Fermented jelly beans. How do I know?"

"Yeah?" Harry got his drink and cigar tangled. His heavy eyebrows knitted in concentration. "Gonna get well pissed. You deserve that much, Wal. Not enough of the old faces here to lay on a good drunk for you. Here's to you, mister. And to our success in wogland. I'm going back inna couple of days. . . . Juss wish Con didn't shell out so much on that

Dirk and his wife. . . . Need every penny spent onna firm, y'know?"

"Sure, sure . . ."

"That De Wit's the one to square. Heesa one with alla clout. See if Harry ain't right, Wal. . . ."

"You're right, Harry."

Wally patted the owlish face and went towards Naomi.

Harry sagged against a pillar and talked to his knuckles.

Margot swizzled her champagne with a pink stick and made Naomi flush when Connie introduced Wally to her by drawling, "I *do* see the attraction, darling." Then, giving Wally her most brilliant smile, she said, "We all congratulate you like mad, Mr. Harold. Such a close encounter. I plan to mark your release by getting as plastered as your friend in camelhair talking to his fingers over there. He has the right idea."

"Traditional," said Wally. "Odd you being here when Con and your husband are divorced."

"But *that's* only business, darling. And poor bastard Malcolm would have attended but for his recent accident. The poor old chap's been in bed with a nasty wrench. I'm being comforted with a night out by my adorable friends here. Aren't I, darlings?"

Naomi moistened her lips with champagne. Unable to meet Wally's direct gaze. Said, "We've all come to be impressed by Conrad's glossy new premises, on Dirk's insistence. We duly are. You look well, Walter."

Wally felt himself warm and rise.

"Look as if you could canter a few furlongs yourself."

Margot's laugh was a spray of tinking barbs.

"You make Naomi sound like a bloodstock mare."

"She could win my two thousand guineas anytime."

Margot arched an eyebrow.

"Such gallantry. And time to melt away. Time I was introduced to some of these theatricals. A little limelight and greasepaint might aid the digestion."

She dragged Connie and the Jorgessons away to gossip with the Welsh toupee and the cockney bosom.

Wally watched Margot take control of the conversation. Saw Connie's arm circle Alicia's waist on Dirk's blind side.

"When did she last jump out of a cake? Mafeking Night, 1899?"

"Margot is highly intelligent. And, like most men, you fear a clever woman."

"Ain't scared of you."

"Which means I'm stupid."

"Means nothing of the sort. But if I was Connie I'd keep well away from that daughter of yours. Must be he feels more confident over here."

"Much like yourself."

Naomi's look simmered.

Wally looked back, his eyebrows hard down.

"Could be you're right. Let's just hope Con's lust burns itself out. With Alicia on one side, your Colonel De Wit in the middle, and Kelly on the other, poor old Con don't stand a chance."

Naomi chafed a wrist.

"I was insane to look forward to seeing you."

"And here's me thinking the same thing. Funny."

"Singularly unfunny."

Wally's frown darkened and deepened.

"I've just had two months of cells, screws, lawyers, heavy filth, and heavier Latin. I could lose myself in a bottle like Harry there. Phone any one of a dozen girls who'd come running to keep me company. One thing I won't do, and that's spend my first evening of freedom with a woman who can't think for herself 'cause her nose is too deep in her daughter's grubby laundry."

"Are you telling me off, Walter?"

Wally pointed at a blank wall.

"No. The female banjo player riding that camel in a bowl of custard. Of course I'm telling you off."

"At which point I melt or stalk off."

"I guess. I know what I bloody want."

"You'll have to say it, Walter."

Wally lit a cigarette and held it away from Naomi.

"Wally," he said. "It's Wally who wants you to stay with him. Not this sodding Walter."

"Very well. Wally it is. But don't dare shorten my name. One of those actresses actually called me 'gnomey.'"

Wally grinned.
"Yeah, they would."
"Your Harry just slid down the wall."
"No law against it."
"Shouldn't somebody see that he doesn't swallow his tongue?"
"Not Harry. He'll sleep for an hour and wake up ready to go again. Don't fret your head about Harry, or Connie, or Dirk, or Alicia, or . . ."
"Point taken. You can be Wally if I can stay being Naomi. Shake?"
"Little fingers," said Wally.
"Now you can buy me a drink, sneak me away, and be very, very animal with me."
"I can but try."
"But very, very hard."
"They won't shoot this horse for not trying."
They hooked pinkies and went looking for the right bottle.

Brixton's wrists and bandaged hands throbbed from the handcuffs. Smiler went past the opened cell door, his face as white and tight as his naked buttocks. The screw at the end of the passage was all the way down in his chair with a dark sapmark on his jaw.
Brixton stumbled at the stairhead. The tape over his mouth made breathing a positive act of will, thinking impossible.
The stairs went down forever, and Brixton's snorting breath was the only sound in the silent cellblock. All the security doors were unmanned and hard open. The surveillance cameras slept with unlit "On" lights.
Then Brixton was outside. Chilled by night breeze and padding on tarmac.
A fat moon rode through mackerel cloud and etched the central prison yard with hard shadow. Brixton and Smiler were herded into the dark lee of high walls, ready to flee from sirens and the heavy tread of the regular patrol. The sudden sear of arcs turning night into day. Harsh commands to halt and lie spreadeagled on the floor.
Nothing happened, and they were safely outside a wing.

No torchlight. No shouts. Nothing.

The soft fall of a rope ladder came next, and Brixton swarmed up it with a hard hand pushing his buttocks. Another in the small of his back. Then the hard heave to flip him over the pitched capping stones. The cold slap of Edwardian slate against the inside of his thigh, shrinking his manhood like the unwanted sexual advances of a stone woman.

Brixton went down the other side of the high wall. Dropped into shadowed clutter. Sweated and shivered and skirted stands of old timber in a builder's yard. Frightened he might step in broken glass. Feeling vulnerable and foolish in his vest.

Was reminded of childhood dreams of flying where the exhilaration of the high swoops across dark skies were spoiled by his partial nakedness and the rudely staring people below who ran to tell his mother about the third member he had grown in flight. And waking in his safe and overheated bed, face and penis blushing beneath the covers. Exploring the mad stiffness of his tiny precocious member. The great fear of angry grown-ups censuring his fledgling sexual fantasies of soft roundnesses hiding dark and damp caves he could enter if he had the courage. Guilt and awe snuggling him in a fetal curl around the hard little monster, paring away another layer of childhood each time it happened.

There was a winding alley of smooth cobbles and then the grass and gravel of a canal footpath. The masked men hurried Brixton and Smiler past narrow boats into trees where two cars were parked without lights.

Smiler was bundled into the back of a Cortina, and Brixton was shoved aside when he tried to climb in beside him. The one with the gun ducked Brixton into a Jaguar and ground the bore into his ribs when he craned to see Smiler's look of mute fear before the Cortina swept him away. A second man took the Jaguar's wheel to drive with fast skill down too many back turnings without his heads on.

"Dress."

Brixton jammed his feet into shoes and struggled into slacks. He was still buttoning himself into a shirt when the car stopped in a darkened road and he was bundled up a side path into a terraced house. Guided into a curtained room, he was sat in an armchair. He felt the thick pattern of moquette under his fingers and took comfort from stroking it.

A telephone was used for several short calls with long codes before it was put down with a light ping.

Then three men came into the room and switched the light on. The one with the gun tore the tape from Brixton's mouth and unlocked the cuffs. Dropped them in Brixton's lap.

"Souvenir," he said. "Cigarette?"

Brixton threw the cuffs from him. Touched his raw mouth.

"Depends who's asking."

"You wanted out. You're out."

"There's out and bloody out. Could be I was better off where I was. Nobody had a shooter on me in C wing."

"There's gratitude." The voice was softly Irish.

The mask was peeled off and Dublin Gerry mocked Brixton with shamrock eyes. Tossed the revolver to the man behind Brixton's chair.

"You'd try the patience of all God's saints, Billy boy."

Froggy Farrell ruffled Brixton's hair.

"Out's out, Brix."

Brixton jerked a thumb over his shoulder.

"That shooter's still pointing my way."

Pimlico came around the armchair to plump the revolver in Brixton's lap, grinning at his jump of surprise.

"There are big kids and little boys, according to you. I just hope this squares a few things between us."

Brixton rubbed his sagging jaw.

"Could be, but why'd you bastards split me and Smiler up?"

Dublin Gerry played with a pack of Gallagher's Blue.

"Bonar's made special arrangements for Smiler. You're a fish of a different color. We figure Tommy Troy wants your train money and plans to lose you in the shuffle."

"Like I shuffle off to give fish dancing lessons in concrete boots, right?"

Pimlico lit one of Gerry's cigarettes and fed it to Brixton.

"And why we pulled you out our way. You're going missing, Brix, but not like Tommy Troy planned. Once we get you out of here, only two people'll know where you are. Me and Charlie."

Brixton looked at Gerry, Froggy, and Pimlico in turn.

"My brain hurts. Are you telling me Charlie, Tommy, *and* Connie are in on this? How long have they been shaking hands?"

"They ain't," said Pimlico. "Tommy and Connie have declared a truce, but Charlie won't give either of them the time of day. And he won't see you feeding the fish, neither. If he sees your dough safely to South Africa along with Bonar's contribution, Connie won't grumble, and Tommy can't. We keep you on ice until the money gets to Cape Town. Then see how long it takes for Camberwell and Bethnal Green to start knocking heads. I'm here for you and Charlie's sake, paying a debt that's owed."

"And your share, Pim?"

"Goes out with yours when Charlie says."

Brixton nodded wearily.

"Let's just hope we're trusting the right man."

"Where's the choice, Brix?"

Brixton sagged as the adrenaline drained away. The seedy room was just another cell, and the three men were jailers without uniforms. He saw a progression of such rooms, strobing past like windows in the longest train in the world. Rolling into a bleak future with him as the only passenger. The past was another train on a parallel track. A weary shuffle of pasteboard dreams, all glitter and no substance. Yesterday's fragments that had tasted of success until reality left ashes on his imprisoned tongue. And now nobody would steal Kaiser Bill's watch.

Brixton opened his eyes and said, "And which of you brave soldiers gets to tell Tommy Troy that Brixton Billy ain't for drowning?"

Dublin Gerry bowed from the waist.

"My pleasure."

"Better make it a phone call or face him on neutral turf. You head his shit list, Gerry."

"Don't worry your head, Brix. Wouldn't Charlie and

Bonar make him eat coal in Hades if any of us earned a hard glance from the man?"

Brixton had no energy to argue. He offered his hand to Pimlico.

"I'll shake now you're one of the big kids, Pim. But it'll cost you a nice cup of tea."

"Thanks, Brix."

Pimlico and Brixton cracked knuckles as Froggy put the kettle on.

The telephone said, "They're out," and went dead.

Killed a heartbeat.

Connie closed his eyes and spread his hands on the teak reception desk. The party lost color and sound and his limbs turned watery.

They're out thudded in his chest.

Brixton Billy had £200,000 salted, and even with a swingeing charge of ten percent for the break itself the balance gave him the capital to bring the Nikex plant from Hungary to the Mkuse site.

They're out pearled his nose with moisture.

And Bonar Tree's escudos would grease the way to owning the Ghost Mountain site he and Dirk had been negotiating for with a prospector from Pretoria.

They're out meant Pimlico's £100,000 would sweeten South African Customs and the Minister of Mines, consolidate his holdings here in London, cover Vic Dakin's thievery.

Connie's hands left perfect misty prints on the gleaming teak, and he had the crazy notion he should preserve them in some fashion. Wanted to mark that single moment in time indelibly. Wanted to celebrate in a darkened room with Alicia and could not. Should tell Kelly and did not want to.

Everything is safe again. Nothing can stop me now.

All the same . . .

Connie crossed his fingers when he gave Wally the news.

They're out.

Ingrid craned to see herself in the mirror above the big golden bed. A stranger with silver hair in a flame kimono.

Dotty played with the strobe lights, and the Tonna brothers lounged in the lounge, ignoring the women. Roger put the telephone down and chinked glasses with Jesus and: "They're out."

Jesus pulled his grey moustache and watched the girl in the silver wig flicker in strobe lights.

"So, okay," he said. "Sadler figures this train robbery money will keep the South African mining deal afloat until we walk in and take over. All too long-term for me, kiddo. I think we should grab and run. Go home before this local head-to-head gets bloody."

"Relax." Roger rang down for more champagne.

"I've got that old feeling."

"You feel shafted if your after shave fails. We're sitting pretty. We've got this Connie Harold's operation taped. Soon we'll own this hotel and the casinos, and the Troys are soldiering the sidewalks. We're in gravy, brother."

"Not with Archie Ogle still upright, we ain't. Our butts are still up for grabs. Don't ask me to swallow what smells bad, Roger. Hung meat ain't always venison."

Roger was dismissive.

"Shadows at midnight. Only people playing grab-ass with us are those two broads Maurice sent over. Archie's browning his belly in Malta. We're in his hotel and he's picking up the tab. The joint is crawling with Troy's torpedoes, and his guys are even working the kitchens. We're gold in Fort Knox. Relax."

Jesus disagreed with a grunt.

"Sadler has ducked us this trip, and that 'accident' of his vibes wrong. Once we get solid control here he gets hit. Going after Archie through his betting shops was smart-assed and dumb."

"So he screwed up. Hell, he's a corporation man. He'll learn street sense."

Jesus turned the empty Krug bottle in the ice bucket.

"You had street sense once, Roger. You even look like a goddamned banker nowadays. The Savoy this joint ain't. First thing I do when we take this place over is get room service jumping."

"You do that." Roger laughed.

"And where the hell is Manchester Freddy? Troy was supposed to turn him up."

"The hell with Freddy. He takes off when Maria's apron strings strangle his drinkbone. He's off on a drunk with a stray piece of tail. He'll turn up with the shakes and a cartload of gifts for his kids."

"You can't party with empty glasses, Mr. Tonna."

Dotty twirled a glass near Roger's face.

Roger patted her cheek as somebody tapped on the door.

"No more than you can, honey. Let the man with the bubbles in."

He watched her sway across the carpet, her dress as yellow as her hair.

"Nice tush."

"A bought-and-paid-for barracuda," Jesus grunted.

Dotty wheeled a trolley across and handed Roger a chit.

"You have to sign this, Mr. Tonna."

"Christ, can't even sign her own name," Jesus sneered.

"You want a chess master from Mensa?"

Dotty dimpled. Eased the cork with a light pop and a wisp of mist.

"We don't have any of them on the books."

"Other talents, huh?"

"Only the best for you gentlemen. Maurice's orders."

Dotty poured wine and whispered an obscene promise in Roger's ear, flushing his lobes.

"The toast is pleasure."

Roger and Jesus drank and their glasses were topped.

"You girls ain't taking the sauce," Jesus said.

Ingrid drifted from the bedroom to tease his shaved neck. "Your pleasure first. We'll have our bubbles . . . after."

"After what?" Jesus leered, feeling the wine.

"Just . . . after."

"You gents aren't just talkers, are you?" Dotty pouted.

Roger grinned and drained another glass of Krug.

"One demonstration coming up. For the honor of Toronto."

He stood and weaved beside Dotty, more fuddled than he thought.

"Lean on me, baby," Dotty cooed.

"Sure thing, sweet pea."

Ingrid offered her hand to Jesus, and he blinked at the brilliant carmine nails. The couch was suddenly deeper and softer, and there was something he should worry about off in one of the shimmering corners of his mind.

Ingrid's oval face was a pretty blank and her bright red mouth was a jiggling red fish. Silver hair shone with alien brightness. All the pieces were there but somehow exploded into separate jewels of detail. Her dark eyes were twin moons hovering in the vibrant air and deep enough to drown in.

In the bedroom the eyes leaped with the crackling pulses of light, and he sprawled on the golden lake of metallic comfort beside somebody who might have been Roger. A Roger who laughed when his robe was stripped away. Laughed at his own sleek limbs and grizzled chest.

Jesus saw his own body jump with electric blue light. Both motionless and in motion. His naked feet were as huge as picket fences and too high to see over. He washed clammy palms and the fingers entwined without his help. The wrongness of it all was hilarious and melancholy, and he wished Roger would stop laughing into his own navel.

Then the lights smoothed into long gentle strobes and dimmed to a cool dusk that no longer swooped him into a thousand dark corners. The circular bed was no longer a spinning carousel and the girls stood quietly, out of reach. Attractive flames of primary color with all their softness gone, watching the man with slate eyes cross the lounge with silent grace.

Jesus screamed without sound and knew true fear for the first time in his adult life. Leaned on an elbow that slid away from him. Leaving him supine and helpless in a fogged drift of lysergic acid.

Jesus pawed his brother, and both men tried to swim away from the bed. Roger still laughed at things only he could see, but the weird chuckles were nothing at all to do with humor.

Charlie Dance drew up a golden chair and laid a long-barreled Savage across a knee.

"Is this how it was for Archie when he waited for you bastards?"

Roger said something that never got started.

Jesus burned to tell his brother not to grovel. But his head nodded over waterfalls of anxiety, and his tongue flapped behind clenched teeth. If he opened his mouth, it would scuttle off into a corner to hunt edible vowels. He fell against Roger and they held each other for comfort. Charlie's words abraded their eardrums, and brain cells jumbled thoughts like balls in a bingo fountain.

"Archie couldn't talk either, could he? Queenie had to find the words for him."

Roger made sounds. The Savage had been used in Malta. Now it pointed its bore at him. A dark Cyclops staring into his very soul.

Ingrid ripped off the silver wig.

"Hurt them, Charlie. Hurt them the way they hurt me."

Charlie's voice had a thousand cutting edges.

"Your animals killed our child. Kicked it to death. They're long dead. But you're still alive. My lady doesn't like that worth a damn."

Jesus mewed into his naked lap. All the words he needed writhed like the hair on his thighs. He got a leg to the floor and cracked his nose against Roger's chin.

"Goodbye, Jesus."

The room roared and flame came at him from a roll of smoke. He fell away as the gun jumped a second time. Felt nothing but nausea and mad dread.

"Goodbye, Roger."

Roger saw the gun swing toward him. A smoking black eye. Tried to push himself away along the bed with legs of uncoordinated string. Wanted to squeeze his eyes closed against the flash and whack of the concussion. Dared not miss the spit of fire and the hard double bark of powder stink. It was all he had. All there was left.

The Troys should come. Anybody. His mind embraced invented pain and he fell back into a last death throe that did not come. Charlie was still there and Roger saw himself in the mirrored ceiling. Naked and wretched.

And alive.

Charlie's voice was the Wrath of God.

"Now she's seen you as you really are. Stinking with fear.

All your manhood gone. The memory of that will mend her hurt. But you'll never forget this moment, will you? You'll take it with you to the grave."

Roger lay with Jesus, both of them leaking sweat and champagne and urine.

Dotty led Ingrid away and they left the hotel suite without a backward glance.

Alive, thought Roger. *Alive with abiding humiliation.*

The same fearful thought glazed Jesus' eyes.

Why don't they come? Follow the shots and drag Charlie's carcass away?

Charlie seemed to read his mind.

"The hotel's closed for redecoration. You animals and just one other are the only guests. I'll bring him. He'll be company for you."

Who will? Who will?

Roger and Jesus wanted a miracle when Charlie left them alone. Flailed onto the floor in a tangle of rubbery limbs. Roger butted the control panel, and lights revolved as he tried to crawl over Jesus and away from the bed.

Jesus sneezed into the carpet. Unable to scratch a nose wider than his face. There were vicious pins and needles in his fingers and toes, and every hair on his body was a barb in his flesh.

Forming consecutive thoughts was beyond both men. Their minds were blank scratch pads that would accept only outside stimulus. And Charlie Dance was written large in indelible neon.

Moving further was beyond them.

And Charlie was back in the room, playing them the tape of their meeting with Sadler and the Troys. Damning them with their own words.

Jesus was flopped onto his back with his head propped against the bed. Roger was rolled in beside him, smelling of funk and defecation, and they found themselves staring at a slight figure in crumpled clothes. His thin face all hollows and his mouth a drooling pout. The eyes were just empty smudges of nothing.

They screamed silently as Charlie sat Manchester Freddy in the gold chair with his feet touching their naked soles.

"In a couple of hours you'll be able to walk. To start running. Don't be here when I come back. Nor anywhere I can find you."

And for ninety-seven minutes Roger and Jesus watched Freddy sit very still and do nothing, wearing an idiot's face.

Naomi came out of her white dress in a long, tanned surge and moaned into Wally's neck on the reclining seats of Sadler's Daimler as they coupled with urgent need and little finesse, crashing to an abrupt orgasm.

"Too soon, too soon . . ." Naomi beat a fist against Wally's chest.

"Can't argue with that, love." Wally fought tender feeling. "Short and very sweet."

"Ninety days over in ninety seconds. Pathetic."

Naomi's bosom rolled in dim streetlight, nipples still crested.

"And now you'll want to smoke and take me straight home."

Wally tucked his cigarettes away.

"Stop telling me what I'll do next, woman."

"Well, you will."

"Maybe I've grown out of gropes in dirty dark doorways and the backs of cars. Even with a class lady."

"Am I a classy lady?"

"There and back and twice on Sundays."

"That's nice," Naomi purred, almost mollified.

"What are we arguing about, then?"

"Us? Nothing."

"Then . . . forget it."

"You're smoking."

"It's me nerves."

"Nerve, yes. Nerves, no."

"Thank you, Princess Perfect."

"Was it awful? In prison?"

"Holiday camp where you get a striped suntan. Boredom and bars."

"Margot tried to find out where you were and what was happening to you. Through a friend in the police force. You know, I don't even mind your cigarette smoke anymore."

Wally kept sudden alarm out of his voice.

"What filth does she know?"

"Filth?"

"The law. Cops. Who does she know?"

"Oodles of them from chief constables down. My God, your chest's gone as hard as a floor. Does it matter?"

"Who she talks to does. Who was it?"

"Chap named Lemmon. He was at one of Margot's Christmas parties last year."

"Just the one?"

"As far as I know. Why?"

"Maybe it's all right, then."

"When are you coming back to Jo'burg?"

"How do I know? Three months off the cobbles is a long time in my business. I'll try, okay?"

"Very, very hard? Promise?"

"You could stay on here. Get an apartment and keep a light burning for me. When I can get away."

"It had better be every night if I did."

"Then, you will?"

"It would end in tears and you know it. Besides, I do have commitments back home."

"Bridge and tennis parties? Christ."

"I'm no social butterfly, you oaf. I have business interests I've too long neglected. Investments need to be tended like any other crop. I am independent and wealthy, and this climate is absolutely filthy."

Naomi shivered and snuggled closer.

Wally grinned and killed his butt.

"There're ways of keeping a woman warm."

"Not when it's over in a trice."

"Over like what?"

"Like this." Naomi's hand fell to find Wally erect. "Where did *that* come from?"

"Probably a hitchhiker. Shall I throw him out?"

"Throw yourself out. Leave him here."

"And do what while you're busy with him?"

"You'll think of something."

Wally reared as Naomi's mouth found him. Closed his

eyes and soared on surges from her clever tongue. Worried about Lemmon in Sadler's house and how much Sadler could have leaked to the law about Connie's business. Knew he'd have to talk to Charlie if Connie wouldn't listen. Knowing Connie wouldn't listen. Knowing Kelly was unapproachable.

What a bloody tangle.

Wally raised Naomi's face and lifted her across his lap.

Why the hell don't I just walk away from it all and live on this classy lady's dough in wogland? Go for the good life and leave the fog and shooters and blood behind . . .

Thought, *why not, why not, why not,* as Naomi came down on him with long and liquid thrusts of need.

Why bloody not?

Roger knew enough to pay the cab off three blocks from their destination. His eyes streamed as he rolled them at street signs in darkest suburbia.

Jesus and Freddy had muddied themselves falling on a grass verge, and Jesus swore at invisible insects infesting his clothes. Freddy drooled and went where he was pushed, and Roger bit on the laughter that hurt his chest and mind. His mouth was bloody by the time he spotted the familiar monkey puzzle trees and Father Time leaning on his scythe above Sadler's roof.

Jesus reached the gate first, stumbled up the flagged drive slapping his jacket, his brown scalp slick with sweat. Roger got Freddy round a gatepost and ducked him under a rake of sharp puzzle leaves. Saw Jesus wore odd socks when he stretched for the bellpull. Heard the dark across the street call his name.

Roger's mind screamed as he ducked and turned.

Saw a man in a navy topcoat point at him with slow deliberation. Saw slate eyes stare along a leveled revolver as light slicked the barrel and air whacked past his face. Saw Freddy jerk and weep at the crack of gunfire.

Roger heard Jesus grunt as he threw himself against the carved front door with half his skull gone and gobbets of flesh and grey ooze spattering the varnished wood. A second report pinned a red rosette between his shoulder blades and arched his spine.

Freddy wept, hating the hard barks of sound.

Roger moved through glue. Started to pull Freddy down as he called to Charlie to stop and think. To talk. Heard his baritone squeal without authority. Saw the shine on Charlie's shoes as he shifted his stance. Saw a knuckle whiten as the bucking gun threw flame. A thermal fist set his chest alight and monumental pain threw him upright to embrace another bullet.

Roger folded over himself as a foggy cloak formed over his eyes. Jesus toppled from the steps and was a big loose doll with an unrecognizable face who dropped Roger on cold flags beside a maroon car smelling of new rubber and body wax.

Roger lay still. Too weary to feel anything but regret for all the fine things he would no longer enjoy.

He thought of breasts and flowers and fierce Tuscany wines. Of racing sulkies. Very long legs and lingerie. Of his grandson and saffron butterflies in a field of white daisies.

Charlie was gone in the darkness, and Freddy held the long-barreled Savage, making Roger smile about cleverness.

Charlie *would* think of everything.

A family feud with two dead and no witnesses save an imbecile driven out of his mind by the man who actually pulled the trigger. With us gone, Toronto will revert to Archie. The new drug circuit will fall into his lap, too.

Neat, Charlie. Very, very cleverrrrrrr . . .

Roger died and his smile stayed behind.

Flecked by Jesus' blood.

Zipped back into her dress, Naomi repaired her make-up as Wally drove through the outskirts of Esher.

"You can have one small drink at Margot's while I call a taxi for you."

"Coo, thanks, lady. Me inside that posh house without leg irons and handcuffs. What a treat. Can I stand on the carpet and sit in a chair?"

"Why must our every meeting turn into a cockfight?"

"I thought class women never talked shabby."

"Rather depends on the company one keeps." Naomi was still smiling when Wally coasted to a halt with deadened heads fifty yards from Sadler's house.

"Not a third time, you goat of a man?"

Wally peered through the windscreen.

"Shut it, love. Just a feeling. There's somebody out there. Ain't that Jesus and—?"

Rapid gunfire made Wally and Naomi flinch.

Wally held Naomi's head below the dash. Saw Jesus slam his face into the front door with his skull losing shape. Saw Roger snap upright and genuflect when two bullets smashed his chest. Skate on his side as Jesus fell across him.

Then Manchester Freddy strolled aimlessly toward the car, his thin face mindless and a gun hanging from his hand. A navy coat showed in the shadows down the block and was gone into the greater darkness.

Wally swerved away from Freddy as he tried to lie along the bonnet. Left him collapsed in the curb as he power-turned in tire-scream, deaf to Naomi's questions. Cutting stoplights until he was deep into the friendly gloom of Camberwell, where he parked far away from his flat, wondering who the fourth man could have been.

Must have been.

Every national but the *Financial Times* made banner headlines of the double escape from Winsom Green Prison and carried their theories about a shadowy mastermind in bold type beside old quarter-tones of Brixton and Smiler.

The death of two Canadian businessmen made the Stop Press of the London papers printed in Manchester, and missed the later editions because of a dispute between managements and the print unions.

The sanity hearing of Manchester Freddy Carpenter was reported a week later, almost as an oddity. Found unfit to plead, Freddy was installed at Broadmoor mental hospital with button-eaters, paper-tearers, and silent starers as his unnoticed companions.

Their bodies claimed by shadowy "relatives" in Malta, Roger and Jesus Tonna were interred in a plot overlooking the sewage outfalls above Marsa Creek. Their police files were officially stamped CLOSED both sides of the Atlantic, and the vacuum their demise left was quickly filled by a subtle power shift arranged by telex.

CHAPTER 7

BRIXTON BILLY'S BEARD WAS FOUR DAYS OLD WHEN PIMlico drove him into the Knightsbridge mews outside Dotty's flat.

The run down from Birmingham had been brightened by radio reports of 150 armed police surrounding a country house in Stockbroker Surrey, and naval helicopters backing a similar operation at the Dorset estate of a foreign royal, which might well have created a minor international incident had he been in residence at the time.

As it was, there were red faces among police spokesmen, some prize dahlia corms were trampled, and an aged gardener was held at gunpoint until his identity could be established by the local vicar, who cycled over for that express purpose.

The evening television news promised to be as entertaining.

Pimlico sounded a triple bleep on the horn and counted slowly to twenty. Dotty emerged with two large suitcases and a frivolous hat. When she had jammed the suitcases in the rear of her Mini, she laid the hat on top of them and drove toward Cromwell Road and Heathrow Airport.

Pimlico told Brixton to say goodbye to his mail train money, and Brixton's imagination peopled the window boxes with angry lawmen.

"Hope it's more a short *au revoir,* Pim. Charlie moves a bit quick, don't he? I only told him where it was buried yesterday morning."

"That's why Chas is Chas."

Pimlico left the Jaguar in Dotty's parking space and let Brixton into the flat. Fitful sunlight played on drawn curtains and flowered wallpaper. Roses twined on upholstery and forget-me-nots patterned the bathroom. The guestroom was a busy mixture of arum-lilies and scarlet pimpernels, and the pine bed was draped with a Union Jack bedspread. A blue sash proclaimed Queen Victoria Miss World, Disraeli held a pint of Watney's, and a sepia Buster Keaton ran from a phalanx of policemen. The wardrobe was full of clothes in Brixton's size.

Brixton bounced on the bed with a can of beer.

"You and Dotty gone to some trouble. But her flying that dough out solo don't feel right. Even if she's your wife."

Pimlico popped a can of Long Life.

"She's got more protection than the Prime Minister. Charlie's got all his heavies riding shotgun. And a few of Connie's lads.That money's as safe as you are. Mine's going out too. Ingrid and Wally got some South African woman to include some in her luggage."

"All that dough in one jump?" Brixton shook his head. "He's something else, that Charlie."

"Better than taking it out in penny packets. The more time that went by meant there was more chance of the Troys jumping it. And you, Brix."

Brixton's gaze inverted.

"Tommy would love to dip his beak in all that gravy."

"No chance of that, Brix."

Pimlico thought of Dublin Gerry facing the Troys with the news the moment the money left British air space. Charlie had wanted Dublin Gerry to go team-handed to see the Troys, but Gerry wanted the privilege of turning the knife with Irish charm alone.

"Another beer, Brix?"

"Too tired to drink." Brixton lay back on the national flag and kicked off his shoes. "Leave it to Charlie," he said, and went to sleep.

Pimlico went out and closed the door. Rinsed glasses and fed the canary. Glad of Brixton's faith in Charlie and disquieted by his own decision to launder his money through Connie's mining company. Musing over a second beer as Brixton snored.

With Dotty and Ingrid safe in South Africa, the cobbles could turn as red as they liked.

Dotty drove through Knightsbridge fighting panic.

The cases she had thought too heavy for her had seemed to weigh nothing when she packed them in the Mini under her flowered hat as Pimlico had instructed. She whirled through traffic trying not to think of the last time she and Pimlico had made love. His stomach had knotted under pink scar tissue and ugly blue puckers. The grains of heavy buckshot still worked their way to the surface to be picked out by tweezers, and he had muttered in his sleep afterward, sweat shining on his face as he gripped the bedhead rails like cell bars. Perspiration running from his wide chest. Water on muscular stone.

The wrench of leaving her mews flat. Skipping down the stairs with Pimlico's assurances rolling through her mind. How the flat was only wallpaper and four walls. And how a canary was only a canary. Replaceable, where she and Pimlico were not. And the new life together in the sun had got to be better than whoring and pimping and robberies that ended with the dawn raid by the police and long cold train journeys for prison visits once a month. The future was making fat babies in the sun.

Wally's green and black Jaguar led Dotty to the start of the A4, where Archie's white Rolls swung in behind her. Two motorcycles brought up the rear as Dotty thought of motherhood and passed some of the finest industrial architecture the thirties had produced, the rows of gabled houses built to overlook green fields that no longer existed. Then there was sun in rusty fields of seeded cabbage. Fishermen on a canal bank. A whip of bare trees and slow Friesians grazing a paddock.

Dotty saw Ingrid and herself with prams in a playground. Was glad Jonas, Brock, and the Tonnas were dead, and that Freddy was insane. Only Maltese Maurice was left, and Dotty hoped he experienced, before he died, the misery he'd inflicted on the girls who whored for him. Life was going to be different. Instead of hiding from the police, Pim would mow a lawn and hang curtains, with babies gurgling in a playpen.

The dream died as the plane she was to catch crashed into a dark mountain in her mind. The motorcyclist peeled off into the approach tunnel to the airport. Dotty followed the Jaguar through a barrier and up curving ramps into a multistory carpark swarming with hard, quiet men. An NPC man waved her into a reserved space and brought trolleys for the luggage.

Ingrid got out of Archie's white Rolls to kiss Dotty, and Froggy, Sodbonce, and Nasty Nostrils took the luggage to the elevators.

Dotty glimpsed Archie's white head before the car door closed and she asked where Charlie was.

"Around." Ingrid reassured Dotty with a squeeze.

Dotty said the tension turned her milk to camel's water.

The NCP man stayed with the cars, eyes too big for his scared olive face, as Ingrid and Dotty followed Wally and Naomi down cement stairs to the covered pedestrian ramp. When Wally paid excess baggage on three of the suitcases at the SAA desk, he made a face and a joke.

"Expensive playing it straight," he said, suggesting a drink.

His humor escaped Naomi, who had already started to miss him.

Quill watched Wally introduce Naomi Leathers to Ingrid and Dotty on their way to the bar. Without Payne there would be no photographs, without back-up, no arrests.

Quill angled closer as Wally took the women up to the horseshoe bar on the second level, unaware Charlie trailed him or that the anonymous call he'd received that morning hadn't been Bulstrode talking through a handkerchief.

A late Lufthansa passenger was paged, Aussies drank from cans with brash flamboyance, and Africans in robes wheeled their duty-frees about in wire carts. Foreign students on "stand-by" slept on newspapers, stoic Germans ate overpriced *gâteaux* in the cafeteria, and Texans waiting for the Dallas flight looked jaded under their Stetsons. An Afrikaans couple watched their baby scream from its folding chair while sullen Asiatics mopped between chairs and smoking stands as though they had done nothing else for a thousand years.

Quill wondered what he was watching. Wished he could translate nods and handshakes into evidence. Have a beer himself or eat another breakfast. Since airport security was not controlled by the Metropolitan Police and the rest of Lemmon's squad was assigned elsewhere, Quill was just another private citizen on private property, and must conduct himself accordingly.

Quill watched a couple of Toytowns walk the concourse below and sneered at them. Long on hair and short on brains, they were just dropouts from the Met. With the Toytown police bungling what passed for security at Heathrow, the wholesale thievery came to millions each year. The Toytowns wouldn't go within fifty feet of a loading or unloading plane for fear of union accusations of "harassment." It was no wonder to Quill that insurance claims and premiums had gone into orbit.

Quill passed kiosks selling things seen only in airports, ducked through a newsstand, and buried his nose in an acre of camelhair. It was Sodbonce's chest, and Froggy and Nasty Nostrils flanked him. Quill swallowed hard. They had all left their smiles at home.

"Hello, Prophet."

"Going on your holidays?"

Nasty Nostrils played with a key ring on a carousel display.

"Keep it clean, lads."

Quill dislodged a Travis McGee and a couple of Chandlers from a shelf. Sodbonce stood closer.

"Seeing somebody off, Prophet?"
"Could be."
Quill swallowed tart bile.
Sodbonce put the paperbacks on a shelf.
"Happy coincidence you being here, Prophet. Right, Nasty?"
"Right."
"Lucky," said Froggy.
"Except it ain't. For you," Nasty told Quill.
Froggy jerked a thumb. "The Man wants to see you."
"Man? What man?" Quill asked. Knowing and unhappy.
"In the carpark. Man in a white Rolls."
"They're both white. Him and the Rolls." Sodbonce grinned.
Quill had backed as far as he could. A counter cut at his buttocks and he jostled a Wrigley's display.
"Out of order, lads," he said.
"Call a Toytown, then."
Sodbonce flicked Quill's necktie from his jacket.
"There's one. Peaked hat and face to match."
"Enough, lads."
"Call Toytown or come quiet." Sodbonce laid a size ten suede over Quill's size seven Oxford. Draped a meaty arm around the slight shoulders as Froggy lifted Quill's warrant card and hid it in a pile of *True Romances.*
"Or limp."
Sodbonce crushed Quill's foot.
"I'll . . . walk . . ."
Quill soaked himself in popping sweat. His foot swelled and an icy fist clenched his stomach. He was taken through automatic doors into dull sunlight, where porters leaned on their trolleys as a Toytown told a motorist he couldn't park on yellow lines even if he was a close personal friend of British Airway's chairman.
Nasty's fingers met around Quill's bicep.
"Take a long last breath, Prophet. Like you told our Charlie when you took him in on that phony charge. Remember?"
Quill was crossed behind a black cab and walked into the shadows of the multistory carpark. Clattered up cement

stairs and between rows of cars. The NPC man was told to make himself scarce, and Charlie came out of somewhere to lean against the white Rolls Royce. An electric window whined open, and Quill saw Archie Ogle in the back seat. Frozen green eyes in a tanned face. Brandy and soda in a freckled fist.

Quill's mind tumbled over itself. Was back in bed with the telephone telling him Bulstrode would meet him at Heathrow to watch the SAA flight desk. Putting aside natural caution because the rest of the squad was on surveillance in Bethnal Green with observers from the Buckinghamshire Constabulary. If Bulstrode hadn't called him, who . . . ? Quill spun back to the carpark to stare at Charlie Dance. Wanted to bluster and couldn't.

Charlie lit a Gold Flake and blew out the match in a hard puff of smoke.

"You've annoyed Mr. Ogle, Prophet. Won't even talk to you, so I have to waste my breath."

Archie growled and sipped brandy.

"You and Maltese Maurice got on well when you were in uniform at King's Cross and he was running his first string of whores. Favors for favors, as Maurice so delicately puts it in his sworn affidavit. Very delicate is Maurice since his accident."

Quill's small eyes widened. *Accident?*

"Maurice's girls were honest, too. Swore in writing you had some fine old Friday nights in their cribs. Dates, times, the lot. You've been a very immoral lad."

Quill blinked.

"Twenty-seven sworn statements before a Commissioner for Oaths and couple of silks from the Queen's Bench. They ought to keep you busy explaining to C12 or A10 or whatever Internal Affairs call themselves nowadays. And then there's your undeclared bank accounts."

Quill wished he could laugh or swallow or break wind. Scared to miss anything. Thought: *What bank accounts?* Said, "You've framed me, you . . . ?"

Charlie laughed smoke.

"Now, who'd believe that? You've been salting money away for two years, Quill. And copies of your bank statements are lodged with a solicitor who doesn't know our firm from a bar of soap. When all that evidence goes to the Director of Public Prosecutions your feet won't touch. And calling Maurice and his girls liars won't stop you getting suspension on half pay until you're dismissed from the force."

Charlie leaked smoke through a tight smile.

Quill found the courage to snarl.

"I'll come back at you, Charlie. However long it takes."

"No, you won't."

Quill sprang back when Charlie flicked ash. Took a short hook to the stomach and fought to keep his breakfast. Suddenly on his knees, he gaped at oily concrete.

"Suicides can't fight back."

Quill's stomach was seared by spits of fire as he was lifted bodily. His ankles were roped together and his arms were pinioned behind his back. Held aloft, he was carried to the elevators and saw the OUT OF ORDER sign was a lie when Sodbonce opened the doors. A rope was tied off to a crossbar in the liftshaft and the dark hole came up at him in a surge of disbelief.

"Lose . . . him . . ." Archie said with slow finality.

Quill tried to call Charlie. Or Archie. But nothing came as he was toppled into the void. Nothing but nausea and fury.

Falling, he embraced the coming end with anger. Found the breath to snarl at it.

Was jerked to a halt. Blood rushed to his head and his neck whiplashed. He spun giddily with oily black cables smearing him. Fought blackout. Knew he must keep his nerve. Find the breath to call for help.

This was just the heavy frighteners. They hadn't meant to kill him at all. They'd all be laughing up a storm, thinking they'd drained old Prophet of courage. *Wrong, you bastards,* Quill thought.

Wrong.

Then he heard the cage whine down the shaft at speed and wondered what his last thought would be.

* * *

Naomi thought she quite liked Ingrid Dakin, but that Dotty Machin-Parsons was a petite blonde with a *petit-pois* mind.

Naomi hated Dotty's fuss about crashing aircraft and not drinking the water abroad as if she expected to squat at a waterhole and slake her thirst in the company of baboons and vervets. Naomi hated the thought of all those air miles with that little goose for company instead of her loving clod, Wally.

Naomi walked toward the whining aircraft. Wiped a slick of moisture from her eye. Touched the bruise of Wally's farewell kiss. Blanked her face and rejected conversation. Stowed her coat, grateful for the aisle separating her from Ingrid and Dotty. For the empty seat beside her. Refused a boiled sweet and buried her nose in an airline magazine. Daydreamed about honest sun on her face and servants who read her mind. Forced herself to forget about the money in the rear baggage compartment. The shooting outside Margot's house. Wally driving her away without explanation. Refusing to let her go back or even to telephone the Sadlers. And keeping Dirk and Alicia away from reporters and the police.

All Naomi had for De Wit were some newspaper cuttings and her own hazy recollection of gunfire. The small man called Freddy falling away from the car to roll in the gutter with empty eyes.

Naomi shuddered, knowing De Wit's debrief would be thorough and unpleasant. She kicked off her shoes and thought that at least playing house in Wally's tiny flat had been fun. Cooking basics on his funny little stove and going to bed in the long afternoons when the sun never showed at all. Even though it had been nothing more than a holiday romance, a shadow dream that would fade like the last frame of an old movie, she had enjoyed every last moment of it.

"Have you fastened your seat belt, lady?"

Wally grinned down into Naomi's upturned face.

"What?"

The Super Constellation taxied toward the apron and the

NO SMOKING signs were lit. There was no possible way Wally could leave the aircraft before takeoff.

"You incredible twerp," Naomi said, realizing he was making the flight with her.

Lemmon climbed into the Post Office van and sat beside Dillman, who wore earphones as he fiddled with a directional receiver aimed at the Martyred Thomas. Payne's thousand-mill lens was trained on the saloon-bar entrance and his Pentax was loaded with 400 ASA film. In the lab it could be boosted to twice its speed with a slight loss of definition. The small mikes they had planted inside the pub the previous night had picked up a whistling decorator who had left when the Troys entered just after high noon.

"Anything new?"

Lemmon didn't light a Player; they'd all agreed not to smoke in the confined space. He had just come from one of his "meetings" at the Home Office where his files were accepted by an anonymous official who gave him coffee in good china without a word and let him out without uttering a single syllable. Now and then Lemmon gave Bunny Halliday an update by telephone, and knew Bunny was pleased with his progress only when Elizabeth received a bouquet through Interflora.

"Nothing yet," said Dillman. "Just mutter and what sounds like drinking."

"Lucky old them. Can't even bust them for drinking out of hours on licensed premises."

"I get the feeling they're waiting for something to happen," said Dillman.

"And we're not?" said Payne.

"Is Buller on station?"

"He's parked in an unmarked mobile east of us, and he's tuned to our frequency. I've had an acknowledge."

"And Quill?"

"No sign of him, guv. No message on his answerphone, neither."

Lemmon scrubbed tired eyes with a hot fist, and his jaw cracked when he yawned. He thought he'd stroll down to

Tubby Isaacs' stall for a bowl of jellied eels in fresh air. A cup of lemon tea in one of the kosher cafés.

"I just hope Prophet—"

Lemmon broke off as Payne began shooting film. He craned to see through the two-way-mirrored window just as a tall and stocky man pushed into the Martyred Thomas.

"I'd know the back of that bullet head anywhere," Lemmon breathed. "Give us some sound, Dildo."

Dillman flipped the speaker switch, and a needle danced on the volume dial as Jesse said, "Hello, Mr. Ax. Pleasant surprise, eh, Tom?"

"A glass for the law there, Gordy," Tommy said.

Arthur Ax cleared his throat. Scraped a chair aside and said, "Nothing to drink on duty."

Jesse laughed and snorted. "Collared, are we?"

"Not yet awhile. There *are* those who live in hopes. I could be one of them if my sweetener doesn't get to Jersey very, very soon. It's overdue."

"We ain't clockwork like your coppers. You can't wind us up and earn a salute. You'll get your hotel in Guernsey, so don't fret about it. We're waiting for news about the money, so you'll have to wait with us."

"Have a drink and relax, Arthur," said Jesse.

"*Mr. Ax* to you, Troy."

"Yeah?" Tommy said lazily. "*Mister* gets earned around here. You're a fucking *mister* when I've moved up west. You're in as deep as we are, Arthur, and don't crack on you ain't. You want tugged forelocks and fucking *misters* and *sirs,* wait until you've got a hotel full of bootboys and chambermaids. Until then, *Arthur,* you're a bought-and-paid-for copper with forty grand coming his way as a kickback. And for that you'll *mister* me, right?"

"Finished?"

"For now, *Arthur.* Just you stay by the phone. By sundown you could be a very rich copper indeed. Money straight from the sugar train."

"And a friendly drink wouldn't come amiss," said Gordon.

"I'll call *you,*" Ax said. "Not the other way around. Get

that clear. I'm not jeopardizing my career at this stage of the game."

"Anything else then, *Arthur?*"

"Nothing, so long as my money's in the bank before the weekend."

"All said, then. Sure about that drink?"

"Certain."

"Bye, *Arthur . . .*"

Lemmon's hand mashed Dillman's shoulder.

"Get me some sharp pictures there, Payne."

"Do we whistle Buller up? Turn Ax over?"

"Not yet, brave lads. This needs sleeping on."

Lemmon watched Chief Inspector Ax hurry into the street turning up his collar. The Pentax took close-ups as Payne panned with the corrupt policeman.

"Tell Buller to follow without making contact."

"Acknowledged," Bulstrode said over the radio patch.

"That's one copper in the world too many." Jesse belched. "Why don't we give him to the Irishman, Tom?"

"Only if they took each other out," said Gordon.

"Wouldn't that be neat?" Tommy said.

"And isn't science wonderful?" Lemmon listened to Bulstrode's engine over the patch.

Sweating and tense.

Wondering if he should swarm the area with uniforms.

Decided yes.

The Martyred Thomas was forlorn in gathering dusk.

Decorators' dust sheets flapped on the scaffolding and hardboard covered the unglazed windows. The fascia boards had been removed, and blackened brick showed between the undercoated cornices.

Dublin Gerry stopped in shadow to admire his disappearing handiwork and gave Payne a chance to hack off some profiles before Gerry crossed the road.

"Anybody know him?" Lemmon asked.

Nobody did.

Tommy and Jesse sat in the dim light of the unfinished backbar as Gerry wove toward them through ladders and scaffold boards. He perched on a sawhorse in the heady reek of french polish and freshly planed mahogany, and Tommy tilted Scotch over shot glasses.

"Welcome to the pub with no beer. You done good at Winsom, Gerry, son. The newspapers are still headlining it as the jailbreak of the century."

Dublin Gerry took a glass and raised it.

"Another nine-day wonder is all. Looks like your insurance paid out on the fire. Let's drink to the grand opening of the old Thomas."

Jesse took whiskey down.

"Be about a month. But some bastard still owes us for torching it. And he'll pay with his legs."

"That right?" said Gerry.

"Yeah, yeah." Tommy hated talking about the fire. "What about Brixton's dough?"

"And Bonar's fee for getting Smiler back?" Gordon added.

Gerry began rolling Old Holborn into a cigarette paper.

"There's good and bad news about that."

Tommy rolled the gold band on his index finger.

"Without the choir and organ, Dublin."

Gerry teased tobacco flakes into shreds. Building tension with the cigarette.

"Straight you want it. Straight you'll get it. Bonar Tree's escudos will get to Jo'burg in about a week. Not bad, seeing as how them Portuguese like the money rolling in and not out. Bonar's got his way with them, though. Now, there stands a clever man."

Tommy stiffened in his chair.

"Since when was that money supposed to go direct to South Africa?"

He hunched his shoulders at Jesse.

Gerry licked the gummed edge of a Job paper and rolled it into a neat tube. Pinched excess tobacco from the ends.

"From the exact moment Bonar knew you planned to hold Smiler to ransom for every penny Bonar took off that mail train. Smiler is the apple of his daddy's eye, you see."

"Fucking touching," Jesse sneered.

"What am I smelling here?" said Tommy.

"Just a clever man being cautious. As cautious as Brixton Billy. And with good reason."

Gerry struck a Swan Vesta on his shoe and waited for the flame to burn evenly before touching it to his smoke.

The brothers exchanged glances with Gay Gordon, and Tommy cracked knuckles.

"How cautious is that, Dublin?"

"All the way, Tommy."

"All what fucking way?"

"Nobody believes your handshake, Tommy. Not Brixton or Pim, not Bonar or Smiler, not Connie Harold. And definitely not Charlie Dance."

"How did Charlie Dance get in on this, for fuck's sake?"

"Charlie organized the money so you couldn't dip into it. Brixton Billy's out of Birmingham and safe. Smiler's on his way to join Daddy in Portugal. And your cut of the money, as well as their full shares, is where you can't touch it. Four miles up and flying at four hundred miles an hour toward Africa. Nobody's reneging, Tom; that's what was agreed. And you'll get yours when it's been laundered, and not before."

Jesse was pale, and his plump mouth was livid.

"Who brought Charlie Dance in?"

"Everybody."

"Not us." Tommy's face was bled meat. "Name me names."

"I have."

"All of them?"

Tommy could not believe it.

"You and your firm ain't popular."

Tommy pointed a thick finger.

"I'm holding you responsible, Dublin. You."

"Why, because there's only me here? I was bought and paid for and paid off. It's the big faces you should pull faces at. Not me. I've delivered their message and there's an end to it."

"You figure you can just throw that in my face and calmly waltz off like nothing's happened?"

Gerry leaked smoke through a lazy smile.

"Stop and think, Tommy. Charlie wanted the heavy money out of the Smoke, and he's done it. You and Connie wanted South Africa, he stood aside. Now he's got peace of mind and you've got wogland. Job done."

"You still owe us one."

"One what?"

"Who paid us out in horsemeat for a hit on Dance and Queenie? You."

"And overdue for repayment," said Jesse.

Gerry hurt his drink and ate smoke.

"Over and done, Tommy. You want to end up like the Tonnas?"

Jesse palmed sweating jowls.

"Manchester Freddy went off his head with a shooter . . ."

"If you say so." Gerry smiled.

"You ain't telling us . . . Toytown tales." Tommy blanched.

"You believe what you want, but look what happens to them as shakes hands with you. Kosher Kramer, Pinky Bellaver, Roger, and Jesus. Maybe Freddy was lucky ending up mad instead of dead. What you touch turns to shit. You want to own all the manors and skim all the mail train dough. Your partners say you can't, so you look for a scapegoat. Count to a hundred and learn to live with how things are."

"The bastard's enjoying himself, Tom."

"I've got eyes."

"So has he. Up to now." Gordon stroked the cutthroats behind his lapels.

Gerry tossed off his drink.

"Anything happens to me, you three'll go down faster than washing on a broken line."

Tommy's hand shook as he drank. The Scotch did nothing for him, but he could see the truth in what the Irishman was saying. It was coming too hard and fast for him, and everything was somehow slipping away. He had to crack skulls until it all fell back into place. He licked Scotch from his thumb and said, "You've pushed your tired Irish charm too far this time. There's just us and you. And here and now. Right?"

Gerry sighed and stayed where he was.

Tommy poked another finger at him.

"Pay back your debt. Give us Brixton. His dough'll fly back fast enough with him under our thumb."

Jesse liked that and said so.

Gerry shook his head.

"Take a drink and forget it."

"That earns you the paper hat," Tommy said as Gordon stroked his lapels.

Gerry shrugged and set his feet.

"You're down and you don't know it. Every mother's son wants you off the streets and out of their lives. How don't matter no more. Their shooters or the law. One way or the other, you're history."

Tommy's mouth worked into a bare smile.

"That earns you a last *drink!*"

Tommy's bottle swung and Gerry went under it in a hard crouch as Gordon's knee came up into his chest. The razors came in as a double blur of borrowed fluorescence.

Gerry dropped a shoulder. Flicked his shot glass at Gordon's mouth. Heard it chink against tooth and gum. The knee skidded on a deltoid and Gerry stiff-fingered Gordon's crotch. A razor flew off into pots of varnish and paint, and Gordon sat heavily, his torn mouth a hole in oatmeal.

Gerry banged the sawhorse into Tommy's next swing. The bottle shattered against steps where his head had been. Scotch stung the air, and Jesse's first punch missed. His second caved Gerry's front teeth in as an implosion of shock.

Gerry knee-dropped. Straight-armed Jesse to the heart through a swinging chairback. The chair disintegrated and a slat cut Gerry's eyebrow. A leg raked his cheek. Gerry rolled and toppled a scaffold board. Rolled again and kicked Tommy's legs out from under him. Pots scattered, and turpentine spilled to make a stinking lake on the bare pine boards.

Gerry swallowed a bloody tooth and gagged as it stuck in his throat. Backed towards the saloon-bar door.

Tommy was coming to his feet and trod on Gay Gordon's hand. Jesse drew a long blade from a cardboard carton. Hurled the scabbard from an antique cavalry sword.

Gerry caught Tommy in the neck with a long kick. Jumped away and tangled an arm in a decorators' dust sheet. Tore himself free as Tommy windmilled punches. Slammed a foot into Tommy's armpit and backed clumsily as Gordon's long forward lunge glittered before contact.

The left hook cut instead of numbing.

A flap of meat hung over Gerry's collar and severed nerves screamed in lazy spits of blood. Gerry took another slash across the upper arm and followed through with combination punches that dropped Gordon in a flail of buckets and falling brooms.

Gerry feinted from the waist. Avoided Jesse's hooks and slashes with the saber. The door was closer all the time and traffic brawled as the lights turned green. A bus changed gear and a horn bipped. Gerry shook blood from his eyes and skipped backward. Kicked a bucket aside and felt for the brass handle. Skidded in turpentine and missed the swing of a balk of sawn pine.

Tommy smashed the four-by-two across Gerry's right arm. Shattered bone. Drove him in a half-spin against the door in a daze that would not go away.

Something cleaved the air, and Gerry's face seemed to burst apart. His knees hit the floor and he fell on his side with his trapped right arm bent the wrong way. Bone splintered near his elbow. Ripped through tendon and knifed through his sleeve. Made him wail as he spattered himself with dark blood. Panted as he got his knees under him again. Only vaguely aware of the arcing knife that plunged into his face and pinned his head to the floor.

I should have listened, Charlie.

Gerry breathed and felt nothing. No sensation save wood shavings rustling under his skewered face. Keeping his eyes open was almost too much for his sapped mind to cope with. One was blinded anyway and wept onto the blade through his cheek.

A longer blade hung in a shaft of light. Dust motes danced like liver spots. Jesse's hands were around the sharkskin haft. A golden tassle hung between the meaty knuckles.

Tommy bellowed madness.

The saber hacked down through rib and lung and jammed in bone near Gerry's spine. The shock turned everything to silence. Gerry no longer owned a torso. No longer had legs. Just one good eye and his good left arm. It took Jesse by the throat and bulged the manic pink eyes. Locked off, the hand squeezed pith from a piece of rotten fruit.

The brothers leaned over Gerry in blessed silence. Turned the saber. Sawed deeper. The point chunked into the floor and metal grated against bone. Splintered a floorboard.

Spitted, Gerry watched his fingers open. His arm fell away. It was nothing to him anymore. Spittle from Tommy's soundless shouts sprayed his upturned face. Pink froths of lung blood foamed in his open mouth. Gerry fell away from it all. Did not hear a last clatter of air form a blood bubble over his lolling tongue.

The dark ceiling came down to smother him and the body on the floor moved with the cut of the crimson blade long after Gerry had ceased to exist.

Dillman ripped his earphones off as Gerry's scream soared with the first downward plunge of the saber. The sound went round the Post Office van as a whirlpool of agony. Payne took pictures of the closed pub door without knowing he wasted film as Lemmon told all vehicles to converge. Now.

Bulstrode's Cortina U-turned to mount the pavement, barely missing a braking bus. Lemmon slammed the rear doors open and turned his ankle on the slick cobbles. Two pandas reached the intersection and began to bring order to the hooting traffic. A small man in a drab raincoat threw his weight against the saloon-bar door as Bulstrode bulled from his car, and tumbled inside with Bulstrode three paces behind him. Payne took close-ups of Silversleeves Sutton before he fell inside the pub. The back of Bulstrode's head as he closed the gap, his necktie streaming with his hair.

Lemmon hobbled through pedestrians, bringing up the rear.

Dillman sat and listened to the chop of metal on flesh with an ashen face, unable to move anything but his rapidly blinking eyes.

Silversleeves had dressed over his pajamas and hurried to the Martyred Thomas as soon as he had put the phone down from his cousin Willie. A porter at Heathrow, Willie had seen Charlie's firm grab Prophet Quill as Wally Harold caught the SAA flight.

"Got to be worth a few sovereigns to Tommy," Willie had said, and Silversleeves repeated that fervent hope as he hurried along Mile End Road.

Then Bulstrode had panicked Silversleeves by burning rubber across traffic and bumping up the pavement, forcing Silversleeves into the pub instead of away in the opposite direction. The door closed on Silversleeves' back at the moment Jesse withdrew the saber to sever Gerry's head with a savage downswing. Spattered Silversleeves with coagulating gore.

Silversleeves stared through blood measles as the head pinned to the floor stared one-eyed and grinned with broken red teeth. Said the world outside crawled with heavy filth and didn't see Gay Gordon crawl behind the unfinished counter. Then Bulstrode was there and allowed Silversleeves to take comfort against his chest as all the coppers in the universe swarmed through the door.

Uniformed and plain-clothes police grappled Tommy to the floor and Jesse was backed against the bar, shedding sweat through freckles of blood and making noises nobody wanted to hear. Cornered, he threw the saber somewhere and tried to punch out through a hard-boarded window. Bowled uniforms aside like inflated dummies. Ash truncheons cracked against his skull. A lignum vitae baton took the strength from his shoulders, and more heavy truncheon blows dropped him in a heap. His eyes rolled over his spread-eagled brother and glared up at Bulstrode and Lemmon. He hawked and spat with manic fury. Hit

Lemmon's sleeve with a gobbet of phlegm before going limp with knees in his back and handcuffs on his wrists and ankles.

Unseen, Gay Gordon had crawled into the bar well and dropped through the opened cellar flap into the dark. With the sureness of practice he squeezed through the gap behind a large wine rack and squirmed into the vaulted cavity beyond. And waited.

Silversleeves smeared crimson across his mouth with a cuff.

"Nothing to do with me, Buller," he said hopefully.

"Cut yourself shaving, did you?"

Bulstrode wished he knew who the dead man was. Ambivalent about being too late to save him. Murder was a hanging charge, and the Troys were caught dead to rights. A thousand Arthur Axes couldn't save them from the long drop and burial in lime.

Jesse wailed in mental twilight like an abandoned child.

Tommy just lay on the floor and ground his teeth.

Bulstrode made Payne take pictures and said, "What a bloody slaughterhouse."

"Definitely nothing to do with me," said Silversleeves.

Lemmon held the saber by the tassle.

"This is one we won't lose in court," he said, going over what he would say to Bunny Halliday and the silent man at the Home Office. Knowing he had most everything he needed to nail Arthur Ax. He bowed his head to let Dillman whisper something about Quill being rescued from a liftshaft at Heathrow by firemen, and as he shook with nervous laughter one of the uniformed men was discreetly sick in a bucket of whitewash.

Gay Gordon did not move until three in the morning.

The CID had sealed the Martyred Thomas and left a constable and a sergeant to guard the building. The sergeant stood on the grating above the cellar and smoked where Gordon could not. Dropped his smoking butts into the shaft where they lay like fragrant rubies until they died. Cussed the cold when his constable patrolled past and hummed Gilbert and Sullivan medleys when he was alone.

Gordon crossed the cellar and quietly broke down a pile of wooden beer crates he had used to seal off the rear vaults. Eased himself over a dusty sill and closed the hole behind him with crates he had stacked on the opposite side.

No point in making the law a present of my way out.

The golden rule in Glasgow. When we were head to head with rival gangs in the derelict tenements. Always have a crafty way out if your mob got skinned. Aye.

Thick dust cushioned his footsteps as he wove through crusted arches scaled with mold. Feeling his way without showing a light. His outstretched hand touched the far wall and found the shutter of an old dumbwaiter. It opened with a squeal and he froze for a millennia of seconds.

Listening.

The constable prowled the pavement overhead and the sergeant whistled to himself.

Gordon crawled into the dumbwaiter and hunched small. Gingerly started himself upwards with the rope pulley. Knew he should have oiled the tackle more often. Waxed the rope.

His tender groin pounded as hard as his heart, and fear of dark enclosed spaces sweated his scalp.

Just to be clean again. To languish in a bath and come out smelling of magnolias. Find somebody like that Penny waiting for me. Don't think about it. Or how bad things are with Tommy and Jesse under close arrest. They'll never get out. Ever. Don't think about it.

The ropes snagged and squealed when he was forced to haul on them with all his strength. Got them running free with a shriek that he thought could have been heard in Brighton.

Don't think about it.

Pray if you must. Hail Mary, full of grace . . .

No, cunt. You're parroting bitch Helen. Dead Helen. Helen in her RC pew with her rosary and her face bloodless in pink bathwater.

Don't think about it.

Just pull the ropes easy. Pull and ease off. Past the gym and on up the shaft. Past this dead air. On and on and up and up to the top-floor offices. All this bad air. Got to breathe.

Don't think about it.

The dumbwaiter bumped to a halt.

Dead air smelled of old newspapers.

Gordon opened the hatch and sliced through wallpaper. Cutting carefully, keeping a straight edge. The square fell away and slithered against a skirting. Fresh air smelled sweet and made his own stink all the more improbably.

To be clean . . .

Gordon climbed out onto a landing, and borrowed street-lights showed him the ladder to the fanlight in the roof. The CID seals on the outer office door.

Gordon gnawed his upper lip.

Cunting coppers. Hadn't banked on them sealing the offices. There's hot water and clean clothes inside. Money and a shooter in the wall safe.

Think, you dumb muggled Jock.

Think.

The filth will be all over Ida like a blanket. You can't go near the Fortress. Or call cunting Arthur Ax. No friends left down at the Leman Street cop shop now.

Think.

Nothing but small change in your pockets and not a single friendly face you can trust in the whole Bethnal Green. No shooter. Not even a razor. Nothing but bare knuckles and your muggled Jock brain.

Think, cunt, think.

You've got enough for cab fare to King's Cross. Hop a train back to Scotland. Wait. King's Cross. Argyle Square. Maltese Maurice. The only man in the whole Smoke who owes you for past favors.

Maurice. Aye.

Gordon climbed to the fanlight and worked rusty bolts.

Maltese Maurice.

CHAPTER 8

THE GIRL WITH THE POCKED FACE CHEWED GUM AND SAID, "IT'S twenty pounds or piss off, sunshine."

Gordon's breath exploded in the early morning darkness of Argyle Street as he snorted. "I'm no Rob Roy kiltie just off the banana boat from Aberdeen, henny lass. That's hard coin you're talking."

The girl sloe-eyed Gordon.

"You say. It'd cost you a fiver for bed and breakfast without clean sheets around here. I'm worth fifteen more than that."

"To who? Not to me. You only keep five. The rest you hand to Maurice."

"Who's bleeding Maurice when he's home?"

"Your pimp. My friend."

"You and him are mates? Never."

"I told you."

"I ain't never seen you with him. Like together."

"You wouldn't have." Gordon's groin ached in the cold. "Twenty? Jesus."

"It's the best room in the square, sunshine."

"That makes it the first-floor front in Maurice's own house, girl. The one with the musical bed and rampant stag wallpaper."

The girl stopped chewing, and her big eyes hardened in a thick ring of mascara.

"Maybe you do know him. Know Maurice."

"Call him on the phone. Wake him up and ask him. He'd mark your stupid face."

The girl looked thoughtful. Bit a nail and wet her lipstick.

"Okay, sunshine. Ten it is. But nothing hard. Nothing violent."

Gordon crackled the last pound note in his pocket.

"Wouldn't draw the wings from a fly. Just up and down and job done, that's me. Come out of the road before we both freeze to the pavement."

"Romantic little sod, ain't you?"

"Valentino never paid for it in his life."

"Another friend of Maurice's, I suppose."

"Aye. A known West Ender like me."

"Come on, Elephant Balls. Let's get you outta the wind before a good sneeze knocks you over."

The girl stuck her gum behind her ear and Gordon made fists in his pockets.

"Gonna mother me, eh?"

"Not for ten quid. Me name's Carlotta. Nice, eh?"

"And last week you were Charmain or Greta."

Carlotta jangled keys.

"You want it or not?"

Gordon took her bony elbow.

"More than a free pint."

Carlotta opened a peeling door onto boiled greens and tomcats.

"After you, Jock. You wouldn't be bad-looking if you wasn't so skinny."

"And Carlotta suits you. Exotic."

"Yeah?"

"Aye."

At the top of a flight of stairs Carlotta fumbled with a light and unlocked her room. Turned to bow Gordon inside and saw the blood and filth on his face. The brown stains on his collar and cuffs.

"Now, listen, sunshine—"

Gordon hit her in the throat. Chopped her hard behind the ear. Caught her and dragged her into the stale room. Dropped her on the sagging bed, glad to let her go. The smell of her made him swallow hard. There were fresh track marks on her wrists, and her nostrils were red from snorting coke.

That's how you keep them tame, eh, Maurice. Give them a habit they can't break. Aye, that's Tommy's idea, too. But he's gone and . . .

Don't think about it.

Gordon tied Carlotta to the bedhead with her own tights. Gagged her with an unwashed pair of panties.

"Choke, you whore," he said aloud, locking her in.

A Negro voice complained in whispers as bedsprings protested. A cockney girl whined back as a strap slapped flesh. Gordon climbed stairs past snoring and the hoarse grunts of copulation. Two flights up he came to Maurice's flat. Used one of Carlotta's hair grips to pick the lock. Took exactly eleven seconds to spring the door, slow by his standards.

Tired, he told himself in justification. Eased the door closed against the jamb and accustomed his eyes to the gloom. A wedge of light showed under a bedroom door, and the air was heavy with lavender polish.

Gordon risked the overhead light and showed himself the small, neat sitting room with its easy chairs and sideboard of framed photographs. Maurice smiled beside the Tonnas at a sulky race in Marsa, walked a horse with a winner's rosette on his lapel, leaned on bars in Canada, Malta, and Soho, popped champagne with Gordon at a party in Manor House, wore funny hats with Manchester Freddy at a Greek restaurant in Peckham. Stood in a tuxedo surrounded by a flock of girls in spangles and feathers, and rode a fairground horse with a girl who might have been Carlotta before horse and smack took her looks and self-respect.

Gordon's stomach growled and he found the kitchen to

rifle the fridge. Ate salami and drank milk to wash down stale crackers. Maurice hadn't shopped recently.

He's letting things slide. Must be snorting himself to sleep with the light on. Nose candy was supposed to be a fine sex aid for the over-forties.

Gordon grinned and helped himself to a sharp kitchen knife. Tucked it into his waistband where it was handy and cracked the bedroom door. Maurice lay on the bed in a dressing gown, and his naked legs ended in white plaster bootees, leaving his toes free to wiggle if they wanted to. His round face was rounder and one ear was the glossy purple of ripe aubergine. Crumbs of eyeball peered through black prunes of discolored flesh, and his mouth was swollen and negroid.

Gordon ran fingers through his hair and stared.

"Who handed you the paper hat, Mo?"

There was something wrong with Maurice's voice.

"Be somewhere else . . . Gordy. They broke me up good. . . ."

Gordon took a step inside, thinking of self-preservation. How to ask Maurice for money without asking who had worked him over.

". . . Said they knew about Brock and Jonas . . . the casino receipts . . . Told 'em I know nothing . . . but that Limehouse kept at me and at meeee . . ."

Limehouse?

Gordon's skin crawled.

Don't think about it. Get the dough and go. Aye.

"Where's your money stashed, Mo? I need—"

Gordon sensed movement behind him. The slap of bare feet on linoleum. Then somebody was on his back and thin legs were around his waist, heels hammering his painful crotch. Nails dug into his face, and Carlotta's stench was all over him as she tried to drive a pair of pinking shears into his ribs.

Didn't hit her hard enough. Must have cut herself free.

Gordon tried to scrape her off against the bed. Got the hand away from his face and turned the wrist until it cracked. Heaved the girl on top of Maurice, who sat upright to bellow softly before subsiding in an unconscious sprawl.

Found the rank hair and jerked the spitting girl's face close to drive a short hook to the jaw. Clicked her teeth together just as she drove the shears into his ribs.

The whore has cut me. Deep.

Gordon hit the girl again. Drove her face away over her shoulder at an odd angle. Smelled Carlotta on his fist when he let the body fall across Maurice. Wiped his hand on the garish pink bedspread thinking of money and where it might be hidden.

All pimps salt their money away. Aye.

Gordon ripped drawers from a dressing table. Left the shears in his side until later when he could stop the bleeding. Let clothes fall in heaps and emptied the wardrobe. Opened shirt boxes and found a coin collection. Emptied the gold and silver ones into his pocket. Discovered a wad of Maltese sterling in a leather collar press and stuffed it inside his shirt. In a suitcase he found the good stuff. Used fives and tens in rolls held by elastic bands.

Bloody thousands.

Gordon filled his pockets, then sat on the bed to look at the shears in his side.

I'll be a stuck pig when I pull them out. Better do it in the bathroom. Staunch the blood with a bath towel and surgical tape. Wash off the blood and clean up. Take one of Mo's clean shirts. Walk down to the railway station and go first class back to Scotland. Aye.

"As God makes them, so he pairs them," somebody said from the doorway, and Gordon turned to Charlie Dance leaning there. Saw him take in the whore and the pimp and made a helpless gesture. Decided to keep the bastard talking until he felt less tired.

"You did that to Maurice? Makes you as bad as any of us, Charlie."

"Limehouse lost his temper. I'd have just killed him."

Cunting Limehouse again.

"You don't want me, Charlie. Not now it's all over with Tom and Jesse. I'm nothing."

"You were in on what they did to Dublin Gerry."

"That was business. Nothing personal."

Gordon needed the bathroom. His bladder was full, and

hot fireflies burned his side. He watched Charlie walk round the bed to feel Carlotta's pulse, taking in the shears when he dropped the limp wrist.

"You did a better job on her than she did on you, Gordy. She's dead."

Gordon blinked drearily. *I only hit her the once.*

"Not for want of trying, Chas. She's fucked me pretty good. Just let me walk away, Chas, eh?"

I can make it once I'm out the door. Throw the lock and be down the stairs before he can bust out. Shiv him through the banisters if he follows. Aye.

Charlie scratched his chin at the dead whore.

"You know where the door is," he said softly.

"You won't regret, Chas."

"Goodbye, Gordon." Charlie just looked at the girl.

Gordon made the door with a lunge and held the lintel as vertigo turned the room on its axis. Saw another man in the sitting room. A man in black with red hair and freckles and nothing in his hands but cigarettes and matches. Nothing in his face but cold hatred.

"A last smoke before you go, Gordy," Limehouse said. He flipped a lit cigarette on the floor at Gordon's feet. "Have that on Helen."

"You'll not see me beg."

Gordon bowed slowly and picked the Player off the carpet. Waited for the pain to leave before he straightened. Flicked the cigarette into Lou's face and punched the kitchen knife at him as he bobbed aside. Felt the blade strike nothing but air as Lou's foot drove the shears deep into his side with a light thud. Gordon was full of air he could not breathe. Unable to lower his right arm, he watched with sad eyes in deep sockets as Lou waited for him to die.

Gordon refused to fall. To give in. He kept Lou away with sweeps of the kitchen knife and made small steps towards the dark staircase. Heard himself grab a final victory as he said, "You never had her, Cunty. I took that away from you. Me. And now you never will. . . ."

Gordon could see the landing, but it stayed where it was. He was sinking to the floor, and something feminine shimmered as distant laughter tinkled from a face with hair as golden as the agony in his chest. Then he pitched forward onto the linoleum, falling into infinity and beyond.

Charlie stepped over the body and found the smoldering Player. Put it in his mouth and drew on it. He had finished Maurice with pressure on his carotid artery, and it wouldn't take the law long to work out how Gordon had murdered him and the girl during the course of a burglary. It was as neat as he could make it.

"Where shall I drop you, Limehouse?"

Lou almost smiled.

"West End Central. Time I gave Mr. Lemmon all he wants on the Troys. Tie up the loose ends for him."

"You don't have to. They're well collared."

Charlie wiped off anything he and Lou might have touched and led Lou out of the squalid house into the start of a bright summer's day.

"Gordon was right. I never had her, Chas."

"No."

"Makes it all the purer, though, eh?"

Charlie nodded at the starlings flocking around the turrets of St. Pancras Station.

"Two away to you, mister," he told the quickening sky. Not adding the girl to his tally.

CHAPTER 9

MARGOT WALKED THE RIVER BOTTOM BELOW CHARTINGS Hall and surprised a heron as mist retreated from the rising sun.

Malcolm would be awake soon, and the Spanish cook would be preparing breakfast for him. Margot cut at the tall reeds with a hazel switch, calming herself after a sleepless night.

She had spent the previous morning in the confines of Lincoln's Inn with her legal adviser, whose conversation had been most illuminating. A dusty thumbprint on his half-glasses had blurred his right eye as he talked in a monotone in his dark, paneled chambers, a desiccated old pedant with the face of an ancient Druid and a voice as dry as his phraseology.

But sweet, Margot decided.

And desperately honest. And as ugly, sober, and dull as Oscar Wilde's view of Dodge City.

She climbed the steps of the sunken garden to her favorite vantage point. The shrubbery was bright with new leaf, and the view over the vales of Sussex was achingly green as the season ripened into early summer. Chartings's Jacobean brickwork and mortar were earthenware lined with biscuit, and the leaded windows were bright lozenges of reflected sky.

Margot knew she would not miss the house in Esher, even the sanctuary of her conservatory. The double shooting outside it had soured her association with that part of her life, but the loss of Chartings would be a tragedy of monumental proportions, far outweighing even Malcolm's previous brutality.

Margot said "Ouch" softly and unclenched her fists.

Her nails had scored her palms with deep crescents.

The gardener's old spaniel stalked flies on the lawn and an early bee blundered into a flowerbed. Pigeons from a nearby copse beat overhead and linnets spiraled from the cottages near the main road. The air was as clear and as fresh as any skiing resort Margot had visited, and she vowed to better Bastard Malcolm at his own devious game in order to keep her home.

Just to breathe rainwashed air and watch clouds chase olive shadows over the vales. Watch an old dog snap at insects on a lawn ruined by mole runs. Be mistress of my own destiny. Dream of another Telephone Charlie who may one day enjoy me on that same lumpy run of lawn. Or anywhere else he might fancy.

Calling herself "Fool," Margot scratched her wayward nose and went into the house to collect Malcolm's breakfast tray and the morning papers, and was sitting on his bed when he emerged from his bathroom smoothing freshly shaven chins and the front of his very purple dressing gown.

"Good morning, wife."

Sadler no longer called Margot "Cat."

Margot poured his coffee and stirred in cream and sugar.

"You're walking better, Malcolm."

"Am I? Yes, I suppose I am."

Sadler drank and smacked his lips, a mannerism Margot hated.

"You'll soon be well enough to travel, I shouldn't wonder. All those foreign parts . . ."

"I?"

"You, Malcolm."

"You surprise me."

Margot plowed on through his negative responses.

"You and another, Malcolm. To Buenos Aires perhaps?"

Sadler stopped reaching for the newspapers.

"Buenos Aires, Margot? Why do you mention Buenos Aires so particularly?"

"The airline tickets in your bureau. Tickets purchased on the domestic account. Not the business. Tickets, Malcolm. Plural rather than singular. You won't be traveling alone."

"Ah."

"Ah, indeed."

Margot held out the pewter pot.

"More caffeine?"

Sadler offered his cup with a lifted brow.

"Two to Buenos Aires? And what might the significance of that piece of information be, I wonder?"

"I imagine it's where you plan to run with some female now that it's all up with your villainous friends."

Sadler drank his second coffee black, as he habitually did.

"Which friends would they be?"

Another bloody mannerism I abhor.

Margot opened the *Daily Express* and laid the *Daily Mirror* alongside it.

"These friends."

Sadler saw Tommy Troy glare from beneath a blanket as police escorted him to a Black Maria. Jesse's grainy portrait sullen beside block headlines, his hair drooping spikes as he was frog-marched through drizzle. Ida cried into a handkerchief on courtyard steps as a beefy WPC held photographers back, their faces bleached by the flash of Speed Graphics. Tommy and Jesse flanking the cockney bosom in their new Bond Street nightclub. Posing with a life peer who shone in popular television programs and wrote pompous articles for the Sunday journals, whatever their political persuasion.

Sadler went the grey of the newsprint.

Margot watched his mouth blush and his jowls shudder. Saw coffee slop from his porcelain demitasse. Saw a thousand truths she had blocked out with brandy and self-delusion.

"How many photographs are you in, Malcolm?"

"Be quiet. . . ."

"Inspector Lemmon wasn't taken in when he asked you about the Tonnas, was he? He *knew* you knew them. And your claim to be too ill to talk made not the slightest scrap of difference, did it?"

"Enough, Margot."

"He knew you were lying from moment one. Saw through my unconvincing tears, too, didn't he? And they say the wife is the last to know. A cliché and a truism both."

"I said *enough.*"

"You and your friends in high places. No such animals exist now, do they? Bunny Halliday hasn't accepted a single invitation since he brought his favorite copper into our circle, has he? Or any of the other self-important characters you so confidently called your friends?"

"Shut up." Sadler scanned the scant details. "I have to *think.*"

"Of Argentina? Of divorcing me for your new traveling companion?"

"You will kindly close your very foolish mouth."

"Yes, Malcolm, three bags full, Malcolm. That's what the old Margot would do. But not this one. Not now she knows she's a serious candidate for divorce or sudden death."

"What drivel."

"Was it to be one of these *Express* headlines who converted me into a plausible 'accident'?"

"You don't know what you're talking about."

"You didn't 'fall' in the conservatory. Was that mauling you took a warning not to cross them further?"

Sadler stood and promptly sat.

"You were dead drunk when I . . . fell. Nobody hurt me."

"Lies, you liar."

Sadler mumbled. Pawed his hair.

"I must think."

"And this sudden flight to Buenos Aires? To sell my darling Chartings Hall to that awful farmer from Cheddington?"

"You know about that?"

"And how I do is simple. You put all your U.K. property

into my name last year. A small matter of bad investment, remember? And yesterday I learned that silly drunken Margot's signature is necessary to release the deeds of ownership so that the sale can go through. I signed over the Esher house, but my Chartings?"

Margot tossed her head. Dislodged a fat black curl.

"Not Chartings, Malcolm."

Sadler's lips curled and quivered.

"You have no choice, my dutiful wife."

"Wife in name only. We're talking property settlements. Not marital bliss. No more threats of brutality, Malcolm. One single bruise and I walk away with everything bearing my name. You'll get your divorce then—after I've taken your last solitary sixpence."

"Will you now?" Sadler's doubled fists trembled in his lap.

"You utterly silly and thorough cow. All the courage in the world now you think you have the upper hand. And a fool of a solicitor to make your money-grubbing legal."

"For the first time since our parody of a marriage started I feel I'm a person in my own right."

"You, you degenerate bitch?"

"Me."

"You joke of a woman."

Margot smoothed her skirt with a sigh.

"Thank you, Malcolm. That makes it easier to leave."

"Fornicatress."

"I accept the gender, but the charge itself you must prove."

Margot forced herself to hold Sadler's crumbling gaze.

He licked a moist upper lip.

"Prove it, my pet? Didn't I see you reflected in the water under those bloody palms? Yes, my dearest dear, I saw. I wasn't sure until afterwards. Long afterwards. And you are quite right; my accident was no accident. I was fucked by the same bastard who fucked you."

Telephone Charlie? Margot thought, not realizing she said it aloud.

Sadler grinned like Blake's Tyger.

"Your penchant for giving pet names damns you. I

thought on my bed of pain for weeks and was never really sure until now. God, if only I'd known at the time. I could have had these men . . ."

Sadler stabbed the half-tone Troys with a forefinger.

Margot thumbed a ticking eyelid.

"Had them kill us?"

"Why not, you bitching bitch? Your Telephone Charlie wants *me* dead. And now you're killing me by inches with your puerile notions of independence. That man, that man, that fucking man . . ."

Sadler paced, his face dark with fear and malice.

Margot perspired. Chill as the sun rose through the leaded windows. Malcolm's fear fouled the timbered room and his swearing was a frightening novelty.

"You deluded bitch. Do you really think you can keep Chartings Hall and live if I die? He won't leave witnesses, not him. You go with me, you dunce of a bitch. We both have to run from that man, that fucking man . . ."

"Run? Run where and why?" Margot did not comprehend.

"From him, from him."

But he made love to me. True, true loving.

Sadler turned on Margot with some of his old spirit.

"But Dance won't have it all his own way. Not by a long chalk. I still have a long arm, wife-in-name-only. I can reach out and hurt him the way he has dared to hurt me. My friends in South Africa will see to that. Charles Dance is about to hurt."

Charles Dance?

Margot spun herself back to Wally Harold's "Welcome Home" party. A Charlie Dance had been mentioned as she beamed through alcoholic mist. Wally had annoyed Conrad by saying, "If Charlie Dance promises the Troys as headlines, mister, you'll *see* bloody headlines."

Margot whirled herself back to an erotic explosion on Korean moss and being cradled in strong arms while she slept. Until Malcolm's torn voice called her back to wade across the pool to where his naked feet jumped on the stone parapet. His chubby torso jerking with fatter testicles and his head cracked against the heated flags in agony.

The awful pleasure of that moment.

The pleasure she took from Malcolm's pain.

Sweat blistered Margot's forehead.

"I don't understand. How deeply are you involved with these criminals to be able to talk of *hurt* in this way?"

"In over my head, wife. I'm dead, and you are equally dead if you don't sign those property deeds and share blocks over to my brokers immediately. Two tickets to Buenos Aires, Margot. For you and me. You can't be left behind. He'd find you. And through you . . . *me.*"

Margot just sat. Very still. Composing herself.

Sadler paced and muttered and dry-washed his hands.

"What a pair we make," Margot said at last. "The man who would steal the world and an effeminate brewery."

"Your salvation lies in signing your name. Not in stolen curtain speeches."

"I believe you, God help me," Margot whispered.

"Then, telephone your lawyer. Now."

Margot studied a silver nail in a sunbeam.

"There will be certain conditions."

Sadler stared. Unbelieving.

"What?"

"Write it all down, Malcolm. A private confession just for me. Then I'll do it."

Sadler's fists drummed his belly.

"You agree, bastard, darling?"

Sadler nodded dumbly.

"Make the call."

Margot went to her room to call Mr. Thrupp. When he came on the line she said, "How long will it take to process those papers I signed yesterday? Yes, all of them, including Chartings Hall. . . ."

"Three days, not allowing for the coming weekend."

"Make that twenty-eight days, will you? And do make something up my husband will believe, should he telephone."

"As you wish, Mrs. Sadler."

"I do so wish."

"My pleasure."

"There is one other thing. . . ."

"Yes?"

"Do you have a discreet enquiry agent? One who could locate somebody without hanging about in a shabby raincoat?"

Thrupp hawed, and his "yes" was cautious. Made it quite clear such activities were more the domain of less prestigious and, ah, lesser men in the lower echelons of his profession.

"But you can offer me such a service?"

Thrupp could indeed, and wrote *Charles Dance* on his memoranda pad before Mrs. Sadler rang off. He pondered the name for a long moment before unlocking a desk drawer, looking up a number and dialing J. C. Hatton in Esher. They talked in low tones for several minutes and came to a ready agreement in less than three minutes.

Margot cleared Malcolm's tray and smiled sweetly.

"All fixed. Now explain, please—about hurting Mr. Dance in South Africa?"

And she listened with a fixed smile as Malcolm explained. Playing with her silver brooch with silver nails.

Arthur Ax feigned a migraine behind *The Times* until his wife went off to a WVS bridge party before allowing despair to drain his face of color. The men from Internal Affairs and the cheerful one called Halliday had been overly polite when they made him read the transcript of the tapes Lemmon's squad had supplied. They agreed they couldn't use the tapes in a court of law when Ax tried to brazen it out, and their polite scorn had told him there were many other ways they could make a case against him if they so chose.

Suspension on half pay, his assets frozen, and a full enquiry. Resignation? Out of the question, Chief Inspector. So sorry.

Sorry, my arse.

Arthur Ax saw his new life in the Channel Islands slip away and knew the lady who had promised to meet him in St. Peter Port would find solace elsewhere with indecent haste.

Too many glands working for that one to live in celibacy or wait for me to come out of prison without a bloody sou. I know what prisoners do to disgraced coppers behind bars. I'd spend all my time in solitary and come out old, broke, and broken. If I lived through it . . .

Ax went into his wife's muddled kitchen, where cakes and sponges cooled on wire trays, and rummaged in the cabinets and drawers until he found the things he needed. Then he undressed in the bedroom and hung his clothes in the wardrobe in his usual neat fashion. He laid his wallet and keys on his bedside table and decided against a note. They would get no help from him, he vowed, and stripped the cord from two pairs of pajama trousers before locking himself in the bathroom.

When he had cleaned his teeth and combed his hair, he sat on the toilet and lashed his feet to the bowl with one of his pajama cords. The second he used to tie his neck to the cistern pipe so that he would not fall when he became unconscious. That was important to his orderly mind. He must maintain some dignity.

He filled a pair of Marigold gloves with cooking oil and trapped them between his knees whilst he prepared the plastic bags that were to go over his head. Four bags together ought to be strong enough, he decided, rolling the edges and fitting them on his head like a skullcap, ready to be pulled down.

Time of death ought to be exact, he thought, and smashed his wristwatch against the wall. The hands stopped at 1:14 and Ax pushed the minute hand forward two minutes to be as precise as possible.

No hesitation, Arthur. Do it.

Now.

Ax pulled the bags down over his face and expelled all his breath. When he breathed in, the bags sucked in against his face and blood pounded in his temples. He drove his hands into the rubber gloves and oil spurted out along his forearms. He rubbed his hands together so that they, too, were slick with oil. The panic he knew would come brought his hands up to tear at the bags, but there was no purchase. He bucked against the cords and they cut into his ankles, tightened around his straining neck. His knees parted and his member rose, a magnificent final erection that would point in accusation at whoever found him. Hoping it would be his bloody awful wife, Arthur Ax bit through his tongue and lost consciousness. His arms and torso went slack and one of the oily gloves slipped to the floor with a rubbery slap he didn't hear. His knees sagged together and he farted long and loudly as his sphincter went slack.

Arthur Ax was clinically dead forty-seven seconds later than he had calculated and was not found until his wife had a neighbor kick the door in just after seven that evening, and Mrs. Ax was still laughing hysterically when the police arrived with an ambulance twenty-five minutes later.

"He always was a pompous prick," she said before they sedated her.

Colonel De Wit thought about Naomi Leathers as she cooled her heels in his waiting room. Her skimpy report lay under his hand, and his displeasure showed as clenched muscles in his long jaw.

Naomi had been a fine mistress when she had been married to Damien Leathers, the financier. A tigress between the sheets and a willing fly on the wall during those business meetings De Wit had been interested in. And just as useful to De Wit in other ways, just as her daughter Alicia was at present. It was clear that Naomi's work had deteriorated since De Wit's interest in Alicia had become more intimate, and it was just as well that her fear of him had not lessened, or even the scraps of information she now brought him would be even more worthless. More footling.

De Wit went to the window to stare down into the police compound where black prisoners washed a fleet of official cars. The big ceiling fan moved the air around without cooling his office, and small roundels of sweat grew under his armpits.

Women's emotions were troublesome, and their motivations were so transparent, so damned dishonest. All delusions without a shred of honesty. No wonder men grew beyond them so quickly and so readily. Women didn't mature and grow like men, they shriveled and wilted like Namaqualand daisies when the dry seasons came. Pretty and vivacious for such a short time, whereas men put down deeper roots and threw up stronger branches to shield themselves from the hot rays of the sun of reality.

De Wit wished he had a decent intelligence network in Great Britain, especially now the damned socialists were in power, with their dangerous and misguided policies of racial equality. Anti-apartheid groups were springing up all over London with the blessing of the Wilson government. Not the wind of change Harold Macmillan had prophesied. This wind blew chill for the only white tribe in Africa.

De Wit went back to his desk and tapped the file with a pencil, sighed, and pressed the bell, and did not stand when Naomi was shown in. Made no comment when she sat across from him without invitation to do so. She was pale from her extended stay in England and wore powder blue to accentuate her blondness. Her generous mouth pouted under the merest slick of lip gloss.

De Wit tapped her report and watched her nervousness grow.

"My men tell me you brought one of the Englishmen with you," he said with suddenness.

"Yes. He wishes to see you."

"Without going through channels? Are you impertinent enough to believe my door is ever open to you?"

"I merely promised to ask if you would see him, Hendrik. Nothing more."

"Hendrik, is it now? Such familiarity. Has his great British heart melted enough for him to give you away in the kirk?"

Naomi's face became scraped bone.

"You can be damned cruel, Colonel. It isn't Wall . . . Walter. It's his brother, Conrad. You wished to see him, and his anxiety for an early meeting merely matches your own. Shall I tell him to go away?"

"I have constables to do that for me. If necessary. Did he tell you, his dear friend and confessor, what he wants with me?"

"Not really. I . . ."

"Perhaps he should explain himself to me. After *you* explain this nonsense you sent me. Three bare sentences and some newspaper cuttings. Nothing I couldn't and didn't get without leaving my desk. Ach, do you take me and our republic for a fool in a nation of fools, Mrs. Leathers?"

"Not at all," Naomi quavered. Chill in the heat.

"This report suggests otherwise. I am not well pleased with your notable lack of zeal. I'm a public servant and a grassroots patriot, and I set aside personal honor to keep your personal fortune from being seized by the appropriate government department. That matter could be resurrected at any time, and I refuse to turn a blind eye without constant loyalty, my wealthy widow. Your late husband's memory would quickly tarnish should the truth about his business ever become known. You'd be impoverished and the scandal would bar you from 'polite society.' And we both know you couldn't survive that eventuality, don't we?"

Naomi felt the familiar weariness of defeat. The fact that she had supplied De Wit with the intelligence that proved her husband's perfidy, albeit unwittingly, crushed her spirit all the more.

Poor dear Damien, I sold us both out, she thought.

"What do you want from me, Hendrik?" she said.

"A small thing. You will stay close to Conrad Harold. Very close indeed. What Alicia cannot glean from him, you will. I hope that is clear."

"Can this wait for a few days? I promised to go upcountry with Wall . . . Walter and his two lady frie—"

"Make your excuses."

"Very well. Is there anything in particular you wish to know?"

"Just keep your wits sharp. We are never dealing with absolutes, my wealthy widow. Keep a bag packed; you and Mr. Harold may well have to return to London in a hurry. Clear?"

Naomi sighed and nodded.

"Then, you may go. And send Mr. Harold in on your way out."

Naomi stood and held a handbag of brilliant blue feathers.

"Am I never to be free of Damien's past, Hendrik?"

De Wit's smile was as bleak as his dismissive nod was curt.

"I very much doubt it, my dear. Run along now."

"Goodbye, Hendrik." *You bastard.*

But De Wit was already looking through her, waiting for the Englishman to come in. He had already forgotten she was there. Naomi heard his cheerful greeting before the door closed on Connie's back, and the offer of a cooling drink before the rickety elevator took her down to the street and quiet tears in her Mercedes, blind to the staring blacks.

Connie Harold quelled nerves as he and De Wit crushed knuckles and he sat in the chair Naomi had warmed for him. De Wit accepted a good cigar and they exchanged opening gambits and smoke across the pristine desk.

"This is all a bit complicated, Colonel."

"Isn't anything worthwhile?"

"It's more than some parking violation."

"Do I look like the Minister of Transport?"

"Two days ago I brought a lot of money into the country. Cash money. To finance the next stage of my mining interests, and I've had a million forms thrown at me by your exchange control people. And well, look, I can't seem to handle them, you know?"

De Wit's smile was sly when he said he thought he just might have heard something about it as Connie shifted from one hot buttock to the other.

"Even their forms need forms to get the forms I have to fill out to get the forms . . . you know? And I can't seem to get around the restrictions over this plant I need from Hungary. My lawyers just run up fat bills and run in circles, and I need it straightened, whatever it costs."

"Are you attempting to bribe me?" De Wit asked.

"I would if I thought that's what it took." Connie found himself by the window, and he stopped himself pacing or raising his voice. "You can't be bought, Colonel. But I reckon you'll trade."

De Wit joined Connie at the window. Stared out at the yellow heat haze and said, "Let us review your situation, my Cockney friend. You've got the best part of four million acres of Namaqualand staked, and swept aside the opposition Jorgesson had allowed to hamstring him. He was fortunate in his choice of partners finally, eh? Not that you gave him any choice, did you? The Ministry of Mines has confirmed your right to prospect and develop the sites at Mkuse and Meir, Portland Cement is very interested in your perlite, and the estimated turnover of your companies during the coming fiscal year is a cool £2.5 million. Correct?"

"Near enough for jazz."

"There are inaccuracies?"

The question was sharp with surprise.

"No," said Connie. Thinking, *Let the man talk. He wants something. Wait for the catch. He's done too much homework on me not to have a hook he wants baited.*

"Too big to go down the Swanee, Colonel," he added.

"You wish to bring not only a plant from an Iron Curtain country, but also two Hungarian experts who are probably agents of the Kremlin. My government's policy on that is very clear: Total embargo. And the many thousands of pounds sterling you brought in *in cash* can hardly be above question, knowing as I do where it must have come from, eh?"

Connie stole a look at the closed brown farmer's face beside him and read nothing there but cool analysis.

De Wit nodded out at the crashing heat.

"Yes, my friend, you do need my protection and a great deal of help."

"That gets it said, Colonel."

De Wit turned slowly and stroked his long upper lip.

"And it must be abundantly clear that your criminal record is no secret to me, either. . . ."

That bloody Clive Spring. Connie seethed.

"From your first appearance at Tower Bridge juvenile court to your recent coercion of an entire jury to secure the release of your brother. Those facts alone should have barred your entry into this country without chance of appeal. So doesn't it strike you as strange that you're allowed to come and go with seeming impunity?"

"Tell me about it."

"Unruffle your feathers."

"I'm calm enough. I can understand you putting me in the same class as Clive Spring, but I don't have to like it."

"Spring has his own peculiar talents, as you have yours. He has made himself invaluable to me, and therefore enjoys the protection of Republican Intelligence. Which is what you need, eh?"

Connie thought jet lag had made him mishear.

"You're like our MI5?"

"More important by far, Conrad. My department is a weapon I've forged to ensure the survival of an entire nation. The only white tribe in Africa. The only true Christians on this dark continent. Republican Intelligence upholds racial and moral purity, suppresses socialism, liberalism, black incursion, and intermarriage with lesser races. All the things you appear to believe in, must believe in if you and your embryonic empire is to flourish. Look at your own country, choking itself to death with its mad notions of brotherhood and equality, giving your black and colored immigrants equal rights in law. England is a museum of yesterdays without a tomorrow in sight. They've given away the birthright of future generations because no socialist has the sense to see the wider issues of a nation within a community of nations. They talk of hospitals, welfare, and schools, but they forget to look beyond their borders and see their enemies for what they are. They are the true criminals, eh?"

"I ain't arguing, Colonel, but that's flying flags. It don't tell me what I need to hear, or what *you* want from *me.*"

De Wit's eyes hooded and flared.

"Obedience. Total and unquestioning. Without it you are finished in South Africa."

Connie felt the floor dip under his feet.

The bastard means it.

"How much money are we talking about?"

"There will be 'donations' to clandestine funds, but they are small nothings for the future. And you almost achieved what I need from you without knowing it, my London sparrow. Those cleverly forged documents you presented to clear your heavy plant through Customs? Next time, you will use that method to bring in items of interest to us. Armaments we are unable to purchase for ourselves."

Connie had chewed through his cigar and soured his palate.

"Just like that?" he said with heavy sarcasm.

"Exactly like that," said De Wit.

"And for that I get my Hungarians and their plant?"

"Why not?"

"And my money?"

"I could have taken your mail train money anytime I chose. Or choose. Never forget that."

Connie's "How could I?" was as faint as he felt.

"There is a man in London who deals with an armaments firm in Hamburg, Germany. You will enquire about the availability of Bloodhound missiles and spare parts for our Centurion tanks. Do you need to take notes?"

Connie wiped his bitter mouth.

"A man who keeps the prices of hundreds of metals in his head can remember that little shopping list, Colonel."

De Wit nodded.

"We should be friends, Conrad. Don't ever make me your enemy."

"No cherries in that cake, Colonel."

"Meaning?"

"You're in charge, Colonel. No contest."

"Keep that firmly in mind at all times. There are several black political activist groups enjoying the protection of the Wilson government in London. Here is a list."

Connie sucked his teeth at the neatly typed addresses.

"And?"

"I want those offices burgled and every scrap of paper in them shipped back to me through this agency. Memorize the list; you can have nothing written down."

"Okay. I can handle this with one hand tied."

"Personally, Conrad. No third parties."

Connie agreed with a nod, too tired to argue.

De Wit opened a cabinet and chinked bottles.

"You'll take a drink now?"

"A big one," Connie said with feeling.
"When can you leave for London?"
"In a couple of days?"
"There's a flight at midnight. Be on it."
Connie accepted a tall Tom Collins.
Said "Cheers," and thought, *The things I do for two and a half million. And who wouldn't?*

Vinnie Castle covered a book of Robert Graves's poems with *Popular Mechanics* when Bulstrode threw a shadow across his wheelchair, grinning at his taste in literature.
"You'll be on Shakespeare next."
"I got tired of *Playboy.* Charlie and one of the doctors bring me things to read."
Bulstrode wadded his jacket and lay on the grass.
"Your Charlie hasn't the time to skim a headline the way I hear it. Busy depopulating the Smoke."
"Is that right?" said Vinnie.
"And Prophet diving down the shaft without waiting for the elevator is a puzzle. Swears he dunno how it happened. How did Charlie get him to say that?"
"Who says he did?"
Bulstrode leaned on an elbow to squint through dappled light.
"He's resigned the force, you know."
"Who has?"
"Prophet. Retired to Dorset to manage some trout streams. Out in the open air away from enclosed spaces. Missed his retirement dinner, too. Couldn't face the ride up to the top floor of the Hilton. Broke down in the elevator and blubbered all over Dillman."
"Poor old Dildo. Bet that took the shine out of his trousers."
"Laugh and I'll kick your one good leg. They saved it, then?"
"And some other bits and pieces. I ain't laughing at your precious Quill. This is a rictus, not a smirk, part of my medical condition. I've got more platinum wire in me than your average jeweler's window."

"Remind me to hold you for ransom."

"Heard Limehouse turned Queen's Evidence."

"Hundred and twenty-eight official statement forms filled with small writing and all usable in court. But never a mention of Argyle Square."

"King's Cross ain't Bethnal Green, so why mention?"

"There's a funny story about that. Gordon and Maltese Maurice were close friends long before Gordon joined the Troys. Maurice liked him around his girls, him being a safe bet being a raving homo. And the fact that Gordon was a handy street fighter. Maurice offered Gordon to Archie first, did you know that? But Archie and Charlie didn't take to him."

"That ain't funny, just sensible."

"What's funny, my unidextered friend, is Gordon killing an old friend and one of his whores for money Maurice would have given him anyway. And that skinny whore finishing Gordon with a pair of scissors just doesn't ring true. Forensic and the Coroner don't believe she could have stuck him that well. Not bang nine inches of steel through his ribs and both lungs. But people do find strength when they're fighting for their lives, a bit like you, my little bantam."

"I love your smiling ways, too."

"Those pinking shears were kicked home. We lifted street dust from them."

"So she was a whore with big feet. So what?"

"She was barefooted when we found her."

"So one of the other girls in the crib stole her shoes. No morality in brothels nowadays. Oh, dear and tut."

"Stow it, Vinnie. We ought to nail all three bodies to Limehouse Lou. Lean on him and get to Charlie."

"Back to Charlie, eh?"

"Back to him."

Vinnie shook his head and accepted a lit Dunhill.

"It's a sunny day, Buller. Plenty of shadows to chase if that's your pleasure. Me, I'd rather fish and wear a flat hat. I've got more chance of catching pike on this lawn than you have of putting a hook in Charlie's mouth."

"No statute of limitations on murder, Vin. That file could remain open for a lot of years."

"Better not hold my breath, then, eh?"

Bulstrode's sudden grin made him boyish in the sunlight.

"There are other fish to net. Like this man Sadler and the Harolds."

"Who?" said Vinnie.

"Damn, but you're predictable. Been around you too long, I guess."

"That mean you won't stay for tea?"

Bulstrode put his cigarettes away and shook grass clippings from his coat. Stood and brushed off his trousers, and watched Vinnie flick his cigarette butt at a nearby chestnut.

"Give me a straight answer for once, Vinnie."

"Maybe."

Vinnie shaded his eyes against glare.

"How is it that Charlie earns such loyalty? You know and I know he's killed a good half dozen the hard way. Yet he still holds Archie up like he's still worth something, and I'll bet he never forgets flowers on Queenie's birthday. He's smarter than the Harolds and rottener than the Troys, and yet you all look up to him. An immoral, murdering bastard like him. For Christ's sake, why?"

Vinnie watched his butt smolder on a root.

"Who else is there?" he said quietly.

Dotty and Ingrid chattered as Wally drove Naomi's Mercedes west towards Zeerust, his face set in a rare sulk.

Bloody women. Say one thing. Do another.

Heat melted the straight brown road into upfalls of dun, and liquid snakes of shimmer layered the lower sky with false horizons. The veld was a winter-yellow sprawl of biscuit and saffron, distant acacias danced in the soft and molten air, and Wally dozed at the wheel with nothing to look at but noonday glare.

"Must be love, the way he's not listening," said Dotty.

"Why wouldn't Naomi come?" Ingrid asked a second time.

Wally caught her eye in the rearview mirror.

"She's a woman, ain't she?"

Ingrid played with her white picture hat.

"Well, it isn't every day you get invited to watch a film being made, and I'm sure she wanted to meet all those stars."

Wally checked the road map against the highway.

"Business, she said. All-fired keen last night. And this bloody morning . . ." He shrugged. "Women."

Dotty bit into a chicken sandwich.

"Haven't *you* got it bad? No, Wally, love, it's me she doesn't like, not you."

"Nonsense," said Ingrid.

"Stupid." Wally swigged chilled beer from a bottle.

Dotty's laugh was a fall of tinkling water.

"Come on, you two. I'm jam jars and she's chandeliers. My old mother scrubbed floors for the likes of her and was glad of the work. Class is class is class, and I ain't got it. I got Pim instead."

"No argument there. You'll have Pim going straight next."

"And why not? Pim could if he wanted. So could Wally. Both of them are halfway there without knowing it. And Charlie's almost a gentleman, Ing. We could all live the good life over here. I may be stupid, but I can see that."

"It was De Wit who talked her out of coming," Wally said suddenly.

"What?"

"De Wit. Naomi goes stiff when he's around. I'd like to know what makes him tick. He's got Naomi and Alicia jumping through hoops. Question is: why?"

"I like him. Even if he is a copper."

"You like everybody, Dot."

Dotty brushed crumbs from her mouth.

"I was born loving everyone. Naomi, too. Maybe being too loving made me a naughty girl all those years."

"Until Pim." Ingrid smiled.

"Until Pim. Yeah."

"How can anybody like De Wit? Or that creeping bastard Spring?"

"Ignore him, Dotty. He's cross because Naomi couldn't come. Don't let his sulks spoil our weekend."

"You're right, Ing. We're lucky to have the men we do. And Wally could do worse than get his feet under Naomi's table. You may frown, Wally Harold, but she thinks the sun shines out of your navel."

"You're right," said Wally.

"I am?"

"Yeah, you are stupid."

Then they were all laughing with Wally trying not to snort beer down his nose as he kept the car straight. There was an odd metallic clunk and the wheel went dead under his hands. The pedals were just pedals under his pumping feet as the car veered and slewed from side to side.

"Can't hold her."

The Mercedes swung right to chop through scrub.

Carved a furrow through a bank of red earth.

Wally yelled, "Hang on," and hit his head on the dash.

The Mercedes crested a rise in free fall. Hung suspended, tipped left, skimmed an outcrop of rock, and sailed on and down. A big grey baobab came up into the bonnet and crumpled it. The windscreen became flying crystal shards, and a gull-wing door opened to throw Wally clear. He thought he saw Ingrid fall away on the other side before he was in red dust with flailing limbs.

Monkey fruit rattled out of the baobab branches and bounced down the incline ahead of the falling car.

Wally heard metal scream like a woman. Stone teeth tore through his clothes and skinned his face. Thorn lashed up like a tangled bed of nails and he was caught up, head down over a long scar in the earth.

Winded and helpless, he heard the final grind of impact before a great brawl of high octane hurled fragments of bodywork into the air. Flame came on a wave of heat, seared the scrub and rock, and the thorn bush that trapped him came alight like an untidy torch.

Wally threw himself outwards and watched himself fall a long way onto his face and shoulders, continuing his long plunge into the dark of unconsciousness.

* * *

Wally came back to crawling in dusk and the smell of scorched earth. One arm was just hanging, and there was a lot of pain in his torn shoulder. He lay and thought about that for a long time before he got sensible enough to use what was left of his shirt to tie off his arm and pad out his broken collarbone. When he saw his blistered hands, they began to hurt, too, and he stopped himself thinking about his face. There was a faint and persistent voice that answered when he called, and he began to crawl towards it.

The gully took a long time to scale, and when he did roll up over the edge he found the shell of the Mercedes in a blackened patch of burned scrub. He stumbled over a burst suitcase and saw what was left of Dotty lying in the back seat on naked springs with its hair and dress gone. The tip of one shoe remained green. The rest was just bone and charcoal.

Wally took the time to be sick and listened for the voice again. Tried to call out and couldn't. Sucked on a stone to bring moisture into his mouth and called Ingrid, hoping the voice hadn't just been inside his head with all the other confusion.

There was darkness now and he had to listen hard.

The voice was low, conversational, and came from the darkness of a deep kloof. Stones rattled when Wally got too near the rim.

"Ing . . . rid?"

Was that me? Pathetic. Try again.

"Ingrid?"

Stronger. Better.

"Don't come any closer."

"I'll climb down. . . ."

"No, Wally. I'm too . . . deep. And the sides keep falling in. I can see the stars and they're a comfort. Go for help."

Help? Where?

"I can't just leave you."

"Yes, you can. And you must. I'll wait here."

"How bad is . . . are you hurt?"

"I can't feel anything, but I can move my head. Go along now, please. Go along. . . ."

"I'll hurry. . . . Swear . . ."

"Take care, my dear."

Wally could find no words. His eyes leaked and salt stung his burned cheeks. He shambled away and stumbled out onto the empty highway to listen for traffic. He thought he heard something in the distance, but from which direction it may have come defeated him. There were no lights. No houses. Just him and the brown road and the sky and the veld.

Wally knew there was nothing the way they had come. Thought he remembered something marked on the road map somewhere up ahead. Began jogging towards the brightest star in the heavens. Stumbled through the Lord's Prayer, missing some of the lines. Tried to remember them to occupy his mind. To blank out the black bones and one green shoe that had been Pim's wife.

"Hallowed be . . . Thy Name. . . ." he chanted as he jogged doggedly on. Knew the Mercedes hadn't gone off the road by itself. Wondered who would want Dotty dead. Somebody getting at Pim through her? Somebody who wanted himself dead to get at Connie?

Keep jogging. Keep jogging.

Or De Wit wanting Naomi out of the way? No, something else. Something other. Just keep jogging, son. Don't fall.

Ingrid? Ingrid to get at Charlie Dance?

Wally almost fell. Saved his face with his one good arm as he scraped more skin from his blistered knees. Rose and kept going as all the stars in the universe wheeled overhead.

Somebody with a long arm reached at and fixed that car.

Wally saw Sadler and Spring with their heads together as they padded along beside him. Thought he heard a car and the wash of heads behind him. Saw Charlie Dance in the shadows with no emotion in his face as a phone told him Ingrid was dead. Saw Charlie come after them all without hurry. All for the sake of the girl lying in a gully with a broken back and only poor Wally to get her out.

Stay alive, girl. I'm running. See?

When Wally's footsteps died away, Ingrid listened to the sides of the kloof crumble in slow dribbles of dust and shale. Kept her eyes on the stars so far above her, wanting to touch them if she could only raise her hand. She could move nothing but her eyes, so she lay quietly with her panic while the small predators gathered and a hyena called his mate from a high kopje.

Come back for me, Wally.

Please?

Mercifully, nerve damage prevented her feeling the first rat begin to feed on her foot.

CHAPTER 10

THE NIGHT SKY HAD PRESSED HIM DOWN AGAINST THE HIGHway too many times, but he had to go on with the blackened thing that had been Pim's wife padding alongside, haunting his conscience. Ingrid kept telling him to take care very quietly, and Wally wished her voice would go away. Begged her to wait as he reared towards the brightest star in a tangle of bedsheets.

A dark kloof split the brown road and became Naomi's cleavage in a dim bedroom as she laid a cold towel on his blazing forehead and hushed him with her soothing voice.

"You didn't come with us, Naomi. You should have . . ."

Wally shook sweat from his face and tousled hair.

"But then you'd have been burned with them. The girls. The girls. Have they found the girls?"

"Long ago. Hush, it's only a bad dream."

"How long ago? When?"

"A week ago. But you knew that, and you will again. Just a lapse of memory. You were in the hospital then. It'll all come back to you."

Hospital?

"Gotta phone Pim, tell him . . ."

"He knows, my dear."

"And Charlie Dance. Explain to Charlie how it was . . ."

"Conrad took care of that when we were in London. I told you about London. I came back yesterday, Conrad's coming today. Any moment now."

"Connie told Charlie? Told Pim?"

"Yes, my dear."

Wally's mind slowly cleared and the burned thing no longer lingered in the shadows.

"You shaved me this morning. Said my face was knitting nicely."

"It is, my love."

Charlie would not go away, was a dark shadow behind Naomi. Wally pawed the air to bring him closer to explain something. But the shadow had not listened before. Would never listen.

"But they do know? They really know the girls are . . ."

"They know."

"And they are, right? They bloody are . . ."

"Yes. The funeral's tomorrow in Kensal Green."

A car door slammed. Steps hurried towards the house.

Wally shrank against the sopping pillows with haunted eyes.

"Charlie?" he whispered.

"No, my dear. Conrad."

"Don't let Charlie in, love. Don't let him in."

"Colonel De Wit's downstairs. You're quite safe."

"Hold me, Naomi. For Chrissakes, just hold me."

And Naomi did as Connie and De Wit locked horns in her living room.

Connie told Harry the Crack and Sailor Mailer to stay in the car, and swallowed a benny to keep himself going as he went up the path to Naomi's house. The return flight had been savaged by storms, and bolt lightning had run the length of the aircraft. Sleep had been a stranger for four days now, and Connie wondered if he would ever close his eyes again.

Another day, another benny, he told himself wryly, wondering how long he could keep going like this. *Just to make love to Alicia before sleeping the clock round. Some chance.*

The houseboy led Connie into a long cream and chocolate living room, where hunting trophies stared down with bright glass eyes. De Wit made Connie a long Tom Collins, his long face somber.

"I hear you're fond of these."

"You hear a lot of things."

Connie rubbed gritty eyes, and his voice sharpened as the alcohol hit home with the Benzedrine.

"Wally first, then we talk about London."

"As you wish."

De Wit jerked his glass at the ceiling.

"Your brother was extremely lucky; that's bad country up there. Just the other month the local Kaffirs burned a man and woman to death for practicing witchcraft. Said the woman had made their children sick and the man had sent lightning to kill their cattle. They'll hang of course; we have to chastise them for the dangerous and savage *skepsels* they are. Your blacks don't do that in the Old Kent Road yet, eh?"

"Not often, no."

We don't have cows trotting down the high street at home. Beef hangs in butcher's shops and milk comes in bottles, you ignorant Dutch prick.

"I had your brother brought back by helicopter and thought it best he recuperate here rather than in hospital. One of our medical staff comes in every day. Walter's strong, and he'll mend quickly. Naomi, broth, and kindness should see to that."

Connie ghosted a smile.

"He's too dumb to die."

But you're covering something up here, Colonel. Something happened out there in Zeerust you need to keep a secret, and keeping Wally here and out of sight is only part of it.

"Let me freshen your drink."

"This one's melting nicely, thanks. I think I'll look in on my baby brother and get some sleep. We'll talk tomorrow."

"Your brother can wait; the talking can't. He's sedated,

and better a woman's breast than yours, eh? Dirk's gone up to Meir for a few days, so you have your own breast waiting for you in Melrose."

Connie said, "Stop talking and say something."

De Wit's harsh Afrikaans accent cut softly.

"Alicia can wait too. In her house surrounded by the English antiques you bought her. I approve of my goddaughter having the best money can buy and, given time, I may approve of your liaison with her. I don't readily give up what is rightly mine, Conrad."

"Nor do I, mister."

"Clive Spring is very valuable to me."

"What's that got to do with me and Alicia?"

"Nothing. Directly. But he has been overly zealous."

"Like talking poetry and using that bloody camera of his? The one that points one way and takes a picture somewhere else? All he's ever done around me is drink too much and boast how he's a friend to the blacks when it suits him. Don't take a big brain to work out what he's doing for you. All them house arrests and detentions without trial he says he's brought about? None of it rates with me, and I don't give a damn what he gets up to."

"You should, Conrad. It was Clive Spring who introduced Dirk Jorgesson to Malcolm Sadler, and had Sadler contact you and the Troys to finance his mining interests. And with my blessing. It was unfortunate that Dirk fell in with Victor Dakin and lost so heavily at the gaming tables, because that brought a man called Charles Dance into the picture."

Connie sat heavily with suspicion reddening his earlobes. He crossed a leg and listened hard with breath whistling in his nostrils.

De Wit stood at the unlit fireplace between long elephant tusks and made the ice in his drink tinkle as he turned the glass with a casual wrist.

"Sadler has made several errors in judgment since then, only matched by your own spectacular stupidity over certain matters."

Connie felt his heart trip and wondered where all this was going.

"I blame myself," De Wit said. "I do not like to deal with Jews, and that clouded my judgment. It was for that reason I refused to deal with this man Ogle. But I knew nothing of this man of his, this Charles Dance. Dance has caused me to revise my plans quite drastically. Cut away a lot of dead wood."

"You including me in your pruning?" Connie asked.

"Not as yet, Conrad. But Sadler *has* become an . . . embarrassment?"

"I dumped Sadler."

"You should have liquidated him."

Connie stared with nothing to say, and the start of a migraine colored his peripheral vision. De Wit could have been lecturing boy soldiers in front of a blackboard.

"You're a petty criminal with delusions of grandeur, Conrad. Your mines and Alicia are lost to you if you aren't of use to me. Recognize that. Also recognize the fact that what I am about to tell you stays between us. You can only listen and do nothing, however much you would like to do something."

Connie ground his teeth. Nodded with marbled eyes.

"Your word, Conrad."

"Okay, for Chrissakes."

"Sadler was ordered not to make himself visible to Ogle. He chose to ignore that advice, that directive. The result was Dance bought and sold Jorgesson like a piece of prime meat. He was also instrumental in bringing the mail train money here to boost your flagging finances, something you could not have achieved yourself. And Sadler, in his infinite stupidity, thought to hit back at Dance for his own warped and selfish reasons. Ergo the car smash, which brings us back to Clive Spring."

"That Welsh offal?"

Connie was standing on shaking legs, his face suffused with rage and hypertension. The glass shattered in his hand, and blood ran down his cuff.

"Yes, Conrad. Spring thought to be of service to Sadler. It was he who effected your brother's accident."

Effected? Connie thought. *What kind of language is that?*

Wally with a smashed face and second-degree burns. Dotty burned to a crisp, and Ingrid dead. . . .

"And you let it happen?" Connie choked. Seeing De Wit through washes of scarlet and crimson.

"I neither condoned it nor was a party to it. You have to see the total picture, Conrad. I needed and *need* a network of agents in London, and who better than men outside the law like yourself? Men who lie, cheat, and steal, and kill for their own ends. Men who will do anything for a profit. In one way you chose yourself, didn't you?"

The truth of that raced through Connie's mind. To revenge himself on Spring would cost him everything he had so far achieved. And with the train robbery money confiscated, there could be no going back to London. He'd be a target for the rest of his life. There had to be a way of pulling his chestnuts from the fire. But how? Connie looked at De Wit for the answer.

De Wit handed him a bar towel to staunch the blood.

"You will continue to work with Spring as I direct, and no harm must come to him, agreed?"

Connie picked glass from his wrist. Wrapped his hand in the towel and nodded.

"Agreed."

"You'll burgle those London offices when you return."

"I've already emptied one. The stuff should arrive next week. And I've put feelers out on the armaments. Hamburg says, 'No problem.' "

"Then, your problems are solved. You can proceed with your mining operation as planned so long as Spring continues to function without fear of reprisals from you."

"I ain't the one you have to worry about, Colonel."

Connie remembered how Charlie Dance had looked when he was told of Ingrid's death. How he had looked from Harry to Sailor and back to Connie himself, eyes like wet slate as he asked oblique questions without emotion or inflection.

"A last drink before you go to Alicia?" said De Wit.

"Why not?"

Charlie would come without doubt. And earn himself a

six-foot hole in the veld if I let Harry and Sailor off the leash. Hmmm. That needed thinking about. But first, a night with Alicia.

The drizzle drizzled and Kensal Green cemetery was a huddle of old memorials and headstones and dripping trees. The man by the railings wore a black armband and did not look at the woman who came along the pavement to share his umbrella. She listened to the reedy voice reading the burial service before saying, "Rather rare, wouldn't you say?"

"It's just a funeral, lady."

"A double funeral I meant."

"Two women. They were friends."

"Close friends?"

"They would have thought so, but they're closer now. That's forever out there, lady."

The woman's veil blew in against a wayward nose.

"Yes," she said. "I rather think it is."

The man said nothing with a closed face.

"You knew them?"

"Yes."

"Well?"

"One of them. But what man knows any woman well?"

"Some have . . . instincts."

A man in black stepped from the distant umbrellas to sprinkle earth to the sound of the carrying pulpit voice.

"Does that man have . . . instincts?"

"Pim? Yeah, but his wife died instantly, they say."

"And your friend?"

"It was different for her. She was blown clear of the car and went down into a deep gully. Her back was broken in the fall but she lingered for a couple of days. By then the rats and white ants had got at her. Both coffins came home marked 'Unviewable.' D'you carry cigarettes?"

"Sorry, no."

"'Unviewable.' That was hard to take. Until I learned to remember her the way she was . . . before."

"A small comfort, but a comfort all the same."

"Some. But not enough."

"You aren't going inside?"

"I don't go to funerals."

"No other car was involved? In the accident, I mean?"

"No other car. Nobody for miles."

"No, that fits. Loss of steering, no brakes. An impact explosion. The middle of uninhabited bush, survival prospects zero. Yes, that's how it must have been. Lonely and very, very terrible for her."

"Are you clairvoyant?"

The man's question was flat. Disinterested.

"Not I. And I'm a complete fool about machinery. I only know what my husband told me. And he only knows what Mr. Spring told him over the telephone. That kind of accident is rare, Mr. Spring said. Rare, but always . . . fatal."

"Sounds like your Mr. Spring was there."

"My *husband's* Mr. Spring."

"Still sounds like he was there."

"Doesn't it, though? He could have been following in another car. To make certain, you know?"

"He could have."

"Was she very beautiful?"

"I . . . thought so."

Drizzle followed a knot of mourners away to the chapel and the waiting limousines. Pimlico stayed where he was, his face wet from more than rain. His coat shone as the sun came from behind cloud to glisten in the droplets on the dark material.

"He'll need a friend," said the woman.

"He's got one."

The man held a railing with white knuckles.

"You?"

The man nodded. Unable to speak.

"I'm grateful you allowed a stranger to share this sad moment with you. Thank you."

The man let his hand rise and fall, making a fist.

"Stopped raining."

He folded his umbrella and shook droplets over the sodden verge.

The woman almost touched his arm before stepping back.

"I have to go. I'm seeing my solicitor, Mr. Thrupp of Lincoln's Inn, at four to finalize things. Leaving the country is such a wrench and, with the servants gone, packing is such a burden for a spoiled bitch like me. Just the two of us rattling around in that huge house for two whole weeks. You do understand?"

"Empty houses are all dark corners."

"Au revoir, then."

"Thanks . . . for dropping by."

"If only things had been . . . different."

"Carry cigarettes next time."

"Next time, Charlie?"

"Goodbye, Margot."

Vic Dakin sat on the veranda in a rattan peacock chair, his feet up on a cane stool, enjoying the cool morning air.

Rain had washed the foothills of haze, and the trees on the distant rim above the Yan Oya river were as clearly cut as Lotte Reininger stencils against an ocean of lapis lazuli sky. A single boa of cloud feathered out from the Buddhist temple on the high western tor, the thinning outer strands marzipanned by brazen sunlight. In the shadowed basin, still heavily dewed by a brisk downfall of seasonal rain, teapickers walked the long rows of *Thea sinensis,* bowing under their woven baskets, quick brown hands pecking out at the ripest plants.

The old woman who came with the rented bungalow brought tea and honey cakes on a tray and went away soundlessly, just another shadow in the heavily carved teak building. Stone elephants guarded the steps of the veranda and a tame mongoose hunted the crevices for snakes, one eye on Dakin's robe pocket, where a fresh chicken's egg might be hidden. The mongoose showed his grey-white belly to the sun and washed his whiskers with hard swipes of his front paws, clucking and sneezing with pleasure.

Dakin sipped dark mashed tea and let honey cake melt on his tongue, cleansing his palate of last night's cigars.

The man on the bicycle would soon join him to drink endless glasses of tea and occasional Manhattans, and polish his rusty English while Dakin added to his Sinhalese vocabulary; each man only too anxious to fill his time with subjects other than crops, weather, and local politics.

Dakin was lonely in exile, and Dr. Ashram Jhanna was his only worthwhile companion.

True, Dakin enjoyed the nocturnal services of a young local girl, but she had no conversation in any language. Once she had bedded "M. Tournier" she was off back to her grandmother's house before the sun rose, her rupees tied in a red handkerchief, too wise to let the village gossips see her leave the fat foreigner's house.

Even the rich silks Dakin had brought her from Colombo had been resold to put food on her grandmother's table for her hordes of brothers, sisters, and cousins, and although she gymnastically strove to earn her money under the whirling bedroom fan, she made no attempt to show Dakin any fondness. She wanted dowry enough to attract a certain estate-worker's younger son, not become permanent consort to an old foreigner who smelled like a wet elephant and tore holes in the night with his thudding snores.

Dakin mourned cynically.

After almost five months in Ceylon, I have a mongoose and Dr. Ashram Jhanna (Retired) as friends.

Dakin no longer saw the *carte postale* view.

The heat jaded him, fear of reptiles kept him from walking the lush grounds, and sex without warm lies was as dull as combing dandruff from a thinning fringe.

Dakin whistled and held out the egg. Listened for Jhanna's squeaking bicycle.

The mongoose came in a short dash. Flowed to a halt with a bobbing head and erect whiskers. Nuzzled the egg and Dakin's plump knuckles, "chitting" with mock anger at the oval "enemy."

"Chit yourself."

Dakin watched the animal roll on his back and lay the egg on the upturned belly. A natural juggler, the mongoose kicked the egg into the air and rolled to catch it between his shoulder blades. Caught it a moment before it hit the polished stone floor. Curled into a ball and bit a hole in the shell to lap the albumin, saving the yolk until last.

Dakin wagged a finger.

"Connie, you're a predator. Just like your namesake."

A car exhaust exploded on the river road as it took a run at the steep gradient to the crest where Dakin sat. A familiar sound signature. The unmistakable sound of Probaka's pre-war bull-nosed Morris.

Probaka delivered mail and newspapers once a week, and shopped in the township when Dakin was too idle to make the tedious journey in the imported Renault he could not get serviced, even though the French attaché in Colombo had done his level best to be helpful. Bringing automobile parts that were not Empire- or British-made into the colony was frowned upon. The staff at the British High Commission had been quite snotty with the plump and balding "Frenchman," as were the tea company officials Dakin had tried to court socially. The wives were the worst. They called him "The Frog" behind his back and thought it to his face, alienating him further from the small and smaller-minded European community.

Even when Ceylon follows Mother India down the road to independence, the tea companies' economic stranglehold will prevail. The British will still rule the island by pursestring. It might just as well be 1864 for the average native, instead of a full century later.

Is this me talking? Dakin wondered.

When have I ever cared for the have-nots in the world? Ingrid and her dead mother wouldn't know me. I'm not sure I recognize myself anymore.

The old Morris stalled outside the bungalow as it usually did, and Dakin heard Probaka kick the offside wing.

"As usual, eh, Connie?"

The mongoose listened with his head cocked.

Probaka loped down the path between butea trees. Called greetings and blessings to enlarge his gratuity. The mongoose took his egg off into a corner. Probaka did not only kick cars.

Dakin stood when he saw the Europeans follow the Hindu delivery man down the path just as the Tamil doctor wheeled his ancient Raleigh bicycle through the gate. Dakin cuffed the wind chime for fresh tea.

Probaka slyly watched Dakin study the men behind him.

Saw him pale under his deep tan and thought he might witness fine gossip in the making.

"I bring you more saabs, Saab. I bring them in my most wonderful very British motor car."

"For which I thank you," Dakin said in dialect.

A languid blond man in white strolled beside a short fussy man with large ears and a crumpled face, a heavy brass-bound briefcase cradled in his arms. Dakin knew the man in white was "something" in the District Commissioner's office, and he had last seen J. C. Hatton when Quill's squad had raided the Windmill Street office and Connie had taken Dakin and Jorgesson back to South London, where he had fed voltage up into Dakin's . . .

Dakin pinched a sweating brow. Paid Probaka for the newspapers, invited Jhanna to lean his bicycle in the usual place, and waved the two Englishmen into chairs.

Is my exile ended? he wondered.

Probaka took his money away to gossip over a glass of *char* with the old woman in the kitchen, and Jhanna took the mongoose onto his lap to play with his silver beard.

Holmes, the Englishman in white, said it was a sticky old day and one never really acclimated, did one? He dabbed at a receding chin with a spotless handkerchief, and Hatton just looked jaded.

Fine rain sped in with the tea, hammered the garden with brief energy, and stopped, leaving the earth to steam as it dried.

Dakin crossed a hot thigh under his robe and sipped fresh mint tea.

"It's very good of you to come all this way to be sociable," he said.

Holmes squirmed.

"Ah, not quite that, I'm afraid."

"If the heat bothers you, perhaps you should have stayed in Surrey, or wherever it was you were born."

"Surrey?" Holmes said.

Jhanna adopted his music hall English.

"Surrey has jolly fine cricket team, jolly very good. But I'm having to be warning you, this very moment and now, India has jolly splendid Test side this year."

The mongoose nudged the cake on Jhanna's plate, smearing the willow pattern with yolk.

"These men will not talk cricket, my friend," Dakin said in rapid Tamil. "Not with you, and most certainly *not* with a Frenchman."

Jhanna wiped crumbs from a troubled mouth.

"They are bad tidings for you?" he said in the same tongue.

Dakin inclined his head.

"Damned if you don't speak the lingo," said Holmes.

Jhanna ignored Holmes.

"Surrey is a rotten side this year anyway. Kent is the better team. If I may excuse myself, my friend, I will walk in your garden until they have gone."

"It is they who should be excused, Ashram. We will talk just as soon as they have gone back to their safe unheathen compound, where we can't taint them with our un-Christian ways."

Jhanna raised a long index finger.

"Take care, Victor, you are turning native."

Holmes made a feeble effort at politeness.

"Don't let us drive you away, old chap. . . ."

Jhanna walked from the veranda with a stiff back.

"We will talk Pali, the sacred language of Buddha. To cleanse your house."

He clucked, and the mongoose followed him into the trees.

Holmes shifted a buttock in a creak of rattan.

"Sorry to have offended the old boy. They are damned touchy, though."

Dakin shrugged and smiled to himself.

"His culture was old when your semi-illustrious forebears searched each other for lice and painted themselves woad blue. He also has a First from Edinburgh University and professed in Bombay for ten years. Not bad for a native, and a bloody sight better than your scraped Third from St. Andrews, Holmes, *old* boy."

Holmes colored.

"But it is best he's gone. And do remember I could have

had you brought down to the Hill Station under escort had I chosen. Made all this very official."

"Decent that you didn't," Dakin mocked.

"It's *you* who has the spot of bother, not I."

"Ah," said Dakin, swearing mentally.

Here it comes, Vic. The hard frighteners in a velvet glove.

Holmes mopped the bridge of his nose.

"Truth is, there's something anomalous about your papers, entry visa, and so on. Even your nationality is in question. And you've caused a bit of a stir amongst the bureaucrats down at the capital. And back in England. All beyond me of course, but they have sent a pretty stiff directive, and it's filtered down to me."

"Ah," Dakin teased again.

"They haven't quite declared you *persona non grata."*

"Yet." Dakin needed a drink very badly.

Holmes agreed with a nod.

"Not quite yet. It's the paperwork, you see. Takes time."

"And I can always appeal."

"Well, you *could."*

"Or take refuge in the French embassy."

"Not that, you can't. Not actually an embassy, old man. And the French aren't *that* keen to take you in. Interpol and all that rot."

Hatton ran a finger round his collar. Cleared his throat and said, "My legal advice to you is to cooperate. In the fullest sense of the word."

Dakin chimed for drinks.

"So Archie's parrot *does* speak. How did you fix this one, J.C.? Interpol *and* the High Commissioner jumping through hoops? You must have greased half the palms in the western hemisphere, you crafty old tosspot of a cheap shyster."

Listen to yourself, Vic. Making noises like some twopenny villain straight off the London cobbles. Holmes looks like he's been shafted by a red-hot poker. Got a face like a boiled baby.

Holmes dabbed at his sweating nose.

"Interpol, yes. Seems they want you back in London rather badly. Scotland Yard were ready to send some policemen, but Mr. Hatton came instead. And the D.C.

thought you'd do the decent thing. Keep it all rather low-key, seeing how things are. . . ."

"The way things are? How would a toffee-nosed little pipsqueak like you know how things are, Holmes? Speak English we can all understand."

Holmes dusted a thigh with his damp handkerchief.

"Very well. You go back to London at the first opportunity."

Dakin slammed the wind chime into dance. The old woman came out of nowhere, and Dakin asked what everybody was having. Holmes wanted a whiskey drowned in soda, and Hatton said he would suffer a small sherry. When they were served, the old woman went back to Probaka and their musical voices drifted on the warm morning air.

Dakin drank deeply to feel the fire of good brandy in his fluttering belly.

"Money buys choice, Holmes. How much do you earn a year? A thousand? Two? I'll treble that in cash if you take that wizened old bastard out of my house."

"Ah, the bribe, The D.C. rather thought you'd try a backhander. But even an *Oxford* Third has *some* backbone. The answer is no, Dakin or Tournier or whatever your real name is, and no apology."

Dakin gulped his drink and padded across for a tall refill. Pleased he poured it without a tremor. Fear knifed the fatty tissue around his heart, biting like colic. The lush garden was a brilliant checkerboard of green through the teak lattices.

"What has London got, J.C.?"

"Milan, New York, Valletta, and Rome," Hatton said through slatted light.

"Rome?" Sweat prickled Dakin's spine.

"The Old Masters fraud that ties you to the Troys."

"And New York?"

"The airline ticket frauds."

"I won't go down alone, J.C."

Hatton scratched his upper lip.

"Events have rather overtaken you there, Victor. Scotland

Yard already has the Troys for murder; they need you to sew up the pieces relating to your involvement with Connie Harold."

"Leaving Ogle and Dance out, I suppose?"

"Do I know those gentlemen?"

Hatton helped himself to another sherry, and Holmes denied himself a second Scotch.

"You have five days to put your affairs in order, Dakin. I shall have to leave a couple of my uniformed chaps with you, of course, for form's sake. They'll be discreet and a bit vague if asked why. Best for you, best for the colony."

Dakin felt giddy. Blamed the brandy.

Holmes dusted his other leg.

"I'll just go and sweeten up old Jhanna. You and Mr. Hatton will want a quiet word alone, I shouldn't wonder."

"Don't bank on it," Dakin snapped, watching Holmes make his way through dappled shade.

Hatton polished his glasses and patted Dakin's hand. An uncharacteristic gesture.

"Five days should be enough time for you to salt your money away, Vic. All you have to do is turn Queen's Evidence and blame everything on Connie. You'll survive; you always have."

"I'd be dead before I reached the dock."

"I can guarantee you won't."

"Backed by whose word?"

"Archie's, Charlie's, and the Home Secretary's."

"Sounds an unholy trinity, J.C. So that's how you found me."

Hatton patted Dakin's hand again.

"We've had tabs on you since you ducked out of Mitre Street and took a plane from Heathrow. You came here via Brussels and Karachi. We could have given you to Connie anytime, but we chose not to."

"Why?" Dakin scrubbed sticky eyes.

"Because of Ingrid. More so now she's dead."

Dakin thought his ears lied, until Hatton nodded solemnly and sketched in the circumstances, misting Dakin's eyes with tears he never knew he had.

"Connie did it. I know he did."

"And you're the only one who can get back at him, Victor."

Dakin made fists for the first time in his life and felt them pulse and swell with anger.

"We'll get him. Promise we'll nail him to the cross, J. C. Ingrid's memory's worth doing five years for, eh? With remission I can do that on my head."

"Charlie thinks so."

"He should have dealt with me from the start."

Hatton just smiled.

Dakin sighed.

"I guess not. Five years of trotting up the interest Connie's money is earning me should make the time pass pleasantly enough."

When Probaka's Morris rattled back along the river road, Jhanna came back to find Dakin weeping with quiet desperation.

"They left policemen. That is bad."

Dakin sobbed laughter.

"Not so bad with the Troys tucked up for murder."

"Tucked up? In bed?"

Jhanna flinched when Dakin embraced him, completely bemused.

CHAPTER 11

THE CHINAMAN IN THE SHINY SUIT TOOK HIMSELF DOWN OLD Compton Street past the phony Post Office van, turned into Eyetie Antoni's delicatessen, and waited for two elderly women to terminate a squabble over the price of mozzarella. When they had wound down into sullen and breathless silence, he bowed, smiled with gold and porcelain teeth, and presented a card bearing his name under the red imprint of his family's *chop.*

"I Fook," he said.

"That's why there's so many of you." Eyetie's maternal aunt took the card through to the back parlor with a show of bad grace.

Fook's eyes glittered at the insult and decided her extreme age was reason enough not to kill her with the edge of his hand. Although a beating with bamboo wands, especially on the soles of her unbound feet, would sweeten her disposition. Masculine shouts sent the aunt scurrying back into the shop, and she was servile when she ushered Fook down the dark passage. He liked that. It proved he was talking to the right people.

Eyetie set his Guinness aside to shake hands and bow and

wave Aman Lee Fook to a seat opposite Archie Ogle. Archie snapped fingers at Fast Frankie Frewin, who served Fook with a properly iced club soda. Archie had schooled Frankie in the art of keeping "face" with his old friend from Hong Kong with, "Chinks are big on manners, Frankie. The more 'face' a man has in a Tong, the worse he dresses and the quieter he is, and the more respect he expects and receives. Modesty goes with power, Frankie, so dress sober."

Frankie found a corner to stand in. Thought: *I'll take my old mother's advice. Keep my mouth closed and let them think I'm stupid rather than opening it and proving it. Archie may be old and smart, but he shouldn't have kept this meeting secret from Charlie. Chas may have smoke in his eyes over losing Ingrid, but that don't mean he's gone soft or addled in the head. If anything, he's harder. You could cut diamonds on his eyes. Him and this hard little Chinaman have the same look.*

Frankie pretended to doze. Listened hard.

The opening pleasantries over, Archie talked opiates with Fook and Eyetie, described a courier network between New York, London, and Amsterdam in such detail Frankie was more than ever convinced Archie had not been idle beside his swimming pool all those months in Malta. And from what Fook said, it was clear he and Archie had met in Valletta and Hong Kong and traveled to Pakistan more than once.

Heroin from the Chinese mainland would come to London in shipments of edible seaweed, ginseng, or frozen racehorse sperm. Eyetie's New York cousins had the East River ports squared through the dock unions, and one of Fook's factories was busily producing hollow madonnas for the first shipment to the New Jersey chapter. There were some problems supplying the West Coast through Baja California from bases farther south in Lima and Buenos Aires, and Fook suspected the interference came from none of the usual government agencies. Archie agreed caution was necessary when they investigated who was blocking them, but his slow voice was confident as he leaned on his heavy cane and held Fook's eyes with a smile.

Frankie was dizzy from all the geography, but he could not fail to see Archie was in top form and planned to present the whole deal to Charlie as a *fait accompli* when he was good and ready.

Frankie thought out his reservations. *Archie's back in the saddle, and looks like he expects Charlie to melt into the background with a mouthful of "yesses" when Archie snaps his fingers. And how long would Charlie swallow all that crow? Ten minutes or ten Christmases? And how will Charlie react to a second stringer like Eyetie acting as a gopher between this Fook character and the powerful New York chapter?*

Frankie thought of blood on the moon and almost missed the profit projection Fook made for the first trading year in his quiet musical voice.

Eleven million plus? That's more than four mail train robberies.

Nobody could walk away from that kind of money, not even Chas. That kind of cash money turns a three-day sulk into a yahoo and a backflip. . . .

Frankie remembered to let Fook refuse a second drink as the meeting came to a close. Caught a vague look of approval from Archie as he levered himself out of his chair and offered a big brown hand to the diminutive Chinese. They bowed with their heads almost touching, exchanging elegant Cantonese as Eyetie toasted their success with a hand over their locked fists. Halfway through a second bow Archie's head snapped back as though he meant to bellow laughter at the ceiling. But his eyes had crossed and his jowls were the color of crusted port. His cane took Eyetie's stout from his hand and dashed it to the threadbare carpet, smashing the glass against the brass scuttle. Fook hissed as his hand was crushed by Archie's grip and he went down under Archie with the suffused face flopped against his thin neck. They hit the floor together and Archie made sounds like brakes binding on a steep hill before he went slack inside his clothes.

Frankie felt for a pulse in Archie's flaccid neck. Let Fook roll from beneath the still body and get to his feet without help. Tried to force a pill through the locked teeth and knew it was too late when the mouth yawned and the swolle tongue poked out at him with a last sigh of dead breath.

Eyetie raked his hair with trembling fingers.

"Say he ain't croaked, Frankie."

Frankie laid a hand on the still chest.

"I can't. He's gone."

"Well, he can't up and die. Not here."

Fook said something that could have been a farewell, an Frankie's mind went into overdrive. With no Charlie c Vinnie to call on, this was one crisis he must handle alone

"Stop whining, Eyetie. Get Froggy in here. We'll ge Archie away to Doc Rudge's in the Rolls. Move."

Eyetie had pulled his hair into spikes.

"But what about our deal? I can't give New York a 'no.' gave my word and my hand on it."

Frankie pointed at Aman Lee Fook as he diale Spitalfields.

"The Chinaman talks to Charlie, that's where your dea is, Eyetie. In Charlie's pocket."

"How can that be?" Eyetie wailed.

"Because there plain ain't nobody else."

Frankie told Rudge to hold when he answered.

"This is true?" Fook asked Eyetie.

"Yes. I mean I . . ."

"Get Froggy, Eyetie. Now," Frankie ordered.

"You will bring this Charlie here," said Fook.

Eyetie yelled for his aunt and Frankie shook his head a the Chinaman.

"He'll find *you,* mister."

"I will not be hard to find," said Fook.

"You can bank on that," said Frankie. "Hello, Doc . . ."

"An unanswered phone is unlucky, Malcolm."

"It's no longer our telephone, Margot. Let the incomin people answer it."

Sadler forced a last suitcase into the maroon Daimler or the drive outside Chartings Hall.

Margot tried not to cry.

"Not until noon. Chartings is still mine until noon. And there are seventeen minutes to go."

"My God, but you're a trial. Are we to have weeping fits all the way across the equator?"

"Shan't be a tick."

Margot hurried through the empty hallway, where Buhl cabinets and tapestries had flanked a grandmother clock with nursery rhyme characters on the face. The telephone rang from the center of the withdrawing room floor, lit by a dusty beam of sunlight. She lifted it as Malcolm slammed the trunk closed, and the growl of a removal van became a persistent dull throb as it halted in the drive.

"You're blocking me in, you dolt."

Sadler's challenge was answered by ripe and righteous cockney.

"Hello?" Margot gave her number for the last time.

"Dolt, your bleeding self. If this is Chartings Hall, we're in the right bleeding place."

"Mrs. Sadler? Alfred Thrupp here."

"But you're blocking my egress!"

"Your what, Squire?"

"My way *out,* you dunderhead."

"Mrs. Sadler? Hello . . . ?"

"Sorry, Mr. Thrupp, my husband is having a last fling in the drive."

A removal man scratched his chin at his foreman.

"Is he talking English or what?"

"I was asked to call you at this precise moment by a Mr. Dance, Mrs. Sadler."

"Who?"

Salt stung Margot's eyes, and she brushed a sleeve across her face as she turned her back on the argument outside.

"Not so much of the name-calling, Squire. We'll back her up."

"Mr. Charles Dance. He has instructed me to wish you *bon voyage* on his behalf. He did not wish to neglect your departure despite being out of the country himself."

"How very like him," said Margot, wondering if it was.

"A very personable gentleman, and I was paid very handsomely for such a pleasant task."

"Did Mr. Dance say where he had gone?"

"South Africa, or was it Malta . . . ?" Thrupp became as

vague as J. C. Hatton had instructed him, and Margot coul
almost see him frown behind misted bifocals. Heard hin
add his own best wishes and ring off a moment before th
GPO severed the service with a loud click.

"Legally, you owe me fifteen minutes."

Margot laid the dead instrument on the bare boards an
listened as the house listened back. The fireplace sighed,
scale of soot fell on the blackened hearth, and a trappe
bluebottle snarled in a pelmet. Margot brushed face powde
from her sleeve and went out into warm sunlight.

The removal van had backed into the trees, its lon
tailboard overhanging the ha-ha above the sunken tenni
court where she had once worked on her backhand volleys
The foreman leaned against the unlettered side of hi
pantechnicon and blew on his knuckles as though he ha
just bruised them against a jaw.

Malcolm used the Daimler's horn to hurry Margot along

"Really, Malcolm, you're the giddy limit. Three minute
is hardly a lifetime. . . ."

Margot slammed into the passenger seat and stared at th
man beside her. Her heart bumped to a momentary halt an
she froze with her hand on the door handle.

"But you're not Malcolm. . . ."

Sodbonce patted his dark wig and the padding around hi
waist.

"Says so on my passport, lady. Chas says I'll pass with m
mouth shut, so you do the talking at the airport, right?"

Margot massaged her right breast.

"Where is . . . Malcolm?"

"Like I said. Right here."

The foreman closed the big rear doors of the pantech-
nicon and banged on the side with, "One away to you,
mister."

Margot had seen him mourn alone at the cemetery in
Kensal Green when she shared Charlie's umbrella outside
the railings. Saw the dead look in his eyes when he nodded,
and Sodbonce took the Daimler out of the gate with a cheery
wave.

"Nice car, lady. Handles lovely."

"But this . . . isn't what I had in mind. . . ."

Margot's mind lurched as the car turned in a shower of gravel, leaning her outwards against the padded door.

"Shouldn't go to double funerals, then, should you?"

Sodbonce accelerated past hedgerows alive with finches, and the removal van trundled away towards the London Road in a spurt of blue diesel smoke. Turned a corner and was gone.

Margot felt the shakes start in her knees and wrists as the enormity of what she had done bore down on her. She thought of asking Sodbonce to turn back, to stop the removal van, to explain that it was all a mistake. Knowing she would only earn herself a short terminal ride beside her doomed husband. She watched the road ahead unwind, thinking of life and the future and the infinite possibilities suddenly opened up to her. Listened to Sodbonce explain the immediate future in cheerful and barbaric cockney.

"When we get to Buenos Aires I'll go missing. A swimming accident, I shouldn't wonder. Clothes on the beach and no body. You throw a fit and have the local coppers searching all over. Post rewards. Generally do it up brown as the grieving widow. Hang about for at least three weeks before coming home. Chas thinks you can handle it. He ain't wrong, is he, lady?"

"Is Charlie ever wrong?"

Sodbonce sucked a tooth with a lopsided grin.

"Only never. Just you relax and leave everything to Uncle Soddy. I'm easy to get along with, and I've always fancied them carnivals down in Rio. We do go through there, right?"

"We do indeed. What would have happened back there if I . . . ?"

"Chickened out? You know the answer to that. Two for the price of one. A shame, 'cause Chas has taken a real shine to you."

"He has, has he . . . Malcolm?"

"That's me now, ain't it? Yeah, he has. Next stop Rio, eh, Margot?"

"Yes, Malcolm."

Margot snuggled as the Daimler quietly ate the miles to Heathrow Airport. Thoroughly content with her lot.

* * *

The solemn blue eyes of the Mares Serenitatis an Crisium regarded Connie from the August moon riding i the dark tidal swell of the Thames below Blackfriars Bridg He had stared at the river for almost an hour, his elbows o the granite parapet, thinking things through, his thoughts a sluggish as the ebbing river waters.

Connie was exhausted physically and mentally, and to many Benzedrine tablets had strung his nerves to breakin point. Fragments of recent events, snatches of wild conve sation, of too many heated confrontations milled in hi mind. A mad patchwork of meaningless complexity furthe confused by his stubborn need to relive them over and ove again, losing himself and the overall picture in flashin jewels of irrelevant detail.

The long and wonderful night of sexuality with Alici before they breakfasted with Wally and Naomi in he sunwashed yard. Wally being fed lightly coddled egg unable to use his heavily bandaged hands or do more tha mumble through blistered lips as he stumbled down the lon brown road under the bright star. Dribbling yolk as he saic "... and all the time there was this green car behind me. heard its tires on the road long before I heard its engine .. always there . . . just out of sight . . . except for a couple o times when I hid in the bush to bring it closer . . . neve really there when I tried to look at it . . . its headlights wer just two more stars. . . ."

And Naomi brushing hair from his skinned and cruste forehead. Dabbing his mouth with a napkin. Wally's despai and the look in his bottomless eyes Connie couldn't mee with his own as Alicia traded looks with her mother an stroked Connie's thigh under the table. Arousing him de spite his guilt as his brother said, ". . . Good you weren' there with me, Naomi. There was nothing left of that side o the car after it blew. Dotty was just black and burned to nothing. . . ."

The image swirled with the river, and Wally slept througl the rest of the day without releasing Naomi's hand, unaware that Connie flew to London that night on De Wit's orders instead of putting a gun in Spring's mouth and blowing his brain over a square meter of deserted bush.

Stealing that last afternoon to bed Alicia when he should have slept, and Dirk suddenly in the bedroom still dusty from the Meir site, the excitement of his discoveries there dying as he watched them bump and grind to a shuddering climax before they became aware of him. Dirk ignoring Connie. Rounding on Alicia with accusations about her affair with De Wit. Screaming, "First the mother, then the daughter. Or did he have you both at the same time? Bloody lucky for me the man's not bisexual, or he'd climb *my* back like the bloody rock spider he is."

Dirk scattering a sample of nitrate bentonite over the bed and his wife's damp body, turning her a dusty grey. Connie jumping to restrain him before Alicia's small fist bloodied Dirk's mouth. Her finger jabbing Dirk's chest as she countered with: "You *blaas japi.* You country boy. Rolling on the ground with Kaffirs instead of white women. You can't even have an affair with dignity, yet you dare to blacken the name of a patriot? You're not fit to lick Uncle De Wit's boots."

The thunder of Alicia's Afrikaans invective coming too fast for Connie to follow as dark wet cherries from Dirk's split lip dripped on the white carpet.

"And a cockney mongrel is better?"

Alicia with fists on her hips like a man. As fiery as her mother.

"Any Xhosa goatherd with an erection is better than you. I'd rather lift my skirts for blacks than let you back into my bed. Go sleep in the garage like the *skepsel* you are. Or will you stay to watch my 'mongrel' take me here on the floor?"

Connie's laugh covering sudden Puritan shock. Pure elfin Alicia tumbled from her pedestal forever, replaced by a woman of earth and passion. Words of his dead mother popping into his mind. Almost the last thing she said on her deathbed.

"A lady in the street, a mother in the house, and a whore in the bedroom. That's the ideal wife, lovely boy. . . ."

And Dirk running into the early dusk pursued by Alicia's snarls. The long flight home and fighting jet lag as Kelly met him on the doorstep, confronting him with the letter she found in a suit she was sending to the cleaners. Alicia's frank sexual expressions in purple ink on lavender stationery. The blazing row that ended with Connie on the living room couch until Kelly walked out the following morning. The crick in his neck that still bothered Connie eighteen hours later.

He flicked a tasteless cigar over the embankment as an empty train ground across the railway bridge to terminate at Holborn Viaduct.

Breaking into the Z.A.P.U. offices in King's Cross had been a breeze. But the offices of Christian Action in Amen Corner are in a different league, and I just hope to Christ I can do better for De Wit at Amnesty International. Dirk's right, De Wit is a bloody rock spider. I can feel him on my back right now. . . . At least I've got duplicate keys to the office block backing on to Amnesty International's premises. . . .

His head pounding, Connie walked back to his Vanden Plas and didn't see Nasty Nostrils's Mini van trail him to Fetter Lane and tuck itself behind a *People* delivery truck.

Connie let himself into the deserted building and climbed to the top floor, reliving his final instructions to Harry the Crack and Sailor Mailer. Sure he had found the solution to his problems with both Charlie Dance and Dirk Jorgesson. With Dirk and Chas dead, Alicia would be his, and no more partners. . . .

Connie crossed to the back of the deserted building and opened a window high above the narrow courtyard separating the two buildings. No lights showed, and one of the windows across the way was open at the top.

Reach in with a wire coat hanger, hook the latch, and I'm in.

Connie fetched the ladder he'd found in the janitor's store and fed it out across the gap. Jammed it against the windowsill opposite and wiped off sweating hands that shook too much. He swallowed another benny and a downer to calm himself, washing them down with water from a faucet in the cloakroom. Waited for the flare of light behind his eyes before ease came in a slow flood of well-being.

Takes longer every time, he thought, short of air.

He crawled out along the ladder four stories above the ground and was across and inside the darkened offices before he knew it. Enjoyed a cigarette before going to work.

An hour later he dropped five plastic sacks of documents and photographs into the courtyard below and returned the way he had come. Tucked the ladder away and had a long swig of brandy from his hip flask. Hurried out of the building just as his euphoria became grinding fatigue. Locked up and buried the keys in a dustbin overflowing with garbage.

He was hauling the first two sacks to his car, when he walked into laughter. Late diners waiting for a taxi watched him throw what looked like rubbish into the back of his prestige car, and a woman in furs giggled.

Nasty Nostrils heard her say "The English eccentric isn't dead after all" as he lay along his driving seat with his mirror angled to see the street.

Connie slammed the trunk and dropped behind the wheel, his judgment warped by the woman and her sarcasm, the constant worry about Wally's pain, Alicia's sleek body, De Wit's all-seeing eyes and his own overwhelming exhaustion. Connie needed to take a nap and return for the rest of the sacks later, and with that in mind he drove away in search of a side street to park in.

Nasty didn't give Connie the chance. He retrieved the sacks from the alley and took them to the Windmill Street office, correctly assuming that Charlie would be more than interested in the contents, and when Connie returned to Fetter Lane he thought the sacks had been cleared by corporation dustmen.

Charlie leaned against a meat locker in Smithfield and watched Sadler drowse at twenty thousand feet as he flew towards the equator on an injection of scopolamine, still muttering after an hour of question and answer.

Sadler was in two places at once, sideslipping from one to the other without moving. Thought: *The passenger with slate eyes made me talk on and on in gathering chill. Pressurized cabins are always cold at this altitude, but why sides of beef hung in the first class aisles is as big a puzzle as the ancient steward checking my pulse and heartbeat with clouding breath that smelled of old books. He should have been retired from flying duty years before. An odd airline indeed, and Margot will have to complain since I'm too drifty to do it myself.*

Drifty, drifty . . .

Even odder was how Chartings Hall exploded with Pimlico's left hook. And being thrown on sacking in a removal van. Mewing behind a gag until a needle in the groin softened anxiety. Coming round strapped to a meat trolley for takeoff. Men packing a corpse in polythene and dry ice and laying it in a bronze casket. The one with slate eyes who might be Margot's Telephone Charlie telling an Oriental called Fook that Archie would die in Malta and be shipped back for burial when the time was ripe. Just a matter of the right documentation and a phony coffin being flown back from Hal Far.

Drifty and odd.

Sadler's eyes rolled with his mind. Realized he had told Dance and Fook how he had balked Ogle's move to bring drugs out of South America by using De Wit's expatriate Nazi contacts there. It had been pleasant airing his knowledge about the Broederbond and Clive Spring's minor role in Republican Intelligence. Amusing to explain how De Wit had recruited Conrad Harold by the use of financial coercion. Satisfying to give them details of how he had paid Spring handsomely to punish the man Dance in that clever and unusual way. . . .

"Shut the bastard the fuck up!"

Doc Rudge's hypodermic slammed Sadler into limbo just as Charlie stopped Pimlico from burying a meat hook in the drugged and garrulous face.

"Your way better be best, Chas."

Pimlico's breath streamed in the frozen air, his face as dead as the face in the casket. Knuckles whiter than his breath. Ready to kill Charlie to get at the man on the trolley who had his wife killed.

Fook watched Charlie's every move. How he was still and quiet and ready. Read every nuance of facial expression and body language like muscular prose. Assessed the cold control of the man beside Pimlico's hot madness and Doc Rudge's clinical detachment. How Charlie expected Pimlico to hand him the meat hook without a word. The outstretched hand both gentle and demanding. Finally getting its own way.

Pimlico drooping at the shoulder.

Saying, "Don't ever face me off like that again, Chas."

"I won't," the response.

Fook grunted deep in his narrow chest at the calm lie. The Buddhist in him offended by the bloody odor of the raw carcasses on their hooks, the Tong in him excited by the prospect of working with the long-nosed and round-eyed Dance. The future could be pondered with serene optimism, he thought. Confident Dance would handle himself well in South Africa, even though the odds against him were enormous. It would be a great test for the man, and in prevailing he would be all the more useful to Aman Lee Fook and the Snake Tong. Eleven million sterling was urine in the wind; his organization made that amount in a single trading day from legitimate holdings. Fook was attracted by the need to expand into other areas for the exhilaration of the new and unknown, the vicarious excitement of seeing a man ready to take revenge without the usual assassin's paranoia.

It warmed Fook's warrior blood, and he was content to leave with the others to give Charlie a last few private moments with Archie's remains.

Night had come and gone, and Sadler was aware of what was happening to him. And he could not scream or fight against what was inevitable.

Sandwiched between Charlie and Pimlico, the white Rolls Royce had whirled him through the City to the Tower of London. Walked inside, Sadler had been sat on a bench by Bell Tower as Charlie and Pimlico puzzled over a crossword and the tourists thinned away. As the evening shadows lengthened, they strolled him into the Chapel of St. Peter ad Vincula and allowed themselves to be locked in by a whistling Beefeater to await the dark of the moon.

Stood in a corner without a cigar to flavor the waiting, Sadler's drugged muscles were too relaxed to form words or cough to clear his gummy throat. Fitful moonglow splashed the painted altar with stained light and mocked his agnostic attempts to make amends, plead, or call on any deity to help him.

The Ceremony of the Keys passed with a brisk exchange of challenge and reply, the ravens slept on their perches below the White Tower, and the moon fell into the vague loom of the Thames beyond the curtain wall.

And Charlie Dance said, "It's time."

Sadler's masonic ring found its way onto Charlie's finger. He felt his clothes being stripped away, and the ancient floor flags struck cold beneath his naked feet. Pimlico opened the door with wire and an Allen key, and Sadler felt night air on his face in a great scald of fear. He was stumbled across cobbles and over metal hoops bordering a square of historic grass. He fell into a clumsy kneel on a square of stone flags, and his head was bowed over a brass plaque with a japanned inscription he knew without needing to read it. It marked the original site of the block where two wives of King Henry VIII had bared their necks for the Great Axe of State. Where his virginal daughter, Elizabeth, had finally rid herself of her tarnished favorite, Essex, after his monumental military blunders in Ireland.

Sadler's sobs emerged as silent trails of spittle.

Wind slapped them across his trembling chins as he tried to make sounds. Noises of any kind. Mucus ran from his nose as Charlie Dance recited the charges against him in a hating monotone of condemnation.

Sadler begged the voice and the trailing sputum to take themselves away. To give him back to himself. Allow him a last vestige of dignity before the end.

Pimlico's legs and an oak shaft formed a tripod of shadow in Sadler's peripheral vision. A dark axehead thumped against the grass, and the leading edge shone. A last crescent of light before the total eclipse of Sadler's world, making him knowing and helpless and afraid.

He could not even flinch when Dance leaned down to speak close to his cheek, each word as sharply etched as the black and brass legend so near his face.

"You get to die twice, Sadler. And dead you'll finally be useful. . . ."

Useful? Useful dead?

The question screamed when Dance's breath retreated.

In God Almighty's name, HOW?

A heel scraped on cobbles. Pimlico's smart alligator shoes shifted. The axe rose and there was a hard grunt of exertion.

HOW?

The screaming question died in a fast whir of steel and the last shock of being nothing. Falling nowhere.

Sadler's head hit the brass plate with its right cheek and spun blind eyes upwards as dark arterial blood blackened the mossy lawn. His body toppled forward, and air bubbled in the neck stump. Ordure soiled the flabby thighs as the arms spread themselves out across the York stone flags with fingers twitching. The head stared and the body felt nothing as Pimlico severed the jerking hands with two clean strokes.

"It wasn't enough," he said.

"What did you expect?"

Pimlico didn't know. He fed the axe into a sack with Sadler's clothes. Dropped the hands in and tied off the neck with stout twine.

"More. Something."

"There isn't . . . anything."

Charlie stripped off latex gloves when he had rolled the head into a heavy nylon container. Hefting it, he led off to the curtain wall near Traitor's Gate.

"Never, Chas?"

"No."

Charlie sailed nylon cord into the dry moat and tested the grapnel's bite on the stone sill before sending Pimlico down into the darkness. Dropping after, he retrieved the grapnel and line and the container and paused to stare out over the rows of cannon defending the reach above Tower Bridge.

"Just a feeling of loss. Hoping it's the last time."

"This ain't the last time. Can't be."

"No. Maybe it never is."

"I'm coming to South Africa, Chas. Nothing's gonna stop me having that last . . . bastard."

Charlie's grunt was almost a sigh. The night was heavy with unsaid things.

"I still miss her, Chas."

"Maybe you won't . . . one day."

"And nothing brings them back, right?"

"Nothing."

They walked west along the embankment in silence and drove the Rolls across Chelsea Bridge to the coalyards of Battersea Power Station. Charlie flashed the heads when he parked and got out to strip naked alongside Pimlico, both of them dressing in new casual clothes. When they had bundled their soiled clothing into another sack, a man in greasy overalls took both sacks away to feed them into the incinerator, reducing the contents to anonymous white slag.

Pimlico took himself home and Charlie went to Windmill Street, where Nasty Nostrils had crated up the Amnesty International documents, ready to be delivered to Heathrow by special messenger, leaving a selection out for Charlie to pack into his attaché case.

There were four hours before his flight, and Charlie had a few things to tie up before he left. And coming back home was something he didn't think about.

Pimlico drove towards Heathrow, sorry he hadn't managed a brighter smile when Brixton Billy brought him tea in bed, his month-old beard shot through with grey and the bacon sandwiches he'd made as thick as doorsteps.

"You're a cross between Old Man Mose and the Ancient Mariner, Brix."

"And too old to be mothering you."

Brixton poured strong tea into mugs and spooned sugar.

"You're looking at a retired schoolteacher just off on a hiking holiday through France. I tried a monocle but it wouldn't stay in."

Pimlico blew on his tea and automatically felt the cool side of the bed where Dotty usually lay. Felt the usual pang of loss and decided Brixton's tweed jacket with leather elbow patches gave him a donnish air.

"So long as nobody asks you about the Hundred Years War or what the capital of Guatemala is, you'll make it."

"Woodwork teachers don't have to know all that bunk.

Once I've cleared Calais I'm off with my knapsack and road maps and down the French canals to Agde. Should get a job crewing a yacht into the Mediterranean from there. Might even make it to Cape Town by sea."

Brixton offered his hand and spilled tea on the counterpane, unable to meet Pimlico's eyes.

"You've been a good friend, Pim. I won't forget."

"Just be lucky, eh?"

"I'll light a candle for Dotty here and there on the way. There's plenty of the old Catholic churches on the Continent."

"Wouldn't hurt," Pimlico had said.

"Yeah," and Brixton had left abruptly, leaving his tea undrunk.

Pimlico parked in the multistory carpark and took his bag across to the terminal. Spotted Charlie at the first class desk as he passed, saw him keep the nylon container as hand luggage when he went through the departure gate with the check-in girl batting her eyelashes at him long after he had disappeared.

Pimlico grinned. It wouldn't take Charlie long to get squared away with something gorgeous once he felt able to put his mind to it. Still grinning, Pimlico slapped his ticket and passport on the tourist class counter.

"Room for a little one?" he said.

The girl ignored Pimlico's wink and checked her passenger list.

Proves you get what you pay for, Pimlico thought.

"Mr. Parsons? John William Parsons?"

"That's me."

Pimlico turned to see an official with a hard salmon face and harder oyster eyes.

"Come with me, please, sir."

"I haven't got booked in yet."

"All the same."

The official pointed the way through a screened door, and Pimlico found himself in a hard white room with a lot of uniforms and Bulstrode.

"Now, what's your game, Buller?"

"Mine or yours?" Bulstrode offered his cigarettes.

"Don't use 'em. And you'd better have a good reason for making me late for my flight."

"To South Africa?"

"Correct."

"You're not going."

"Who says?"

Bulstrode tapped forms and a fat reference book.

"Me and the regulations. We did get an anonymous telephone call last night, telling us about how you hadn't declared your known previous convictions on your visa application. Then the South African embassy called because they'd had a call about this villain trying to enter their country illegally. But their call was from one of the Sunday muckraking tabloids, and the question the reporter asked was: Is South Africa a haven for British convicts? Very upset they were, and wanted us to sort it out at this end, it being our problem rather than theirs."

"And you're obliging."

"Put it down to my sunny disposition, Pim. That and the fact that you're in violation of your parole by attempting to leave the country. Your passport is forged, and the airline ticket you hold is suspect."

"That ticket came straight to me from—"

"Yes?" Bulstrode looked interested.

Charlie handled everything. Passport, visa, tickets . . .

"Nothing," said Pimlico.

"Funny thing, coincidence," Bulstrode said.

"What coincidence?"

"You turning up with the last of Vic Dakin's naughty airline tickets on the very day we fly him home to face charges. I'd say that was a real coincidence."

Except it ain't. Charlie's turned me in to keep me off that plane. Away from the trouble he's flying into. Alone. I had the stomach to back you, Chas. More than I have for the hoops the law's gonna have me jumping through. A strip search and shining a flashlight up my anal canal to see if I'm smuggling illegal aliens. Put me back behind bars for parole violations, uttering forgeries. . . .

In a surge of black despair Pimlico thought of having

Charlie pulled off the plane for putting him back into prison. Caught himself as he remembered the severed head he carried. How Spring would go free without paying for Dotty and Ingrid. Found one of Bulstrode's cigarettes between his white knuckles. Drew flame from a match and said, "Haven't smoked one of these for three years."

Bulstrode killed the match with a flourish.

"Talking could keep you out of prison, Pim."

"Snitch? Me? Put the cuffs on, for Chrissakes."

"Just tell me why you fancied a trip to South Africa."

"To see an elephant that ain't in a zoo."

"You wouldn't have murder on your mind, then?"

Pimlico shrugged to loosen tense shoulders. Imagined a forensic squad around a headless corpse at the Tower of London. Knew he'd not left a single clue behind.

"Murder? No," he said.

"Vic Dakin's talking murder."

"And these things are suicide." Pimlico stubbed the cigarette and didn't know what to do with his hands. "Dakin's talking through the back of his hat. As usual."

"Not when it comes to his daughter's death. You and he ought to talk bereavement. You have that much in common."

"Let him scratch his own fleas."

"You villains don't share your manly tears, then?"

Pimlico shook his head and watched Bulstrode swing in a swivel chair. Heard the Tannoy announce the departure of Charlie's flight.

Be brave for both of us, Charlie. And lucky.

"Caution me and be done with it, Buller."

"Vic wants Ingrid's death nailed to Connie's coattail, Pim."

"Using me as the hammer? No chance."

Bulstrode pointed a finger through smoke.

"Just talk to Dakin off the record. Or you get eighteen months for trying to skip during your parole. You serve the year and a half of your sentence that's outstanding, and another ninety days for the naughty passport. That's without this phony airline ticket. All I want you to do is convince Dakin he's right about Connie Harold's involvement in Ingrid's death. He'll turn Queen's Evidence, and you go free. My word on it."

"That's all?"

"That's all."

Pimlico wanted more nails in more coffins. Needed Dotty to tell him to trust Bulstrode. The scream of a jet taking off sounded as distorted as Bulstrode's sense of justice.

"Well?" Bulstrode asked.

"Where is he?"

"In the next room."

Pimlico nodded. "Alone. In private."

"Just be convincing, Pim."

Bulstrode held a door open and Pimlico went through, hating himself. Thinking, *Do it for both of us, Charlie.*

CHAPTER 12

CHARLIE SHAVED AND CHANGED HIS SHIRT ON THE LONG descent to Jan Smuts Airport and was back in his seat for the bumpy landing. The Super Constellation taxied and the temperature aboard soared when the doors remained closed for fifteen interminable minutes. The first class passengers milled about until they were asked to stand aside to allow a uniformed airline official aboard. He strode to where Charlie sat and frowned at him over a clipboard.

"Mr. . . . King?" he asked officiously.

Charlie said he'd got that much right.

"Your passport please, Mr. King?"

Charlie watched it being riffled through, was asked to "Please follow me," and went out and down steps into blazing noon shimmer. The concrete apron burned up through his shoes, and his scalp broke into sweat when security men with sidearms fell in on either side of him. They ushered Charlie through glazed doors into a shaded Customs hall, ignored the "Whites Only" channel, and lost the airline official when they turned Charlie up a flight of marble stairs. In a carpeted lobby they snapped salutes and sent Charlie into the shuttered light and expensive furniture of the VIP lounge, an over-cool haven after the slamming heat of the airstrip.

"Welcome, Mr. King. I'm Lorenz Krepp. Treasury."

The Afrikaaner wore an expensively cut suit of pale grey lightweight worsted, and the rose in his buttonhole was as waxy as a slick of butter in his narrow lapel. He waved Charlie into a pneumatic chair with a lethal Irish, sat opposite, and made a tent of tanned fingers to beam over.

"This is Spring, my assistant," he added.

Charlie nodded as if nothing mattered and made ice tinkle in his glass.

"Welcome to the Republic, Mr. King."

Clive Spring did not offer to shake hands. He stood behind Krepp and toyed with a camera. A man who did not sweat, he licked a pale smile with a paler tongue, his skin untouched by the African sun. His bronze eyes flicked at Charlie as if he peered from under a rock.

Charlie ignored him and stared at Krepp.

"They kept my passport."

"Naturally, Mr. King. Why should you be plagued by mundanities conjured by the bureaucratic mind? There are enough of *them* to take care of such trivia for you."

Krepp oozed anxiety to please like sweat, and Charlie lashed at him with cold sarcasm.

"Aren't you one of *them* yourself?"

"Technically, my dear sir."

"I made my own arrangements to be met. I hadn't banked on—"

"Our hospitality? Come now, Mr. King, a leading financier like yourself cannot expect to come and go without some notice being taken. You must allow me the honor of oiling the way for you, eh? A small gesture reflecting my humble regard for the great aid your people have afforded us in the arena of the . . . clandestine, shall we say?"

"I don't know what you're talking about."

Krepp liked that.

"You see, Spring," he said over a shoulder. "Discretion, the hallmark of international banking. Hong Kong was most insistent that your privacy be considered sacrosanct. Most insistent, and quite rightly, may I say. True power does not need bread and circuses to amuse itself, eh, Mr. King?"

Charlie savaged his drink and played along. It was clear that Fook had made himself useful by telex without being asked, and the nylon container by Charlie's foot began to burn a hole through his sock. It would have been pleasant to reach across and make Spring eat the camera he was so busy with.

"Hong Kong should not have bothered you," he said.

"No trouble at all. They simply afforded me the pleasure of being useful in my own poor way." Krepp skimmed his gold cigarette case at Charlie. "Turkish on the right, Virginia on the left."

"Thanks."

Charlie hoped his smile was enigmatic enough.

Krepp lit a Perfectos Finos for him with a gold Dunhill that tinkled a tune, and returned Charlie's smile with interest.

"I should have offered you hospitality in my own home, but it was made clear to me that you would prefer the Langham Hotel. Also, that your social calendar had been firmly sketched in."

"Wordy old Hong Kong," said Charlie, his head buzzing. "Shall we go?"

Krepp apologized for the short drive they took to the bonded warehouse where Charlie's off-loaded luggage was being processed through Customs. An air-conditioned limousine swept them across the airport to a long steel building where Customs men scurried with bills of lading and apologized for the several signatures needed to release the five crates and the long leatherette boxfile with ribbons and seals containing Bonar Tree's escudos. Krepp countersigned with a gold pen and saw the crates loaded aboard a carrier vehicle to be delivered according to "Mr. King's" sealed instructions. Spring obligingly carried the boxfile of escudos on his lap when Charlie kept the container and his briefcase on his lap, and on the way to the hotel Krepp launched into his fondly held views on the current financial and political scene, summing up with:

"And is it not a tragedy that the international banking

community is so hamstrung by the short-term placebos of the so-called Popular Left? Free trade was always the backbone of any successful regime, whatever its political hue, and no traditional statesman of the old school was ever so woefully ignorant of the need for a balanced foreign policy as these socialists we see in power in Britain these days. They see no further than the rickety fences surrounding their own national backyard, and ignore the needs and requirements of their international neighbors. They destroy honest argument with naïve hyperbole, bully when they should listen and discuss, and sulk when they do not understand. And does not their blanket offer of equality for all and sundry, without the need to earn it, kill off the individual's right to strive for excellence? To work for recognition in any field of endeavor like the arts, music, and statesmanship? The trouble with the common man is that he is so very, very common, and cannot perceive that only an informed and select élite can truly function for the common good. Am I to be considered no better than my clerks, my Kaffir gardener? Must we all sit in the dust with bowls of mealie-pap and deny our God-given talents by dropping standards to the lowest common denominator? Must excellence be swept away for the sake of the specious views of the mental pygmy? Should individual genius be lobotomized for the duration of this Golden Age of the Puerile? Shall we level all the mountains and live on the dull plain of mediocrity, subsisting on a diet of unrelieved boredom? Kill off all the eagles and allow the humble sparrow to prevail? Interbreed so that we leave the future to a mongrel race of small brown birds? Ach, the orchestra can only follow one baton, eh? And men such as you and I are born conductors, Mr. King, and let those who can follow the score keep up as best they can on their chosen instruments, eh?"

"That gets it said."

Charlie's bemused nod pleased Krepp.

"I knew you for a kindred spirit, Mr. King."

"Almost a Broederbonder?" Charlie raised a hand in peace. "The organization that has no members and doesn't exist? But if it *did* exist, you'd be a senior member, I'm sure. Not that you can comment on that, eh?"

"Your own anonymity is precious, is it not, Mr. King?"

"No more than yours."

"A mere servant of the Treasury? Hardly."

Charlie favored Krepp with a blank smile. "A man can own more than one hat. But wearing more than one at a time is a hell of a trick, wouldn't you say?"

"The Langham Hotel," said Krepp. "Allow me."

Charlie burned through another of Krepp's Perfectos Finos, allowed him to bully the hotel staff with teutonic efficiency, as Spring fixed them drinks and black busboys filled the suite with fresh flowers. When the door closed them out, Charlie laid a large manila on the arm of Krepp's chair without comment.

"This is what exactly?" Krepp asked warily.

"A sample of something that needs to find a home."

Krepp weighed the big buff envelope on a palm.

"It bears no name or address."

"Because it's for eagles, not sparrows."

Krepp's geniality thinned.

"You're teasing me with my own words, Mr. King."

"Because it's time you wore the right hat. One with colonel's stars on, maybe."

Charlie moved Spring away from the bar and stiffened his drink, watching Krepp's reflection rip the manila open in the mirror to leaf through papers and photographs before fanning them out on the floor at his feet.

"May I ask how you came by these?"

"Connie got careless. I got lucky."

"You, too, wear more than one hat, Mr. King."

"Oh, blimey, yeah," said Charlie, letting a silence gather as he met Krepp's eyes in the mirror. Krepp looked at the silent Spring and back at Charlie, put his drink aside, and damped a cigar between pursed lips.

"Just what do you suppose these buy you?" he asked.

"Enough good will to get out of here in one piece."

Spring started to say something and thought better of it. Charlie found complimentary cigarettes in a hardwood box and lit one. Shed his jacket and rolled his shirtsleeves. Turned on Krepp and grinned down at him.

"Customs men don't jump through hoops for bankers, mister. That makes you this toad's boss, right, Colonel De Wit?"

Krepp disappeared as De Wit shed the last vestiges of the assumed persona. He fingered the cigar, stroked a long upper lip, and sat very straight in his chair.

"Quite an assumption, Mr. Dance. Unfortunately for you, I've already taken custody of the five crates from the airport. That leaves you with very little to bargain with."

"Waste paper. Check it out."

De Wit snapped fingers, and Spring used the telephone to speak in clipped Afrikaans. Listened, rang off, and made a face at De Wit.

"Confirmed," he sighed.

"Are we to know where the A.I. documents are?" De Wit asked as he decided on another drink.

"Spread between here, Cape Town, and Durban. I don't know how many law offices there are, but it'll take you at least three months to ferret them out without my help. And even I don't know their exact location."

De Wit nodded over the ice bucket, was generous with soda and sliced limes, and sat with a ramrod back.

"But your people in London do, eh? And they'll inform us when they know you're . . . safe? Very thorough, Mr. Dance, but why did you consider such prudence necessary?"

"With me as the young lady of Riga and you as the smile on the tiger, Colonel? You've got Connie Harold under your thumb, and I represent a lot of people who've sunk capital into his mine. I can't watch their interests under your hammer, can I?"

"Assuming that that's true, I take it that your pretty box contains the final payment from Portugal?"

"Yeah, so let's hope Connie's hole in the ground ain't just a hole in the ground."

De Wit allowed himself a short laugh.

"Come now, Dance. It would suit you very well to see this entire venture fail miserably. My sources are very definite about that. You wanted the money out of England, preferably lost forever, if for no other reason than to teach your opposition a salutary lesson. You're a simple reactionary, aren't you? Admit it, you want to avoid the revolution of change."

Charlie pointed a finger around his drink.

"Exactly what you're doing right here. Keeping the status quo because your people can't handle change. Knowing you won't exist inside ten years if you allow a softening of attitude to your policy of minority rule. Don't kid a kidder, Colonel."

"Do I sense disapproval?"

"No feelings either way. But you made waves in my town. Had idiots like Sadler start a shooting war. Used amateurs like Spring there to cause me aggravation. They're minnows in a river of pike. You should have come to the professionals first."

Spring muttered and fingered his camera. Spots of dull peach burned his sallow cheeks when Charlie sneered smoke at him. De Wit leaned on an elbow, his farmer's face blank and brown, nothing in his narrow blue eyes.

"Are you planning to cause me some small . . . inconvenience?"

Charlie killed his stub in a ceramic tray.

"Where'd the profit be in that? You got it right the first time, Colonel. I want Connie's pack of cards to fall apart right enough, but I figure it will without any help from me. I just have to look like I'm keeping my part of the bargain. Walk around Mkuse and Ghost Mountain, inspect what there is to inspect, and go back making happy noises. Let this 'enterprise' grind to a halt in its own time and say 'Shame' when all the long faces come looking for solace, hand out the fivers and put them all back to work for me. And in future, De Wit, you want something in my town, you come to the organ grinder, not to his monkey."

De Wit showed mild surprise.

"You propose we should work together?"

"You think our worlds are so different? It's the winner who writes the histories, Colonel, not the loser. The Americans run around the globe pretending to be Coca-Cola salesmen, make noises like convenience food and bottled pop was the backbone of democracy when they subvert unacceptable regimes for their own ends. The Russians are close behind with their guns and butter and cynicism when they destabilize their poorer neighbors for *their* own ends; and the British have been playing the same game for three hundred years, so what's so different about what you're doing? You just joined the club a bit late, that's all. You want your patch, I want mine, how bad?"

"Well if crudely put, Mr. Dance. Perhaps we ought to put your alleged power to the test?"

"So long as I can drink while you talk."

Charlie mixed himself a gentle Irish and water.

"Do you know of a man named Dominic Keogh?"

"I do, as it happens." Charlie wondered why De Wit was interested in Dublin Gerry's brother.

"A man capable of murder, would you say?"

"Very capable."

"And competent?"

"He gets the job done."

"That confirms my information. If I want him stopped from fulfilling a contract, could you handle that for me?"

"Money would have to change hands."

De Wit shrugged that aside.

"Keogh and two other men have contracted to assassinate a political figure friendly to this regime. And since he is one of the few black friends we have amongst our neighbors, we cannot afford to lose him. I have warned our friend's security personnel, but it would be simpler if the dogs were called off at the source, wouldn't you say?"

Charlie thought better of lighting a fresh cigarette. He had checked with a contact in Fleet Street after Nasty Nostrils had brought him the sacks from the Amnesty International offices, and learned that Connie must have burgled one other building during his time in London.

"Those Z.A.P.U. papers came in handy, then?" he said.

De Wit put a lot of control into not reacting. Spring did it for him with hot cheeks and haunted eyes.

"Being well informed does not mean you can do what I ask," De Wit said.

"I'll see what I can do. Is there a time limit on this?"

"Yesterday would be soon enough."

"And I get what?"

"Freedom of movement, unless you want me to lay on transport."

"And have your tame constables breathing down my neck?"

De Wit had the grace to smile.

"Anonymity, Mr. King?"

"A precious commodity, Mr. Krepp."

"You'll liaise with Spring here in the event you cannot reach me."

"Fine," Charlie said without shaking hands. And De Wit took Spring away, leaving Charlie with silence and the heady perfume of dozens of prime blooms.

De Wit watched Spring sag in the elevator to the sound of Muzak violins.

"A knowing man, our Mr. Dance," he said.

Spring's mouth was dehydrated.

"He knows, Hendrik. The man *knows.*"

"Guesses perhaps. You got enough pictures?"

"What good are pictures if he . . . ?"

"If he decides to wring your neck? Pray my people find those documents before he finds you, eh? Ach, Clive, the man is alone and friendless. What can he possibly do?"

Kill me, thought Spring. *Unless . . .*

His brow creased in thought, he followed De Wit to the black limousine.

Unless . . .

Charlie had breakfasted and dressed when Harry the Crack and Sailor Mailer came to collect the boxfile of escudos. They sat on the balcony under a striped awning with cold beers and their first cigarettes of the day, Sailor dark and withdrawn, Harry all smiles and suntan, Charlie quietly urbane.

"Playing Buffalo Bill up-country seems to agree with you both. How's Wally?" Charlie asked.

"Being nursed silly. Big girl, that Naomi, eh?" said Harry. He picked peeled skin from his nose, and Sailor gave him a silence to do it in.

"Never met her," said Charlie.

Harry pulled a ring from a second can and skyed it into space.

"He's missing something, eh, Sailor?"

Sailor shrugged in dismissal.

"Just another woman with more money than sense after a bit of rough trade. Wally'd be better off at home in the Smoke than being cozied up with her."

"Sour grapes, Sailor." Harry laughed.

Sailor wiped froth from his mouth with a callused palm.

"Swallowing ale here won't get Bonar's dough deposited in the bank like Connie wants. Forgotten who you work for, Harry?"

"No, but it don't take two of us to make out a deposit slip, neither. If you've got itchy feet, take the motor and go. Too hot to go rushing about."

Sailor stood and crushed his can. Pointed at Charlie.

"He's still the opposition, Aitch. This is just a truce until Connie says otherwise."

"So long as he lets me know, too, Sailor," said Charlie.

"He will."

Sailor went away with a closed face and a stiff back, and Harry waited for the suite door to slam before he shook his head at Charlie.

"Misses his wife and kids. Misses fog, being nagged, and living on pie and potatoes, our Sailor. All this clean air and sunshine gives him a fidgety mouth. No offense meant, Chas."

"None taken. Don't you miss the comforts of home?"

"Me and marriage never mixed. I tried it once, but it never took. Me on the couch and her upstairs in bed with six cats ain't what I call wedded bliss. This country suits me fine, but I ain't that taken with the way Connie's running things."

"Really?" Charlie sounded disinterested.

"What's back in the Smoke for me, eh, Chas? Nothing. I still dig buckshot outta my gut from that fight in that

Catford nightclub. I can't keep doing that much longer. I'm coming up to forty, too long in the tooth for handing out broken arms, right? I need something I can stick to, something with a future, you know?"

"Why tell me?"

"You're the Man, that's why."

"Tell that to Archie Ogle."

Charlie thought of Archie lying frozen in Smithfield among sides of beef. Thought of him living in Harry's mind, as Harry said, "He ain't here; you are. Look, Chas, now Bonar's money's safe in Connie's bank, you could get to be yesterday's man very sudden. Connie's talking of fixing your wagon permanent. Here, before you get back home."

"Sure of that, are you?"

"Sure as milk comes in pints."

"So I'm listening."

"With a shrug in your voice. Shake hands with me, Chas, and we could do each other some good. I keep your tail safe out here, you keep a place warm for me on your firm back home if this mining thing goes wrong. I'll tell you what I told Wally: De Wit and Dirk Jorgesson have got Connie surrounded. He won't see it, and Wally's too ill to listen. Shake hands, Charlie?"

"What good would that do you?"

Harry reared back in surprise.

"You're joking. You shake on something, you stick to it. Your whole reputation's based on your handshake being binding. Firmer than concrete."

Charlie listened to the rap of the striped awning. Sipped beer and lit one of Harry's Gold Flakes.

"Keep talking, Aitch."

Harry scrubbed his head and opened another can.

"Connie don't like partners. Not in business. Not in bed. That's Jorgesson on both counts, right?"

"So?"

"Connie's had me and Sailor giving Dirk the midnight frights. Broke his windows in the middle of the night. Set fire to his fence. Threw a load of stinking offal over his garden. Pumped a few rounds into his house. That sort of thing."

Harry swallowed beer and belched softly.

"And?" Charlie prompted.

"Jorgesson fired back, and he's got this bloody great Alsatian. Me and Sailor barely got away before the local law was swarming all over the place. But Dirk's gotta go, Chas. And not just because our Connie's got the heavy hots for Alicia, neither. With Dirk dead, I earn the top spot out here, and that's me set up for the rest of my natural life, ain't it?"

"If it doesn't all go wrong like you said."

"How can it if I'm taking care of things? You see?"

"So go for it."

Harry reddened and looked shifty.

"Not that easy, is it?"

"Not if your stomach's hollow, no."

"That ain't the problem. It's where the blame gets nailed when Dirk's the *late* Mr. Jorgesson. Who the coppers *charge* with murder. And that could be somebody you *want* nailed, get me?"

"Your tonsils are lubricated with all that beer, should be you can spit out what's on your mind, Harry."

"Don't act simple, Chas. You want who did for your Ingrid, and I know who that was. How about *he* takes the walk to the gallows for Jorgesson?"

"You talk a good fight, Harry, but the sweat coming out of your face looks yellow to me."

"You'd make a statue sweat with them cold looks of yours."

"Name me a name, Harry."

"Won't do you any good. You can't lay a glove on him without my help. Now will you shake on it?"

Charlie rapped Sadler's masonic ring against an eyetooth. Stopped himself from kneeing Harry in half and throwing him bodily from the balcony. Flowing upright, he touched the tip of Harry's peeling nose. Made Harry crush his can and soak his flannels with spilled beer.

"The name."

"Spring."

"That milksop? Forget it." Charlie sneered.

"As God is my judge, Chas. Connie let it slip when he saw how bad Wally was burned. But you try and touch Spring and De Wit'll hand you the final goodbye-Charlie. I can make it look like Spring triggered Jorgesson."

"How, Harry?"

"Spring loaned me a nice little Beretta when I lost my old Webley up at Mkuse. You see? We use the Beretta on Jorgesson and have the police find it under Spring's pillow. That way, you ain't laid a finger, and De Wit can't save Spring from facing a hanging sentence. Sweet as a nut."

Charlie offered his hand.

"I'll buy it. But it's 'we,' Harry."

"Sure, Chas, sure." Harry pumped Charlie's arm up and down until Charlie looked at his wristwatch.

"When were you last at Jorgesson's?"

"In Melrose? Four, no, five nights back."

"Have your car around front tonight at six. And bring Spring's shooter; we'll drive to Melrose and check the place over."

"At six then."

Harry drank up and saw himself out. Took the elevator to the ground floor and leaned into a green Volvo in the carpark. Spring ate pistachios at the wheel, his face stained green by tinted sunglasses.

"Dance bought it?"

Spring's bony Adam's apple bobbed in his thin neck.

"Used all his pocket money, my old Welsh harp."

Harry already saw himself as Connie's partner, with Jorgesson and Charlie Dance dead at his feet.

"But, Clive, you'd better make sure you can keep De Wit happy."

"No problem."

Spring knew he would sleep well for the first time in days.

Charlie had binoculars trained on Jorgesson's house as he filled Harry's car with dribbles of smoke. Melrose was a constellation of glowworms in the warm and velvet night, and cicadas trilled and warbled in the brush beyond the grass verges. Harry took a long nip from his hip flask and shivered.

"Lay off that stuff," Charlie said, bobbing a Gold Flake on his lower lip.

"Settles my stomach, I told you."

"You told me."

Charlie lit a fresh cigarette and tossed his stub away.

"For someone who don't buy cigarettes, you get through the bastards at a fast rate of knots."

"They settle *my* stomach. Where's the gun?"

Harry washed his mouth with brandy.

"Where it always was. In my pocket," he mumbled. "A shooter's only a shooter. You've seen it. You've oiled it. You've reloaded it. You've even polished the bloody bullets. And it's *still* only a shooter."

"It's a tool like any other tool, Harry. A dull chisel cuts the carpenter, not the wood. A lazy spring can jam a pistol. Dust can do the same. And forgetting to take the safety off can leave the man pointing it with more than egg on his chin."

"You told me all that twice already. And how you'd have preferred a revolver on account of how they don't jam. Christ, Chas . . ."

"Nerves, Harry. Just nerves."

Harry wiped off his hip flask and drained it. "I've seen more nerves in a pulled tooth. Nerves, the man says." He shook the last drops of brandy from the hip flask. "Satisfied?"

Charlie streamed smoke. "They've just sat down to dinner. I say we go."

"And have a decent drink at your hotel."

"No, Aitch. Go in. Do it now."

"But I ain't—"

"Had enough to drink?"

"I don't need a drink to—"

"Then we make the hit."

"Don't push me, Dance."

"Then, forget it. Let me out."

"Oh-fucking-kay, but it's—"

"My responsibility. Yeah, it would be."

"Bloody bear's breath."

Harry drove the car off the verge and coasted down into Melrose without lights. Hoped he sounded scared and drunk enough. A sideways glance at Dance reassured him: Charlie leaned back in his seat with half-closed eyes, humming something tuneless. He flicked his cigarette through the quarter-light, and sparks cascaded over the curb.

A man in control, Harry thought. *For maybe five more minutes.*

He halted the car with his hand brake and let the motor idle as Charlie had insisted. Opened the door and left it open when he stepped out, the Beretta a hard, cold friend in his hand as he waited for Charlie to round the hood and walk ahead of him down the front path of Jorgesson's house. He smelled roses and other fragrant blooms when he stepped into the bushes and let Charlie ring the doorbell.

The bastard's half in shadow.

"In the light, Chas. Where he can see you're friendly."

Charlie centered himself under the porch light when it snapped on, and a dog bayed from the side of the house. Chains rattled and a lock was sprung, and a shadow cut light from the yellow glass lozenge set in the plain wooden door as it opened inwards.

"Who's there?"

Recognizing the voice, Charlie leaned farther into the light.

"Hello, Dirk. Couldn't pass without stopping."

Dirk flung the door wide and brought a heavy rifle up to waist height. Blinked and sneered at Charlie an instant before he found Harry off in the shadowed bushes.

"You?" he said to Charlie. "And Harry? Christ, man . . ."

Harry pointed the Beretta off into the flowerbed and suddenly sounded both amused and sober.

"That's the bastard who shot up your house, Dirk. Shoot the bastard, why don't you?"

Alicia called from somewhere inside, and the Alsatian went crazy against the side fence. Dirk pumped a .30/30 round into the breech and cuddled the stock into his shoulder. Breathed out and hissed instead of shouting, "You hairy-backed *rooinek . . . donner . . .*"

His finger curled against the trigger.

Charlie moved. Skimmed his hat back at Harry and

ducked aside. Harry fended off the trilby and brought the Beretta around to bear. Swung a shade too wide and was correcting for a shot when Charlie went in low to mash Harry's larynx with stiffened fingers.

Harry tottered and took a knee up into the scrotum that raised him off the ground and turned his legs to rubbery tubes of hurting tissue that could not support him. He was puzzled when he tried to fall and couldn't do that either. Wanted to grovel on the path and let it all happen to somebody else. But Charlie was in behind him and a shot squeezed itself off before Charlie took the Beretta away. Harry thought it lost itself in the hallway where Dirk was coming forward ready to shoot back.

Harry lost all interest when a steel arm locked across his impacted throat and he found himself sucking air through wells of salty warmth with Dirk planning to shoot Charlie despite Harry's being between them.

Then the Beretta came up from somewhere below Harry's chin and put a spurt of flame into Dirk's waistline, jarring him back on his heels. A second shot blew a hole in flowered wallpaper as Dirk shook hair from his face and resighted. The bore of the rifle leveled with Harry's spangled eyes and stayed there until a third shot hit the big belly and drove a pearl button into Dirk's spleen. The rifle slid away down the path, and Harry slumped in Charlie's arms.

Dirk found himself looking at the hall ceiling, wondering why he had been allowed to be taken by surprise. Spring had promised something other.

Damn that rock spider of a Welshman, Dirk thought. *Didn't he promise Dance would come tomorrow . . . the next day? Give me plenty of warning? It was a householder's right to shoot in self-defense? And weren't Harry and Clive supposed to witness that right?*

Pain drifted Jorgesson away. He did not see Charlie stamp Harry's feet into the soft flowerbed, leave perfect shoeprints in the soil, and haul the big man away down the path.

Alicia's looking down at me . . . asking things I don't want to answer. . . . Of course I hurt. . . .Of course she should call the police . . . stupid carnal woman . . . well rid of her . . .

Jorgesson drifted towards death while Alicia became

hysterical on the telephone and Harry gave hand signals to Clive Spring's house, unable to talk.

Mrs. Hannie De Wit left the telephone on the hall table and stalked back to the dining room, where her husband waited for her to serve dessert. She stood with hands on her ample hips and no longer cared that she sounded disagreeable.

"By the worm in God's apple, Hendrik," she said, "can we never have one hour of peace for dinner without some *dassie* of a government clerk calling to ruin our digestion? I love my country enough to have you go out and die for it twice a week, but not during dinner, eh?"

De Wit looked over the half-glasses he used for reading.

"It's good of you to sacrifice me for the cause, Hannie. But who is calling?"

Mrs. De Wit sat to dab her mouth with an orange napkin.

"When does one of your people give a name? I was schooled for too long to ask for names."

De Wit pushed away from the table and wished his wife into a black Hades where nobody played bridge or spoke a single word of Afrikaans. Somewhere like London, where even the Kaffirs played card games like Christians. He listened to the voice from his office, grunted several times, and massaged his long upper lip as it slicked with moisture. Said, "Send my car and escort," and went to the dining room.

"Important, I *don't* suppose, eh?"

Mrs. De Wit expected the usual sour negative.

"Our goddaughter is widowed. I'd say that was important."

"His heart?"

"Gunshot wounds. Don't wait up for me."

De Wit went to change back into uniform and left his wife at the table, where she smoothed her dress over her round belly and smiled at the candles.

The smile held a malicious and long-awaited delight.

"Well," she said aloud. "Two less legs in her bed for him to worry about."

She reached for her husband's untouched dessert as his

car raced away down the drive without sirens, convinced the wrong person had died in the Jorgesson household. To compensate for that, she ate three more helpings of *gâteau* and clotted cream to ruin her heavy figure further.

It was a comforting revenge.

Spring's Doberman went across the moonlit lawn in a silent run, guided by the man's scent. It located the dark figure against the storm fence under an old euphorbia tree that bowered there, and leaped for the throat. Something whipped in the darkness and tightened around the dog's neck, bringing it up short in midair. The wire tied off to the tree bit into the hard muscles and skidded the dog on its side just short of its target.

Charlie let it jump again and brained it with a rock. Struck again to make sure and left it where it fell, listening to the night. There was just the wind in the wild bamboo hedges and the slower shush of the gums and acacias beyond the bungalow. The single-story building was dark, and Charlie circled it twice before choosing a window with shutters and mosquito netting, where the red steel alarm was located. The circuit was good by South African standards, and Charlie took fifteen minutes to bypass it before he slipped through into a modern kitchen that smelled of antiseptic chemicals instead of cooking. A bachelor smell no Bantu cook had been allowed to dispel with okra, yams, or spiced meats, or brighten with singing.

Charlie hummed as he neutralized a separate alarm system outside a photographic darkroom, sprang the locked door, and lit a viewing plate to give him light to work by.

Strips of newly exposed 400 ASA film dried in a cabinet and Charlie found shots of himself at the airport with De Wit, the nylon container on the floor by his foot. Charlie laid the film across his lighter flame and watched it frizzle to black poodle hair.

Hundreds of negatives in a row of steel files were cataloged alphabetically. There were candid shots of Connie and his associates, hundreds of others of people Charlie neither knew nor cared about. Black faces talked earnestly with white, churchmen looked solemn over drinks, and exterior shots showed mixed ethnic groups entering or leaving buildings, all of them listed with care in a spiral bound book in Spring's spidery script. The man was nothing if not thorough, but there was nothing under D for De Wit save for a small red star beside the initials D.W. and a cross-reference to A. Charlie leafed back and found another red star beside A.J./D.W., which was meaningless until he found a thick album in a secret drawer of an escritoire in the living room.

"Bingo," Charlie whispered to himself. "Very gymnastic. Who'd think the old goat had it in him?"

The naked bodies were fuzzy on the beds in the three locations, but De Wit was clearly De Wit, and Alicia was very much Alicia, and Spring had tucked the negatives into the album's spine. Humming softly, Charlie took the album out to the car and brought Harry the Crack back into the house, sat him in a chair, and went looking for the master bedroom.

Clive Spring came awake gaping for air, with Charlie's fingers pinching his nostrils together. The Beretta slid into his suddenly opened mouth. His eyes opened slower but wider, and Spring tasted gun oil as he tried for night vision. Tasted the burned powder of spent cartridges. Smelled the peaty tang of good Irish. Knew the man drank and the gun had recently been fired.

"Get up, mister."

Spring nodded and cut his gum on the foresight. Gobbled when he tried to speak, muddled by the sleeping draught he had swallowed. The gun and a hand in his hair walked him into the living room on tiptoe. The lamp on his escritoire was lit and showed up dust he had never noticed before. Made the nylon container into a bell jar of luminescent light.

There were groans as hollow as promises, and Spring's brain was no longer dreary when he saw Harry flopped in a chair. Lying there as if his clothes were all that held him together. Hands on his lapels like broken crabs. Heels drumming on a nerve.

The gun sat Spring at his escritoire. Pressed against his balding temple and made him look at the container.

"Open it."

The voice brooked no argument.

Spring's trembling hands released the astringent smell of chemical. He peeled hard nylon edges apart and the pressure seal hissed, stinging his nose and eyes with formaldehyde. Breathing was a grudging thing as he squinted down through tears at the bloated thing drowned in stinking liquid. A muddy dead eye stared back, and its twin made a lazy half-wink. There was congealed blood in the nose, and the mouth was parted in a humorless rictus that bared a long white molar and a chipped bicuspid. Facial hair had grown after death, and Sadler's head needed a shave.

Spring fought vomit and lassitude as his mind formed mad arguments. An opening statement for the defense. All logical men were open to persuasion. He lifted his head to deliver it, but Charlie's fist drove him and his unspoken equivocation to the floor. Through the shock of pain the voice was as chill as a school prefect in charge of a detention.

"Just say goodbye to your partner, Spring. Then it's all been said."

Spring's mouth was too small for his tongue. He rolled his head against the floor, his need to find answers to these terrifying conundrums keeping him conscious. He had to know where his dog was and why the alarms had failed. Why Dance was looking up numbers in a telephone directory, and why Harry pawed at his coat with sausage fingers. It all seemed so futile to Spring. His mind couldn't walk the tightrope of linear progressions, and the fault lay with everybody but himself. With Dance and De Wit and Sadler. With Harry, who opened a small black wallet as if it contained the answer to something important. What good was the sharpened silver nail he balanced in a shaky hand? No good at all.

Dance was dialing and listening and talking to a police station, reporting a prowler on the premises, giving Spring's own address and telephone number. And that was stupid, with Spring's files open and his darkroom ready to be searched when they came. That must be stopped, but Spring's tongue scraped against coated teeth and would not articulate when Dance rang off and looked down at him like some worthless thing.

There was a flick of silver light and Dance ducked with a dart buried in his upper arm. Harry was selecting another nail, and Dance was no longer where he had been. A long leg had struck out and Harry was smashing his chair to tinder as he took it back into the wall and drove the back of his head through a windowpane. Glass fell around him as he hit the polished boards with his face, and his second nail had set the lightshade swinging above Dance's head. Dance turned Harry with his foot before hissing through clenched teeth at the nail buried in his deltoid. He mumbled something Spring did not catch and went away to root about in the darkroom. His shadow used pliers on the nail with a grunt of exertion, something metallic clattered in the sink, paper tissue was ripped from a roll, and cold water ran as the shadow washed and packed the wound with a wad of mashed tissue.

Spring crawled for the door, unable to raise his head. He had reached the doorsill before he was chopped across the shoulders and hauled back inside. There was no feeling in his arms or torso as he was forced to watch Dance dab the Beretta with Harry's prints and drop it into the unconscious man's pocket with spare ammunition and negatives selected at random from the darkroom files.

"Understand now, do you, Spring?"

Dance moved toward the paralyzed man.

Spring did without wanting to. Jorgesson must be dead, and Harry was the prowler the police would find when they arrived. Forensic tests would tie him and Spring to the shooting in Melrose. Trace the Beretta back to him, find Harry in possession of negs of Connie Harold in compromising situations, opening a barrel of worms that would compromise them all. Unless he could think of a way out. Spring was still working on it when Dance took him out to a hired car he had parked down the block earlier in the day.

By the time the police had contacted De Wit, Spring, Charlie, and Sadler's head were well on their way to Zeerust.

* * *

Day grew out of night. Wally's bright star was no longer a staring chip of ice in glacial velvet above the brown road. A bloated sun climbed out of carmine haze, and wind stirred the veld like an old man breathing in shallow sleep. The eastern mountains had blued to ultramarine, and a red scar of light spread bloody fingers into low, melancholy clouds, transforming them to bright banks of drifting peach.

Charlie's hired car threw a long shadow down the longer brown road, and a buzzard sailed in an early thermal like a ragged black pennant, too high to be disturbed by the sudden monumental grind of falling rock or the thick boil of dust throwing itself upward from the collapsing sides of the deep kloof. Brush and rock and shale slid into the depths, and the rumbles were still dying away when the flutter of a distant helicopter grew out of the rising sun.

Charlie climbed back up to the road, rolled his shirtsleeves down, and brushed off his trousers. Lit Harry's last Gold Flake and held the wound in his shoulder as he leaned against the car.

The helicopter sideslipped to circle the kloof and landed on the road in a stew of brown dust. The rotors feathered, and men in olive fatigues dropped to the ground with leveled automatic weapons. The dust pall thinned, and Colonel De Wit came out of it stroking his long upper lip, a thumb hooked into a heavy black gunbelt.

"Mr. King, I presume," he said.

Charlie ignored him and the rising heat. Turned a masonic ring on his little finger.

The kloof gave off a last rumble and dust drifted over the blackened Mercedes below them. The scarred baobab it nuzzled shone like dirty milk, and De Wit sighed.

"Spring's down there," he said. A statement.

Charlie said nothing. Savored the smoke in his lungs.

"A gang of Kaffirs digging for a month might find him, I suppose. I think you'd better walk down there and join him, Mr. Dance."

Charlie looked at De Wit then. Streamed smoke and shook his head.

"No," he said.

"But I insist."

De Wit's nickel-plated army Colt came out of its holster, and Charlie's smile was a bare thing in his dust-streaked face.

"No, you don't. The police have Harry Cracknell nailed to a murder charge, and he'll talk to save his neck. Pass on what he tells you, and you could end up with a lot of new friends at Scotland Yard. Better friends than Spring or Sadler ever were."

"Sadler is to be spoken of in the past tense, Mr. Dance?"

"Another dead joker in your house of cards, Colonel. You're just not seeing the bigger picture, for all your clever talk. If you're sensible, you'll not allow Harry into a courtroom. He'd only tie himself to Spring, and Spring to you. And if my name gets mentioned, how will you explain Messers Krepp and King to the judge and jury? The newspapers would have a field day."

"Not if you go into that kloof after Spring. You fall and die and never existed. Simple."

"Simple-minded, De Wit. Open the trunk of the car. See what I liberated for you as a friendly gesture."

De Wit turned the key and flipped open the album to see Alicia and himself in grainy black and white.

"You and the widow Jorgesson bonking your brains out. How would that have looked in court or in the wrong minister's hands?" Charlie did not mention the negatives he had posted to himself in London.

De Wit's eyes and mouth slitted. He had enemies within the Cabinet who would have used the material to catapult him into disgrace and obscurity. Spring's death no longer required a reaction from him. He need only consider the best way of neutralizing Dance.

Charlie slapped an envelope across a shot of Alicia's rump raised in a dark motel room.

"There's the first of the letters of introduction you'll need to collect the Amnesty International documents. You'll get the rest when I'm out of South African airspace."

De Wit looked at the mountains beyond the kloof, and his Colt went back into its holster.

"You're on the next available flight. You were never in this country, *verstaan?*"

"Suits me, Colonel."

"Congratulations, Mr. Dance. You appear to have won."

De Wit could have been admiring a carefully tended garden or a prettily engraved heirloom, and was taken aback by Charlie's savage reaction.

"Won *what* exactly? The right to stand here with you? We can only win by making others lose. When did you last laugh hard enough to crack a rib? Make love without awarding yourself points? Or just get drunk without using the booze to turn off your brain? Don't talk to me about winning."

De Wit gave no sign he had heard. "It's been a long twenty-four hours," he said, lost in far blue escarpments.

Charlie took a last draught of fragrant smoke and flicked his long butt down at the baobab without seeing the view.

"I just hope she knows I did the best I could."

"Who knows?" said De Wit. "One of my men will take care of the hired car." He led Charlie back to the helicopter with the album clamped under his arm, and they were whirled back the way they had come.

And below the baobab, strapped to the wheel of the burned-out Mercedes, Clive Spring gnawed at his gag and felt the first pangs of terminal thirst as the temperature climbed higher than the circling buzzard.

Knowing what must come with the darkness.

Charlie dumped his soiled clothes and padded into the shower with a bottle of Irish to lay the dust, too tired to care that the scalding spray stung the wound in his arm.

Like iodine, he thought. *The more it stings, the more good it does you.*

He lathered the knife scar Red Bellaver had given him in the yard of Brixton Prison and did not care that the whiskey tasted of soap as he scrubbed himself pink again. He just wanted to be clean and get drunk enough to sleep through the long flight home.

Two of De Wit's men had packed his case and waited outside the suite for him to dress and join them for the drive to the airport. It was refreshing to let someone else do the thinking for a change, and Charlie promised himself a long holiday after Archie's funeral. His limbs shook with exhaustion, and the bottle was heavy when he tilted it over the dark blue hole in his deltoid, cleansing it with alcohol, shuddering when it burned.

A ten-year-old kid could take me now.

Charlie shook spray from his hair and was liberal with shampoo. Aman Lee Fook and Eyetie Antoni's New York cousins could damned well wait until he was ready to finalize the drugs deal. Charlie was only going along for Archie's sake, and planned to bow out as soon as he possibly could without alienating the Chinese in Gerrard Street. There was enough money in the world without dealing in refined opiates and the hallucinogens the trendies experimented with nowadays.

What the hell was wrong with broads, booze, and bedrooms? It's a hard combination to beat, and where's the fun in giggling over the whorls in your thumb or finding patterns in a lamp more interesting than the girl you're turning on with? Dumb and antisocial. Kills brainbuds and conversation. People are alone enough without retreating inside themselves. Ingrid agrees, she . . .

Charlie rinsed off and reached for a towel.

Don't think about it. About her.

He sensed movement through the plastic curtain before something bellied the clinging folds towards him. Slammed into his raised shoulder and ducking head. Snapped his face aside and numbed his whole right arm. Charlie fell with the curtain popping off its hooks and another blow took him in the lower back, skidding his legs out from under him. Powerful arms caught him in a headlock and hauled him out across slippery tiles, where he was systematically kicked in the spine and behind the knees. Draining him of strength.

Charlie still held the bottle and punched it back over his shoulder. Felt it impact against muscle and roll off somewhere. Heard breath expelled as the arms around his neck slackened. Turned and popped a knuckle against a skull before the pressure came back and the knee in his back turned his legs to useless meat. Heard his own bawl of pain as he held on to the soil pipe below the vanity suite with the last of his sapped strength until weakness and suds allowed him to be lifted bodily.

Charlie let his whole weight hang on the straining arms and saw Sailor Mailer's dark face beside his own in the mirror above the wash basin before he was turned away and hurled out onto thick living room carpet. Realized that Sailor had hidden himself somewhere in the hotel suite while De Wit's men gathered up his personal effects. A kick rolled Charlie into a loose curl, and breeze from the balcony cooled his damp hair. The sliding windows had been closed when he went to shower, he was sure of that, and Sailor must have—

Charlie was kicked in the chest and heard himself try to draw breath into lungs turned solid by pain. Knew that Sailor meant to finish him with boot and sap before hurling him out and down onto the hot road surface fourteen floors below. Knew he was too used up to do much about it.

Charlie scrabbled away from the next kick and almost made it.

He upended a chair, and used the cushion to absorb the blow of the sap aimed at his jaw, but not enough to stop him from being spread-eagled without the will to cover his exposed genitals.

Sailor's boot rose in deliberate slow motion above Charlie's crotch, ready to destroy his manhood. Charlie saw the back fillings in Sailor's open mouth, the stiff hairs in his nostrils. Silly details that took his mind off the heavy boot. Then the contorted face jerked at the outer door as it splintered open and the doorknob bounced across the floor. Sailor hacked down and his heel slammed into Charlie's upper thigh, missing his testicles by millimeters.

Charlie jack-knifed over himself like a broken doll and fell away from another wild kick to the head, sensing the men falling into the suite behind him. Black shoes circled him and Sailor was backing away, thinking of survival instead of maiming and killing Charlie.

Sailor knocked against an ornamental table, and a crystal lamp shivered its pendants. He launched himself forward, and his sap whirred as he swung it at the nearest head. It passed through thin air, and a solid fist mashed his mouth, spraying saliva from loose lips. The men were in close then, and all Charlie could see or hear was milling feet and the hard thud of fists on flesh. Then Sailor was down, and the men had his arms up his back as they dragged him toward the sliding windows. The curtains were drawn back and sunlight seared the room as Charlie tried to get a knee under him. He was still trying when Sailor sailed out over the balcony to make the traffic brake and horn from the street below.

"Another bloody suicide."

The first man got Charlie upright and fed his useless legs into his underwear.

The second man laughed softly and got Charlie into his shirt.

"We put it down to the heat," he said, buttoning carefully.

Charlie swayed between them as they zipped him into his trousers and knotted his necktie.

"Can you handle your socks yourself, *boet?*"

"Oh, blimey, yeah."

Charlie passed out lacing his shoes and came to as the black limousine turned into the airport.

CHAPTER 13

CONNIE WAS POURING HOT WATER OVER INSTANT COFFEE when the front gate swung on its rusty hinge and post flopped through the letter box onto the hall mat. He went down the passage licking marmalade from a thumb, with Kelly's cat figure-of-eighting between his legs and mewing for his breakfast.

"Time Kel came and claimed you, face-ache. Unless she figures that by leaving you here, she's got a claim on being allowed back. Some hopes, old puss. You can tell her that from me. This time tomorrow I'll be back in Jo'burg, and won't be coming back to the Smoke for a very long time."

Connie stooped to gather the usual bills and a large yellow envelope with a local postmark. He left the bills on the hall table and opened the yellow envelope with a kitchen knife. The cat pawed his foot and wailed pathetically enough for Connie to discard the post and spoon cat food into a bowl.

"Here I am, the hardest face in the Smoke, being hagridden by a bloody cat. Now, who'd believe that?"

The cat went rigid when it was stroked, its nose deep in fish and meal. Connie straightened as the room spun, and rubbed his aching head. Leaned against the fridge to let his vision settle as the cat refused to purr in gratitude.

"Typical woman. Get what you want from a man, and that's it. Nothing. Forget the bedroom, mister, we're going to church. Well, cat, at least you're some kind of company with my kids at my sister's and the woman I want in another bloody country, where I can't get at her."

Connie glanced at the clock as it ticked past eight. Knew it was the time the law made their arrests, catching villains with the sleep in their eyes. Realized he said as much aloud as if talking to a cat was normal.

"Maybe I should be locked up," he told himself. Gulped coffee and remembered the yellow envelope. Picked it up and slid glossy prints into his palm. For a moment they were just candid pornos of a couple in various beds. The man had the start of a belly and the woman was small and very agile. Then Alicia's face leaped at him as her nails dug into a muscular back and her legs clamped a thick waist. Her big eyes foggy with need as her teeth nibbled a grizzled neck. Biting as only she could bite. Straining against somebody who wasn't Connie Harold. Wasn't her husband. A man who looked as though he wore a uniform under his clothes.

Hendrik De Wit.

Connie spread the prints as if they burned him. Laid them out on the work surface and stared at them, ashes in his mouth and the start of a sick headache clouding his mind. He barely made the sink to vomit and kicked the cat's bowl apart without noticing. Stayed there until he voided nothing but strings of sour bile.

He ran the tap and took cold comfort from the icy water streaming over his neck and face and swirling on the aluminum close to his eyes. Droplets running in eccentric circles like wet lightning on the brushed alloy, no two configurations the same, darting and dancing in liquid anarchy like his disordered thoughts.

Somebody had done this to him. Connie reared upright to spatter the kitchen with water and soak the cat, sending it streaking away. Tore the envelope apart for a note, any clue as to who had sent the filthy evidence to him. There was nothing. Only the rows of grainy prints. Connie ripped them into smaller and smaller pieces. Ran to the lavatory an flushed them away. Pushed the bobbing pieces through th trap with a lavatory brush until there was nothing there bu innocent colorless water and featureless white porcelain.

Connie's head ballooned and split as his heart pumpe blood too hard and too fast. He hyperventilated withou knowing it, and his gorged face was bloated and feveris under his hands. He slumped on the toilet with nerve tapping his feet on cold linoleum. There was nothing t strangle but the cat. Nothing to hammer with his fists bu tiled walls. Only yesterday he had received a long and fon letter from Alicia that mentioned Dirk's death almost i passing. Skimmed over Harry's arrest in favor of bal descriptions of her need to bed her beloved Conrad. Gav no reason for Sailor's silence.

Lies. Lies I swallowed. Lies marching like soldiers. Rank after rank of them. Snapping salutes that gave me the finger Lies only a woman could tell. Rudyard Kipling had it righ when he said: A woman is only a woman, but a good cigar is a smoke.

Hammering came from outside Connie's head. Outside the house. Hammering that had been going on for too long He staggered to the front door, hoping it was somebody he could vent his rage on. He ripped the door open. Blinked out at the tall man holding a search warrant like it was a blue riband for breeding a pedigree animal.

"Conrad William Harold?" he said. "Are you Conrad William Harold?"

"You know it is, Mr. Lemmon." Connie hid his fists behind his back. "You're a bit late for the dawn frighteners, ain't you?"

"Traffic," Lemmon said, easing Connie aside.

CID men were in the passage, and the cat streaked up the stairs ahead of them.

"In here?" Lemmon led Connie into his disordered lounge, where chaos had gathered in the weeks since Kelly's departure and the remains of a forgotten meal congealed on top of the television. "Not much of a bachelor, are you, Connie?"

"Who is?"

Lemmon perched on the arm of a fat flowered chair. Lit a Player and handed Connie's passport and airline ticket to Dillman. Pointed at Connie's packed suitcases in the hall.

"Won't need them where you're going."

"And where would that be?"

"West End Central to be charged formally. Then somewhere safe from harm. In a nice warm cell like your ex-partners."

Connie thumbed a pounding temple. Needed to clean his teeth. Use mouthwash to cleanse his palate.

"Get one of your brave lads to find something for this blinding headache, will you?" he asked.

Lemmon sent Dillman out of the room.

"A quiet word before we go, Connie. Just you and me."

"For that I'll sit down."

"Wouldn't hurt." Lemmon's voice was as dry as the dust in a locked room. "We've got you dead to rights on charges that range from criminal conspiracy to serious fraud, and your jury-rigging is described as conspiracy to pervert the course of justice. But what is so sweet to me, and is so bitter for you, is that your ex-partners all point the finger at you. Nobody's your friend anymore."

"That's twice you've said 'ex-partners.'"

"You want names? Miss Kelly Ketchum comes to mind."

"Kel? I don't believe for one second—"

"Believe it. You're cooked in her slow oven. She was typecast for the part of a woman scorned. She hates your guts."

Connie blinked at his fists. Opened them and said, "And?"

"Victor Gideon Dakin."

"But he's—"

"Yes?"

"Nothing to do with me." Connie bit his lip.

"Dakin says differently, and at length."

"I can believe that."

"You face about a hundred and seventeen charges so far. All provable. All substantiated by documentation and the oral and written statements of the aforementioned Ketchum and Dakin. But our star witness is one Harry Cracknell, your Harry the Crack. He was very forthcoming when interviewed him in Johannesburg. I've just had a week o there, and he ties you to ordering a murder he denies doin The South Africans are dangling a rope for Harry to swir on, and he'll do anything to have a death sentence com muted to life imprisonment. He did do a lot of wild talkin about some tie-in with Republican Intelligence, but that wa just wild talk."

Connie stood and trembled.

"There is a link, and you know it. I can prove . . ."

Lemmon watched Connie's mind catch up with hi mouth. Watched him sag into his chair with a solicitou smile.

"Wild talk, Connie. You couldn't put all those stories c spying and gunrunning in front of a jury. They'll have a har enough time following the straight evidence. You'd bes swallow that bitter pill right now."

Connie wiped bitter scum from his mouth.

"What about Colonel Hendrik De Wit?"

"His name was mentioned. Harry talked at length abou him, but the South African police I liaised with said he wa retired from the force and lived on his farm as some kind o a recluse. I was even shown the records of all the servin policemen in the South African force, and no De Wit wa listed. Unless we counted a seventeen-year-old trainee con stable in Pietermaritzburg. But that's as wild as Harr saying Charlie Dance was a 'Mr. King' who was at th Jorgesson house when the fatal shooting took place. I'd lov to believe it, but wild talk isn't proof, is it? And I checke thoroughly; Charlie Dance was in Malta during that time I've even seen the entry and exit stamps in his passport."

Dillman handed a glass of water and two Alka Seltzer around the door, and Connie let them fizz as he ordered hi thoughts.

"No De Wit and no Mr. King, eh? I have enough to swallow without swallowing that. I can prove De Wit exists I've got pictures of him in bed with . . ." Connie coasted to a halt. He had no pictures.

"With?" asked Lemmon.

"With nobody."

"Best you stick with the straight stuff, Connie. I did turn one odd thing up, though. A Mr. King stayed at the Langham Hotel, but he committed suicide the day after Jorgesson died. I saw the police blotter on that, and he tried to fly from the fourteenth floor. There were photographs, but not the sort you'd stick in the family album. Landing on your head from that height leaves little you'd want to remember."

Connie drank his seltzer down and knew who Mr. King must have been. Sailor hadn't made it, and Harry was singing to save his neck. Everything Connie had held together with sheer willpower was draining away like his own vitality. The millions and Alicia were lost to him. All he had left was the animal cunning he'd been born with. The street sense he'd taken a lifetime to learn. Potent weapons once he'd rested up. Would see him through the coming ordeal. Had to see him through if he was to avoid a long sentence in a maximum security prison.

"How long am I looking at, Mr. Lemmon?" he asked.

"Your electric torture machine will make the headlines. All the toenails you used pliers on. But the heavy sentences will come from the insurance and airline ticket frauds, the unpaid purchase tax and the monies you defrauded the inland revenue out of. Then the judge will not take kindly to your interfering with the due process of law. Property before people, that's the law, Connie."

"A couple of tens running concurrently, then?"

"More likely to be twenty-five long years."

Connie shuddered. Felt his face pale.

"Then, I'll do what Dance did. Sit quiet and refuse legal representation. It worked for him, right?"

Lemmon almost nodded. Almost smiled.

"With a little help from his friends. And from a few who weren't. Yes, Charlie made it. That one time."

"You're still after the bastard, then?"

"More than ever. With you collared, there is only Charlie left."

Connie's wild laugh startled Lemmon. Brought Dillman's face around the door until Lemmon waved him away. Connie stopped laughing and said, "You get this Charlie, and another Charlie will pop up. I ain't the last Conni Harold in the world, neither. The world's filled with Kc shers, Bellavers, Tommys, and Connies, copper. And yo and ten armies won't root them out in a million years. Ain' enough straight coppers, and never will be. I've bough members of Parliament. Peers of the realm. They've all gc their price. And so have you, Lemmon. How does a hundre grand in cash sound? Paid anywhere in the world if you le me walk out of here and catch that plane to South Africa?'

Lemmon just frowned. Leaned in and said, "It's time fo you to pay your dues to the great British public, chum You're going to a prison, where you can't bribe or intimidat anybody ever again. You are well and truly arrested."

Connie shrugged. Felt the last of his energy leak away.

"Funny how big things fall apart in a hurry."

"Not funny. Inevitable."

Connie took a last look around the stale room.

"So caution me. I hate this house. Let somebody else pa the rates and do the washing up. One of Her Majesty' guests has some rights, right?"

"A few."

Lemmon called Dillman in to read the formal caution just as anxious to leave the stale room as Connie.

Golders Green crematorium lay in early morning shadow and a line of funeral limousines stretched back towarc Finchley. Traffic was diverted for two miles in either direc tion, and security along the funeral route was tight enougl for a royal progression or a visiting head of state. Uniformec police patrolled the perimeter and plain-clothes CID mer mingled with the crowds of invited mourners. Press photog raphers were restricted to a roped podium, and keen stray looking for exclusive shots were escorted away by bouncer without a "please" in them. Floral tributes covered a quarter of an acre inside the grounds and lined the white path winding up to the memorial chapel, where D.C. Payne took candid shots of Queenie Ogle being escorted to her pew by Kensington Kate and Electric Raymond. The pall bearers were Nasty Nostrils and Sodbonce, Fast Frankie Frewin and Foggy Farrell, Pimlico Johnny Parsons and Aman Lee Fook, yetie Antoni and his American cousin Salvatore Castile.).C. Brian Bulstrode wheeled Vinnie Castle, Johnny the uilder and Barry the Blag flanked a weeping Armchair)oris and Manchester Freddy's wife Maria, and they in turn vere followed by Stripes Flynn's contingent from mithfield, bookmakers, diamond merchants, club owners, nd publicans, and those who could not be seated lined the valls or gathered outside, silent witnesses to the passing of n era.

J. C. Hatton gave a long and poignant eulogy, and a rabbi rayed for the departed soul as the bronze casket slid away etween slowly closing plush curtains. Queenie gave Electric er black-edged handkerchief to weep into and toured the nass of wreaths before being driven away to the funeral reakfast Charlie was to host in Park Lane.

Lemmon found Charlie back in the trees, where he could ee without being seen.

"You mind company?"

"Not if you're carrying cigarettes."

"Smoked my last one."

Lemmon crumpled his pack and put it back in his pocket.

"The king is dead, long live the king, Charlie?"

"Ends are only disguised beginnings, Theo. How did you ike South Africa?"

"You should know."

"Never been there."

"That's what they told me, and I've learned to compromise. I learned that lesson from you and Bunny Halliday, ven though your trademark was stamped to everything I ouched in Johannesburg and Melrose. But cynicism and olitical expedience decided the day, and my masters have old me I can't touch a hair on your sanctified head."

"I didn't make the rules, Theo, they did. Count your victories and your enlarged pension. You've got the Troys nd Connie Harold, don't get greedy, there's a nice Commander."

"You can't hold the cobbles forever, Charlie. One day hey'll be taken away from you."

"Meaning you?"

"Maybe."

"And when Queenie goes, maybe I'll let you. Just mal sure you don't want change for change's sake. The who world hated the Union Jack when it flew over half the worl but the Pax Britannica lasted a hundred years. And whe the last honest villain goes, you'll have nothing but a lot hard-nosed amateurs to deal with. A whole screed of nas bastards with no loyalty and no standards. Then you'll thi back on today as the good-old-bad-old days. Better the dev you know, mister."

"You wouldn't want me to give up the good fight, wou you, Charlie? Let you and your new friends from Hor Kong and New York have it all your own way? You' paraded them today for my inspection, and I'm ready come at you any way I can."

"That gets it said, Mr. Lemmon."

"What happened to Theo?"

"He talked off the record. You've just drawn the batt lines. Let's leave it at that."

"See you in court, Charlie."

"That's only a maybe, Mr. Lemmon."

"A positive maybe. Oh, one last thing."

"Get it said, then."

"Two things actually. As a Commander, they've given m carte blanche to get you any way I can."

"Can't wish you luck, then, can I?"

"Not sincerely, no. I've got a message for you, from a M Krepp. You remember him, don't you?"

Charlie's smile flitted, gone before it had formed.

"How could I? Never been to South Africa."

"So Mr. Krepp told me, but I'll tell you anyway. He sai and I quote, 'Tell Mr. King I found the loose spring in th Mercedes too late to mend it. He owes me a replaceme part.' Does that make sense?"

Charlie's eyes hardened as briefly as he had smiled.

"It makes sense."

"Keep your back to the wall, Charlie."

"And you, Theo."

Lemmon walked down the line of limousines and becam just another bobbing head in the crowd. The last cars pulle away, and the stragglers on foot followed in their own goo time. Charlie listened to pine trees sigh in the breeze, crackling as they shed their needles around his feet. A cone thumped to the ground, and a grey squirrel flicked from sight.

Charlie took the masonic ring from his little finger and ground it into the needles, no longer needing a trophy. He found a patch of sky through the nodding trees and smiled up into watery sunlight.

"One away to you, mister," he said softly, making his final farewell to Archie. "The best one."

"I wasn't sure of the brand."

A gloved hand offered Charlie a Player and he glimpsed a wayward nose through a black veil.

"You said to carry cigarettes next time."

"Did I now?"

Charlie accepted a light from a gold Dunhill.

"Is this too soon?"

"For what?"

"Too soon for next time?"

"Only one way to find out."

"How delicious. Do you plan to throw me to the ground here and now?"

"I think I'll contain myself until I've seen the floral tributes."

"But there are thousands. Won't that take hours?"

"Half an hour maybe."

"Then will you . . . ?"

"We'll see, won't we?"

"I'm trying not to pout."

"There's a party after that in Park Lane."

"Lovely. And after that will you . . . ?"

"After that? Yes."

"D'you think I can contain myself until then?"

Charlie took Margot's arm and nodded.

"Oh, blimey, yeah," he said.